The Squib's Apprentice

William Wilkin

Bell Street Publishing, LLC

This is a work of fiction. Names, characters, places, and incidents either are the product of the author's imagination or are used fictitiously. Any resemblance to actual events, locales, organizations or persons, living or dead is entirely coincidental and beyond the intent of either the author or publisher.

Published by Bell Street Publishing, LLC,
P.O. Box 836044,
Richardson, TX 75083-6044

Copyright © 2016 by Bell Street Publishing, LLC

ISBN: 978-0-9903164-1-1

First Published in the United States,2016

Contents

Acknowledgements

I owe an immense debt of gratitude to several people who have contributed substantially to this book's artistic integrity.

There are my two sons, James Wilkin and Matthew Stone.

James and Matthew contributed a number of graphic design suggestions that are incorporated in the cover design and interior of the book.

They exhibited attention to detail and artistic consistency far beyond my capabilities.

My wife, Lou, contributed in both obvious and subtle ways to the completion of the book. She is a Spanish teacher and has extensive experience editing and correcting texts – both student and professional. Any remaining grammatical and spelling errors must not be accounted to her. They proceed from my eccentric ideas about the value of deviating from standards occasionally to accurately portray a state of mind or emotional content. A subtle way that she supported the completion of this book was her endless patience with those eccentric ideas.

In addition, she was willing to endure the many, many times that I worked into the early morning hours pursued by my characters who insisted on telling their stories at the most inconvenient hours.

She has always been emotionally constant in the shifting winds of our lives throughout the long thankless years of the struggle to bring these stories to print. Bravo Lou!

Prelude

For those of you who have not read any of the preceding books, I will warn you that this preface contains spoilers. If you want to learn about the story line to the point where this book begins, you could read the stories in sequence—*In the Realm of the Blind, The Chessmaster, The Spare Wizard, The Ministry Witch and Other Tales of Perfidy, Wandering with Wizards, and The Boy Genius*. However, reading the first book by itself would give you a good grounding in the Realm of the Blind.

This story takes place in the universe of the Realm of the Blind where Hogwarts School for Witchcraft and Wizardry exists. It is a residential finishing school for magical youth.

The main character, James Wendt, is an English Literature Professor and Muggle (non-magical). He has been hired by the Headmaster Albus Dumbledore to bring diversity to the school and the slightest touch of liberal arts education to an institution that is basically a vocational school. Dumbledore has been assassinated by Severus Snape.

Wendt and the Headmistress, Minerva McGonagall, are "an item." However, the astronomy Professor Aurora Sinestra seems to have designs on Wendt.

The cousin of Harry Potter, Dudley Dursley, turns out to be a wizard himself. Too old to be a student at Hogwarts, he has instead been offered the post of Assistant to the Janitor, Argus Filch. Filch is a "squib", a non-magical offspring of a magical family. He is happy to finally have someone who knows even less about magic than he does as an assistant.

This story chronicles Dudley's beginnings as a wizard and employee of Hogwarts School of Witchcraft and Wizardry. The questions that face him are: Can he learn to be a wizard at his advanced age? Will he be accepted by students and teachers? Is there romance lurking somewhere at Hogwarts for him? Is he doomed to be the assistant to a squib forever?

Other teachers at Hogwarts include Rubeus Haggrid (Professor of Magical Creatures), Severus Snape (formerly Potion-Master), and Professor Flitwick (Professor of Charms). Other staff at Hogwarts include the Janitor, Filch; the Librarian, Ms. Pinz; and the Nurse, Madame Pomfrey.

This story follows the close of the parallel lines of narrative of James Wendt and Harry Potter. Everything that follows opens completely fallow ground in the saga of Hogwarts.

The Interview

The day of the interview began as usual with me mum waking me ten minutes before my alarm went off. She hustled me downstairs to what she called a "hot nutritious breakfast". It was enough to choke an elephant. It had kippers, scrambled eggs AND omelets, fried potatoes, muffins with marmalade, French toast and biscuits and gravy. I had gotten out of the habit of saying "no" to mum and today I tried to start new. I had some scrambled eggs and muffins with marmalade and a little orange juice and started to get up from the table. Me mum told me not to pick at my food and finish breakfast.

At the same time me dad was telling me how I should dress for the interview. "Dudders, you've got to prove you're serious by dressing for the job. Now, you go up and change from those jeans and trainers and come back down in a suit and tie. I think the dark grey pinstripe would be very appropriate."

Dad was always sure he knew best on every subject but this time I stood up to him, "Look dad, this is a job as groundskeeper not a bank manager, jeans and trainers are the work clothes. I'd look foolish in a suit."

Mum had been spooning more eggs on my plate and urging me to eat more as I was talking with Dad. Meanwhile Dad was going on and on, "Everybody expects a job applicant to wear a suit these days. Now you get upstairs and change into that grey pinstripe."

I started to get up and Mum shook the spatula that she'd been using to spoon the eggs out at me, "Now, young man, don't you leave the table until you've finished everything on your plate."

Dad interrupted, "Now, Pet, Dudders doesn't have time for that. He's got to go up and get changed so he'll be ready when *THEY* arrive to pick him up." He said the word "they" as if they were from another planet.

I got up while I still could and ran upstairs with Mum shouting after me, "Now, you finish this breakfast before you go anywhere with those w . . . w . . " She trailed off without finishing the word. She never could bring herself to say the word. I didn't know if it was because she hated them or because she was jealous of them.

I ran up the stairs and opened my closet door and stared at the grey pinstripe suit. It didn't fit me very well. I'd lost some weight since we'd been away from home and I wasn't anxious to get it back. Mum was though. I wished that I could just stay up here and then walk down when they arrived still dressed in jeans but I couldn't go against the two of them. I slowly took off my jeans and put on the suit pants. I might be wearing the suit but I didn't have to go down until I absolutely had to.

As I slowly tied my tie, I remembered why I didn't like the suit. I always needed help with the tie. I could never get it the right length. Either the wide part went down below my belt or the narrow part did. This time it was the narrow part. After the fourth try to get it right I almost decided to ditch the tie. When I started to slip it off, I noticed that it was the right length – sort of – if I just left it really loose around my neck. What the hell, I decided. I'll just leave it that way. And just in time. I'd been ignoring my Dad's calls to come down but this time he said that they were here. So I ran down the stairs and found that Mum, Dad, and Professor McGonagall were in the living room.

When he saw me, Dad's face turned red but he didn't quite dare blow up in front of the Professor. Instead he came over to adjust my tie. I just dodged him and said, "No time, Dad, we've got to go." The Professor nodded and said, "No time to waste. Off we go."

As we left the house, both the Professor and I breathed a sigh of relief. She turned to me and said, "Well, it's good that we got away when we did. Now, our next step is to get to Hoggwarts. Just what do you prefer? We could disapparate directly there or we could use the floo network."

I just stared at her. How did she expect me to choose? I had no idea what either was. I was about to ask when she shook her head and said, "Of course, you don't know what either of them is like. Well, let me see. If you disapparate, you go immediately to where you want to, but Professor Wendt says that it's the worst way to travel. But he says that about every way that he travels with magical people. On the other hand. . ."

I decided that he was pretty smart and if he didn't like disapparation, then it was not for me either. So, I said, "Professor, let's do the flu network." I hoped that I didn't have to get sick to use it.

The Professor sighed and said, "We'll have to take the Underground then. Do you know where the nearest station is?" I was having a hard time deciding what to call the Professor, but she settled it for me right then.

She took me by the arm and swung me around, "Dudley, you're now part of staff or shortly will be. We usually call each other by our first names except when students are present. Please just call me Minerva."

"Yes, Professo. . . I mean Minerva." I had a hard time getting her name pronounced. It wasn't that I couldn't say it, it was just that it was the first time that I'd used an adult's first name to her face. And she was pretty . . well . . intimidating. You had this feeling that she was someone that you didn't want to play games with. She always said things in a way that told you that you'd better believe her if you knew what was good for you. Anyway, we were walking down the street and I just realized that we were going the wrong way to get to the Tube. I stopped.

Professor errr Minerva immediately asked me, "What is it now? Did you forget something?"

"Well, yes. . . not exactly. . You see."

She was beginning to sound cross, "Just out with it Dudley."

"Well, we're going the wrong way to get to the Tube." I turned around and headed back toward my house. We passed it and kept going at a fast pace. For an old woman, she could move when she wanted to. I was actually having a hard time keeping up.

We reached the tube station and I bought the cards for us. I stopped right then and realized something. Minerva scowled again, "What is it now?"

I just realized that I'd bought a woman a ticket. This was spooky. Was it like a a a date? I walked over to the gate to the subway and led the way down to the train platform. This was really spooky. The train approached after a minute and when the doors opened, I took her hand and led her in. It happened kind of sudden-like and I dropped her hand as soon as we were inside. This was the craziest thing. I asked her if she wanted to sit. There was just one seat.

She smiled and said, "Why thank you Dudley. That's very courteous."

My cheeks turned as red as a beet. I stammered out something – I don't know what. My eyes were stuck to my feet. Suddenly, someone shook my arm. I looked up and found it was Minerva. "This is our stop. We've got to get moving."

I looked around, found the exit door that was opening and we exited. Minerva said, "I think we want to get out of the tube by that exit." She led me up the stairs and when we reached the street we went to the right for two blocks and turned down a narrow side street. After we walked fifty or sixty feet, she asked, "Do you see the sign of the Leaky Cauldron?"

I looked around and pretty quickly saw an old sign that seemed a little hazy but it seemed to clear up quickly. "Uh, yes. Right there." I pointed and she smiled broadly.

"Good. I was wondering if you'd be able to see it. Good."

I didn't see what was so amazing. It was there as clear as daylight. I found myself holding the door open for her. I did that so that I wouldn't

4

have to be the first in. The inside was old. Old wood. Old fireplace. Old man standing behind the bar. Minerva went over to the bar and said, "Well, Tom, is it a good day?"

He answered, "Any day that brings you through the doors of my establishment is a good day. And who's your young friend? If I may ask?"

She introduced me as a new member of staff at Hogwarts and bought two 'butter beers' – whatever those were. I found out pretty quickly. It turns out that butter beers are not alcoholic (too bad) but are like a butterscotch cream soda. She drank most of hers in a hurry and said, "Come on Dudley, we don't have all day." She got up and led me over to the old huge fireplace.

She explained, "The floo network is connected to most wizarding fireplaces in England. The way they work is that you take a small amount of floo powder." Here she took my hand and dipped it in a little pot that had dust in it. "Then you step in the fireplace, speak the name of your destination clearly, and throw the powder to your feet."

I stared at her and said, "You do what?"

"I thought that I was very clear. In this case, you say the name of our destination – Hogwarts Headmistress's floo. And take my hand before you do it – just in case."

I was worried by that "Just in case." I asked, "Just in case what?"

"Oh, you and Wendt are such sissies. Just do as I say."

With such encouragement I took her hand that she'd reached out to me and we walked into the fireplace and I said, "Headmistress, Hogwarts fireplace." I threw down the powder and it exploded in a burst of green flames. I'd have jumped back out of the fireplace, it surprised me that much, but before I could, I spun around and found myself covered with soot and in a much larger fireplace than I just had been.

Minerva was hacking and coughing as much as I was, but managed to say, "Not bad. Really not bad."

While she was saying that, I was rubbing the dust out of my eyes and looking around the room that we'd ended up in. It was amazing. It must have been as large as a church and had some crazy painting in the ceiling that I would have sworn was moving. Then I saw that the ceiling was somehow a window into the sky. I staggered at that, almost slipping and falling, but I caught myself and gasped, "This is your office!"

Minerva had gotten her bearings and grunted, "No. It's the Great Hall of Hogwarts, where we have meals. My office, indeed!" She saw the expression on my face and added, "Well, you needn't be sad. You got us to Hogwarts. That's an accomplishment for the first try."

She laughed and said, "I think that even Potter almost missed Diagon Alley completely at his first go. He ended up in Bourgan and

5

Burke's in Knockturn Alley. I wish I'd seen the expression on his face that time. He was aiming for Flourish and Blots."

She'd gotten my expression wrong. I wasn't disappointed. I was marveling that I arrived anywhere at all. She grabbed my arm and dragged me after her. We quickly left the Great Ballroom or whatever it was and were headed down a long hallway. We reached stairs down there. As we went she was speaking, "We've got to find Mr. Filch before he leaves his office.", "Don't let him intimidate you. He hates change. He's always saying that he wants to go back to the old discipline, you know, the rack, locking students in stocks, that sort of thing." And then, "Just remember, it's mostly bluster."

After going down two flights of stairs, we reached a hall with several doors. One was marked, "Potions". Another was labeled in faded gold letters, "Argus Filch, Caretaker." Minerva knocked rapidly on the door and called out, "Argus, it's Minerva. Are you there?"

A voice answered from inside. I couldn't make out what it said. It seemed to be a very loud mumble. Then the door opened and on the other side was an old man who stood erect and was wearing a suit that seemed to be even older than he was. I was tempted to ask him if it were his father's but decided not to.

He opened the door wider and invited us in. Minerva introduced me and explained that I was applying for the job of assistant caretaker. When he heard that, Filch scowled at me and asked, "I don't remember you being a student here. Are you from one of those fancy foreign schools?"

He squinted at me as I answered, "No, sir. What schools are you talking about?"

He waved his hand in the air as though he were swatting a fly away, "You know. Durmstrang, Beau Batons. One of those?"

Minerva broke in and explained, "Now, you remember that I said that Mr. Dursley never attended a magical school. Anyway, I want you to explain his duties as your assistant and show him around. If he is favorably impressed, he'll take the job and you'll have your assistant that I promised you."

While she was explaining this, a sly smile crept across his face and he pitched his head sideways a bit as he stared at me. Minerva left and when she did, Filch looked me up and down. Then he asked me a question. "If you've never been to a magical school are you uh . . ." He hesitated, as though looking for a word. Finally he finished, "Magical?"

"Well, people tell me so. But I've only used a wand once and it didn't seem such a success to me."

With that Filch's smile broadened. "Wellllll. You've come to the right place. Hogwarts is a great school for magic and you've got yourself a good guide to magic."

That was reassuring. "Great. Do you mean Professor McGonagall?"

He shook his head dismissively, "No. She's way too busy to spend much time with the likes of you and me. I was talking about me."

I couldn't help smiling. He seemed to be the last person that you'd go to if you wanted to learn magic, but he mistook it for a smile of gratitude. Thus encouraged, he went on, "Yes. I might say that I'm the real brains behind magic at Hogwarts. All the great professors used to come to me for advice.

"They'd say, 'Mr. Filch, what do you think of this spell for curing spatter goit?' and I just tell them right off the go what to do."

He then gave me a tour of the castle. We started in the dungeons where the Slytherin dorm is and worked our way up to the basement and then the main floor. We stopped by Mr. Wendt's office. He knocked on the door and when we were invited in, he asked very politely if we could come in. He tried to introduce me but Professor Wendt said that we were already acquainted.

Professor Wendt spoke to me, "I wouldn't believe too much of what Mr. Filch has to say about students. They're mostly not bad."

Filch sort of looked down at the ground and asked, "Seeing as it's Mr. Dursley's first day here at Hogwarts as part of the staff, I was thinking that we might celebrate with a little, uh . . . you know, drink?"

Wendt seemed to be having trouble holding back a laugh. He said, "Well, Mr. Filch. I'm surprised at you. You know that we don't drink during working hours or in front of the students."

"But this is such a special occasion, I thought that we could like stretch the rules a little bit and just have a wee dram of your good whiskey." He nodded jerkily and had a big smile on his face.

Wendt just shook his head and said, "Oh, you know far better than that. Now. If you were to drop by after dinner tonight, it might be a different case."

"Yes, sir. We'll be back for sure."

Filch just said that he was taking me for a tour and we should be getting on our way. We did. We worked our way up the stairs and he had a comment for the dorms of each of the "houses". "Now, you take Hufflepuff there. They are deadly dull. I never saw any students that had a harder time playing a practical joke on you."

At the Ravenclaw dorm, he muttered something about, "damn stuck-up egg-heads."

Finally when we reached the Gryffindor tower, he spat out his dislike for those student, "Rapscallions all. They are constantly playing tricks on the staff. The worst were the twins – those damn Weasley twins."

He stopped walking and then suddenly began kicking the wall underneath the portrait of a fat lady.

He almost screamed, "Those damn twins. They were terrible."

He went on and on about them, about how they'd invented these fiendish potions that would give you hives or a tongue that swelled up like a watermelon or make you throw up and I don't know what else. By this time, it was getting close to lunch time. So, I asked, 'Do they feed you around here?"

At that, Filch's face brightened and he said, "Indeed they do. Come with me." He lead me down the stairs and past the Great Ballroom and seemed to have no intention of going in, even though there was obviously tables laid out with food and people in there eating.

So, I asked, "Mr. Filch, aren't we going to eat?"

He stopped and looked back at me and said, "Of course, Come with me."

"But isn't that the dining room?" I asked, pointing back at the Hall.

He shook his head and said, "No, no. We've got much better, come on."

So we walked back to the stairs down and went to the first level below the Great Ballroom.

The House Elves

We walked on to a broad stairway that led down below the main floor. When we reached the bottom, we turned and went along a hall for a short distance and Mr. Filch held one of a pair of broad doors open for me. As we entered, the most wonderful smell that I'd ever sniffed filled my nose. Just once, me Mum and Dad had taken me to a fancy restaurant in the City. It was one of those that had fancy white tablecloths and waiters that stood behind you as you ate. That seemed kind of creepy to me at the time. You would be eating and enjoying your steak when suddenly this bloke appeared without warning next to you and was scraping the bread crumbs away from the tablecloth next to your plate. The first time it happened, I almost choked on the mouthful of spuds that I was eating.

But the smells of the food in that restaurant were like the smells in the room in front of me. And then, I almost choked again. In front of me was a . . . a . . . thing that was no taller than my knee. It was looking up at me and said something like, "Begging your pardon, master. Is there something that we can be doing for you?"

I was too stunned to speak but Mr. Filch acted like he saw these things every day. As a matter of fact, I learned later that he did and that I would too.

Filch looked at the space above his head and said, "This here is my NEW assistant, Mr. Dursley. Fix us each a plate of food. We'll be eating in my office today."

Filch turned to me and said, "Them things are House Elves. They do all the cooking and most of the cleaning hereabouts, leaving the more important things for us to do."

I wondered what those more important things would be. But I didn't have long to wonder because the Elf had returned with two plates piled high with the most savory food that I'd ever smelled. As we left the kitchen and walked down a flight of stairs on our way to Filch's office, I asked a question that seemed obvious to me, "We've got plenty of food. What are we going to drink?"

Filch brightened noticeably and simply said, "I've got something really special for tonight – it being your first day on the job."

▽

We arrived at the office and Filch handed me his plate while he unlocked the door, commenting under his breath about the sneaking kids who sometimes broke into his office. After he had the door open, we went in. He pointed at an old guest chair that might have been upholstered in red leather at some time in the distant past.

He cleared a space on his desk by pushing miscellaneous papers off the desk. He opened a drawer of his desk and pulled out two glasses. I wondered when they'd last been washed. However, the elves had provided napkins. I used mine to wipe out my glass.

As it turned out, I hardly needed to do that. I doubt that any microbe could survive the stuff that he filled the glass with.

After filling both our glasses, he raised his glass and said, "A toast. A word to the wise – never trust a student."

I lifted my glass and said, "Nothing ventured, nothing gained." I took what I thought was a cautious sip but what went into my throat seared it and rendered it incapable of either speech or even breath.

As a matter of fact, Filch actually noted, "Takes your breath away, don't it?"

I could only nod.

I commented to Filch after finishing our libation, "I've had the tour. I've eaten and drunk. There's just one thing left missing."

He stared at me and asked, "What could that be?"

I couldn't believe that he couldn't guess. "Where do I spend the night?"

He stared a moment and said, "Oh." After a moment, he said, 'I guess there's only one thing to do. Follow me."

I did. We worked our way up a couple of floors and reached a spiral staircase. He led me up and knocked on the door. A voice that sounded familiar but I couldn't quite place said, "Come."

Filch opened the door and I went in first. It turned out to be the office of the Headmistress. When I was with her away from school, I could force myself to think of her as Minerva. Here, I couldn't help thinking of her as Headmistress.

Filch came forward and said, "Begging your pardon, but Mr. Dursley needs a room to stay in."

10

I was gazing about the room as I listened to them talk. There were bookshelves with lots of books. There was a fancy sofa and several yellow antique arm chairs. There was one red leather chair that looked newer. There was a large desk made of dark wood that she sat behind. The walls were covered by painted portraits. Many of them seemed to be paying attention to our conversation. She was speaking.

"Well, Mr. Dursley, I think that you'll have to stay in one of the dormitories. We may get a room of your own some time, but for now, it's got to be something less grand. Which do you prefer?"

I stared at her and asked, "How can I choose? I don't know anything about them?"

She gazed at me appraisingly and asked, "Are you bothered by heights?"

It seemed a strange question. "What do you mean?"

She said, "Well, both Gryffindor and Ravenclaw dormitories are located in high towers. On the other hand Slytherin is in the dungeon and Hufflepuff is near ground level."

I thought a second and said, "Heights don't bother me."

"Do you prefer them?"

I shrugged.

She thought a minute. "Well, you'll be spending lots of time in your dorm. Ravenclaws are smart and you have to solve a riddle every time you enter their dormitory."

It didn't take me any time to say "No, thank you" to that. I'm not one for riddles.

She went on, "Hufflepuffs are very friendly and well, I guess, some would say that they're boring. But you can be sure that you'll never be short-sheeted."

I laughed at that and decided that boring was bad. She went on, "Slytherins tend to be both smart and devious, some would say."

I thought a while about that. I was certainly devious at times and I knew how to deal with tough coves, but that smart thing bothered me. What if they were so smart that I was always being "put upon". Maybe that wouldn't be so good. I asked, "What about Gryffindors?"

The Head smiled, "I was a Gryffindor. As a matter of fact, I was the head of that house for many years before I became Headmistress. They are strong, brave and true – if I do say so myself. You couldn't want anyone better to watch your back."

I nodded and thought. Gryffindors sounded like the kind of guys that I would like to have had as part of my little gang. I asked a question to give me more time to think, "Can I change my mind if it doesn't work out so well?"

"Certainly, Mr. Dursley."

"But the students can't change."

"No, not usually. But you aren't a student. You have other privileges that they don't." She waited while I thought and after a couple of minutes added, "We don't have all day."

That decided it for me, "Better be a Gryffindor."

She smiled again and said, "Good man! You know that Potter was a Gryffindor."

I shook my head, "No, I didn't know that."

She then shooed me out. Filch took me down to his office to pick up my things and then led me back to Gryffindor. I wouldn't have found it by myself, but I was sure that I could pick up the ways around Hogwarts in a while. We arrived and Filch spoke to the painting that covered Gryffindor's entrance, "Let us in, you old witch."

She had been facing away. She turned to us and said, "Password, please."

"Look, the Headmaster wants Dursley here to stay in Gryffindor. Just give with the password or I'll go get her and she will not be happy!"

The lady pouted and said, "Oh, be a spoil sport then. It's 'Starry Night'."

Filch told me, "Don't forget that. She'll not give it to you again." Then he led me through the door and up one of a pair of stairs. We reached a level with a circular hall and doors facing off it. He stopped at one that had a plaque that read, "Male Resident – Mr. Wigglesworth."

He knocked on the door and it was answered by a man that I had seen at a distance in the Great Ballroom having a meal. I'd not met him. Filch explained my need of a room. Wigglesworth smiled and said to follow him. Filch left us and Wigglesworth led me down the hall to a door labeled 'Grassmere". He explained, "This will be your room. We'll not put any students in here. There are a couple of beds. You can take your pick. Use any of the armoires. Welcome to Gryffindor, Mr. Dursley. If you have any questions, be sure to ask me."

I thanked him and he left me and my things to myself. I unpacked and settled in.

The Beginning of Term

I had a variety of duties as Filch's apprentice. Mostly they were doing the jobs that he normally did. The first day of the week, Monday, we met in his office after breakfast and he pulled from a drawer of his desk a worn piece of parchment that he posted on the old corkboard on the wall near his desk. It had a list of days and tasks associated with each. After he'd finished he explained.

"You need to learn all the tasks that we do. The best way to do that is by practicing. So, we're going to practice."

The first task on the list was cleaning the boys' WC's. I had a feeling that when he said that "we're going to practice." The "we" was really going to be me. I wasn't disappointed in that expectation.

The first thing we did was to go to a huge walk-in closet on the 2nd floor. It had buckets, mops, brooms of all descriptions (but not as I learned later a single broom that you could fly). There were all sorts of "magical" cleaning products. I think that these "magical" products didn't have any more magic than the "magic" cleaning products that Muggles used. As a matter of fact, after a week or two, I came to the conclusion that the "magic" in the "magical" products was what my Aunt Marge calls "elbow grease". I can still remember her instructing Harry Potter to apply more "elbow grease" when he was scrubbing the kitchen floor as he frequently did when she visited.

My Dad wanted to prove to Aunt Marge that Potter wasn't a free-loader as she frequently suspected that he was. Potter actually got to be a decent cook. I preferred his bacon and sausage to me Mum's. He would have made a good house elf.

Anyway, after we collected ONE mop and ONE scrub brush and ONE bucket and ONE bottle of Zonko Magical House Cleaner, we left for the boy's WC on that floor. We arrived and Filch gave me explicit and lengthy instruction on how to apply the mop and brush to the floor and so on. This repeated the next day when we did the women's loos. Was there a difference between the women's loo's and the men's loo's? According to Filch it was subtle and I had to train on both.

The rest of the week was spent on polishing floors and dusting the suits of armor. At one point, getting rather bored with constantly doing all the work, I asked Filch, "Mr. Filch, the House Elves clean the Great Hall, right?"

He agreed..

"And they also clean the various dorms, right?"

Again, he agreed but asked, "Where is this going?"

"Well, it seemed to me that they could do all the cleaning, couldn't they?"

That threw Filch for a loop. He looked at the floor hoping that an answer would rise from the flagstones, maybe. Finally, he said, "Well, you see Uh." He was stuck. I was about to declare victory, when he looked bolt upright. He had an idea and didn't want to lose it, "But, the dorms and even the Great Hall are not common areas. We have to have a better standard of cleaning in the PUBLIC areas where the visitors will be!

"Dumbledore doesn't trust the cleaning of public areas to House Elves. That's got to have the human touch."

I stared at him and he seemed to realize what he'd said and he corrected. "I mean Dumbledore never trusted the common areas to House Elves. That's why he hired me all those years ago." He hesitated and turned away, as if inspecting the hour glasses with the scores of the House competition points. Then he looked back and went on, "And the Head keeps to Dumbledore's ways."

That seemed to settle it, but I knew that the House Elves were just as good as any person at cleaning up. I wondered why Dumbledore did keep Filch on and why would the Headmistress have hired me to help him? Why not just retire him and let the House Elves take over all duties? I wondered about that a lot over the next couple of months. However, I never could come up with a good answer and over time, I let go of the question.

▽

The next week, we had a letter delivered by owl. Actually, it was Filch's letter but it affected me, so I thought of it as our letter.

We were sitting in his office. We were taking an extended lunch hour as he called it. Actually we'd finished our work on the normal schedule early for once, because Filch, for the first time, had decided to actually work rather than just complain about my inept performance on the job.

He slit the seal on the note with a pocket knife. I asked him why he didn't use a spell like, Relashio. He just stared at me and said, "You don't use a sledge hammer to drive a thumb tack."

Embarrassing, of course - for me. It was one of the few spells that I actually knew and I was anxious to prove that I wasn't a complete moron about magic. That didn't work out so well.

However, the owl had come through the crack in the door that Filch always left open because he was paranoid and thought that students were always sneaking around looking for opportunities to do bad things. He claimed to be able to smell mischief at a thousand miles. The owl nudged the door open and hopped over to the desk and leaped up onto it. It held out a claw on which a note was tied.

Filch had removed the note, shooed the owl out of the room and opened the seal and read, 'Mr. Filch and Apprentice." He nodded at me and went on, "Please attend the annual beginning of year business meeting and party to be held on the 27th of August, 1999 at 4PM in the Teacher's Lounge. RSVP is unnecessary as attendance is obligatory. Attire is casual. Best Regards, M. McGonagall, Headmistress, Hogwarts School for Witchcraft and Wizardry."

I laughed, "What kind of party is obligatory?"

Filch said, "A good one. Unlike most events at Hogwarts, this one includes beverages – GOOD beverages, if you know what I mean."

I had to admit that I was curious to see what Filch would consider a "good party". Fortunately, I didn't have long to wait. This note was delivered on Wednesday and the party was only two days away. As the time approached, I realized that I wasn't perhaps quite so anxious for it to come after all. It was the last event on the last weekend before school started and I felt some fear about students being present. It wasn't so much that I didn't think I could hold my own among them, but it was new and they all – even the youngest – knew more about magic than I did.

Time has an amazing nonchalance about our feelings and Friday came despite my growing wish that it wouldn't. Filch couldn't have been happier. I couldn't see that he dressed differently than he did any other day, but I put on my newest jeans and a dress shirt and went with Filch to the Teacher's Lounge.

I asked Filch, "Is the Lounge really only for teachers?"

Filch sneered, "Of course not. Anyone can come to it what works for Hogwarts, if you take my meaning."

I admitted that I did, but I couldn't remember ever seeing Filch there, although I occasionally saw real teachers enter it and leave it.

We arrived before most of the teachers had arrived and Filch picked a spot for us at a table near the rear of the room. Half a dozen tables along with chairs had been set up. These chairs and tables came from somewhere else because the walls were lined with armchairs, sofa's and smaller tables that would seat four. There was a large fireplace and a fire was blazing brightly in it. I enjoyed the cheery fire despite the fact that it was still summer by the calendar.

"Tell me, Filch, who set this all up. I thought it would be our job."

Filch stared at me as though I'd just declared that Christmas should come in July, 'Well, the House Elves, of course. Who else? Ain't it our party, not theirs?"

I had to agree. By then, the rest of the teachers started flowing into the Lounge in numbers. I'd seen them all but had met only a few. Finally, the Headmistress arrived. She looked around the room sternly, nodded as though she'd just verified something and strode to the center of the room near the fireplace. She then began her speech.

"I see that you are all here and in good time too. As most of you know, this is a meeting where I provide you with last minute announcements, and we have introductions for the new staff. After all that business is finished, we have a wonderful meal, followed by pleasant conversation and convivial spirits."

Filch nudged me in the ribs and whispered, "Especially the convivial spirits if you know what I mean."

I had to admit that Filch might be a man of few ideas but he stuck to them with a tenacity that was admirable. But the Headmistress was going on.

"First, let's introduce ourselves to the new staff and vice versa. I'll introduce each, and then each of you will take turns standing, providing an interesting bit of information about yourself and greeting the new staff members.

"In alphabetical order, there is the new Defense Against the Dark Arts teacher, Stephani Appelcart." She rose uncertainly, stood a moment and sat quickly, "She occupied that post several years ago. Eight, I believe." Stephani nodded agreement. "She left us because of an injury and now is back to give it another go. Please, make her welcome with a good round of applause." We did.

"Next is the new Muggle Studies professor, Joseph Arne. He is the child of two Muggles and has written a column for the American newspaper, the *Magic Report*. The column was an advice column dealing with proper protocol and dress when mixing with Muggles. I think it often dealt with Muggle/Magical Romance issues, didn't it?"

Arne stood and agreed about the newspaper column. Filch punched me in the rib again and said, "I doubt our Miss McGonagal needs much advice about that," and sniggered. I supposed that she must be involved with a Muggle and wondered who it could be.

Then, I realized that my name was being called out. I was introduced as an apprentice of Mr. Filch and helper who maintained the Castle. Then, the bottom fell out, "Mr. Dursley is a wizard but has not had the advantage of training at Hogwarts or other magical school." She gazed around the room like Medusa and proclaimed in a voice that frightened me, "I trust that the ENTIRE staff will support the Hogwarts policy that EVERYONE, staff, teachers and students, all deserve full respect." Here she hesitated and added, "Variances from this policy will be handled swiftly and with discipline befitting the seriousness of the breach.

"Now, each of you, new staff and old, will stand and give a quick fact about yourselves." That nearly panicked me. What could I possibly say that would be interesting? That I was a middle school boxing champion? Stephani was showing off the body part that she'd lost when she was a Dark Arts teacher.

Fortunately, I was seated near the back and had time to think. When Arne stood, he told everyone that as a reporter he'd once interviewed the President of the United States. Nearly everyone seemed puzzled or bored but I burst into applause. I knew who the President of the United States was, anyway. I even shouted out a question, "Which one?"

He hadn't expected that, so he fumbled a minute and then said, "Why, President Clinton. It was during the time that Valdemort was running the show over here, and we wanted the President's reaction for American Wizards and Witches."

Eventually, it was my turn and I was still stuck for an idea. I stood up, cleared my throat, looked down and noticed my glass of water. I picked it up and took a swallow that I could barely force down so that I could gain time, but then I was stuck.

The Headmistress looked at me quizzically and then mouthed something at me silently. I gave my head a little shake in confusion, and she, showing her consternation, almost spoke out loud, "Potter".

Then I got it, and I almost slapped my head in relief, "Of course. Uh. I mean I am Harry Potter's cousin, and we grew up together." That resulted in some genuine applause as though I'd achieved something noteworthy. I quickly sat in embarrassment. I can't even remember what Filch said. It was something about keeping kids in line.

Then the Headmistress made a few announcements – the dates of the Holidays, parties, Owl and Newt exams – whatever those are – and so forth. After those announcements were over, she made a little speech.

"As all of you know, this is the first school year that I am Headmistress, but I consider it much more significant that this is the first REAL school year after the loss of Professor Dumbledore.

"Professor Snape who replaced him was a flawed person, and for all his virtues, he was not able to lead Hogwarts as it should have been. I hope to bring back a bit of the spirit of Professor Dumbledore. Almost all of you knew him and have an idea of what I mean.

"One of his traditions that I can't emulate was giving a word before each meal. Each word was whimsical and often had meaning for that particular moment when it was given." Here her voice caught in her throat, and she stopped for a moment. "Instead, I will simply ask each of you to be silent for a minute and remember Professor Dumbledore in you own way. That will be the custom at every meal in Hogwarts during this school year whether students or professors or staff are present. After that moment, I will sound my glass to signal that the feast has begun."

Some lowered their heads, some closed their eyes, others just seemed to simply sit in quiet repose. Then suddenly, the Headmistress dipped her finger into her wine glass, ran it around the rim of the glass and produced a brilliant, sharp, clear sound.

Then food appeared on the platters before us on the tables, and the Headmistress said, "Dig in."

⋈

The work was easy until the students arrived. On my third week at Hogwarts, the students arrived on the Hogwarts Express. I didn't realize that was going to happen until the day came that they were supposed to arrive. It was getting late in the evening, and I wondered where the students were. My experience at my own school was that parents drove up with their kids all through the afternoon of the first day before school started, and there was no order to it at all.

I asked Filch about it, and he said, "Haven't you never heard of the Hogwarts Express?"

I had to admit that I hadn't.

"Well, how did you think they'd get here?"

I scratched my head and realized that I'd not thought about that. Then I said, 'By floo or maybe their parents would disapparate them."

Filch only shook his head and said, "No. No. That's all too dis-order-ly for Hogwarts. Everyone arrives at once by train." He hesitated a minute and then took my shoulder and pulled me off toward one of the stairs. "Come on with ye." He led me up the stairs that turned out to be the ones that went to the Astronomy tower. No one was there, but we stood on a parapet and looked out over the Lake and toward a train station.

Filch said, "They should arrive shortly. We'll just stay here so you can see what happens when the train arrives."

Eventually in the waning light I could see the smoke from the stack of a train, and then I could hear the train itself pull into the station. Filch commented, "It's hard to see from here, but if you look closely, you'll see

18

there are a bunch of boats on the lake near the station. You can't see them, but there are carriages near the station as well."

I looked hard and barely made out the boats. Then, the boats were filling up with people. I watched them sail off. Filch then pointed down to the road from the station to Hogwarts, "Watch there. The carriages will come into view shortly."

They did. There were carriages and people in the carriages but no horses that I could see pulling the carriages, "Mr. Filch, are the carriages going by magic?"

He laughed, "No, sir. You can't see what's drawing them?"

I didn't like the way he said that, "What's drawing them?" I admitted that I didn't. But then, I did begin to see something as though through a haze. They seemed like horses, but I was pretty sure that they weren't.

He laughed again, "Well, some folk think it's bad luck to see what's pulling them." I couldn't help gagging. What were they?

Filch laughed again, having noticed my expression, "Oh, nothing to be afraid of. It's just that you can't see the Festrals that are pulling those carriages unless you've seen someone die. They look a little like horses – nothing really scary."

I then understood. I had seen someone die, but it was so dark and murky that I perhaps almost hadn't seen the deaths.

I changed the topic back to the boats, "And I suppose the boats are pulled by invisible porpoises?"

He laughed again. I was giving him lots of opportunities for fun. "No, that's real magic that's pulling them. It's all 1st years as ride in them."

"Why's that?"

"Oh, it's good for morale if they come over in boats without anything visible pulling them. It scares most of them good, and it makes our jobs easier for the first term or even longer. Sometimes one or two of them will fall into the water.

"That's usually good." He noticed my stare. "It's good for the ones who don't fall in because it lets them know that punishment's always right around the corner."

I had gotten the gist of it and finished the idea out loud, "And it's good for the ones who do so that they have something more to be really afraid of."

Filch just smiled and said, "Right you are, boy-o."

As we were gazing down at the carriages approaching the castle, Filch suddenly came to life and said, "We're burning moonlight. We've got to get down to the Great Hall. We have to be there when they arrive." We both sprinted to the stairs and down the stairs as fast as we could go. We arrived before everyone except a few professors who were sitting on the stage.

Filch hurried over to one of the long tables. I followed him. He sat at the end of the table nearest the entrance where I sat across from him. I was curious about his choice of tables, "Why this table?"

Filch nonchalantly said, "Oh, any of them would be alright, but I always like to sit at the Slytherin table."

"Why?"

"Well, the professors that came from Slytherin always seem to have a better idea of discipline than all the others. Oh, I'll give you that sometimes a Gryffindor has a good idea of discipline, but all the others are just Nancy's about discipline."

Shortly after that speech, students started filing in and taking seats. To make conversation as we waited, I asked, "I suppose the 1st years know their house assignments before they arrive."

Filch looked offended, "Oh, no they don't. They have to get sorted out by the . . "but he was interrupted by the arrival of a troop of students that I guessed must be 1st years. They marched to the front of the hall and stood as a group. Professor Grubbily-Plank was leading them.

Filch jumped up and whispered, "Be back in a minute. Just wait here."

When'd they'd gotten in order, at the front, the Headmistress stood and greeted everyone to a new school year. She then proclaimed that the sorting into houses would begin, and she called for the Sorting Hat. Just then Filch re-entered the Great Hall carrying an old, tattered, tall, pointed hat. He carried it up slowly and as he passed me, I saw that the hat had eyes! AND a mouth! The eyes looked over to me as it entered the hall and the mouth spoke as it passed me, "What I wouldn't give to sit on that head for five seconds."

The strange comment overwhelmed me. It was obviously talking to me and about me. What in the world did it mean?

Shortly I learned, because the 1st years were called one at a time. Each sat on a stool. The hat was placed on its head and after a shorter or longer interval it named a Hogwarts dormitory House. Apparently that was the way that the 1st years were sorted into Houses.

At the moment that I realized that I went into shock. What in the world did it mean? Did it want to "sort" me out? I missed most of the rest of the sorting. I couldn't remember the little song that the hat sang. As a matter of fact, I was so much trying to understand the hat and what it meant that I didn't notice when Filch had returned or remember where any of the students had got sorted.

He nudged me, and I looked up. The Headmistress had just said something, but I didn't know what it was. Filch prodded me and said, "Stand up."

I did and the Headmistress repeated a question that was apparently directed at me, "Mr. Dursley, would you please tell us something interesting about yourself?"

It was lucky that she'd asked the same question as at the Teacher's Banquet. I remembered what she'd prompted me to say, "I'm Harry Potter's cousin, and we grew up together."

There was a gasp through the hall and then some applause that mostly came from one table. Then other tables joined in the polite applause. I was still stunned. Filch kind of punched me in the back, so I did a half bow. Then he dragged me into my seat. He mumbled something from behind me about "dolts".

The Headmistress gave a short speech that was pretty similar to the one in the Teacher's Lounge about this being her first year as Head and our having a short period of quiet before every meal. The moment of quiet came and went, and she urged us to "Tuck in."

The meal was again spectacular, and the rest of the time in the Great Hall was fun – except that every now and then one of the people near us at the Slytherin table would ask me if I really were Harry Potter's cousin. When I admitted to that, which seemed to be generally regarded as a crime at that table, many a student sneered and asked a question that usually was along the lines of, "How could you stand living with that creep?"

I was, at first, speechless when presented with that question. I had hardly expected it, and I just sort of gaped at the questioner. Later, I admitted that at first it was pretty miserable having him in the house, but I got used to him after a while.

When the meal was over, the Head sent all students to their dorms. I wasn't sure what to do, so I just hung around as the students filed by. More students, mostly from other tables, asked a similar question as they passed me, "What was it like living with Harry Potter as a kid?" The general impression I got was they expected me to say something about how wonderful it was. Sometimes the question was posed as, "What was it like living with the "Boy Who Lived'?" I didn't have an answer at all for those.

As the last of the students filed past, they tended to be the oldest. One of them, a girl with long jet black hair asked me, "Are you really Dudely Dursley?" As far as I know, neither the Head nor anyone else had mentioned my first name.

I answered, "Yeh, how do you know my first name?"

Her face compressed into a mask of anger, and she replied between clenched teeth with more force than I could have believed possible, "Ginny

21

Weasley is my best friend." I was trying to figure out the significance of that when she punched me in the nose. She did that with a whole lot more force than most of my boxing opponents had used. I tripped backwards over my chair and felt the warm sticky feel of blood running down over my mouth.

Filch was at my side to help me up, but before he could say anything, the Head was standing between me and the girl, "Ms. Stern, did you think I was kidding when I said that anything less than total respect for all staff would not be tolerated. Twemty-five points from Gryffindor, and you will see me tomorrow night in my office for detention."

Stern was obviously getting a reply ready but something in the Head's look must have warned her that this was a field of battle that she didn't want to stay on. She glanced at me and then back to the Head and her teeth were not clenched when she said simply, "Yes, ma'am. But fifty points?"

The head's head of steam had not decreased, "One more word and it's one hundred points, Ms. Stern."

Ms. Stern's face turned ashen, and she just walked away.

Filch had a big smile on his face that quickly turned to one of solicitous concern when the Head turned to him. He quickly said, "I'll take you up to the hospital wing to have that looked at."

I picked up a napkin from the table and stopped the free flow of blood. Filch looked at me and said, "I don't think I've ever seen a house start off in negative territory before the first day of classes." He was smirking again. He clearly enjoyed the discipline being meted out.

We reached the hospital wing and found Madame Pomfrey reading some sort of magazine. As we approached she looked up and clucked her tongue, "Not even the first day of classes and already the first casualty." She looked at the blood and me and asked, "What happened? Did some first year try some stupid spell?"

Filch was laughing, "No, Ms. Stern of Gryffindor threw a punch that hit Dursley here square on the nose."

She asked, "What in the world caused that?" Then she turned to me accusatorily, "What did you do?"

Filch wouldn't let me answer. He was laughing so hard that I was amazed that he could get words out of his mouth, "He admitted that he was Harry Potter's cousin and lived with him for years."

She seemed puzzled, but she got straight to work. She pulled the napkin away and the nose started oozing blood slowly. "Well, this is simple. I'm surprised that Minerva didn't do something right on the spot."

Filch started laughing again, "Oh, she did. Gave Gryffindor a minus 50 points."

Pomfrey frowned at me and said, "Well, I hope you don't admit to being Potter's cousin again."

I said, "Are you kidding. If one kid asked me what it was like living with Potter, then a hundred did. I don't want to hear that question again as long as I live."

Then she took up her wand, touched my nose, and said, "*Episkey.*" My nose hurt far more than it had when Stern hit me. I squawked, "That hurt! What the devil are you doing? I thought you were fixing me?"

Pomfrey said, "I did. Your nose is set and it is no longer bleeding. Don't be such a sissy." Then she added, "Oh, yes. I like Potter, and most of the upper classmen and teachers know how you treated him."

I thought about objecting to the unfairness of that, but decided I shouldn't argue while Pomfrey still had a wand in her hand. She said, "Go clean up that blood before I decide to do it myself."

I didn't need further hints. Filch and I left immediately, stopping by a sink in a boys WC to clean the blood off my face.

The Room of Requirement

I was walking on the third floor looking for a suit of armor to polish. That was my job that morning, but I wasn't thinking of armor, really. I was thinking about a desk for Mr. Filch's office for me. He said that he'd find one for me, but it had been a couple of weeks and I was darned if he had done anything to find one. I was thinking about how much I needed a nice desk. I had no idea what I'd put in it, but I wanted one.

I turned a corner and there was still no armor in sight. There weren't even any of those strange paintings with moving (and talking! for goodness sake) people in them. As I was walking slowly along the hall, I noticed a bit of something out of the corner of my eye. I turned suddenly and found that next to me, there was a door where there had never been one before. I stood for minutes on end trying to decide whether to just keep walking or run as fast as I could or go over and open it.

I decided finally that I'd walk over and open it ever so slowly and carefully. If there were the slightest reason to be scared, I'd run for all that I was worth. I stepped up to it slowly, and as I did, the more real it seemed. I reached out, afraid to touch it, as though I could still escape until I touched it. Then, once I did touch it, I'd be trapped in something that I had didn't understand.

I reached out and touched the door handle. It was not strange in the least. It might have been the door handle to my home in Little Winging. I swallowed a lump that had formed in my throat and turned the handle. It rotated easily, and I had no sense of impending doom. I pulled slightly, and it moved on its hinges without the slightest creaking or effort. I kept myself behind the door for as long as I could. There was a dim light streaming out from the opening onto the castle floor.

I pulled the door past me, and I looked into the interior and saw the most jumbled mess of things that I'd ever seen in my life. My mom would have fainted at the mess. There were chairs, boxes, bookcases complete with books, brooms, and things that I couldn't even guess what they were.

They were piled precariously and randomly. As I looked on, they all seemed to have been damaged, many by fire. I was about to turn away and close the door when I noticed a desk. It seemed to be undamaged, though it was hard to tell from a distance. It seemed to be made of a rich dark wood. It was just the sort of thing that I would have liked to have had for Filch's office.

I wet my lips and tried to decide if I should go in to investigate it. It did look beautiful. Perhaps too beautiful. Filch might just think it was nicer than his desk. I walked over and opened a drawer. It had a stack of parchments in it. I pulled one out and read. It seemed like a letter from home but it was in very strange English. I closed the drawer again. Since I was here, I decided to do a little looking around. I wanted to keep the door that I'd entered in view. The room was very large, and I wasn't sure that I could see the far wall.

I walked around a bit, though. The further in I went, the more fire damage there seemed to be. Parchments were little more than piles of ashes. The chairs and brooms and piles of books were charred deep below the surface. I picked up a book and it crumbled in my hands.

On the way back to the door, I took a different aisle. There the damage wasn't so bad. There were armoires and coat racks and everywhere stacks of books. Finally, I made my way to the door and closed it behind me. I was sure that I could find the fine desk again that had somehow escaped serious damage. I went on down the hall looking for armor to polish.

▽

The next day while Filch and I were taking a break, Filch with his feet up on *his* desk and I sitting on the other side. I asked him how the search for a desk for me was going. He glanced over at me and said, "Well, not well. I've not found a good one yet."

I persisted, "What about the Headmistress? Have you asked her?"

He became shifty, "Well, not exactly, but I've started thinking about how to ask her."

I shook my head to myself. This would never happen if I didn't do something myself. So, I started my speech that I'd been thinking about all morning, "Wellll, I was keeping my eyes open, you know, just in case I happened to run across a desk. And, . . ."

Filch broke in, "You didn't find one." Then he added, hesitantly, "Did you?"

"Well, as a matter of fact, I did find an old desk in a strange room."

Filch became suspicious, "Just where was that strange room that you found?"

"On the third floor near. . . "

Filch actually stood up and almost came around the desk, "Let me guess. The room was large. You didn't see the door at first. It had dueling equipment and lots of open space."

I wondered where that strange description had come from. At first, I thought that he'd seen it, but then, I didn't think so. "Well, sort of. Leave off the open spaces and dueling equipment, and you might have it."

"Yeh. That's the room all right. I call it the. . uh . ." I could tell that he was making it up on the spot. "The Room of Finding. That's because you can find the things you need there. You. You. You found that room."

I stood too, "Let's go find that room and that desk."

He looked at me with that look that says, "Do we have to now?" I just walked to the door, opened the door, looked back, and watched Filch reluctantly follow me.

We worked our way up the stairs and reached the hall where THE room was. I walked up to the spot where the door was, but nothing happened. I stared at the wall and it hit me that I didn't really know how the door had appeared. I thought that my just being there would open it up, but it didn't.

Filch just smiled and said, "Welp. Don't feel too bad. It's happened to me more than once. Back a couple of years ago. I was trying to find that Potter most of the year when he was in there."

We trudged back down to the office, and I wondered how I could find THE room again.

The next few days, I spent a lot of my free time up there. It didn't do any good. I decided to give up for a while.

Continuing Education

The next week I was walking down the 2ⁿᵈ floor hall and passed Professor Flitwick's classroom. The door was open, and there was a class going. It was the strangest class I'd ever seen. Everyone was standing with wand in hand. They were waving their wands wildly and saying *"winguardium levioso"*. They were standing there staring down at the feather that was sitting on their desks. A few of the feathers were drifting lazily in the breeze.

Flitwick was apparently losing his temper. He walked around from his desk and went to one student and said, "No, no. It's *winguardium levioso* and don't wave your hand so . . so . . . .oh, wildly. Smoother. Like this." He pulled out his own wand and waved it in a smooth compact motion.

The student tried again. The result was that the feather fluttered up into the air a moment and then fell again. Flitwick enthused, "Yes. Much more like it should be." He moved on to another student. Just then someone grabbed the back of my shirt and pushed me away from the open door. He whispered in my ear loud enough to break my eardrum. "Mr. Dursley, let's not forget that you're not a student here. Now, what about that suit of armor up ahead? That deserves your attention rather than Professor Flitwick."

I moved on, but I didn't forget Flitwick's lesson. That night in the Common Room of Gryffindor after lights out, I put a sheet of parchment on a sofa, stood over it. I pulled out my wand and stared at it a minute. Then in a voice that was even squeakier than Professor Flitwick's, I tried the spell, waving my hand in an imitation of the easy swooping motion of Flitwick.. Nothing happened. I kept at it for a while, trying different motions and different pronunciations of the spell. Nothing happened, so I went to bed.

The next couple of days when I was on break, which was pretty often because Filch was not a really hard master, I would try the spell on whatever was at hand – a gum wrapper, a scrap of parchment, a dead fly. I had no luck.

Then one night in the Common Room, I was practicing again. However, this time it had been a long day, and I'd lost my temper. I was bellowing out "wingardium levioso" and waving my wand so fiercely that I didn't notice when someone was coming up behind me. My wand smacked him on the nose. I swung around, "Sorry! So Sorry! Did I hurt you?"

The person that I'd hit was Mark Nowand, a 6th year that I'd met the first day of classes at Hogwarts. But he seemed to be apologizing too, "Sorry, sir. I didn't mean to sneak up on you. Are you OK?"

The idea of someone "sir-ing" me struck me as so funny that I couldn't help laughing, "Oh, sorry, ha ha ha, I'm not laughing at you. I'm laughing at the idea that you called me 'sir'. Oh ho ho. To think that I'd live to be 'sir-ed'!"

Mark could only say, "Sorry, sir." again. Then he laughed once also. That set me off and we both were guffawing like loons. When we regained control of ourselves, he said that he'd heard someone making an awful racket and came down to see what was going on.

"Well, Mr. Nowand," and here I blushed, "I was trying. Well, I was trying to do this wingardium levioso thing, and I just couldn't get it to work and I kind of lost my temper."

He took a step back and stared at me for a minute and asked, "Uh, no offense intended, but you aren't a. . . a. . . a. . . "

I supplied the word that he seemed to be afraid to say, "Squib?" Nowand sighed with some relief and nodded. I went on, "No. It's just that I haven't really gone to school much. It's a long story, and I don't want to talk about it."

Nowand smiled a little and immediately suppressed it and said, "Well, then, maybe I could just give you a little pointer or two." With that, he walked over behind me and said, "Just let me guide your hand." With that he took my wrist and swung it throw a small loop that ended with an upward thrust. "OK. Do that a couple of times without saying anything."

I did. Once or twice he took my wrist again and made a small correction. Then he seemed to be satisfied and said, "OK. Let's try it with the spell. But first, just say the spell. No motions with the wand. As a matter of fact, why don't you set your wand down?"

I did and tried just saying the words. He made slight corrections a couple of times and then he said, "OK. Put the motion and words together, and let's see what happens."

I did and couldn't believe my eyes. The parchment that I was practicing with fluttered a bit. It was hard to see, but I could tell that it had. But Nowand didn't seem to be pleased. "You did the words and the motion pretty well. That parchment should have flown off the coffee table." He seemed to be pondering. He looked down at the coffee table as though he could move it with just his thoughts. Then he whacked himself on the side of his head, "Of course. What were you thinking about when you said the spell?"

I shrugged, "Oh, I don't know. I guess I was just trying to be sure I got the words and the motions right. That's what I should have done, right?"

He nodded in triumph as though that explained everything. "No. No. No. If you concentrate on doing things right, it won't come off. You have to be... Oh, I don't know." He seemed to be searching for words. "Oh, oh, you have to be . . . visualizing. Yes, that's it!" He almost shouted as though he'd made a brilliant discovery. "Yes, you have to visualize the parchment rising up."

I frowned, "But, if I do that, I'll get the motion and the words wrong."

"No, you won't. The most important thing is KNOWING that the paper is going to fly up and letting your body do the remembering about motions and words."

I shook my head. "I don't think I can just KNOW that it's going to work."

He paced around and then said, "It's like my granny used to say when I was little. 'If you're having trouble, just close your eyes and imagine.' You do that."

I imagined how stupid I'd look with my eyes closed and waving my hand, pointed at who knew what. I started to shake my head, but Nowand just stared at me. I finally gave up, "OK. I'll do it. Just promise you won't laugh at me."

Nowand smiled but agreed. So, I closed my eyes. He said, "Now before you do anything, imagine for a second, the parchment rising up." I did. Then he said, "Now go ahead with the rest."

So, I kept imagining the parchment flying up, and my hand moved, seemingly without my telling it where to go. A voice that I recognized as mine said, "winguardium levioso." Then I heard Nowand laughing. I opened my eyes, and in front of them, the parchment was sailing off somewhere. Also, the coffee table was higher than my head. Then, instantly, the coffee table dropped and would have hit the floor with a crash, but Nowand had his wand out. Hedid something, and it gently lowered to the floor.

His smile was as wide as the Thames. "You see." There was triumph in his voice, but not triumph over me somehow. It was triumph over the world and all the things that are always going wrong.

All that I could say was "Wow!" Then, I thought and added, "Boy, what I wouldn't give to be able to impress a girl or two that I used to know with that trick! But it'd be their skirts not a coffee table."

"Yeh. I have a girl that I'd like to impress here."

I asked, "You have trouble impressing girls? I'd have thought you'd have them eating out of your hands."

"Maybe some girls, but it would take something a whole lot more impressive than that to get her attention. She's pretty darn good at spells herself."

I was curious. "If you don't mind, who is that?"

His face turned red and he looked down at the floor. "There's a 7th year here. Here in Gryffindor. She's Pamela Meyers."

I couldn't help whistling, "No kidding. Who wouldn't want to impress her?" He nodded, and we both thought for a moment about the blond Pamela. She was just the right height, had shoulder length golden brown hair, and was smart. Everything she wore made her look like she'd just walked off a magazine advert. I realized that I'd said some of that out loud, so I just finished up, "Yeh. Everybody in Gryffindor would like her to go with them on a Hogsmead weekend."

Nowand swore, "Bloody Hell. Every guy in the school, you mean."

I laughed and nodded. "Bloody likely that's going to happen with either of us!"

He stopped laughing and seemed to be in deep thought. "Maybe not. Hmmm."

"What did you say?"

"Oh, nothing. I was just thinking of class tomorrow. I've got to get some sleep. See you later." He ran up the stairs. I followed and went to my room.

▽

The next few days, I practiced the *levioso* spell and found that I could do it pretty well and even control what it was that flew up in the air. I was sweeping the floor on the first floor one of those days when I heard a strange conversation going on. At least, it seemed to be a conversation. I couldn't make out the words, so I walked down the hall to hear more clearly. I discovered that Professor Wendt had left his classroom door open and I gazed in to see several people standing with books in hand and reading out loud.

What I noticed most was Pamela, she was just saying something like, "Then poor Cordelia! And yet not so, since, I am sure, my love's more richer than my tongue."

In that moment my heart melted, and I said to myself (I think), "Oh you are far, far richer, Cordelia! In every way. In form, in mind, in words, in dress, in graceful movement, in the love you bring to my heart." I really had ears and eyes only for her. I heard her say, "Unhappy that I am, I cannot heave my heart into my mouth: I love your majesty according to my bond; not more nor less."

Oh, dear Pamela, you say it so well. But my problem is that my heart does heave into my throat and keeps me from speaking when you are near.

I don't know how long I stood there, stared, and listened and listened and stared. Thank God, Mr. Filch didn't happen along just then. In a little while the class ended. Professor Wendt gave an assignment and reminded them to keep practicing their parts. The class started to pack their back packs and get up.

I was still standing and staring when the first left. I suddenly realized that I should at least pretend to be working, so I started to push the broom. I suddenly wished that I was doing anything other than pushing a broom when Cordelia, er, Pamela came out. She stayed behind a minute to ask Wendt something and then came out by herself. A couple of her friends were waiting for her. She smiled and for a blessed moment, I thought she was smiling at me. Then I realized that she was smiling at them. I immediately turned so red that my face felt like it was on fire. My eyes shot to the floor but not before I'd caught her eye for a second. At least, I like to think it was my eye that she was smiling into.

The rest of that day, I stayed there in that hall, hoping she'd return to ask Wendt a question. Stupid. I know.

That evening at dinner in the kitchen, I asked Filch a question, "Mr. Filch, does Hogwarts have a library?"

Filch shook his head, and then a broad smile came across his face, "Of course, it has a library. What would a school be without a library?" An idea seemed to occur to him. "Would you like to see it?"

That was the last thing I expected from Filch. I had seen no sign that he liked to read or even owned books. But he was actually stuffing the last bits of supper down his throat and actually grabbed my arm to hurry me along. We reached the library and he even held the door open for me to enter. Inside, he led the way to the desk of the librarian. Filch introduced me to Ms. Pinz whom I'd seen around Hogwarts but we had not really been introduced.

She was very courteous toward Filch, but when she heard that I wanted to have a library card, she was rather short. "Well, Mr. Dursley, why do you need a library card?"

I was surprised by the question. I'd never had a librarian ask me that question. At the school libraries, they practically force them down your throat and try to get you to take books out. I just stammered for a minute.

She said, "You see! He doesn't need a library card. He doesn't even know what he'd do with it."

I regained my tongue and said, "Yes, I do. I want to take a book out."

She continued to regard me with suspicion and asked, "What book?"

I was back to stammering, "Well, uh, uh, I don't exactly know."

She didn't even dignify that statement with a comment but just threw her hands up. I regained my tongue again, "I don't know what it is, but I can describe it."

Still suspicious, she said, "Go ahead then, and we'll see if you need a library card or not."

"Well, it's a play." I hesitated while I tried to think of something else to identify the play. She just stared down her nose over her wire-rim glasses at me. "Uh, it's got a woman character named, uh. . Cordelia."

"Oh, wonderful! How many plays do you suppose have a character named Cordelia?"

"I don't know. Do you?"

It was Ms. Pinz's turn to be befuddled. "Well, I. . . " Filch sniggered briefly and quickly stopped. Then her expression changed. Her grimace relaxed, and she asked in a gentler tone, "This isn't the play that Professor Wendt is doing with the 7th years?"

I blushed a bit and nodded. "Well, why didn't you say that at first? That's Lear."

I was puzzled. "I'm not leering."

"No, no. The name of the play is 'King Lear'. It was written by William Shakespeare. Now, let me see. I don't know if I have a playbook with just Lear in it, but I'm sure we've got a Complete Plays of Shakespeare. Let me see." She got up walked to a cabinet that had dozens of tiny drawers, pulled one open, and began riffling through the cards there. She quickly found one and said, "Ah, ha! Come with me."

We all followed her to a bookshelf and watched as she ran her forefinger down a shelf and pulled a thick book off the shelf. My heart sank as I thought about reading the whole book, and I asked, "The play's that long?"

She actually chuckled, "No. This is all the plays that Shakespeare wrote. I think something like two dozen. *Lear* is one of them."

I breathed a sigh of relief and reached for the book. She drew it back and said, "Ah ah ah. Not until you've checked it out."

We went back to her desk where she opened a drawer of her desk and pulled out a sheath of papers. She handed them to me and told me, "Please fill out this application and bring it back to me during normal library hours."

I was dismayed again. Amazingly, Filch noticed and said, "Can't we help him fill it out now?" His smile would have lit the room up. She looked at him and said, "Will you stay and help?"

"Of course."

"Then, certainly." She turned to me and started asking questions. There were the usual – name, address (how could she not know that I lived here at the castle?). There was birth date, age, character reference. Filch volunteered himself. Ms. Pinz's smile would have lit the library. Then there were the strange ones: sign of the zodiac (which I didn't know), was I a wizard, Muggle or Squib, was I staff or student (how did she not know this?), was I an Animagus (?). The questions went on and on and finally ended with: What Quidditch team was my favorite.

She admitted to Filch that that was just a little joke of hers.

She took her time filling those answers in and announced that she would have a decision within a week. Filch frowned at her, and she giggled and took a small piece of pre-printed parchment from a drawer. She filled in the date, my name and asked me to sign it. It was my library card. She smiled, wished us a good day, and turned her attention to Filch.

I pointed out that I hadn't gotten my book yet. She frowned and said, "Oh, yes. Well, since this is your first book, you have to take the Library Cardholder Oath."

"O.K."

"We used to make kids take this as an Unbreakable Oath but Professor Tippet didn't allow that. But you still have to take the oath."

I didn't want to known what the Unbreakable Oath was and was glad that I didn't have to take it. She recited the oath, and I repeated after her. "I Dudley Dursley swear, affirm and agree to return all books as soon as possible but certainly before the due date. I swear, affirm and agree to treat all books as the valuable property that they are. I swear, affirm and agree to not break the backs of books. I swear, affirm and agree not to write in books. I swear, affirm and agree not to lose library books. I swear, affirm and agree not to talk in the library. . . "

It went on and on. Just when I thought it wasn't going to finish, it did. She handed me the *Collected Plays of William Shakespeare* complete with a card in an inside pocket that announced that it was due back at the library on Oct. 18. I headed back to Gryffindor to find a quiet place to start reading. I was determined that when I ran into heavenly Pamela next, I would be able to discuss the wonderful play, *King Lear*.

I picked a prominent chair in the Common Room. I hoped that Pamela might just notice what I was reading as she walked past. I spent a day or two with the book open in front of my eyes but not getting much read as I surreptitiously scanned the room for signs of her. She actually did walk through a couple of times when I was in the Common Room, but she was always with friends who briskly walked by on their way up to the girl's dorm. Fooey!

Back to the Third Floor

Filch sent me up to the third floor one day to sweep. While I was up there, I wasn't even thinking of finding the room. I was wondering if I'd ever get my own desk when I felt something happening. I couldn't say what it was, but I immediately looked up from the floor and scanned the corridor. Sure enough, there was the door that I had been looking for so long and hard before. This time, I didn't hesitate but ran directly to it and flung it open.

It did open. Inside I found things much as they had been. There was the desk at the end of the aisle. There was the profusion of junk of various sorts. There was no clear sign of a far wall. This time I decided to spend a lot more effort looking around. It was an amazing collection of junk. Now that I had time to look, I found everything that I'd seen around Hogwarts: broomsticks, desks, chairs, beds, armoires, quaffles, blodgers, books, cauldrons, vials, etc.

Almost all of them had one or more defects – broken legs, bent handles, torn covers—you name it. There was even one poor snitch with a broken wing that was just wobbling crazily in circles. However, there were a few items that seemed unaccountably whole. They stood out like sore thumbs even in this menagerie of miscellaneous mistakes.

There was a strange glass display case. At least, it would have been a display case if it had had some shelves, but it was at least seven feet tall, was glass on all sides and had never had any display shelves. Then, there was my (I'd begun thinking of it as mine) desk - beautiful and with no flaws that I could find. I took a very careful look at it. All the drawers worked. There was even a set of keys taped to the bottom of the wide shallow drawer above the knee hole.

Then there was the strangest of all items. I don't know what attracted my attention but it seemed to stand out. It was a book resting on the top of a broken down dresser. It was old, and the exterior was fairly worn as by frequent use, but there was no real flaw to it. I walked across the way to pick it up. It was a text book.

The title was _Advanced Potions._ It had a sort of sketch of a cauldron on the front cover. I opened it and thumbed through it at random. It was marked up as though the owner had thought every page filled with errors. The notes were in a sort of italic printing. A lot were difficult to read. After a few minutes I thought there wasn't a single page that wasn't heavily annotated.

I glanced at my watch and found that I'd already spent 45 minutes here. I made a snap decision that I would keep this book. I didn't think it would be a good idea to leave it here for when I returned with Filch to get the desk. Besides, who knew if I could get in again?

▽

I got back to work. When Filch and I had supper in the kitchen that evening, he wondered if I'd read anything interesting lately. That scared me. Had Filch seen me wasting my time in the mystery room?

But it turned out that he had something different in mind. He winked at me and said, "I was walking by Professor Wendt's classroom and I saw the class practicing a play. _Lear_ it was." Then he nudged me and went on, "I can see why you might be interested in the character Cordelia. Quite a looker that."

I was so relieved that I actually admitted that I wanted to have something to talk with her about. So, I was reading the play. He nodded wisely and said, "Not a bad idea, but you'd do better if you were more athletic, you know, played Quidditch, eh?"

I nodded mutely. Shortly afterwards, Kretur came to the table and sat with us. "How are you gentlemen doing?"

Filch mumbled something. I don't think that he entirely liked Kretur. But that question got me to thinking. "Kretur, can I ask you a question?"

He just shrugged, and I went on, "Do you know anything about a strange room on the third floor. . ."

Kretur interrupted me before I could finish, "Yes, yes. The Room of Requirement it is. What is it you are wanting to know about it?"

"How do you get into it?" Then, another question occurred to me, "And why do you call it the Room of Requirement?"

Kretur swelled up a bit with pride, "The name, the house elves of Hogwarts knows about it for longer than anyone knows. And some students and teachers knows about it too.

"We calls it the Room of Requirement because it always comes when someone is needing something."

That was amazing. I couldn't help asking who made it.

36

"Nobody is knowing who created it, but some house elves think it was one of the founders – Rowenna Ravenclaw maybe. They's is believing it was created as a sort of logic test. Only people who could figure out its secret could get in."

This was crazy. How did the house elves know so much about it? But I asked, "OK. What is its secret?"

He looked at me with a sort of disapproving frown but answered anyway, "I shouldn't be telling you this, I'm thinking." He hesitated and went on, "The enchantment of the room is that it will provide whatever a magical person needs if he thinks clearly about that need. But, and this is the real trick, the need has to be something that is real, uh, made of something.

He seemed to be thinking a minute and then went on, "So, if you just said, I want the room that Harry Potter uses, it won't open for you. You have to have a real need of some thing."

I thought about that. Then I asked, "So, if I thought, 'I want the room that I was in last week', it wouldn't work, right?"

"No, it wouldn't."

This was really exciting. Then a thought occurred to me, "You know that the room is full of all sorts of junk. . . er . . things. Does someone own them?"

Kretur thought about that for a long time. "Well. Kretur thinks that all those things were things that people wanted to hide, get out of the way like."

I added, "Most of them are things that are broken."

"Yes, that make sense to Kretur." He slowly drawled the answer out. "They is things that someone broke and wants to hide. Maybe they thought that they would come back and fix them. They never did."

That made me really excited, "Then if these people didn't want anyone to find them and they never came back for them, they must not want them any more?" I nodded my head hopefully.

Kretur shrugged and agreed, "Maybe. You sees something in the room you like to have?"

I was a little embarrassed but I answered quickly, "Yes."

"Well, they've been there for a long time. I think they belong to whoever claims them."

"Great."

All this time, Filch had been listening, and now he said something in a sort of sing-song voice, "I see what you're thinking. You've seen a desk in there haven't you?"

I nodded, "Yes."

He slapped his arms on the table and said, "Well, then. Let's go up there tomorrow and see what we can find." He was actually excited by the idea. Maybe he was a sort of pirate at heart, ready to appropriate whatever was not nailed down.

⧖

Later that night, when I got back to Gryffindor, I was planning to take up my usual post reading *Lear* and keeping an eye open for Pamela, but somehow I couldn't get my heart into it. Instead, after sitting in my habitual chair for a few minutes reading, I got up and went back to my room. I pulled the middle drawer of my dresser open and took out the other book.

I thought about going down to the Common Room. This book might be as interesting to Pamela as Shakespeare, but somehow I just didn't want to share it right now. Maybe I was afraid that someone would claim it as their own. What would I say?

So, I sat in the old leather chair in the corner and began to read it.

I found that the inside cover had an inscription. It was apparently the property of the Half-Blood Prince whoever that was. Across from that inscription was the title page. It was the only page that didn't have some sort of handwriting on it. The table of contents showed that the book was organized into sections of increasing difficulty. The first section had the easiest potions. Even these pages had notations. But they were comments on the book itself. That first section had a little note that said, "You'd think they'd get these right!"

Apparently the author of the notes didn't think much of this textbook. But still, he'd filled it with notes. The first potion was one to make people laugh. I read the directions. They didn't seem all that simple. I thought about it and decided that maybe even I could do this first one. Anyway, the page had several corrections. The brewing time was decreased slightly and the ingredients were not to be mixed thoroughly. I shook my head at the idea of making such minor changes.

I poured over this book in the evenings of the next couple of days. After the first couple of potions, the going got much harder. For one thing, there were many more notes and they were harder to read. They were smaller so that they could all be fit on the page, of course, but there was something else that made them harder. The author had a sort of shorthand that he used for phrases that he used often. It took me a while to figure out.

Even after I'd realized that, I still found the corrections harder and harder to comprehend as I went along.

The Desk

After a few days of laboring over the potions book of the Half-Blood Prince, it occurred to me that it would be better if I had that desk down in Filch's office where I could read with more comfort. So, I asked Filch one night to come with me to get the desk.

He wasn't anxious to help, claiming that his arthritis was bothering him. I begged, "Oh, come on. Please help me. I have a right to have a desk. It's just sitting up there waiting."

Filch smiled a smile that I wasn't completely happy with and said, "Well, laddie, since I'm likely to make my arthritis worse, it'd only be fair if you took on a larger part of our work for a while. Oh, say for the rest of the term."

"You are a pirate, Filch. No way. I'll give you two weeks."

His face screwed up in an imitation of pain, "Oh, I can feel it coming on even now." He hesitated and said, "Two months. That's final."

"One month and you'd better take it while it's still there. I might just ask a house elf to help me."

"Six weeks and it's a deal."

I thought it over and finally decided it was the best I would get. So, we agreed to do it Saturday morning. I've heard Professor Wendt describe breakfast at Hogwarts on the weekends. Breakfasts are very good. When I was living at home, I would have loved it. I haven't quite had the appetite that I once had. But this morning, I had an appetite. On weekends, Filch and I sometimes went to the great hall to have breakfast. This was one of those times. We sat at the Gryffindor table because I wanted to. I live with them. I'd actually started liking them. Not too surprising, really. For a long time I hated Harry Potter and every thing that he was associated with. I'd heard him mention Gryffindor once or twice, and I hated it because he loved it. Then he saved my life.

Filch was staring at me and he asked, "Harry Potter saved your life?"

I hadn't realized I'd said that out loud. "Uh, yeah."

"You're kidding me."

"No, he really did. There were a bunch of Dementors going after us, and he saved my life. He sent them away. I don't know how."

Filch was still staring at me. He shook his head and said, "Here I thought you were on my side."

I didn't know what to say. I just shrugged. He shrugged too, and we dug into the wonderful strudel on the platter between us.

After it was over, we walked up the stairs to the third floor. I said out loud what I had thought the other two times that I'd been on the third floor, "I need a desk."

Filch just shook his head and said, "Well, let's go back to the office and have something good to drink."

But I saw a door appear in the wall – just like the last time. "Come on Filcho, Filchee old boy. Here it is. Let's go and have some fun." I ran over and grabbed his arm. He looked up and stared.

"What are you talking about?"

I looked from him to the door and back again. "Don't you see it?"

His eyes wrinkled up, "What are you talking about?"

"The door, man, the door, what do you think?"

Filch just shook his head. But then, he looked again at the wall and his face changed. "Yeh, I see it. Where did that come from?"

"That's the Room of Requirement." I walked over to the door and opened it. Filch just said, "Shit." Inside, there was everything that I remembered including the desk. I started to walk over to it, releasing Filch's arm. He shouted and looked around as though I'd disappeared. I suppose I had. I walked out and took him by the arm again.

"I think that you need to hold onto me to come in." I practically had to drag him in.

Once inside I released his arm, and he walked around, ogling everything. After a while he delivered his verdict, "What a pile of junk!"

"Yes, but my desk is right over there, and it's just perfect." I walked over, and he touched it, feeling its smooth, cool, solid surface.

We both took an end, and we both lifted – without effect. Filch groaned and said, "I feel me arthritis coming on."

"No, you don't, Filch. You agreed and you're going to help me! I'm not going to be your slave for six weeks if you don't."

He stared at me and growled a low growl like a dog that my Aunt Marge had once. It was not an angry growl. It wasn't quite a whine either. That dog had expected to get something, and it was hoping to remind me that it expected it. Then he said, "Well, what do you expect me to do? Even working together we didn't budge it."

I leaned back and thought. As I did, an idea formed in my mind. "OK. Filch. Stand back I'm going to try something."

He stared at me warily and seemed about to growl again, but he backed off a couple of paces. I took hold of my wand in my jeans pocket and pulled it out. I stared at it a moment hopefully and pointed it at the desk and said, "*Wingardium Levioso.*" For a moment nothing happened, and then the desk shifted and slowly lifted off the floor.

Filch shook his head unbelievingly and whistled, "Well, I'll eat my head if that desk ain't floating in air."

I was pretty surprised too. My mouth dropped open, my arm fell, and the desk did too with a thud.

Filch smiled a crafty smile and said, "Well, it doesn't look like you need my help, do it?"

I frowned at him and said, "I certainly do. I can get it off the ground but I don't know how to move it. I think that you'll have to push it or pull it while I lift it."

His smile deflated into a frown, and the frown became a hard line across his face. "How do you know that will work?"

"I don't know that it will, but we're going to try it and see." I must have said that with a lot of determination because Filch just nodded. I lifted the desk again with the spell and told him to pull it. He did. It turned out to be easy for him to pull it. As a matter of fact, too easy, he could give it a pull, and it would float along without any further pulling. The first time that he pulled it, it quickly sped up and would have knocked him over if he hadn't jumped out of the way. Before it went far, it slammed into a pile of broken chairs and stopped.

"Be careful, Filch, you'll run it into something and scratch it."

He grumbled something, and we got started again. This time, he was careful as he guided it to the door. We went through, and once we had it completely out and had started off down the hall, the door to the Room of Requirement had disappeared.

Filch smiled another crafty smile, "Sometime we should go back up here and do a little exploring. I'll bet we could find a bunch of useful things."

I wondered about that but didn't deflate his good spirits by pointing out that to get back in, we'd have to come up with something that we needed that was in there. That might not be really easy, but we kept working our way down the hall. Both Filch and I had begun to think that this was going to turn into a snap.

Then we reached the first flight of stairs. I guess that we both thought that the desk would just glide down the stairs the way it had glided down the hall. Well, in a way, it did. The only problem was that after the desk had gotten a little more than half-way over the stairs, the desk tipped over and started to accelerate down the stairs like a sled down a snow-covered hill. I had this strange experience of seeing it happen in slow motion. I tried to think of something to do to stop the inevitable. I failed. I kept my wand arm up. I was afraid to drop it, but there were a couple of seconds in which the desk kept going faster and faster.

Filch jumped up on the desk, which kept him from being bowled over like nine-pins, but I could see that the desk was going to hit the turn in the stairs and it wasn't going to turn. In those few seconds I saw the end of my career at Hogwarts, the end of Filch, and maybe the end of me. He screamed something that would have been a curse if he weren't overwhelmed with terror.

I watched frozen on the spot, waiting for the inevitable.

The inevitable didn't happen. From behind me, I heard someone say in the clearest voice that I'd ever heard, *"Arresto Momentum."* And both the desk and Filch rapidly slowed to a stop. When I was sure that a terrible collision hadn't occurred, I turned to see who had saved my bacon. My heart immediately dropped back down into the depths of my stomach somewhere.

It was Headmistress McGonagall. "Well, Mr. Dursely, I see that you've been practicing your *'Wingardium Levioso"* spell. Let's get you, the desk, and Mr. Filch down to his office and then we'll go back up to my office and have a little discussion."

That was it. My career was all over. For a moment I thought about Pamela. Then, I realized that when word got out about what had happened, I'd just as soon see her as I would want to see McGonagall in a few minutes. I couldn't avoid that meeting, but I would resign if McGonagall didn't fire me to avoid the other meeting.

We walked down and found Filch dusting himself off. When he saw who his savior was, he eyes went down to the floor and they didn't get up again for a long time. McGonagall quickly got us sorted out. She even showed me where I'd gone wrong with the spell. She showed me how to keep the desk from tipping over. She was actually pretty nice about it.

We went down another two and a half floors together. She let me take the final flight of stairs, practicing what she'd shown me. We got down to the lower level, and she let us proceed on our own to Filch's office. However, she insisted that we come back up to her office as soon as we'd put the desk in place.

▽

Filch and I moped our way up the staircases to the Head's office. He was constantly grumbling as we went. He seemed to think that it was all my fault, and he shouldn't have to come up with me. We eventually reached her office, and I knocked on the door. For a moment, we both thought that she might have had some important business that took her away, but just when we were about to turn and go, we heard her clear crisp voice, "Come. You've taken long enough getting here."

We entered the office. She invited us to sit. We all sat there for a good minute and she finally asked, "Well?"

Filch looked at me, and for once, I knew he was right. So, I started, "I'm sorry Headmistress. I'm ready to quit. If I owe the school anything for the damage . . "

I couldn't bring myself to look her in the face. "Oh, don't be such a whiner, Dursely. You didn't do any damage, and I think you showed some cleverness, using the *Levioso* spell."

I looked up for the first time and found that she had a little smile on her face. When she saw my eyes, she immediately turned off the little smile and said, "But, if you're going to use magic, you'll have to practice it thoroughly under controlled conditions before you try using it in the 'wild', yes?"

I could only nod and agree. Filch started to get up but she now turned toward him. "Did I suggest that the interview is over, Mr. Filch?"

He lowered himself back into the seat and shook his head, "No, ma'am."

"Well, then. Why in the world were the two of you moving a desk down the staircases, where did it come from, and why didn't you ask me for a desk?" She turned to me as she asked this last question.

Filch's mouth opened in apparent astonishment, and nothing came out. I looked up at her and asked, "Would you have gotten me a desk?"

"Of course I would," She quickly added, "and even if I didn't, I'd have helped you get one for yourself. But where did it come from? I don't want you to tell me that you 'found' it in someone's office."

"The Room of Requirement." When I said that she stared at me and was silent for a while. She seemed to be focused internally on something. Then she looked up at me again and said, "I think I've only heard that term used once before. You don't mean the room where . . . "

I decided to finish her statement for her, "Where Harry Potter practiced with the D.A."

A look of amazement came over her face, "Do you mean you got into that room?"

I shrugged and was about to speak when Filch ended his silent period and said, "Of course, that's what he means. We found it a couple of weeks ago, and we were deciding how to get the desk down from the Room of Requirement."

She had been watching Filch deliver this amazing statement and started to ask him, "Since when are Squibbs able to . . . oh, never mind

Filch." She turned to me again and went on, "How DID you get into the Room of Requirement?"

I glanced over at Filch, unsure as to how much I should verify his crazy claim. Before I decided, the Head decided for me, "I'll not hear any more of this cock and bull story about Filch finding that room. How did YOU find it, Mr. Dursely?"

"Well, it was really mostly luck. I happened to be polishing armor up on the third floor, and I happened to be thinking about wanting a desk when I heard something behind me. I turned and noticed a door where there had been none before. I went into the room and immediately saw the desk at the end of an aisle of broken furniture."

She shook her head slowly, "And you had no idea that such a room existed?"

I shook my head, "No."

She steepled her fingers and stared in them for a while. Then she went on, "I've never been in that room. Oh, I'd heard rumors for years but I didn't fully believe in it until Potter and his gang actually used it." Then a thought seemed to occur to her. "Tell, me, did you see a glass cabinet in there?"

I agreed, "Yeh, with all glass sides and no shelves and a fancy handle?"

"Exactly." She leaned back and thought a moment. "OK. I'd heard a rumor that it was used by Deatheaters to get into the castle. I didn't believe it."

I was confused and asked her, "What was the cabinet?"

She nodded, "It's a vanishing cabinet. You put something in and say the spell and it vanishes, to return later. This vanishing cabinet supposedly had a twin somewhere. People could travel between them. I didn't believe that rumor. Now, I'm not so sure.

"Well, I hope you've learned something from this experience – both of you."

I nodded eagerly. Filch said, "Yes, ma'am. I'm not going to trust Dursley here again."

"Well, the two of you are dismissed. See that you don't get in trouble again. . . At least not soon."

We left her office together and Filch invited me, "Let's go down to the office and have a shot." I didn't object.

Potions

The next week was quiet. I had my desk. I spent a lot of my spare time at it puzzling out the potions book and its odd inscriptions. Well, that was my idea but the truth was that I had very little time to puzzle out the book. Filch never let me forget that I'd promised him 6 weeks of slave labor.

One day near the end of October, Filch came into the office while I was working the book and said, "Laddie, guess what happened in the girl's bathroom on the 2nd floor?"

I sighed. I didn't know what the answer was, but I knew that I would find out in the most intimate way shortly. Filch went on, "Well, there's this awful stench coming out of it. Just trot along up and clean up the mess, whatever it is."

I trudged out of the office with Banshee cleaner (it scares the dirt right off the floor), mop and bucket. I hated to think about what I might find up there. I rounded the final flight of stairs and walked down the corridor toward the girl's loo. I arrived and opened the door trying to prepare myself for whatever it was that caused the awful smell that I could smell from the moment I reached the 2nd floor.

Behind the door I found something that I would never have believed if Filch had told me. It was Knowland, bent over a huge black kettle with a fire under it and a steady stream of noxious smoke wafting away toward the open window. He didn't notice me enter. I cleared my throat, and he practically jumped over the cauldron—he straightened that quickly. 'Don't you ever announce yourself when you come into the girl's loo?"

"Well, not usually. I don't usually come into a girl's loo. Now, see here. What is it you're doing here making that awful stink?"

He looked around as though he were afraid someone were likely to hear him. "Do you promise not to tell?"

I was getting unhappy about this guy acting like he had every right to be in the girl's loo, but I said, "It depends."

45

He seemed to see me for the first time. Then he said, "OK. Here's the thing. I'm really not supposed to be here."

I shook my head. "Do you think?"

"I mean. I've got a good reason. I just don't want to tell."

"Well, you'd better if you don't want me to march you to the Head's office."

He thought about that for a moment. "Would you?"

A single look at the expression on his face told me that he knew the answer to that question. He went on. "You see. I'm brewing a potion that's . . . well. . . maybe not exactly part of an assignment."

I was rapidly losing my temper. "Let's just go up and see Professor McGonagall and see what she thinks."

"OK. OK. Here it is. I'm brewing a love potion."

I couldn't help laughing. "You think that you're going to get a girl to drink some of that awful, smelly, mess in that pot?"

He looked down at it and he seemed to realize that it did seem pretty hopeless. "Well, I'm following the directions exactly in the Advanced Potions book."

That rung a bell in my head. "You mean the textbook by . . ." I had to think a minute to remind myself of the author of my copy, "Somebody by the name of Cleaver?"

"Sure, that's it. Why?"

An idea formed in my head and while it was solidifying, I started to pace back and forth. Meanwhile Knowland said, "Well, come on. If you're going to turn me over to McGonagall, just do it and let's get it over with."

I shook my head, "No. No. I just got an idea. Give me a minute to think it through."

He stared, "You mean that you're not going to turn me in?"

"I didn't say that. . . yet. Just let me think." As I paced the idea became more and more solid, and I liked it the more that I looked at it. His attention was now fixed completely on me. He was beginning to have a hopeful look on his face.

With a decisive nod, I looked over at him and said, "Yes. I'll do it.

"Now, I want you right now to put that stupid fire out and open the windows as wide as they'll go. Then poor that awful mess down the toilet."

He was still staring at me, and I said, "I mean now. It's not too late for me to change my mind."

He immediately used his wand to extinguish the flames and went over to the windows. I went on, "Stay here until I get back. No. No. Go back to Gryffindor, and I'll meet you there in the Common Room." Then I ran out the door. I went down to the office and found Filch there with his feet up on his desk.

"What was it?"

"Oh, it was a stupid student playing with his chemistry set."

He ogled me and asked, "What do you mean chemistry set?"

"Oh, you know. He was trying to make a potion and was screwing it up."

"What did you do?"

"I had him clean up after himself and go back to his house."

Filch nodded and returned to his contemplation of the glass of fire whiskey that he was slowly sipping, "Good. I hope you gave him a good detention."

"Oh, I did better than that."

He looked up, smiling craftily, "Something really nasty, I hope."

"He's going to work for me for a while."

"Blackmail, eh? I like it. A little subcontracting."

I nodded absently, pulled my potions book out of my desk, and began thumbing through it. I reached the page that I wanted, pulled out quill and parchment and began making a list.

I finished the list and headed off to Gryffindor. The student was sitting in an armchair. Since it was a nice day, there were not a lot of people hanging around the Common Room. I came over and sat down in a chair next to him. I handed him the list. He stared at it for a few minutes and shook his head. "What's this?"

I tried smiling a superior smile. "This is a list of ingredients for a potion that will really do what you want."

"You're crazy if you think I'm going to go out on the limb again, sneaking some of these out of the supply cabinet in Potions class. I had enough trouble getting the ones I had before." He tried to have a hard, determined look on his face, but the slight quiver in his lip gave him away. When I was in Muggle schools, I got to be pretty good at judging people's faces. I figured that he was pretty determined, but I could tell that I could turn him fairly easy. He reminded me of one of the gang members in my last school – nice fellow but a little starved for friendship.

I decided to play Mr. Nice Guy. "Well, you know that I'm going out on a limb for you not reporting you for this infraction of rules that you were doing. ... " After a minute, I added, "And I'd really like to help you with this little project of yours. Who knows, it might be useful for me to have some of that potion when we're done."

He brightened a bit at that idea. "Oh, yeh. Who do you want to use it on?"

"Oh, no one in particular. I just like to have a thing or two in my hip pocket should the need arise."

He smiled a broad smile at that. I knew the smile. The co-conspirator smile. Each has a little bit of blackmail material on the other. I was offering him a little additional safety for this joint venture of ours. "OK. But have you ever made this potion yourself?"

Here was a question that I hadn't anticipated. He had a point. How did I know that it would work, that it wouldn't poison the person that it was used against? This was the point of no return. How would I answer his question? I decided in that moment that I was going to have to trust the Half-Blood Prince, whoever he was. I couldn't believe that he would go to so much trouble making those extensive notes just to trick someone into making a fool of themselves or worse. It just didn't make sense. The first time someone used one of these crazy potions it would backfire, and he'd never try another one. No this had to be for real. And, come to think of it, I'd never heard of a student anywhere making such lengthy notes in their book – even to pass a course. This guy had had to be doing it for himself. God, I wish I had a drink or something in my hand to pretend to be doing something while I was doing this thinking.

I smiled my best bluffing smile and said, "No, I've never made this potion, but it comes from a lot better book than that thing that your teacher uses."

He was surprised by that answer, "What do you mean? The potions book we use has been used for the last 15 or 20 years. I'm using one I got from my older brother when he took the course. It's just like the fancy new ones from Flourish and Blotts."

This was getting easier as I went, "I'm telling you. I've got the real shit. I know a bloke who's writing a new book that will blow the pants off of that piece of dreck that you're using. He lets me look it over to sort of like edit it to make sure that it's easy to read. I have to admit that I wasn't great in school. If I can get it, anyone can."

He sort of looked me up and down and said, "I guess you'd be good for that." He quickly added, "No offense intended."

I smiled a broad happy smile, "None taken." I gave him a minute to make sure that he believed that and then said, "So, when can you get the ingredients?"

He looked up as though he saw something over my left shoulder and said, "I have a potions class tomorrow, but we won't be doing anything new. I wouldn't have a reason to go to the supply cabinet. But the next class I should." He seemed to be almost bold, "It's getting close to the Halloween party. Do you think we can brew it right away?"

I leaned back in the chair and pretended to consult an imaginary calendar that I kept in my head. "I've got a lot of work to do, but maybe we can manage it before the party."

He jumped up and then sat down quickly as though remember that he needed permission to leave. "That would be great! We'll meet at the girl's loo on the second floor that night right after dinner."

He again got up, and I shook my head and he sat down again. This was just like my last school. I was actually a little scared. When I agreed to come to work here, I thought that I'd left all that behind. But here I was. I was doing the same stuff from before. It was almost like some people who were selling drugs at school. They used the addiction of kids to get their "highs". I promised myself that after this was over, I'd stop.

"We're not going to work in the girl's loo. I've got a better place. Just meet me on the third floor after dinner."

I told him to go study and slapped him on the back as he got up and left for his room.

▽

Back at my (that is, our) office, I got some parchment out and the Half-Blood Prince's book and found the love potion. I looked at it and realized that I was crossing another bridge that I might not be able to go back over.

Filch was taking a little nap, but his cat, Mrs. Norris, jumped on his lap and must have dug her claws in, because he shouted and sat up. "What the . . ." Then he realized where he was and saw me sitting at my desk staring at the parchment in front of me. He stared at me a minute and something struck him as funny, "Cat got your tongue?" He laughed so loud that I had a little time to think about an answer.

Before I could say anything, he had another idea. "No, no. I get it. It's a love letter, isn't it?" He was slapping his knee and was practically bent over, gasping hard to get his breath.

While he was still laughing, I just decided to start writing. It was difficult. Even the title was hard! The Half-Blood Prince had crossed out the original title, *Amortensia*, and written in his own title. Apparently, he'd decided that he didn't like that title, had crossed it out, and had written another. He'd crossed out his first title so completely that I couldn't read it at all. But I was determined to know what he'd been so anxious that no one know. I stared at it from different angles and had finally guessed that maybe if I looked through the page by staring at a light through it, I could make it out. It was strange. I wasn't absolutely sure. His first title seemed to be something like "With Lilies" or maybe it was "For Lily". I pondered that. Maybe, the idea was that there should be Lilies present when someone took it. I never figured that out.

His final title was simple – just "Love Potion # 9". Maybe he'd tried several other formulas before he ended with this one. Fortunately, the rest of the instructions, including his corrections, which changed almost every step and ingredient were easier to read.

I had to re-write several drafts before I was satisfied with everything. The longer I worked on them, the easier it got to read his cramped handwriting. But I was determined that my version would be much easier to read. After I was satisfied that I'd got it all right, I wrote a final neat copy.

By this time, Filch had calmed down and looked to be ready to leave for dinner. I put the book, my neat copy, my unused parchment, and the quill and ink back in my desk. I tossed the draft copies into the fire that was almost always going in the fireplace. I followed Filch out the door, and he asked if I was ashamed of my love letters because I had burned them. I was getting tired of Filch's "humor" but a question occurred to me, "Hey, Filch, have you ever heard of the Half-Blood Prince?"

I caught him up and could see his face. He seemed to be taking the question seriously. He scratched his chin and said, "Can't say as I have. These young whippersnappers get all sorts of fancy ideas. You know that Harry Potter used to call himself 'The Chosen One'?"

"No, I didn't know that. What was that all about?"

"Oh, nothing worth talking about. He just got a swelled head, the way lots of them do."

The next day was Thursday before Halloween weekend. That year, Halloween came on Sunday. Sunday is a school night, so no parties then. The party was the day before. Henry was getting nervous. He stopped me in the hall after breakfast that day.

"Dursley, do you have those instructions yet? We need to get working on them."

He was anxious. He had run to catch me up and still had a few drops of sweat on his brow. I said calmly, "This is a school night. We're not doing anything until tomorrow after dinner. Really, the instructions call for a solid six hours of work without break. I'm not going to stay up until 3 AM on Friday morning OR Saturday morning to work on this with you."

He had an answer for that, "That's OK. Just give me the instructions after dinner tonight, and I'll do the rest."

We had been walking. I stopped and turned to face him directly, "I am NOT doing that."

He began to wheedle, "Why not. I don't need YOUR help." He immediately regretted saying that, but I pretended that I'd not heard the emphasis on the "YOUR".

I explained in my best "I'm just being reasonable" voice. That almost made me laugh. When had I ever used a voice like that before? Anyway, I explained, "In the first place, you don't know how to get into the place that we're going to. And I won't show you. It's way too dangerous for a student to use by himself. And it's the perfect place to do potions. You'll see. It's even better than the potions classroom."

I mentally crossed a finger when I said that. I didn't even know if it could be a decent place to do potions or not. I just had a hunch that it would be.

"Secondly, you screwed up the last potion that you worked on by yourself. I'm not going to have to help clean up the mess again. I'm going to be there to make sure that you get it right." I expected an objection to that. I had never mixed a potion or whatever you call it. I couldn't believe that he didn't call me out on that one, but he didn't.

"And," I hesitated here. I'd forgotten what number I was on. So, I just finished, "finally, I want to make sure that I get my share."

"What do you mean 'your share'? It was my idea, I had to get the ingredients, and I'm doing the work. Why do you need a share anyway?" Then an idea seemed to occur to him. He squinted at me, as if seeing me for the first time. "You have a girl that you want to use it with, don't you."

I tried to keep a straight face but he said knowingly, "I knew it! You've got a sweetie that you want to impress." Then eagerly, "Who is it anyway? Surely not one of the teachers. They're all ancient. Maybe that new waitress at the Three Broomsticks? Eh?"

I tried to look dignified, "No. It isn't the new waitress at the Three Broomsticks or anyone else. I just like to have something in my hip pocket. You know, just in case."

"Oh, sure. Just in case. That's what I always say when I don't have a chance in heck."

I just shook my head. He came back to practicalities. "OK. But we get together before breakfast. I can wait for the last minute, but I need at least a little time to use it before the dance."

I agreed, and we parted company.

I heard something. I tried to shake my head and roll over. The noise kept going and actually sounded louder. I tried to blink myself awake. By that time, I identified the noise. It was someone knocking on the door. I struggled up and looked at the luminous dial of the alarm clock on the table next to my bed. It was 4:37 AM. What the hell was going on?

I mumbled, "Hold your horses. I'm coming." Whoever it was must not have heard because the knocking just kept going. I mumbled louder, "Just a minute." With that the knocking became more insistent. I finally was on my feet and staggering toward the door. I kicked something on the floor. Later, I realized it was the trunk at the foot of my bed. But I didn't really care at that moment. I just shouted, "Bloody Hell."

51

I reached the door and opened it, "What is it?" My eyes weren't completely open, but I realized that it was Henry. I was mad now, "What the shit are you doing waking me up at 4:37 in the morning?"

He had an eager flushed expression on his face, and he admonished me, "No need to swear. I told you that I wanted to get started before breakfast."

"You moron! This isn't before breakfast. This is after dinner!"

He looked a little sheepish at that and said, "Well, I couldn't sleep any more. I must have rolled over in bed for an hour. I figured that you must be as excited as I am, so I came to get you."

By this time I was thoroughly awake. "Ok. You're here. It's morning, sort of. I suppose that we might as well get going."

"Wonderful. We can finish the potion in time for lunch. Maybe I can give it to her then."

It was then that I noticed that he had his cauldron, a gas bottle and Bunsen burner as well as a sack that I guessed was full of the ingredients. "Just leave all that stuff here."

He looked at me as though I were a raving lunatic. "We need that. How will we brew the potion without the equipment?"

"Look, I told you. Where we're going has all the equipment that we'd ever need, right? Just put it in my room. You can take it back later."

He looked at me very doubtfully, but finally agreed and put his stuff in my room behind the door. Then we started off. I led him down through the Common Room. As we opened the painting of the Fat Lady she addressed us, "Where are you two going? This is after hours. Do I need to report you?"

I grimaced and thought a second. Then I realized that I was staff. "Look. I'm a member of staff. I and Mr. Knowland are off so that he can serve a detention with me."

She looked puzzled and then said, "Oh, I suppose so. He must have done something very awful."

"That is a confidential matter. We never discuss student discipline except with the Head."

She looked a bit embarrassed, "Of course, I didn't want you to break confidentiality. I was just . . uh . . wondering . . " She trailed off and we went on down the stairs toward the third floor.

Knowland looked at me with something almost like respect. "You handled the old bat pretty well."

Something about the attitude struck me the wrong way. I frowned at him and said, "You are never to talk about any staff or teachers that way. Do you understand?"

He was surprised and just stuttered, "Well, uh, well, I didn't mean any harm."

"See that you don't forget."

We continued in silence to the 3rd floor. When we got there and Knowland realized that we were headed there he spoke, "Oh, the famous 3rd floor."

I asked him, "What do you mean 'famous'? Do you know about this?"

He studied his toes and shook his head, "Not really. It was just that two years ago, all the 'in' kids were heading off to the 3rd floor. I couldn't get anyone to talk about it?"

"Why was that?"

"Oh, I was new." I must have been staring because he quickly added, "That was the first year I'd been here since before the great Goblet of Fire."

I tried to look knowing and smart and didn't say anything. I didn't have to. He went on, "I'd been out of the country for several years. My dad was an ambassador. The last couple of years we were in Paris. I had to go to the 'great' French academie. You know, Beau Batons."

I nodded as wisely as I could. Then a thought occurred to me, "But surely the potions classes there must have included love potions?"

He chuckled, "You'd think so. But they don't let kids do those until 7th year. Before that they spend a lot more time on food related potions."

We had reached the spot that the door seemed to appear and I closed my eyes and thought, "I need a room with lots of potion brewing stuff." This was it. I would really look stupid if nothing happened.

For a minute, nothing did seem to happen but then Knowland gasped, "Wow! Blimey. Where'd the door come from?"

I just smiled and walked over and opened it praying to God that there would at least be a cauldron on the other side of the door.

———

What I opened the door on made me gasp.

I had taken about 2 weeks of chemistry my last year at Muggle school. I'd survived through the introduction to chemistry equipment and basic techniques. It was just enough for me to get the names of some of the equipment and to learn how to light a Bunsen burner. That actually was the end of my chemistry career. I'd lit the burner. While my lab partner had been getting the flask filled with water for our first experiment—boiling water—I had sort of set the lab table on fire. It wasn't easy to do. The top was made of something that wouldn't burn, but the base was wood.

Anyway, I'd learned the names of some of the equipment. So, I recognized a lot of stuff. There were cauldrons that weren't the dirty, rusted iron that Knowland's cauldron had been. There were several of different sizes from smaller than a flask to large enough to boil a side of beef in. They all shined in a dark lustrous way. The color was a sort of grey.

There were all sorts of glass flasks and pipettes and retorts. There were Bunsen burners of various sizes. There were all sorts of tools. There was a rack of tools. Each was labeled with the metal that the tool was made of. There were silver knives (what in the world were they for?), tongs, measuring spoons and cups. There were a set in platinum. I'd never seen platinum before. I'd heard about platinum from another gang leader. He'd stolen some things made of platinum and got a lot of money for it.

And then there was a set of dark grey tools that reminded me of the cauldrons. I'd never heard of that metal. They were made of titanium.

Knowland was even more impressed than I was. "Wow, I've heard of titanium but I've never seen anything made of it. And look at those tiny cauldrons. Blimey, why don't we have potions' class here?"

The only thing that I said was that we needed to get going.

I pulled the parchment with the instructions out of my pocket and opened it. He wanted to hold it, but I insisted that it was my sacred duty to the author to keep it and only read the instructions. So, we sat down on adjustable stools, and I read the recipe from the beginning slowly. First was the list of ingredients. He checked his bag and laid them out as I named them.

Then I read the directions. He listened carefully and insisted that I read them again. After the second reading he said, "OK. It's not really hard, but the timing there at the fourth step is pretty tight. It's a good thing there's a nice timer here. I didn't think to bring one."

So, we agreed that he'd actually do all the steps and that I'd keep my eye on the process and the time. By now it was already 6:30. I commented that we'd better get going if we wanted to make lunch.

Knowland sort of grimaced, "Let's forget about lunch. I want this to be perfect. Just don't look at the clock until we're finished."

I agreed with him and we got started. Things went OK. The fourth step that required tight timing gave us both goosebumps as the timer counted down and I read off the time every ten seconds. But after that ticklish spot, the rest seemed easy.

The final step was to let it cool for 30 minutes before removing it from the cauldron and putting it into glass flasks. While we were letting it cool, he commented, "You know the original recipe?"

I smiled at that. I'd had to read it a dozen times while I was modifying it and copying. "Sure."

"You know what it's supposed to look like and smell like?"

I laughed, "Sure. It's got a pearly sheen, and the smell depends on the individual.

"Lots of girls say they think of chocolate when they smell it. Others think of horses. A few smell different things.

"Most guys smell freshly mowed hay or hairspray or . ."

Knowland interrupted me. "What is hairspray?"

I smiled, "Oh, my mum uses hairspray all the time. But I don't know why. Her hair's short, and it doesn't need anything to keep it in place."

Knowland seemed puzzled, "But most girls use one spell or another to keep their hair in place."

"Well, you see." Suddenly I found myself reluctant to say the simple and, really, obvious truth, "You see, my mum's a Muggle."

Knowland's eyes immediately locked on the floor. "I didn't know."

I suddenly found my feelings battling between shame and pride of my mum, "You weren't to. I've never told anyone that."

Knowland looked up and said, "Oh, oh. It's OK. Lot's of wizards and witches have Muggle parents. That was the whole point of the great war, wasn't it? Muggles are OK.'

A fierce burning fired up in my chest, and I found myself wanting to beat this little shit who thought that me mum was just "OK." But I managed not to say anything. It's a good thing that his embarrassment had caused him to study his shoes again. I don't know what he'd have seen in my face if he hadn't. I swallowed deeply.

Knowland glanced up and said, "This stuff doesn't look or smell anything like that. Have I failed again."

That surprised me. But then, I hadn't read him the end of the instructions, "No. The instructions say that," Here I stopped and picked up the parchment and read, "The resultant potion is perfectly clear and colorless. When brewed to perfection it has no odor whatsoever and tastes like distilled water."

"What does distilled water taste like?"

I thought a second and then another nugget came back from my brief tour of duty in chemistry class. "Nothing. Distilled water is perfectly pure water. It certainly looks and smells right. Do you want to try it?"

He laughed and said that I could sample the batch. I laughed too and we waited silently for the half hour to be over. When it was, we poured it out into two titanium flasks. I took one and he asked, "How much are you supposed to use."

I glanced at the parchment, although I didn't have to. "It says that you use a standard shot glass for someone weighing 10 stone."

He rolled his eyes, "Like I'm using standard shot glasses every night. And how do I know how much this girl weighs?"

I tried to look judicious as I said, "I think most school girls weigh about 7 stones. I'd be careful. Keep the dose low."

Knowland nodded and slapped me on the back. "Are you coming to the party tonight?"

"Oh, I don't know. I've not really got any good friends among the teachers yet and students are, well, you know, kind of out of bounds."

Knowland had suddenly become really happy, "Oh, come on. You should at least come to see your potion in action. It can't be that bad. Maybe you'll get lucky!'

I thought about what "Getting Lucky" would mean for me. Even if I did, it would probably turn out awful, but I decided that I ought to be there to see the stuff we'd made in action for the first time. I might learn something – like not to ever use it."

Lockhart

I had a long hard afternoon. It seemed that the longer I thought about it, the more I was scared about the future of this little experiment. Finally, when the banquet started, I couldn't stomach eating anything. I sat at the Gryffindor table. Nobody objected. I slept in the dorm. I probably spent more time in the Common Room than any real Gryffindor. I was one of the first to arrive. As the students filed in and took places around the tables, I just wanted Knowland to arrive, use the potion and, I hoped, everyone lived healthily ever after.

Shortly the food started appearing on the tables. Shortly after that the students flooded in. I spotted my buddy, Knowland coming in with Pamela and chatting her up. Great! He'll give her the potion, we'll see what we'll see, and it will be over. But almost as soon as they'd entered the Great Hall, she spotted some friends, waved at them and went over and joined a gaggle of half a dozen giggling girls. Knowland seemed to give up and came over and sat opposite me. He leaned over the table and whispered, "This isn't quite going as fast as I'd hoped."

I thought to myself, "Great. Who knows how long it will be before he gets this done?"

There was the usual little speech that the Headmistress gave on banquets. The party was to start at 8PM that would give everyone a chance to go back to their house to change into costumes if they wished. There was a minute of silence. Everyone should enjoy the banquet. Done. Finished. Then I stared at my plate and looked around at the platters piled high with food. None of it looked good to me. None of it could I put into my mouth without gagging. My neighbor to the left asked me if I wanted some pumpkin juice. I decided that I should appear to be eating something, so I nodded silently, and he filled my glass. I looked into the glass and steeled myself to force some of it down my throat.

I thought about trying to talk Knowland into giving up the plan. I had a bad feeling about what was about to happen, and I really wished he wouldn't do it.

Actually Knowland didn't look much better than I felt. He had a little food on his plate. He was constantly glancing over at where Pamela was sitting, talking in high spirits with her friends. The banquet dragged on and on. I forced some pumpkin juice down my throat and answered in monosyllables the few questions that were directed my way. Finally, people started leaving to change or not for the dance. I looked across at Knowland and asked him what he intended to do.

He sort of opened his mouth like a dead fish I'd once seen and said, "I'll go up to the house and change into something different and come down. I'll try to get her to take it in some punch sometime at the dance." I nodded absently and decided that I'd just stay seated until the dance started.

That plan didn't work out so well. Shortly before the last students left, a couple of house elves came in and started moving tables and benches over to the side walls. They brought up trays of snacks, punch bowls full of punches of various sorts and some decorations that flew up into the air and hung suspended from nothing below the invisible ceiling and the stars that had begun to show through gaps in the clouds. I had to get up when they didn't have another bench to move. I walked over to where they'd placed the bench that I'd been sitting on and sat back down.

I'd been trying to decide whether to ask Knowland to give up on his plan when the Headmistress came over to me. "Well, Mr. Dursley, this is your first party here, isn't it?"

I nodded wordlessly.

"Well, you don't look like you're enjoying yourself even though you're sitting here as though you couldn't wait for it to start."

I shrugged and looked forlorn, I suppose.

The Head looked at me speculatively and then surprised me. "Get up, Mr. Dursley, I want to take a walk around the hall."

I stared at her but got up, and we started to circumnavigate the hall counterclockwise. She watched me as we walked and after a few minutes said, "These Halloween parties always have something unusual happen." She hesitated and said ruefully. "Usually it involves Professor Wendt. Have you heard about him and Halloween from Mr. Filch?"

I shook my head, "No."

"Well, he almost always comes disguised as someone unusual. Sometimes he goes through most of the night without anyone realizing who he really is."

I stared quizzically at her, and she answered the unspoken question, "You don't know about Polyjuice Potion, I suppose. Of course not. You can be the perfect image of someone else for a few hours with Polyjuice Potion.

Once, a Hogwarts professor (not Wendt) spent almost the whole year disguised as someone else, and no one guessed until the end of the year.

"But Wendt's tricks are only for the night, and people usually guess who is. He's very funny." Under her breath she added something like, "For everyone but me."

By this time, we'd circled the room, and she said, "Well, we're back where we started." She walked on, and I sat down again.

▽

After a while, the band arrived and started setting up. Then students started appearing. The first seemed to mostly be Huffelpuffs. They gravitated to the food and drink tables. They stood around in small groups and talked. The Ravenclaws appeared next. They congregated along the opposite wall and also talked in small groups.

The next group to appear was the Gryffindors. By this time, the band was set up enough that they started to tune up and do some riffs on their instruments. They could have passed for a heavy metal band in the Muggle world. The Gryffindors tended to come to the center of the room and congregate there. I wondered where the Slytherins would land.

Just about that time, the band started playing. I have to hand this to the band. They seemed to be pretty much jacks of all trades. They started with what sounded like a blues song but unlike any that I'd ever heard. It seemed to be a song about a girl whose guy had left her for a Vila – whatever a Vila is. A lot of the Gryffindors paired up and started to dance. A few were with Huffelpuffs and Ravenclaws.

The music seemed to be a cue for the Slytherins. They walked in with their noses in the air Some paired off and danced while others went to the food and drink.

I hadn't noticed her before, but now I noticed Pamela standing with a group of Gryffindor girls. Just then, when I was afraid that he wouldn't show up, Knowland walked in through a side door. He seemed to be looking for someone. I knew perfectly well whom he was looking for. He seemed to spot her, but just then someone elbowed me in the ribs. I whirled around to see Filch standing next to me. "Well, Dursley, how long are we going to hang around here before we head back to the office and do a little serious drinking?"

I just shook my head and waved him off. I whirled around to see what was happening with Knowland. He had walked over to the group of girls. I had to admit that he had more courage than I took him for. He and Pamela seemed to be splitting off to head for the drink table.

This was it. I started off myself to get a better look. I tried to pick a vantage point that would let me see both their faces clearly in profile but would let me stand off a good distance. I hadn't taken into account the tendency of girls to run together like a herd. There were a couple who were trailing after, and it looked like they would get in the way of my view.

Bloody Hell! I wasn't going to miss this, even if I had to jostle a couple of girls out of the way. I managed to get a better view. I was pretty close, and the girls that I'd nudged out of the way had made a little fuss. Pamela looked around to see what had happened and I saw that she held a full glass of punch in her hand.

She focused on me and shocked me by saying, "Mr. Dursley, isn't it. Would you join us for some punch?" As she said that she lifted the glass to her lips. Behind her, I could see Knowland shaking his head violently and waving a hand, but there was nothing I could do if I wanted to. She'd downed the whole cup as though she had just walked off an all-day hike on the Sahara. She had closed her eyes as she tilted her head back. When she lowered her head, her eyes opened full wide and stared into mine. Just then Knowland shoved through and pushed her out of the way. She stumbled toward me but regained her poise.

She paid no attention to Knowland even though he'd nearly knocked her over. Instead she took a step closer and asked a question of me! "How fortunate that you happened by. I was just thinking of you and hoped that we might dance."

Just then the band started a new song, a slow wordless tune. She smiled wider. I don't see how that was possible. Her expression had been one of luminous glory. She said, "Perfect. Let's dance."

I had no idea what to do. She stepped the final step to me and placed one hand on my left shoulder and took my right hand with her left. Then she started to dance.

Once, when I was twelve, my Mum had signed me up for a dance class. It was one of those where there are two dozen kids – boys and girls who stand in a line and practice dance steps. Then they pair up by the numbers and practice with a partner. I'd lasted about two classes, but that had been enough to teach me how to stumble through a slow dance. For the first time in my life, I was happy that she'd done that.

Her amazing glorious smile was what kept me on my feet during that dance that was full of mashed toes—all hers. Somehow she turned all those missteps into graceful turns. I don't know what my face looked like, but it must have been shocked incredulity. After a timeless eternity she said something. That shocked me into a response, "Whuh?"

She laughed as though I'd just made a witty answer, "I was just wondering if you ever talk when you dance?"

I tried to decide what to answer since I never dance. Was it "No, I never dance, so I don't talk all those times when I don't dance". Or maybe, "Yes, I always talk when I dance, which is to say never." Or, maybe, "I don't know." That probably would have been the right answer but I didn't get to use it.

She said, "Well, if you did, I might ask how you like the band."

"And you might say 'The band is only so-so.'"

"And I might answer, "But this is such a charming evening that I can't tell whether the band is good or bad.'

"And then you might say, 'The way they . . .'"

The one-sided conversation went on for a while that way and eventually turned to the weather. There must have been at least a couple of dances while this conversation went on. Then something happened that interrupted the conversation. The band stopped and switched to something really heavy metal. She released me and switched to a much more exuberant dance style. I did my best to follow. At the end, somebody called out a name of a song, and the band picked it up. It was the first song they'd played.

Pamela stepped close, but when she walked into my arms, she was much closer than before. She put her head on my left shoulder and had her hand around my waist. After a silent moment, she whispered into my ear. "Don't you think it's getting hot in here?"

It definitely was, but it didn't have anything to do with air temperature. She asked, "Why don't we go out in the courtyard after this heavenly dance ends?"

That caused me to think fast. I only had a couple of minutes until I had to say something or just go along to tragedy. I came up with the answer. When the dance ended, I said, "Why don't we go get something to drink?" She pouted a little but seemed willing. Yes, willing. Way too willing.

We started over toward the drinks, but before we got there something happened that I didn't expect—as if I'd expected any of this. There was a little commotion over toward the main entrance of the Great Hall. A man appeared who was more flamboyant than any I'd ever seen in a world of flamboyant wizards and witches in bizarre costumes. He had flaming gold curly hair and was wearing purple robes. He was walking with a witch with long black lustrous hair. I recognized her as Professor Sinistra. They were apparently headed for the drink table, and I thought they would make a good diversion. So, I picked up our pace. We arrived at about the same time they did.

Professor Sinistra had just received a glass of punch from her strange partner. I closed distance and asked her, "Professor Sinistra, would you introduce us?"

She smiled wickedly, "Of course. Miss Myers, a 7th year student and Mr. Dursley, on our grounds staff." Pamela frowned at that. "This is . . ."

61

Before she could introduce him, the wizard said, "Don't give me a hint. I just lost it for a minute. I am. . . I am Gilderoy Lockhardt, the famous." Again he hesitated. Then said, "Don't tell me. It's on the tip of my tongue. . . I'm ready to tell you any minute now. . . Yes, yes, it's coming. . . It's almost here."

I was ready to move on when his face brightened and he said, "I've got it. It's something to do with books. I'm a book reader. No. No. Wait. It's something like that. I copy books. Yes, that's it. I copy books."

Sinistra shook her head and said, "Close enough Gilderoy."

He then reached into his robes and pulled out a sheaf of small parchments. He handed one to each of us as he said, "I know that you all want my autograph and are just struck dumb by my presence, so I'm saving you the embarrassment of asking. Here you are. Here you are."

I looked at the one that he'd stuffed in my hands. It was a printed form that said, "Dear," there was a blank there followed by, "my close friend and loyal fan". Then it was signed in a scrawl that I could almost not read, "G. Lockhardt."

He was going on, "You needn't thank me. No. No. The least I can do for my loyal fans. You no doubt are wondering why I've already signed them. I've only just gotten back cursive writing in my fine round hand. This saves us time. It would take ever so long, if I didn't sign them in advance."

Just then, Pamela exclaimed, "Of course, I know you. My Mom used to love . . ." She thought better of what she was saying and smoothly finished it, "your books."

"Of course, she did, dear. Everyone did. Any time now, I'll be back to copying books. Just you wait and see."

It seemed like a good time to move on to somewhere else – anywhere else, when I remembered that the next place would be out in the courtyard in the moonlight if I didn't think fast. But it turned out that I didn't need to think at all because just then someone new arrived. She had long dark red hair and I thought she was a 7th year.

She looked around the group and said, "If it isn't the two people in the world that I hate the most."

That surprised me; I looked around and inventoried the people. There was Pamela, Professor Sinistra, the poor sap, Lockhardt and me. Who could she be talking about? Maybe Lockhardt in a different life and Professor Sinistra? He certainly looked as dumbfounded as I.

I didn't have to wait long because she told us, "Lockhardt. Do you remember abandoning me in the caverns under Hogwarts and trying to obliviate the memory of my brother and my boyfriend?"

Sinistra intervened and said, "Of course, he doesn't girl. He's just been let out of Saint Mongo's on an overnight pass because he's just beginning to get a little memory back."

Then the girl turned to me and really snarled, "And you."

I racked my brains to understand what in the world she would have against me. I couldn't even remember her name. But she made everything clear quickly. "Yes, you, Dudley Durseley."

At that Pamela took my arm in hers and whispered in my ear, "Ooooh. Dudley. My wonderful Dudders." I didn't have time to think of it at the time, but later I realized two things. I'd hated it when me mum had called me that, and I now loved hearing Pamela say it.

"You needn't play as dumb as Lockhardt. You remember your cousin Harry and the way that you used to abuse him for the first 12 years of his life and then every summer afterwards. Well, he's my boyfriend and he's not here to give you what you deserve, so I will."

In the meantime, Pamela had tightened her grip on my arm and pulled herself around in front of me. She hissed, "Ginny Weasley. You take that back. Dudley is the kindest, gentlest, most loving man I've ever met. He would NEVER do any of the things you say."

At that Ginny started to open her purse, and Pamela was fast following suit. In that moment, the three "cat fights" that I'd witnessed while I was a gang leader in school flashed into my mind. Two had been barehanded and neither girl had come away very badly hurt. One involved knives. That one was different, but nobody had left in a body bag. With both girls armed with wands, I had no idea what might happen. I briefly thought about pulling my wand. If I did, what could I do? The few spells that I knew were just not useful.

Luckily a cooler head prevailed. Sinistra had seen something like this coming. She'd already pulled her wand out, and she pointed it between them and said, "Ladies, I think we should all just take it easy and wait for the Headmistress to sort things out."

Just at that moment, the Head appeared and looked around the strange scene. She said, "Right you are, Professor Sinistra. I'll take over here. All three of you are coming up to my office this minute."

As if I'd not seen enough bizarre things for one night, they just kept piling up. Knowland came around from behind me and said, "Uh. . . Headmistress."

The Head was clearly losing her control on HER temper. "What is it Mr. Knowland?"

"Uh, I think I could clear up a lot if I were to come along."

She rolled her eyes and said, "Well, the more the merrier for this party. Come along if you must, Mr. Knowland." Then she turned back to Sinistra and said one more weird thing, "Professor." Her mouth stayed open and she didn't say anything for a moment. Then she went on, "I can't believe I'm saying this. Professor, please stay here and look after Wendt. I don't want him getting in any more trouble."

Sinistra just nodded demurely. The Head thanked her and turned back to us. "Let's go."

We went directly to her office. On the way she said, "Just go on ahead in. I'll be there in a minute. And, all of you, don't do anything until I get there."

Weasley asked, "But isn't there a password on the entrance?"

"There is not. Girl, don't you listen to beginning of term announcements? I said that we have an open door policy. My outer office is open at all times of day and night. You simply walk in. I'm notified that you're there, and either I see you then or we set up an appointment for later."

She dropped back for a couple of minutes. We arrived at the office and walked straight in, bold as brass. We waited a few minutes and the Head arrived. She opened the door to the inner office and went in.

"Please pull up a chair and sit around my desk." I sat in the middle on the Head's right. Pamela sat next to me immediately on my left. Knowland sat next to me and Weasley next to him. All of the chairs were upholstered in yellow.

She seated herself, "Ordinarily, I offer drinks to my guests, but I don't want to waste any more time with you four than I have two. Let's get started." She looked at the four of us one at a time and then began. "This is the most bizarre group that I've seen in this office in my career. But I have to admit being fascinated by you, Mr. Knowland. You don't have any apparent connection to this incident, and yet you volunteer to come along. Let's start with you."

This was my point of greatest fear. Depending on what he said, I was in a ton of trouble or none at all. He stuttered, "Uh, Headmistress, I'd like to discuss this alone. I'm sure that I could clear up the situation . . ."

She frowned at him and he fell silent for a moment. She looked around us and said, "This is my house and we're going to play by my rules." Her face broke into a brief smile, and she went on, "Yes! This is my house. I was the Head of Gryffindor before becoming the Head of Hogwarts. And you are all of you Gryffindors, even you, Mr. Dursley. Even you live in Gryffindor. I'm terribly ashamed of all of you." She fell silent.

Then he went on, "OK. Here's what happened. I brewed a batch of Love potion and gave a dose to Ms. Myer." At that, he turned toward her and said, "Look Pamela, it was completely wrong to do, and I'm so sorry that I ever did it, but . . ."

The Head's frown deepened, "You're right, Mr. Knowland, that was completely wrong, and you and Gryffindor will pay dearly for it. One hundred points from Gryffindor and you will serve detention with Professor Slughorn. I hope he has you clean out every cauldron and flask and utensil in his classroom."

Then she turned to me. "And you, Mr. Dursley. You must know that it's wrong for teacher or staff to have a romantic . . uh . . liaison with a student. This would be serious indeed if you both weren't adults. . ."

She was interrupted by Pamela who said, "Oh, Professor." She reached out to take my hand but the Head's withering look stopped her in her tracks. But she went bravely on. "Dudley is not at all at fault here. The whole evening, he didn't say a word to me. Certainly nothing to encourage me. I guess that I must have taken some love potion if Mr. Knowland says so, but it was pure luck that the person that I fell in love with is the kindest, gentlest, most wonderful man that I've ever met. I swept him off his feet. I didn't give him a chance to object."

At this, Weasley sneered, "Some kind, gentle man. He . . ."

Pamela didn't let her finish. She broke in, "You don't know anything. Haven't you seen him in the Common Room, reading all the time? And what does he read? He reads Shakespeare, don't you Dudders?" Again, she reached a hand out toward me, but the Head's glance stopped that. She seemed to be bemused by this unusual conversation.

Weasley said, "Shakespeare! Sure! What play were you reading, lover boy?"

I thought everyone might have forgotten that I was in the room. But, I had an answer and best of all, it was a true answer, "King Lear."

Weasley rolled her eyes, "Can you quote a single line from Lear?"

I thought I was cooked, until the words that I heard when first I laid eyes on Pamela sprang into my mind, unbidden. "Then poor Cordelia! And yet not so, since, I am sure, my love's more richer than my tongue." With that, Pamela sighed very audibly and said, "Oh, Dudders. My first lines." This time, she did squeeze my hand before the Head intervened.

Weasley said something under her breath, and the Head's voice sounded like a crack of thunder, "That will be enough Miss Weasley. Through your whole career at Hogwarts you've been skating the fine line of being suspended for a term. I will have no more. Is that understood?"

Weasley looked down at her feet and nodded silently. Then the Head went on. "Back to you Mr. Dursley. You and Mr. Knowland. He is not implicated, and yet he volunteers to come and implicate himself. You are implicated, and you don't object to coming. This is strange."

All that I could do was smile and hope that Knowland didn't add anything to his story.

The Head said, "I suppose that you are basically innocent, but you too are skating the fine edge. You will not look at Miss Myers as long as she is a student here. You will not talk to her here. You will not stay in a hall that she is walking in. You will not eat in the Great Hall except between terms. If you break any of these instructions, you're finished here." Then she seemed to soften. "At least until Professor Slughorn has given her the antidote. Even then, you will stay away from her. Now, after she graduates in the Spring, you two may do whatever you like. You are adults. Is all that heard, understood and agreed to?"

"Ma'am, yes, Ma'am".

She nodded and said, "After we're done here, you'll have to spend the nights out of Gryffindor. Until I find something better, you'll have to stay with Professor Wendt. Just go to his office. It's unlocked. He probably won't be back there until much later. I'll have your things sent down to his office."

"And you Myers will have to see Professor Slughorn tomorrow after breakfast to get him to brew an antidote for you. Do you have a class immediately after breakfast?"

"No, Headmistress."

"Then be sure you follow all these instructions."

"Yes, Headmistress. I understand perfectly. The hours will fly like the wind until my darling and I are re-united. The time will be like being in heaven. The . . ."

The Head shook her head sadly. Pamela closed her mouth. Nobody else made a sound, not even Weasley.

She turned to Weasley. "All right, Miss Weasley. Start talking. I saw you and Miss Myers about to square off with wands. I want a complete explanation, now."

Weasley obviously wasn't happy but she told it straight, "I found these two . . ." She couldn't find a word that satisfied her sense of justice, so she went on. "These two people who have wronged me terribly together – Lockhardt and Dursley."

The Head frowned and said, "Respect, MISS Weasley."

"Mr. Lockhardt and Mr. Dursley. I would have held my piece but MISS Myers insisted on defending Mr. Dursley. She . . . " Here she stopped and looked at Pamela.

Pamela didn't flinch from her gaze but simply said, "Oh, Ginny, you know I HAD to defend Mr. Dursley." She didn't amplify on that explanation.

A change swept over Weasley's face. She took a deep breath and said, "I know, Pam, that rat gave you love potion. You couldn't keep yourself from doing it. I'm sorry for what I said and almost did. Maybe we can be friends again before school is over."

Pamela's face returned to its former radiant smile that she'd worn ever since drinking the potion. "Oh, Ginny, I've never stopped being your friend."

"Yeh, I guess."

The Head looked from one to the other. "Look ladies, I'm going to give you two one chance to be honest with me. Can the two of you survive together in Gryffindor for the rest of the year? If you can't, I'm going to send one of you to Huffelpuff and the other to Ravenclaw, God help them."

Weasley and Pamela looked at each other and something seemed to pass between them. They both nodded silently at the same time. The Head accepted that. She gave us final orders, "All of you are to return to your quarters for the night. Don't stop at the party, don't stop in the kitchen and no breakfast for any of you."

My mouth dropped, and I would have said something if I'd not seen the glint in the Head's eyes. I grumbled to myself that I'd not eaten since Friday night, and it looked like I might be lucky to get something before Sunday night.

We went our separate ways. The other three headed together for Gryffindor and I headed for Professor Wendt's office. I arrived there and, as the Head had said, the door was unlocked. I called into the open door so that I wouldn't startle the Professor, but no one answered. I went in, shut the door and decided to wait in the leather chair. It seemed like hours, but I suppose it was less than one when the door opened.

I had started to doze off when the door slammed open, waking me. In the door, I saw Professor Wendt staggering, supported by Professor Sinistra. I jumped up, and Sinistra just said, "Oh, stay seated. I got him all the way here from the party. I can get him the rest of the way to his bed."

Professor Wendt seemed to have some gold in his hair and was wearing a bright purple robe like Lockhardt had. He seemed to have trouble focusing his eyes and asked, "Who is it?"

Sinistra stared at me and said, "What in the world are you doing here Dursley. Shouldn't you be at the party or Gryffindor or anywhere else?"

"No, I can't stay in Gryffindor any more. The Headmistress sent me here until she could find someplace else permanent for me."

Sinistra looked around, saying, "Drat that McGonagall." Then she started to walk Wendt toward the bedroom.

"Should you be doing that?"

She looked at me and said, "Double Drat. I suppose you look healthy enough to put him to bed." Her mouth turned into a hard straight line as she said that. Then, with one last longing look at the bedroom, she turned back to me and said, "Come on, give me a hand, and we'll put him in bed and . . ." She trailed off.

I jumped up and went to them. I helped get Wendt into the bedroom and we rolled him onto the bed. She looked at him lying there, apparently dead asleep. She shook her head, and her long black hair shimmered. Then she walked out of the bedroom and on out of the room.

I closed the door behind her and decided to lock it. Then, I went back to the couch and slipped my shoes off. I put my feet up on the sofa and arranged a cushion as a pillow and lay back, hoping that my stomach wouldn't growl too loudly to let me sleep.

The next morning Wendt staggered into his office in the same robes he'd worn last night. He shook me awake and asked, "What in the world are you doing here, Mr. Dursley?"

I shook myself awake, yawned, and asked him if he didn't remember going to bed last night. He shook himself again and took a quick look around. "Did anyone sleep with me last night?"

"If you are thinking of Professor Sinistra, no she didn't."

He sighed relief and asked me, "Was there someone else? Oh, surely not. What are you doing here anyway?"

"Do you remember the 'cat fight' last night?"

He looked at me suspiciously, "No? Should I?"

"I suppose not. It's just that. . ." Here I stopped to think about it. The two of them had been about to fight over me. In my wildest dreams, I hadn't imagined that any pair of girls would fight over me. Of course, one of them wanted to kill me, but the other wanted to save me. "Well, these two girls. . . "

Wendt interrupted me, "You mean Miss Myers and Miss Weasley?"

"You saw it then?"

He scratched his chin, "Yeh, I guess so. So, they both wanted you, and they were about to fight over you? But how can that be? Miss Weasley and Harry Potter are like this." He twisted two fingers together.

"Not really. It's complicated, but the Headmistress decided that neither of them could be in the same house with me. So she sent me here, at least for tonight. Sometime, she'll find someplace else for me to stay."

"That's OK. As long as you sleep on the sofa, you can stay with me. Hey, let's go down for breakfast. Sunday mornings the food's fabulous here."

"Sorry, I can't. It's part of my punishment. I have to wait for lunch."

"OK. I could sneak a little something up for you."

"Don't. I'm in enough trouble with the Headmistress as it is."

He left, and I tried to think of something, anything other than food. I decided that I had to wait until someone brought my things, so I just

68

browsed through Wendt's bookshelves seeing if I could find something interesting to read while I waited.

There were a whole stack of *Scientific American* magazines. There were a whole shelf of American books by Twain, Faulkner, and other people that I'd not heard of. There seemed to be a British bookshelf too. I walked over to his desk and found a copy of the *Times of London* – yesterday's. I picked it up and looked for the sports page. I wondered what Man U had done yesterday. It turned out to be an early edition and didn't have results, so I just paged through the paper looking for something that seemed interesting.

I went back to the bookshelf and found a small collection of vinyl records. There was a strange assortment. There was Pink Floyd and Yes. There was one "best of" collection of Huey Lewis and the News. There was a "best of" collection of Blue Oyster Cult. There were a few by groups that I'd never heard of. There was a group called "The Monkeys".

Then there was the classical group. There were several by Bach. When I looked closer I saw that almost all of them were recorded by Glenn Gould. That pulled at a heart string. There were some by Rachmaninov and Brahms. There was one by Beethoven. There were a couple by Dvorak. I'd heard all the names, but except for the Bach, I'd never heard any of the pieces that he had in that group.

I guess that the time passed pretty quickly. It was almost time for lunch when there was a knock at the door. I wondered who would come to see Wendt on Sunday morning. It was a 6th year, a Creavey. He said, "you've got to come down right now to the Headmistress' office."

I looked at the clock. It was 11:15. Was I going to miss another meal?

I looked at Creavey and asked, "Can I stop at the Great Hall to grab a roll."

He shook his head, "She seemed quite mad. I don't think I'd keep her waiting."

I nodded and left for the Head's. I arrived and walked right in. As I did, the inner door opened, and I could see the Head through it. She signaled me in. I walked in and found that there were already three guests seated around the desk – Knowland, Pamela, and Professor Slughorn. Pamela was as white as a ghost. Her eyes went to mine and somehow still had love in them.

The head motioned me to the lone remaining chair. I sat and she began. "Professor Slughorn, would you please explain what happened when you prepared an antidote for Miss Myers?"

"Of course. I prepared the standard antidote for Amortensia. When I administered it, Miss Myers had an adverse reaction."

"What!" I practically shouted.

Pamela said, "Oh, dearest, it wasn't bad. I just threw up a little." She smiled, and the radiance melted my heart.

The Head said, "It was rather worse than that."

Slughorn went on. "Apparently, the love potion wasn't the standard Amortensia but something else. I understood that you brewed it, Mr. Knowland. Would you please provide us the recipe?"

He opened his mouth, and I couldn't stand it any longer. I stood and started to talk. The Head said, "Mr. Dursley, please sit. I like eyes at a level."

I did, and I took a deep breath. This could be it—the end of my job. "I provided Mr. Knowland with the recipe. I'll go get it. You can brew an antidote." I turned to Pamela and said, "Please forgive me. I wouldn't have hurt you for the world."

She still smiled at me. "You weren't to know."

I shook my head and said, "Let's see how you feel after the antidote."

She actually laughed gaily. "Yes, we will see." And I had to admire her determination—even if it were not hers really.

The Head, tight-lipped, said, "Go."

I ran down the stairs to the office and threw open the drawer with the recipe. I pulled it out and ran back. I arrived and handed it to Slughorn. He opened the folded page and examined it. He stared at it long and simply said, "Interesting. This may take a little time."

The Head said, "What!"

Slughorn looked around and said, "Well, this is quite an unusual formula. It's unlike any love potion that I've ever seen." He hesitated and said, "I'm sure. . . Yes, sure that I can brew a counter."

He looked up at me and asked, "Where did you get this unusual formula?"

I found myself reluctant to take a chance at losing that amazing potion book. An idea struck me, "Well, sir. In a potions book."

He rolled his eyes. "Of course, it was in a potions book, but which one."

I thought quickly. "Well, I have a library card, you know. It was in the library."

The Head said, "Good. Miss Pinz will have a record."

"No."

"Why not? She's very efficient about keeping her records. Of course, we'll find which one it was."

I took a slow breath and said, "No. I was browsing and picked one out at random. The formula was in it. I didn't borrow it from the library."

The Head seemed very perturbed, "Mr. Dursley, are you 'jerking us around' as the Americans say?"

"No, ma'am."

She looked over to Slughorn, "Do you need the book?"

He sighed, "No, but I was hoping the text might also have the antidote. We'll just have to go slowly and carefully. I'll test every antidote with very small doses to make sure that they're safe before using a full strength version."

Mr. Knowland said something for the first time, "Does it really matter? Won't it wear off eventually?"

Pamela sighed and said, "I hope not. This is the happiest I've ever been in my life, and I'm not convinced that it was a real love potion anyway."

"Yes, it will, but I've no idea how long it will take. It could be a few days but it could also be a few months. She might still be affected by it after her graduation."

Pamela showed the first real gumption at that, "Hey. I'm in the room. You keep talking about me in the third person. Don't my desires count here?"

The Head turned to her and was sympathetic. "I'm sorry. Yes, your feelings do count, but the real problem is knowing just what your real authentic feelings are."

Pamela said, "I'll tell you what my real feelings are. I've always liked Mr. Dursley, and this has just let me express those feelings."

The Head looked pained, "I know it feels that way but you really won't know what they really are until you're out from under this potion."

On that very unhappy note, the meeting ended. I asked to stay behind for a few minutes to talk with the Head alone. She let me. "Go ahead. I'm all ears."

"Well, ma'am, I was wondering how you were getting along finding me a new place to stay?"

She stared hard at me. "I'm working on it. You'll know as soon as it's ready. You're dismissed."

All that I could say was, "Thank you, ma'am."

71

Filch's Prelude

I thought that it might be a day or two before I was relocated but a week passed, and then I was into the second week without a permanent place to stay. I was beginning to wonder if Wendt's office might be my permanent place. One night I was sitting on my bed in Wendt's office. He was at his desk grading papers. I had decided to read one of Wendt's books. He recommended "Huckleberry Finn". It was hard reading at first, but Huck started speaking normal English after that, and it wasn't so hard.

After I'd read a couple of chapters, I was pretty tired out, so I asked Wendt a question – "Can I listen to some of your music sometime? And, why is it all LP's."

He looked at me quizzically. "You must know the answer to that."

I puzzled a minute and then said, "I suppose that you mean that you couldn't play CD's here because electrical things don't work in Hogwarts but somehow LP's do?"

"Right."

I went on to the other question, "Well, can I listen to some of the LP's?"

A strange crooked smile appeared on his face. He took a deep breath and said, "No. Please let me explain."

I shrugged. Why not? I said, 'Sure. This ought to be good."

He opened the left lower drawer of his desk. I knew what that meant. "Can I offer you a glass of something? I have some Dewars and Seagram 7. Sorry. No warm beer. I also have a few cans of 7 UP if you want something non-alcoholic. I don't offer that to everyone, you know?"

I wondered what had brought on the alcoholic beverages but I wasn't about to object. "I'll have some Seagram."

He pulled out two shot glasses and poured a shot of Seagrams for me and the Dewars for himself. He took a sip and leaned back in his chair.

"OK. Here's the deal. LP's are unique. Even though they are not as faithful to the original music as most CD's are, they somehow have a sound quality that makes up for their lack of scientific accuracy."

He looked up at the ceiling and seemed to be contemplating something or just falling asleep, but he did lower his eyes to me again. "The other thing about LP's is that they are very susceptible to wear. You can probably only play an LP a few times before you begin to get scratches, pops, skips."

He hesitated again and said, "These LP's are rare pressings, played only once. After that first playing, I planned to copy them to cassette tapes. Then I'd listen to those." He sighed and stopped again.

I thought I knew what he was going to say next. So, I said it for him, "You love that music so much that you can't stand to ruin it."

"I have just one question. Have you transferred the music to cassettes yet?"

He shook his head. "That's the irony. I couldn't afford to start collecting these rare LP's until I had a good job that paid well. Now that I have that job, I'can't even do the transfer because electronics doesn't work here." He shook his head again.

He laughed mirthlessly. "Do you want to hear something really funny?"

I wasn't sure that I really wanted to hear what would come next, but I was his guest and decided that I ought to humor him. "Sure, go ahead."

"Well, there is only one machine in this castle, probably in Hogsmead as well that you could use to play those. It's an old crank gramophone. Guess who owns it."

I scratched my head and tried to think of someone who would appreciate music enough to have a gramophone. I made a guess, "The Head . . . uh . . . mistress." I'd almost made the mistake of referring to her familiarly.

Wendt smiled, "Good guess, but no."

I thought again. "What about Professor Sinistra? She seems like someone who'd like music."

Wendt frowned, "I can see where you're coming from. You think that she'd do. . . uh . . . anything to please me."

I hadn't thought that, but I wasn't going to contradict Wendt. I tried my last guess, "I suppose that only leaves Professor . . . oh . . . what's his name, the conductor of the chorus."

Wendt shook his head again. "It was your boss – Filch."

All I could say was, "OH!"

Wendt went on, "Yes, it's surprising isn't it."

He hesitated again and said, "He noticed those same LP's one time when we were drinking together and wanted, like you, to listen to them.

"I, of course, pleaded that I didn't have an instrument to play them.

"He shocked me by revealing that he owned a gramophone. I had to do some quick thinking to come up with a reason for not running down to his office right away and bringing it up.

"Of course, he thought he was doing me a great favor."

I could understand that. It would be hard to deny the old fart something as simple as that once you got to really know him. I asked, "Was he too disappointed?"

Wendt smiled, "I had an inspiration. I told him that I couldn't let him take a chance of ruining his fine instrument with my old scratchy records. There was that and the other thing."

I was happy to be the straight man, "What other thing?"

"The other thing was the bottle of Johnny Walker Blue Label that I opened."

I nodded sagely.

Slughorn

Another day, as I was reading, something occurred to me. "Professor Wendt, you know the Headmistres pretty well, don't you?"

He laughed. It must have been some sort of private joke that I didn't know about, but he answered. "Yes, I do."

"Well, I was wondering if you could kind of ask her to get me a permanent place to stay."

He laid his pen down and looked at me. "You and I both would like to put this partnership to an end."

"But can't you just tell her that you'd like to have me somewhere else."

He shook his head, "No. You see, you're here as part of your punishment because you're in the dog house."

"But what about you? That's not fair to you."

"Oh, Dursley, I'm in the doghouse too. Maybe if I could help you get out of the doghouse, I'd be out too."

I didn't understand that, "You in the doghouse? I thought she was, well, kind of sweet on you."

"Yeh, that's the problem. But that's not something we can work on. Maybe we can work on your problem though. Tell me just how you got in the doghouse."

I leaned back on the couch and thought about the simplest way to tell the story. I then leaned forward and began, "Well, it's just that I helped Mr. Knowland with brewing the love potion and then. . ."

Wendt cut me off and said, "Wait a minute. You helped Knowland with the love potion? You who couldn't spell Thaumaturgy three months ago helped a 7th year magic student with a tough potion?"

I wanted to make it clear, "Sir, I still can't spell Thauma-whatever."

"That's my point. How in the world could you help him?"

I had to think about that. He was patient. He didn't hurry me. Then I got up, pulled the red leather chair over to the desk, and looked at him. "Tell me. The truth. Would you keep what I tell you a secret?"

It was his turn to pause. After a bit, he said, "If you promise me that what you're going to tell me isn't illegal in a major way or immoral in a major way or fattening in a major way, yes."

That was good enough. "OK. Do you know about the Room of Requirement?"

Wendt shrugged, "Sure."

That surprised me, "What do you mean, 'sure'. There are a lot of people who don't know about it."

"Well, I do, anyway. Go ahead."

"I found a book in the Room of Requirement. A potions textbook. I think it's the one that Slughorn uses for his advanced classes. I started reading it a bit because it was completely covered with notes and corrections. I'd never seen a textbook that had notes in it that weren't funny cartoons or drawings or notes to the pretty girl in the next row.

"Anyway, one day Filch sent me up to the girls bathroom on the 2nd floor to checkout an awful smell that was coming out of it. I found Mr. Knowland in there brewing something."

Wendt smiled and said something that sounded like, "Chemistry Labs-R-Us."

"Pardon."

"Oh, a little joke. This is not the first time that the girls WC has been used to brew potions. So, go ahead."

"Well, he'd made a mess of it. I had him clean it up and sort of in exchange I promised to help him brew a love potion that would blow the socks off anyone who drank it."

Wendt nodded eagerly. "Yes. So you went back. Got the Potions handbook and let Knowland use it."

"No sir, I didn't want him to touch it." I'd said that very loud. What was that about? I went on. "The book's very hard to read. I'd gotten to the point where I could make out most of it. I made a copy of the corrected formula and . . ."

Wendt broke in, "And you gave that to him."

"No, sir. I wanted to be sure that he got it right. I didn't want to be cleaning up the girl's bathroom again."

"You mean that you didn't want him to be cleaning up the bathroom again."

"Well, something like that. Anyway. I read him the instructions, and he followed. I made sure he did it right, and then on Halloween he used it."

"OK. So, what's the deal? Slughorn must have brewed an antidote and Miss Myers is back to normal and . . ."

"No, sir. Slughorn hasn't succeeded yet. He tried brewing the standard remedy for the standard formula, and it made Pamela. Uh. . . Miss Myers sick."

Wendt nodded. "I see. There's more than meets the eye here. You have feelings for Miss Myers?"

"Yes, sir."

"And now she has feelings for you because of the love potion."

"Yes, sir. I gave Slughorn the real formula, and he's been trying to brew an antidote but . . ."

"Not so much luck, eh?"

"No, sir."

Wendt thought a moment. "Well, what about an antidote from THE book?" He stopped speaking and went on quickly, "Hmmmm. About that book. Whose was it?"

"I don't know. Whoever owned it said that he was the Half-Blood Prince."

Wendt jumped up at that. "What did you say?"

I repeated it, and he stood up and started pacing. I got half-way up but he just waved me to sit down. "Dursley. I think I know who owned that book."

"Who?"

"Never mind. But the answer is simple. I'd bet that the Half-Blood Prince has an antidote for it in the book. Just go show it to Slughorn and we'll all be out of the doghouse."

The smile that was beginning to form on my face turned to a frown. I don't quite know why, but I just didn't want to give up that book and I was sure that I would have to if I just showed it to Slughorn. "I'm sorry. I can't do that."

Wendt just shrugged and said, "Oh. Of course. It couldn't be that easy. Why?"

"Well, I'm sure that he'll keep the book. He'll claim that it's the property of the Potions Department or whatever."

Wendt sat down again and seemed to be deep in concentration. He leaned back in his chair, and his lips formed a thin hard line. Then he closed his eyes. That went on for five minutes, and then he suddenly sat up and opened his eyes. "That's OK. Slughorn is a vain man. He will do anything to claim a triumph – even if it isn't his. I think that we can get him to go along with us and let you keep your book.

"Here's what you do. Tomorrow, go into his office and talk with him in private. Tell him that you found the book that has the antidote. But, you'll only let him use it if he promises to let you keep it and not tell anyone about it. I'm pretty sure he'd agree to that. . . "

I interrupted, "But, but. Can we really trust him?"

"Oh, just wait and listen on . . . "

Wendt continued on with his plan.

$$\triangledown$$

The next day I was waiting outside the Potion classroom for Slughorn's last class to end. When it did and everyone had left, I went in. "Professor Slughorn, do you have some time to talk?"

He shrugged as he packed away supplies, "Sure. What do you want to talk about?"

"Suppose that I had a way for you to brew an antidote for the love potion?"

At that Slughorn put down what he was doing and came over to the door to the hall, closed it and came back, "Just what do you have in mind?"

"Well, sir, I think that I've found the Potions book that I used."

"Wonderful, let's get started."

"But there's a catch."

Slughorn's face fell, "Somehow there always is. Go ahead."

"Well, I can get you the antidote formula but you've got to agree to never tell anyone about how you got it. AND I have to be able to keep the book."

He exclaimed, "That's blackmail."

"Yes, sir, it is."

"But don't you want Miss Myers to get better?"

I smiled at that. I was used to bargaining this way. "Don't you? Just agree to my conditions."

He paced up and down. Then he stopped and turned to face me again. "And YOU agree to not reveal to anyone how I did it or contradict me when I say that I invented the antidote? When I take total credit for the cure?"

"Of course, that fits perfectly with what I want."

He paced a moment more, thinking over all the ways the deal could go south, I suppose. He stopped, turned, and extended his hand, "Deal?"

I took the hand, shook it and repeated, "Deal."

I added, "Let's do it on Saturday morning. That gives us lots of time and leisure to brew it carefully."

"You aren't just going to give me the book and let me do it?"

"No, sir."

"Hmmm." He went back to putting supplies away in the cabinet. "Are you still staying with Professor Wendt?"

"I'm afraid so. It seems like we're both trapped until Miss Myers gets cured."

"Well, then we're certainly in a hurry, aren't we?"

"Yes, sir, we are."

"Well, I'll see you Saturday morning."

I answered, "Bright and early."

"Yesss."

I left his office and went back to report to Wendt what had happened.

The dark figure walked in the dark halls of Hogwarts after midnight. He was in the basement and walked slowly, carefully, and most importantly, silently. He reached the door that he was searching for. He took a deep breath and grasped the door handle. Ever so gently he applied pressure to make it turn.

The click of the handle catching on the lock told him that he'd have to use force. He reached inside his robes and pulled out a wand. He wasn't good at subvocalizing but this time it worked. No one could have heard the *aloe ahora* spell. The handle turned freely, and he entered the room. There was no light. He closed the door behind him and then spoke the spell, "Lumose Minima". His wand lit, and he walked over to the two desks that were side by side. As he approached the wan light of his wand showed the name plates of each. He walked around the one that he was interested in.

He made a quick search of the desktop. What he was looking for was not there. He carefully slid the top drawer of the desk open and lowered the wand toward it to give him a better view.

Just then a voice that he immediately recognized said, "What yer looking for Perfesser? Maybe I can help?" It was the caretaker, Filch.

Slughorn turned and said, "Oh, I guess I have the wrong office, you see, I was uh . . ." His voice trailed off and simply stopped.

"Maybe you were looking for someone else's property. Maybe it was Mr. Dursley's, eh?"

Slughorn immediately replied. "You can't prove that."

"Well, let's see here. We've got you entering a locked room and rummaging through the desk of Mr. Dursley. I think that's pretty clear, don't you."

Slughorn made one last try, "It's just your word against mine. I just entered a room in the dark that was unlocked, and by accident it was yours and . . ."

Just then, I walked out from behind a supply cabinet toward the back of the room. "Hello, hello, hello. I guess it isn't just one man's word against another's, is it?"

Slughorn's contenance fell. Looking at Filch he said, "I thought you were always out looking for evildoers at this time of night."

"That's exactly what I was doing, and it looks like I found one, yup!"

He turned toward me. "I thought that you would be with Wendt." Then he brightened, "But it's just the word of one old wino and a juvenile delinquent against me."

Just then, Professor Wendt walked out from behind the same supply cabinet that I was hiding behind. "You were right Slughorn, Mr. Dursley was with me. And it's the word of the caretaker of Hogwarts, his assistant and a professor against yours."

Slughorn sunk into the old red leather chair in the corner, "OK. What do you want? I'm ruined if you choose. None of my old friends will be caught dead with me if you reveal this episode."

Wendt walked around the desk and sat on it. "Slughorn, we're not cruel or unreasonable. We just want you to keep your agreement with Mr. Dursley. You two go ahead and brew your potion. We don't reveal where it came from, and you let Mr. Dursley keep his book—and whatever other agreements you made. That's it. If you break any of them, then we talk to the *Daily Prophet*."

Slughorn looked up, "You're dealing square with me?"

Wendt nodded in the dim light, but there was no doubt that he meant it.

"OK. That's good enough." He turned to me and said, "Get a good night's sleep tomorrow night. We'll start right after breakfast."

I nodded, and we went our separate ways.

That Friday night I got the first good night's sleep I had had on that old lumpy sofa of Wendt's. The both of us got up early. We had breakfast in the Great Hall. He said that he'd stand up for me if the Head objected. Wendt was right about the breakfast being grand on weekends. Then we went our separate ways. I headed down to the Potions classroom.

We'd not seen Slughorn at breakfast, but he seemed to be enthusiastically ready to go when I arrived. I had my book along and had it open to the right page. "OK. The formula is on this page. Just look there. No peaking elsewhere."

He took the book and exclaimed, "This is just a standard advanced Potions text. We use it in this classroom even now!"

"Take a closer look. You'll see that the formula has been uh 'improved'."

He did look and as he looked, his eyes widened. "This is incredible. I had no idea that this was the way to counter that other potion." Then he looked up at me and asked, "Just whose book was this. It's obviously not yours."

I shrugged. "I don't know. It says on the inside cover that it's the property of the Half-Blood Prince" whoever that was."

Slughorn gasped, "I taught him. He was probably one of the three best students that I ever had. There was he, Lily Evans and Harry Potter. Funny really. He was Lily's boyfriend for a while and Lily was Harry's mom."

"Yeh, yeh. It's a small world. Let's get going with the antidote."

Slughorn started to read carefully now and started making notes on a fresh piece of parchment. After a bit he asked, "Is this word wolfsbane or wolfram?"

I went over and looked over his shoulder. "Wolfsbane."

He wrote that down and then went on. After a few minutes he said. "This is hard going. I wished he had a clearer hand."

I was getting disgusted with the delay. "Oh, just let me do it. I've been reading it a lot and I've got his handwriting pretty well scoped out. I'll just write the whole procedure on a piece of parchment and then read it to you as you do it."

He stared at me, "Are you sure? You've never taken Potions have you?"

"Believe me. I know what I'm doing. When I finish you can look it over and we can talk about whatever you think looks wrong."

He was shaking his head but finally let me do it. I sat and started writing. Pretty soon, I was writing as fast as I could clearly. When I finished, I handed it to Slughorn.

He looked at it, his eyes traveling up and down it several times. The first time was rapid. Then he went slowly. Then he concentrated on a couple of spots. Eventually, he looked up and said, "Yes. I think this is right, but when we've finished, we'll give Miss Myers a very small dose and wait overnight for reactions. If there aren't any, then we'll give her a full dose." Then he asked, "Do you agree?"

I was startled that he'd asked my opinion, "Oh, sure. That sounds good, but one thing. Before she takes any dose, I'm taking a full dose."

Slughorn stared at me as though I were a Lepricorn. "What in the world for? I don't know what it will do to someone who's not taken the original love potion."

I found that I was really determined, "I don't care. I'm doing it. If you don't like it, we can always go talk to the *Prophet*."

Slughorn swallowed several times and then said, "Really. I don't want to be responsible for another person using an untested potion."

"I know the risks. I'm doing it. Just don't get in the way."

Slughorn made a face and said that we should get going on the brewing. He went to the store cupboard, got out supplies and organized them on a table. Then he got a cauldron and a few utensils. He gave a sigh and said, "This is it,"

I took my parchment with my copied formula and read off the directions, one at a time. Slughorn asked me to read them off three at a time – the one that we'd supposedly just finished, the one that we were about to do, and the next one.

This time it was much easier than with Knowland. I usually had to repeat ingredients several times with Knowland, but with Slughorn, he recited them from memory along with me. We almost never disagreed, and when we did, it was usually I who'd made a mistake. I'd get the name of some ingredient wrong or out of sequence. At the end, the formula called for 30 seconds of heating and then immediately removal from the fire. Slughorn swore and said, "My timer isn't that precise. We'll have to count the seconds together." I thought ruefully of the wonderful timers in the Room of Requirement but it was too late for that.

We counted off the seconds, pulled the small cauldron, and poured it into a vial. The final product was a vile green stuff that had a pungent odor. Slughorn looked at me then at the stuff and back to me. "That's what the instructions say it will be like. Do you still want to try a full dose before Miss Myers. You don't have to."

I glanced at it, and there was no doubt. "Yes, I do. Just measure out the dose." He poured it into a small graduated cylinder.

He nodded at me and said, "It's all yours."

I glanced at it, picked it up, and downed it in one gulp. It didn't taste at all as I expected. It reminded me of peppermint toothpaste. I shrugged. I didn't feel any different. "So far, it's OK. If I'm still walking tomorrow, we can try it with Miss Myers."

Slughorn was downcast, "Don't talk that way. I won't sleep any until tomorrow morning. Make sure you're always with someone. You could stay with me if you wanted to."

I laughed at that. "I've just broken in a new roomie. I'll stick with him."

I was making a joke of it, but I had to admit to myself that I was a bit nervous. I didn't make a big deal of it, but I was always sure that I was close to someone the rest of the day – just in case.

The following day was Sunday. Wendt was up even before I was. He was dressed and headed for breakfast even before I was quite dressed. "What's the big deal?" I asked. "Later today, we're going to try the formula on Ms. Myers but that's afternoon."

"Oh, on Sundays I always try to get up very early for breakfast and stay on after I've eaten to do some meditation. The Great Hall is pretty quiet, and the invisible ceiling makes for good contemplation of the wonders of God's universe."

"Oh. Hang on a moment and I'll go with you."

All he said was, "Good." We went down, and he had a quick breakfast and immediately went for the furthest corner of the Great Hall. I lingered over breakfast, and when Wendt finished his contemplation of the universe, I joined him and asked if it were OK if I accompanied him. He shrugged approval and commented, "I'm just going back up to my office to do some lesson planning. Then I'll be back down for lunch. Then what happens with you?"

"I show up at the Potions classroom right after lunch to be examined. I guess if I'm OK, we'll give the antidote to Pamela." I realized that it had leaked out. I'd said her first name. It was out, and I couldn't call it back. Wendt didn't act as though he'd heard. We went up to his office. At 11:30 we returned to the Great Hall for lunch.

By this time, I was sure that there was not going to be a problem. But the Head dropped by along with Madame Pomfrey to see how I was. She said that Miss Myers, Professor Wendt, and I were invited to the one o'clock event. It appeared to be optional for no one. Wendt seemed unconcerned.

We all showed up over a quarter hour surrounding 1 PM. There was Mr. Knowland as well, and even Miss Weasley was there. Slughorn looked me over. He measured my pulse and asked me a bunch of numbskull questions. I guess they were to determine if my head was working OK. He proclaimed me fit, and then things started for real.

The Head asked Pamela if she were ready. It seemed like a formality, but she looked over at me with longing in her eyes and said, "I don't want to do this if it's going to take away my love for Dudders. You can't make me."

Wendt rolled his eyes and sat down on a lab bench. Slughorn spoke first, "Miss Myers. I assure you that it's perfectly safe. Mr. Dursley took a full dose yesterday at this time. You can see he's . . ."

She interrupted, "He's dreamy."

"Uh, yes. He's perfectly fine."

She repeated, "I won't take it if it takes my love away."

Minerva came over to her and took Pamela's two hands in hers, "I'm sure that it won't take away anything that is really yours."

She considered that for a few minutes and then she said, "All right. I'll do it." There was no wheedling, no begging, no bargaining. She just said it.

Then, Slughorn came up to her with the vial and said, "This is the antidote. We've tested it thoroughly, and I'm sure it's safe. Mr. Dursley insisted on taking a whole dose yesterday. I want you to just take the tiniest sip. We'll wait an hour, and then if you're fine, you can take the rest. Do you understand?"

She nodded and said, "Of course. I'm to take the least amount I can and then we wait an hour before I take more."

Slughorn nodded and said, "Very good, young lady. You're very brave. Are you ready?"

She nodded mutely. He handed her the vial. She threw her head back, as she had at the party that seemed so, so very distant in time. She swallowed the entire dose in one gulp, eyes closed, before anyone could do anything. She slowly lowered her head and gazed into my eyes.

Slughorn quickly asked her, "How do you feel Miss Myers? How do you feel about Mr. Dursley?"

Her eyes never left mine as she said, "He's strong, brave, gentle, kind, generous."

Slughorn seemed dumbfounded by that answer. The Head asked her, "Miss Myers do you love Mr. Dursley?"

At that question, Pamela tilted her head slightly as if seeing me for the first time. But still her eyes held mine. She opened her mouth to answer and hesitated. Then she said, "I don't know."

Slughorn immediately celebrated, "That's it. No man or woman under the influence of a love potion could answer that question that way. They would compose a sonnet on their love. Case closed!"

The Head didn't seem quite so sure, "Strange. Very strange. I don't see how you could be wrong, Professor." Then she turned to Wendt who appeared to have been bored by the entire proceedings. She asked him, "Wendt, what do you think?"

He looked up with a slightly startled look as though the possibility of his being consulted was the last thing in the world that could happen, but he immediately answered, "You're right." Then he stood up and walked out of the room without a moment's hesitation.

The Head frowned and said to no one in particular, "I suppose that is that." Then, she turned to me and said, "Come over here where I can see you both at the same time."

I had to come over next to her, practically touching Pamela. Pamela kept her attention on the Head, who said, "On the night of the party, I gave you two instructions, and nothing has changed them. You, Mr. Dursley, will be transferred elsewhere besides Professor Wendt's office. You are not to speak to Miss Myers or spend time together until after she's graduated. Miss Myers, the same goes for you. Do you both understand?"

We nodded and she said, "Get out of here then." As we left together, I held the door for Pamela. She nodded thanks and we went different directions.

I'm glad no one asked me how I felt about Pamela. It raised goosebumps on my arm just being next to her. But I was going the opposite direction from her and arrived back at Wendt's office, somehow hoping that instructions would have been delivered as to where to go. But that didn't happen. That evening at dinner, a 3rd year found me in the kitchens where I was having dinner with Filch. He handed me an envelope. I opened it and discovered that I'd been transferred to the Huffelpuff house. I could report there tonight or tomorrow night at my convenience.

After dinner, I consulted Wendt about it. I told him that I wanted to stay this final night with him. For, frankly, I hoped he would give me some pointers about getting along with Huffelpuffs.

He smiled, "Well, you've got the easiest house to get along with. You'll find that they are easygoing and enjoy being helpful. You're lucky that you didn't get Ravenclaw."

I was puzzled by that but Wendt explained, "Oh, you know that with all the houses except Ravenclaw, you have to learn a password to get in. It's changed at irregular intervals, but you always have notice. That's not the way it is with Ravenclaw."

I puzzled at that, "No password?"

"Not exactly. You have to solve a new puzzle every time you get in. Sometimes, it's a math problem. Sometimes it's a logic puzzle. Sometimes it's a simple puzzle that depends on you knowing some fact like when America was discovered by the Norse."

All I could say was, "Shit."

On the other hand, the Huffelpuff password works the opposite way. If you don't remember the password, the door painting gives you hints about what the password is. In the end you have to be really dull not to be able to get in."

"I wouldn't count me completely out on that."

"The Huffelpuffs will expect you to be a good 'citizen'. They'll expect you to keep the Common Room clean – even if you didn't make the mess. There will be a room inspection every week to make sure your personal space is neat and presentable to company if it were ever to show up."

I laughed hard at that. Wendt wasn't laughing. "You're not kidding, are you?" He nodded. All I could say was, "Oh, shit."

He shrugged and said, "You'll get used to it. The only question is will it happen sooner or later."

We talked more about Huffelpuffs. Wendt talked about their Quidditch teams, their other competitions and so on, but it really all boiled down to what I'd heard in the first five minutes. I looked around our office – at Wendt's messy desk, the few photos on the walls that weren't all straight, even at his bookshelf where the books were not neat. I thought that I might just miss staying in his office – old lumpy sofa and all.

Huffelpuff

I arrived at Huffelpuff during the noon hour. Mr. Wendt helped me carry my things down the one floor to the Huffelpuff entrance. He offered to help me carry them up to my room, but I wanted to do that on my own. So, we parted company there at the door to Huffelpuff. The door picture, which was of an only very slightly plump, red-cheeked, merry-looking maiden asked for the password.

"I'm afraid that I don't know it."

She was not troubled in the least. "Then, you'll be happy to know that it's the name of a former headmaster here at Hogwarts."

"I'm afraid I don't remember any of their names."

She was completely up for that. "Perhaps you'll think of it by remembering that it's a color."

I saw what he meant about them being accommodating. Of course, I didn't know any of the names of Hogwarts Heads other than McGonagall, so I had to guess, "Is it Blue?"

"A good guess, especially since it starts with the same first letter."

I tried, "It's not Beige, is it?"

"Another admirable try, but not right."

That seemed to only leave, "Black?"

"Right you are. It's actually Nigelius Black for future reference."

The door opened, and I thanked her.

I'm not sure what kind of reception I expected, but it was certainly not the reception that I received. When I entered through the door, there was a cheer and applause. I looked around to see if anyone else had arrived. I was it. The applause was not lengthy, but it seemed to be heart-felt. Someone who looked like he might be a 7th year approached me and said, "I'm Brock Evans. We in Huffelpuff want to welcome you to our house. We know that you aren't a student but you are known to all of us, and now that you are here, we all treat you as a fellow Huffelpuff. There was another round of applause and, not knowing what to say, I simply said, "Thank you all. I'm sure I didn't receive a welcome like this at Gryffindor."

Another cheer sounded. I looked around at the roomful of happy, friendly faces and wondered what I might have missed when I was at school. Then there were a flood of questions. The ones that surprised me were about Pamela. Someone asked, "What's it like to date the prettiest girl in the school?"

My mouth dropped open at that one. When I recovered, I said, "Well, first off, I haven't dated any girls at Hogwarts."

Some guy said, "We saw you at the Halloween party With Pamela Myers."

"Well, you weren't paying much attention. I didn't come with her and although I left with her, it was also with the Headmistress. I wouldn't exactly say that I was 'dating' either one." After a few more denials, a couple of guys grabbed my bags and we all went up to my room. I unpacked and came back down to the Common Room.

I saw a newspaper on a table in the Common Room and I was hoping against hope that it might have some soccer scores. It turned out to be a *Daily Prophet*. I gagged and started rummaging among the magazines there. As I was looking, a trio of girls, yes, a trio of girls came up and started to talk all at once. The upshot was that they wanted to know what Pamela was like. I sat down on an armchair because I figured I'd have to talk about this and I might as well get it done with now rather than later. Also, girls are more effective at spreading gossip, so I could maybe get it over once for all by talking with a couple of girls.

One of them started the conversation, "What is it about that Myers that guys like so much?"

I was so tempted to just say, "You have to ask me that! Don't you have other guys you can talk to?" But what I really said was, "Let's start with some simple truths. Guys prefer blondes to brunettes. Redheads are a special case. It can go either way with them. Second, guys prefer straight long hair to short curly hair." All of them had short hair. "Sorry, I don't make up the rules. It's just life as it is.

"Now, all of that counts, but what most attractive women have that you may not have is confidence." I got blank stares all around. "I'm not kidding. You don't have to be perfect to be confident. That's the problem that most ladies have. They think they have to have perfect hair or perfect clothes or a perfect figure to get anywhere with guys. Not true."

One of the girls asked, "I've got confidence, but there aren't any guys that pay attention to me."

I looked over her. She actually wasn't that bad looking. She was a redhead with a deep auburn color. I nodded and said, "Yep. You don't look bad and. . ."

With that she sniffed and I thought I saw a tear forming. I moved fast to cut that off. "OK. Let's see your confident approach to a guy."

She was flabbergasted. She asked, "You mean now, here?"

I was tempted to give a smart-ass answer but I decided that they weren't ready for that. So I said, "Yes. This is a play. You're going to act a role as a confident lady approaching a man for a date."

She stared at me. I went on, "What did you mean that you were confident?"

She sort of shrugged, "Oh, I meant that if a guy asked me for a date, I'd smile and decide whether I wanted to go out with him before answering."

I nodded. "Good start. But to really become confident, you have to be willing to start it. OK. Let's practice. You want to meet a good looking guy. So, you walk up to him and introduce yourself. Let's see how you do."

She stared again and then realized that I meant me, now. "Uh. Oh, damn, I didn't mean to say that. Let me try again."

I held up a hand. "No. Everyone makes mistakes. No one notices the mistakes except the person making the mistake. No one else knows what they intended to do or say."

"But how can I be confident if I'm not perfect?"

I scratched my head. "OK. If you're perfect, you don't need confidence. It's only the imperfect who need confidence. Try it again. No do overs, no retakes. You just start talking, and whatever comes out comes out. Don't worry. Just keep going."

She clearly didn't believe me, but I have to give her credit. She tried. She said something like, "Hello. . .uh . . .hi. My name is Marigold . . . er Mary. What's your name?"

I nodded and clapped. "Good job."

"Oh that was horrid. I made so many mistakes."

I said, "OK. That was OK. Let's try something different. Same situation, but this time, after your name, say the first thing that comes to your mind."

She turned blood red, and I knew that I'd hit pay dirt. She had something that she actually wanted to say. "Step right up and say your piece."

She shook her head. I stared at her. "You have to do this."

Her mouth dropped open. "Really." I couldn't believe my ears. She actually accepted that stupid lie.

"YES."

"Well OK." She took a deep breath. What she said came out in a rush that would have had me laughing except that I didn't want her to think that I thought it was funny. Anyway, she said something like, "Hi. My name er I'm Mary, and I think you're cute."

I had to reward her. She had zero confidence but she actually did what she needed to. I answered her, "Hi. I'm Dudley and I think you're cute."

Her mouth fell open, and she spoke naturally for the first time, "Really! I've been watching you all night and hoping that I could talk to you."

That deserved an A+. "Great. You know I noticed you, too." Her face turned a shade that I'd never seen before. Then she laughed. I guess it was relief of tension. I don't know.

I went on. "OK. That's the key to confidence ladies. Not caring that it hurts."

One of the other girls said, "What do you mean, not caring?"

An idea hit me as I was talking. I thought of the perfect example. "OK. Have you seen the movie, 'Lawrence of Arabia'?" I looked around and realized that they didn't know what I was talking about. I thought fast. "Have you read the book?" They all shook their heads.

"OK. Lawrence of Arabia is about a Brit in World War I. He's stationed in Egypt. One day, he's in a bar talking with a couple of buddies, and he shows them a 'magic' trick."

Mary interrupted, "Is this real magic?"

I thought a moment. Was it? I didn't know. "I don't know. I'll tell you about it, and you tell me. Anyway, his trick is this. He lights a match, holds it in one hand, and with the thumb and forefinger of the other hand puts it out.

"One of his buddies asks to try it and shouts and drops the burning match. Then he says that it 'bloody well hurt' and asks Lawrence what the trick is.

"Lawrence answers that the trick is not caring that it bloody well hurts."

The three of them stared at me, and one of them asked, "What do you mean?"

I know that some people think that I'm dense but this goes beyond me. However, I was patient, "I mean that the key to confidence is that you have to stop caring that it bloody well hurts when you fail. You have to be perfectly willing to go up to nine guys in a row and introduce yourself and say, 'I think you're cute.' And have all nine say goodbye."

"Why would I want to have all that pain?"

"Well, I give you that it hurts the first couple of dozen times that it happens, but after that it becomes a sort of game. You want to see how they turn you down, and then you begin to see that a lot of them don't turn you down."

I could see doubt in some of their eyes. "I'm not saying that you'll ever hit it off with more than half. Most will still turn you down, but before long the guys see the confidence in your eyes, and then things get fun."

Mary said, "No way!"

"I'm not kidding. Go ahead and practice for real."

Then, one at a time, they tried introducing themselves. It was mostly positive, but I would throw in a flat turn down. After a while one named Gerry asked, "What's a good pickup line with a guy?"

I nodded and said, "There is no good pickup line."

They all stared again.

"I'm not kidding. Far better than any pickup line is to say whatever comes into your head as you're talking." They were still doubtful. "Look, the reason that you want to pick up the guy you're talking to is that there's something that you like about him. Let that come out. You'll be surprised.

"Now, this is the final exam. Each of you introduce yourself and say the one thing that's at the top of you head at that moment. Don't try to dress it up. Just say it."

Mary just blurted it out, "I'm Mary, and I really want to meet you. You're more fun than any guy here."

I nodded. Then Gerry said, "I'm Gerry, and I really want to go to bed with you."

"OK. That's it for this session, and we never talk again."

The third said, "That's unfair. I didn't get my turn."

How could I say other than, "Sure. Do it."

"I'm June. I see why that Pamela wanted you."

I had to finish this with a clear understanding about the Pamela thing. "OK. Here's the straight truth. Pamela got a dose of love potion – not from me! I was the first guy that she looked at taking it. She was just magicked. That's all. She got the antidote, and she says she doesn't love me. Over. Out. Case closed."

They all seemed sad at that. Strange. I don't understand women at all. "Now, it's almost curfew. I need to get up and work tomorrow. Good night. Good bye. Sleep well."

They all got up, waved goodbye and walked up the stairs to the girl's dorm.

———
▽

It was only a couple of weeks to Christmas Holiday, and I began to wonder what I'd do over the break. I knew that Filch lived at Hogwarts all year round, and I wondered if I had to as well. So, one day I asked him about it.

He was getting into the Christmas Spirits early and was in a good mood. When I asked him, he explained, "Well, buddy, almost all the kids are gone, and so are my greatest duties. You don't have to work hard to catch the bad guys if they're all off at home with visions of dancing elves in their heads. I can get the house elves to do most of the regular maintenance work and cleaning. . ."

"Yeh", I thought to myself. "That's the way it works all the time."

"So, if you want to take the whole Christmas Holiday off to visit your family, it's OK. I'll soldier on alone and forlorn, but you go enjoy yourself."

My answer was simple, "Thanks. I will." And he was right. As we approached Christmas it was almost as if all the J.D.'s just had decided that they should be on good behavior. The older ones were busy buying Christmas gifts for friends, and family and the younger ones were trying to prevent that last minute owl sent to home by a teacher or – dreadful – the Head.

I had gotten into a routine that kept me from thinking about Pamela. I don't mean that I'd forgotten her existence, but I was doing everything I could to keep myself busy. But then something happened that brought her back to mind. I was eating in the kitchen with Filch and the house elves when we had an unexpected visitor.

Professor Slughorn looked jaunty marching up to our table with a wide smile on his face. "Ah, good to see you Filch. How are you Mr. Dursley?"

I glanced over at Filch. He apparently didn't have any idea what this was about. He just shrugged and said, "Happy Holidays without kids."

Slughorn laughed and said, "Quite. Quite. Now, Mr. Dursley, I was wondering if you could join me at my annual Christmas Party this year."

That had come out of the blue and I was a little suspicious. "I didn't know that you threw a Christmas Party. There wasn't anything on the staff bulletin board."

"Oh, it's not a formal school thing. It's just a little personal tradition that I have."

Stranger and stranger. "Well, do you invite most of the school?"

He laughed again like old Saint Nick. "Oh, no. I just invite a few personal friends, mostly students and a few outsiders. You know, influential people that I've befriended along the way."

I thought to myself, "Where do I fit in this zoo?" But I actually asked, "And is there a dress code?" Hogwarts had one for staff, so I thought that he might.

"Oh, nothing fancy. If you've got formal robes that would be good. But if you don't, just come in something nice."

I wondered what counted as "something nice". And what about guests, so I asked, "Can I invite a guest?"

This was the first question that seemed to be scary to him, "Oh, you're not thinking of inviting that girl?" He couldn't bring himself to say her name.

"No, no. I was just thinking about a friend. You know. Maybe, Professor Wendt."

He was back to old Saint Nick, "Oh, yes. Wendt. Perfect. He's always good for . . ." Apparently, he was having a hard time thinking of something that Wendt was good for, but he found it. "He's always good for one of his funny Muggle stories."

"I'll see."

Slughorn apparently had a thought that bothered him, "But. He's your guest. He can't invite a guest. I mean, not anyone like Professor Sinistra, you know."

I smiled and said, "I'll let him know."

Slughorn drew out his answer, "Goooood. Yes. Just don't offend him."

I smiled again and said, "Don't worry."

He backed away from our table a good bit less jolly than when he arrived.

Filch had been looking at me as though, I were the Creature from the Black Lagoon. "You mean to say that you wouldn't invite me?"

"Now, I didn't say that. I just asked the question. I might not invite anyone." I thought a second, "Do you want to come?"

He shrugged elaborately and said, "It really doesn't matter to me one way or the other."

I thought, "Like hell it doesn't." However, I only smiled.

He went on, "Well, I suppose if you don't have anyone else to go with . . ."

I had an extremely hard time keeping from smiling, but I succeeded, "Good. Don't forget that we need to wear, 'something nice'."

He shook his head, "I don't know where you get the idea that I might not wear something nice."

The next day I was walking through the Common Room of Huffelpuff on my way to my room when I felt a finger tap me on my back. I turned around and found that it was Maribel . . er . . Mary. I started to say something when she simply said, "Mr. Dursley. I've heard that you are invited to Professor Slughorn's Christmas do."

How in the world had she learned that? She went on, "I'd really like to go with you to that party."

I really had to admire her. She'd said it without a shake in her voice or a glance at her feet. I congratulated her, "Very good. That was real confidence. I couldn't be more proud of you."

She kept going, "Thank you, but this is not practice. I mean it. I want to go along with you to Slughorn's party."

I didn't intend to, but I reacted immediately, "Wow! That is really good."

Her mouth closed tightly into a hard line, "I'm serious. Why don't you take me seriously?"

I apologized, of course, "I'm sorry. Yes, you're exactly right. It's a serious proposal, and I need to take it that way." She smiled a smile that would have melted an ice-cold heart.

"I'll answer seriously by saying that I can't invite you."

"And why not!"

I liked her more and more the farther this went on. "Well, the first and most important reason is that I've already invited someone. But there's a second reason that's really quite as important. The Headmistress would fire me on the spot if I dated a student."

She was undeterred. She looked down for the first time, "What girl are you taking?"

At that I couldn't help laughing. I quickly explained, "I'm sorry, the funny thing is that it's not a girl at all."

She seemed to be offended by that and asked, "Well, then, have it your own way. What woman are you taking?"

"Oh, this is too rich. I'm taking Filch."

Her reaction was instantaneous and direct, "You're lying."

It was awful. I just couldn't keep from laughing, "No. No. It's true."

It just kept going on and on. She hesitantly asked, "Are you gay?"

That sobered me some, "No. I'm not, but he wanted to go. And he's never been in his whole career here that goes back farther than Slughorn does, I think.

"Don't forget that Filch is my oldest and maybe best friend here. It would be disloyal to turn him down when he wanted to go.

"Also, at least as important, it is strictly against the rules for someone on the staff to date a student.'

Mary seemed about to say something. I quickly added, "Even if both are adults. It would mean my job."

That seemed to mollify her some. Finally, she asked, "Did I really do well – asking you out?"

"You were superb. I doubt there are a handful of boys here at Hogwarts that could resist you."

Her eyes seemed to grow wider by the minute. "Really. You're not just saying that to make me feel good?"

"Really. I meant it completely."

She reached a hand out and touched my arm. I took a step back and said, "Don't forget that I'm staff, and I can't even have a long conversation with students."

The light went out of her eyes, and she nodded and backed away. "Good night."

Over the next couple of days, she was not the only adult 7th year lady who thought that she could skirt her way around the ethics of the school, but she was definitely the most self-assured, confident one.

Someone who wouldn't even sign her note slipped it under the door of my room and never revealed to me who she was.

The next Saturday, immediately before finals week, was the party. I had gone into Hogsmeade and bought an inexpensive set of dress robes. I was afraid of what Filch might show up in. However, I was pleasantly surprised when he showed up in a presentable, if approaching threadbare, set of robes that weren't quite formal but were nice.

We arrived a little late. The room was already fairly full. That was good because there wasn't any attention paid to Filch and me when we arrived. Before Slughorn had even greeted us, Filch had made a beeline for the refreshment table. I wandered in and was found by Slughorn who insisted on introducing me to his guests.

The editor-in-chief of the *Daily Prophet* was there. Gwynnock Jones of the Holyhead Harpies was there, although she didn't stay late. Shortly after Slughorn introduced us, she left. There was someone whom Slughorn insisted was a vampire. He looked fairly normal if somewhat pale. I suppose that Slughorn wasn't kidding. He was kind of spooky.

However, the real surprise was a guest that I didn't need to be introduced to. Gilderoy Lockhardt was standing near the drink table with a woman in an odd white costume. There were a couple of other people also there apparently talking to him.

I walked over toward him, and as I approached, I heard Lockhardt ask the others if they wanted an autograph. They backed away offering apologies. The woman in white stayed with him. When I arrived, Lockhardt turned to me with a smile. I asked him, "Do you remember that we met several weeks ago?"

He studied my face and said, "Well, my memory is not fully up to snuff. I'm afraid that I don't remember."

"Oh, it was right here."

"In this room? I don't remember being here before."

"No, I mean here at Hogwarts."

"Oh, yes. They tell me that I taught here one year. Was it then?"

"No. No. We met on Halloween weekend in the Great Hall. Yes?"

He shook his head slowly. The lady with him introduced herself, "I'm nurse Baxter. I go with him whenever he travels away from St. Mongo's. We are encouraging him to visit places that he stayed as his memory improves, but Mr. Lockhardt was not here on Halloween weekend."

I stared at the both of them. "But surely he was. I saw him and spoke with him briefly. And he wasn't with you. He was with one of the professors here – Professor Sinistra."

This time, she stared at me, "I'm sure not. We never let our memory patients travel with different people." She leaned over toward me and whispered, "It's too confusing for them."

I gave up, "Sorry, I guess I confused Mr. Lockhardt with someone else."

At that, he became more alert and said, "Well, I'm sure we met somewhere. I can't recall either. I'm sure that you want my autograph."

I tried to refuse, "I already have one, so you don't need to bother."

"Oh, it's no bother." He drew out a small notebook and pen and started writing. As he did, he asked, "How do you want the inscription?"

That confused me anew, "You don't have pre-printed ones?"

He almost seemed offended. "Of course not. What would the point of that be? Now, how do you want it?"

I shrugged and said, "To Dudley, an old admirer from St. Brutus'."

He smiled, "Very good. I always like to run into old school chums. Did we ever play sports together?"

This was becoming bizarre, but I decided to see how far I could push it. "Only on the old football squad. You were a great sweeper."

Without the slightest hesitation, the old faker said, "I certainly was, wasn't I."

I begged leave to find my date, and I left him.

Of course, I didn't go out of my way to find Filch. However, someone found me. It was Slughorn. He pulled me over to the side and said, "I don't have time to talk with you right now – too much hosting to do. But, I want to talk with you later about a little business proposition. Would you stick around after the party so that we can talk a bit? I won't keep you long."

I agreed and wandered off trying to avoid Filch, and Lockhardt, and his keeper. It really wasn't hard. There were a lot of guests at the party. I found it hard to believe there was room for everyone.

I also ran into Professor Wendt. He was talking with a woman whom I'd seen around, but I couldn't quite remember her name. When he saw me, he invited me over and asked me if I'd met Madame Pomfrey.

"We never formally met, but I remember you from the anti-love potion."

She asked, "You don't exactly fit the profile of a mover and shaker of society."

Wendt smiled, "Nor do you, come to it."

"Right-o. So what are any of us doing here?"

Wendt went on, "I'm here because you had mentioned to Slughorn that you were interested in inviting me, and he wanted to make it possible for you to invite someone else."

Pomfrey added, "I'm here because I invited myself. It seems like there are lots of minor injuries and poisonings here and I wanted to have a head start on the trouble."

"Well, I don't know why I'm here. By the way, did you see Lockhardt?"

Both of them had. "It's hard to believe that he's the same guy who was here at Halloween."

Wendt looked around and then said, "There's a good reason for that. He isn't."

"What do you mean, he isn't? I talked to him both times. Both times he was screwy but in different ways. Still, both times, he looked the same, sounded the same. Everyone said he was Lockhardt."

Wendt chuckled, "Still, they were different people."

"Oh, come on. How do you know?"

"It's simple. The first time, I was Lockhardt."

I was dumbfounded, "How is that possible. You two aren't anywhere near the same height. You've got different color hair. You're sane. He's not."

Wendt shook his head, "Crazy, but true. I was Lockhardt the first time by using Polyjuice Potion. It lets you imitate anyone."

I still thought he was pulling my leg, but Pomfrey backed him up, "Oh, yes, Mr. Dursley. Wendt has impersonated lots of people. Once he even impersonated, the Headmistress."

I wasn't absolutely convinced but I decided to take them at their word until I could check in some way. "OK. Why do you do that?"

Wendt seemed a bit uncomfortable, "Well, I wish I knew myself. I started off doing it as a joke, and after a while, it just seemed to take on a life of its own. I'm not sure I really know now. Sometimes it just seems easier doing it than not."

I thought to myself that this was a screwy place if there ever were one. We talked a bit about plans for the holidays. It seemed that Wendt returned to London and usually spent a few days with the Headmistress. I found that hard to believe, "You talk about it being unethical for staff to date students. Well, OK. But what about teachers dating the Headmistress!"

Wendt chuckled, "Oh, I give you that it's dangerous but I started dating her when she was just another teacher and one of us didn't report to the other. Then this year when she became the Head – well, it just seemed like we'd sort of established a precedent, and we just kept going. What about you, Pomfrey? Are you staying at Hogwarts as usual?"

She shrugged and said, "Like you say, after a while, it just gets easier and easier doing the habitual thing. I guess I may change some day, but . . . . " She trailed off and then turned to me, "And you, Mr. Dursley. Do you have plans for the Holiday?"

I shrugged and said, "Well, I guess I'll go home for the Holiday and maybe see if I can look up any of my old gang. I guess it will seem pretty tame compared with life at Hogwarts, but it will be good to see my Mum and Dad."

After a while I left them, and Filch found me. He'd had a good time. There was lots of good food and drink. That was as much as he wanted. We compared notes. When I told him about seeing Lockhardt his reaction was, "What, is Professor Wendt play-acting again? I thought he never did one more than once."

"Oh, no. This is the real Lockhardt. I talked to Wendt tonight too."

"Oh, that Wendt is tricksy. I don't know how far you can trust him when he starts with the Polyjuice."

The party was starting to break up, and Filch wanted to head for his office/rooms. I told him to go ahead because I had a little business with Slughorn. "What? Don't you want to come down to the office and have a nightcap?"

I shook my head no. He seemed to be truly sorry that I wasn't coming down, but he cheered himself up with the thought that maybe he could get Wendt to join him for a nightcap. Where he got that thought I have no idea.

I started to clean up while we waited for the last stragglers to move along. They finally moved along. By that time, I'd tossed all the party junk into the garbage bins that were strategically placed around the rooms. When he saw what I'd been doing he said, "Oh, you should just have left that for the house elves."

I smiled at the idea, "No. This is my job. It doesn't really matter much."

Slughorn accepted that and invited me to come over to a pair of armchairs. When we'd sat, he flicked his wand, the lights went down, and a fire burst into life in the fireplace. He asked me, "You want, a snifter of brandy with me, don't you?"

I shrugged, and a pair of snifters appeared floating along a few feet above the floor and deposited themselves on the end table between our chairs. It looked like I was going to have a nightcap after all. "Now, we can talk in comfort."

"Yes, I've been wondering what you wanted to talk about."

He glanced around as though he thought someone might be listening in and said in a soft voice, "I have a little proposal for you."

"Go ahead."

He steepled his fingers under his nose and seemed to concentrate for a moment before proceeding. "First, let me ask you not to come to a snap decision. I'm sure you're not quite ready for the suggestion that I have. Take time to think about it.

"As a matter of fact, think about it over the Holiday." He then added an unusual request. "Please promise me that."

This was truly bizarre, but I agreed. Then he went on.

"Good. That love potion that you brewed was pretty unique."

"Well, first of all, I didn't brew it, and second. . ."

He interrupted me, "No. No. My boy. You are the force behind that potion. It would never have been brewed without you. The way you supervised the brewing of the antidote was quite impressive."

He hesitated again before continuing, "I have a much larger project in mind for us to take on."

I wondered what in the world he could have in mind but I was more than willing to listen. Seeing no objection, he went on, "I've been thinking of your book, the *Advanced Potions.*"

I shrugged. Was he thinking of updating a few more potions to use in class or something? Once expressed by me, that idea seemed to disturb him. His brows knit and his mouth compressed. In frustration he asked, "Doesn't that excite you?"

I had to admit that it didn't. His face switched to a picture of confusion. "Don't you have any idea how much those potions in the book are worth?"

"No. How would you make them worth something?"

His mouth dropped open in what I supposed must be amazement. He leaned back and gazed toward the ceiling. I took another sip of the brandy. It was pretty good. After a minute or so, he lowered his eyes to mine and said, "OK. Let me explain to you.

"First, what I propose that we do is complete the process of converting Snape's notes to complete revised recipes. I admit that even just that would be a major undertaking. You'd have to take the lead on that because you've clearly got a good idea of how to decipher that cramped writing style that he uses.

"But, the payoff could be tremendous."

I still didn't get it, "OK. You're going to have to explain that in more detail to me. Just where does this payoff come from?"

Slughorn began to have an eager glint in his eye. "Oh, the opportunities are amazing.

"In the first place, we'd edit the book and get it published. The revenue from that alone would be very tidy. This would be such an improvement from the standard text that we use that every magic academy in the world would eventually adopt it. Just think of that. I use the standard text in all my advanced classes. Each student would buy the book only once, but that amounts to 50 to 100 texts each year. There are at least a hundred schools like Hogwarts around the world. I feel confident that they'd all quickly adapt the text. That would be five to ten thousand sales a year. The book price would be over 100 galleons apiece. That could be a million galleons a year. Of course, the authors don't get all of that, but I think we could conservatively count on getting a few hundred thousand a year.

"Now, that's only the beginning of book sales. We'd publish a beginning text and an intermediate text using this book as the basis. They wouldn't make as much money, but I think that we could certainly count on more than a million in revenue each year from total book sales.

"That's just student sales, of course. There are lots of experienced wizards who would buy these books so that they have the best formulae. And then there are library sales. These wouldn't amount to huge numbers but they would be respectable."

I sat in amazed silence. Could he be serious? Millions per year income! But he wasn't done. He kept on going.

"Of course, that's just book sales. If the rest of the formulae are like the two that I've seen, most would be truly unique." He hesitated for effect, "Sooo unique that we could patent them!"

He obviously expected me to be astounded, but I wasn't. "Don't you see!" He was obviously a bit miffed and spelled out the details for me.

"The ones that we patented would be ones that are used in manufacturing processes. The businesses that use them would have to pay us license fees!

"Now, how large might they be? First, let's make some reasonable guesses. In the standard text there are a little over five hundred pages. The average number of pages per recipe is about two and a half, so there are about two hundred formulae. About a third of them are just for fun. You know, impressive effects but nothing profitable. Another fifty percent are probably used for profit but aren't worth a lot. We could patent them, but the improvement wouldn't be enough for manufacturers to adapt them over what they use now.

"But that still leaves ten or even fifteen percent of them that would be solidly profitable if patented." He hesitated for effect again, "So, you ask, what is solidly profitable?

"At a conservative rough guess, I think that they might yield 25,000 to 50,000 per year each. That's anywhere from a half million to maybe well over a million per year."

I had to whistle at that. He was beginning to talk real money. He nodded approvingly and went on, "But, ah ha! That may be a low quaffle estimate. It's likely that among those twenty to forty winners there are two or three real gems.

"How much, you ask. Oh, I'd say, for starters at least 10 times the average value. We could be talking several million per year all together.

"Pretty impressive, you say, but that might just not be all." Here he actually rubbed his hands together. I'd heard of people doing that, but I'd never actually seen it in action.

"If just one of those couple of real gems were quite valuable, we might not patent and license it at all. We might just keep it for ourselves and sell it to the highest bidder or license it to the highest bidder for a really large fee." His eyes got a far-away look. "We might even start a company around it ourselves."

He slapped his palms on his knees and leaned back in his chair. "Now, I made you promise to not give me a decision until you'd had a chance to think it over during the Holiday. I'm going to hold you to that. Go home, relax, spend some time with your family. Talk it over with your parents if you care to. But make sure they keep this confidential. We'll talk again when you're back."

I agreed and walked away from Slughorn's lair with quite a lot to think about. I had a hard time sleeping that night, and Sunday night was not any better. But on Tuesday of Finals Week, I thought of something that I could do before leaving for Holiday.

I went to Professor Wendt's office that night. He invited me in but was not in a great mood. "Well, Dursley, I hope this is important. I'm trying to get through grading essays. This is the busiest time of year. What is it?"

I didn't want to rush this, so I apologized and said, "It's just that Slughorn told me what he had on his mind, and I wanted some advice. But I'll leave, since you're so busy."

That grabbed Wendt's attention. "Really? I have to admit to being curious. Can you tell me about it? Don't rush."

He motioned me to take a seat in his shiny red leather chair. I took it and began, "You know the Love Potion that I brewed and the antidote?"

"Sure. Go ahead."

"Well, they came out of the Half-Blood Prince's Potions book."

Wendt nodded. "Yes, Snape's. Go ahead."

"Well, the Professor thinks that we could edit the book to include Snape's notes and then publish it and make a bunch of Galleons. What do you think of the idea?"

Wendt scratched his chin and stood up. He started to pace. "Well, well. Does he, then?" After a couple of minutes of pacing, Wendt went on, "Well, Slughorn is the current past master of potions around here. Snape was before. He should know what would sell and what wouldn't. As a matter of fact, I'd say that Slughorn is the past master of making money. IF he says that something will make money, it will." He paused and continued pacing. "Did he tell you how much he thought that you guys could make?"

I was almost embarrassed to name the figures but I forced myself. "Well, the thing is that he thinks that book sales alone would bring in hundreds of thousands each year."

Wendt gasped, "You're kidding."

"No, sir. That was his conservative estimate."

"But that was not all that he thought you might make?"

"Oh, no. He thought that some of the processes could be patented and licensed for . . . " I hesitated to name his figure but I gave the low-quaffle figure, "possibly over a million a year."

Wendt stared and took his seat. "You're not kidding me?"

I could only smile and say, "No, sir."

Wendt swiveled his chair away from me so that I had a side view of him. "Well, what does he want you to do – decide before the Holidays?"

"Oh, no sir. He insisted that I think about it over the Holiday."

"Good."

"But there's something I want to ask you." Wendt nodded quickly and I went on, "Do I own the formulae?"

"Tell me more about how you came upon this book."

I took a deep breath and started the story. I told him about the Room of Requirement and looking for a desk. I told him about finding the book. I told about finding the desk and being given permission to keep it by the Headmistress. During the whole time, Wendt was sitting motionless with his eyes closed. When I finished, he opened his eyes and asked, "Do you think you own the book?"

"I don't know. I do feel very . . uh . . jealous of it. I don't want to show it to anyone. What do you suppose that means?"

He just shook his head, "no." Then he said, "This seems to me to have more of legerdemain about it than of legality. Let me consult a friend about this, and I'll get back with you before the end of the term."

I agreed.

The next couple of days were quiet, and then Thursday night I found a note in my mailbox in the Staff Lounge. It was from Wendt. He wrote to ask me to meet him at the Headmistress's office on Friday after lunch.

Most of the students had left the school by Hogwarts express shortly after breakfast. I sat at the same table with the teachers, but Wendt was surrounded by teachers. So, I didn't get to talk with him until after lunch. I approached him, and he got up from his chair, nodded at me, and pointed to the main entrance.

After we'd exited the Great Hall, he spoke. "We'll go see Miner . . . that is, the Head. Let me do the talking. After I've finished, then we can all talk."

We arrived at her office, but the door from her outer office to her inner one was locked, so we just took seats and waited. She walked in from the outer passage, bustled over to the inner door, and opened it. "Come on in and take seats."

She asked if we would like some sherry. Wendt agreed, but I declined with thanks. Wendt began the discussion. He told my story briefly but accurately. After he told the story, he asked THE question, "Minerva," I'd never heard anyone refer to her as Minerva in school, but I supposed that now that the term was officially over, people could be less formal. "Mr. Dursley wants to know if he has the right to sell the secrets in "his" book. Is it "his" at all?"

The Head showed some exasperation, "Why is it, Wendt, that you always save these puzzles for the end of term when I think I can take it easy?"

"I really don't know."

She ran both hands through her hair as she stared down at the desk. Then she straightened and began, "Well, most people put things in the Room of Requirements to lose them – get rid of them. That would seem to make them fair game for anyone else who comes into the room. But this is different from most things . . ."

Wendt asked, "How so?"

"For one thing, most of the contents of the Room of Requirement were destroyed at the end of last term when one of those Slytherin idiots loosed a fire demon in the place. However, some things survived. Why? They should have been destroyed."

Wendt smiled an uncertain smile and suggested, "Luck?"

"Oh, Wendt, do you really believe in Luck – especially in a case like this?"

He just shook his head.

"Then, I think that something wanted it to survive AND to fall into hands that might do something with it."

Wendt sniffed, "Well, Dursley did do something with it. He brewed a love potion that got people in trouble."

The Head nodded and then added, "But that got it into the hands of Slughorn."

"I rest my case." Wendt laughed.

"Oh, I don't know." Then she turned to me, "Dursley, let's just suppose that it is yours to dispose of as you wish. Take your Holiday and decide what you want to do. Then we'll see what happens."

I wasn't sure that I was happy with this experimental approach but I didn't have much choice. We all wished each other a Happy Christmas. I announced that I would pack and take the floo from the Great Hall to the Leaky Cauldron and then go on to Little Whingeing. Wendt was not very encouraging, he just wished me, "Good Luck. See you after New Year's."

I left the office and headed for Huffelpuff. I didn't see either of the others leave.

Little Whingeing Suffers

I made my way home rather easily. The floo system got me to the Leaky Cauldron easily. Then, I went into Diagon Alley to visit my bank – Gringotts. I withdrew some of my earnings as galleons and some as pounds sterling. I walked to the nearest tube station and worked my way by Underground and train to my parents' home.

They had a big reception planned. Aunt Marge was there along with Ripper, and we had a good dinner featuring Yorkshire Pudding. Aunt Marge wanted to know all about my job as the understudy of the Security Manager of Barclays in Edinburgh. Apparently, that was what Mum and Dad had told her about what I was doing.

I had to think fast. "Well, you know, it's not quite completely 100% true. I am the assistant to security in a Scottish institution. It's just not Barclay's."

Of course, Marge had to know what bank it was. I was in a tight spot, so I sort of stretched the truth, "Well, it's ING."

Marge waved it away. "Well, everyone has to start at the bottom. Just be sure that they treat you well, and you'll work your way up to Barclays before you know it."

All that I could do was give her an uncertain smile and thank her for her good advice. The rest of the night went well – except for one moment. She asked me, "What ever happened to that cousin of yours? You know, Harvey or Harcourt or something like that."

Dad saved me the trouble of answering, "Oh, he's graduated from St. Brutus' School for the Criminally Insane and is making license plates."

I almost suffocated trying to keep myself from rolling on the floor with laughter. Aunt Marge responded, "Good. I had to spend six months in that German Concentration Camp before the British ambassador got me out of it."

Dad just smiled weakly and explained, "I think it was actually an American air force base. They were trying to keep you safe."

She harrumphed like a bull elephant, "It was in Germany, and I was held against my will. That's a concentration camp."

Dad rolled his eyes when Aunt Marge wasn't looking and changed the subject.

After Aunt Marge left, we caught up on what had happened while I'd been gone. As the night went on, though, there was a strange way that the conversations went. Mum and Dad kept asking if I didn't have any news that I'd not told them about.

The next couple of days they were in the best mood that I'd ever seen them since we all got back from hiding out from the Deatheaters. They acted as if they knew something that I didn't think they knew and that they were pretending not to know, but they were wishing that I would tell them.

I tried to worm it out of them while they were trying to worm it out of me. It made for some very strange conversations. Toward the end of this time, the conversations were going something like this:

Mum: "Dearest Dudders, do you have something that you'd like to tell us?"

Me: "I don't know anything that you should know that I haven't told you."

Dad: "But, Dudders, we are just sure that there's something that you know and we should know."

I had no idea how long this would have gone on, but we were getting close to Christmas and I sure hoped that we wouldn't be having that sort of talk while we were opening presents.

▽

Finally, on Christmas Eve, Mum announced that we were going to have a guest for Christmas dinner and wouldn't it be nice if we all knew who it was.

"Yes, and it would be best of all, if I knew who it was." I pointed out. But no one was talking, certainly not me. As the evening approached, Mum insisted that I dress for proper company. So, I dug around in my closet and found a gray suit. I decided to wear a blue shirt, and I found a red bow tie that took me most of an hour before dinner to tie properly.

When I came down stairs I found that there were hors d'oeuvres on the coffee table in the living room. Mum was wearing a black dress, and dad was wearing his best suit. I looked around wondering if I'd wandered into someone else's home. Usually, when there's an important guest, like a business contact, the evening was planned to the second. I hadn't heard anything other than a guest was coming. I thought maybe it was our next door neighbor, that spooky old biddie who always used to watch our house out of her living room window.

Mum approved my suit. She said that our guest would be here any minute. And wasn't there ANYTHING that I had to say. I had no idea what she was thinking of, so I just smiled and sat down.

Sure enough the doorbell rang, and I jumped up to see whom this mystery guest was. I went to the door and discovered that it was a package delivery service. There was a small oblong package. It was addressed to me. The return was some sort of mail order house that I didn't recognize, WWW.

Mum shouted, "Who is it dear?" in that sort of sing-song voice that she reserves for special occasions when she wants to appear especially hostess-like

As I walked into the living room, I said, "Oh, it's just a package for me. I'll leave it on the table with the other Christmas gifts." I supposed that it was just another Christmas gift from Mum and dad or maybe my Aunt Marge. I casually tossed it on top of the pile and sat down.

Dad started to say something, "Well, Dudders, I guess you're not going to come clean about what you've been doing at that school." He'd not yet completely come to terms with the name of the school or that I was working there. I wondered what I could have done that required, "coming clean". He went on, "So, I'll just have to jog your memory a little." This sounded bad but I never discovered what he was going to say, because just then the doorbell rang again. I was already standing, so I walked back to the front door, wondering aloud, "I suppose another present."

I opened the door and got the shock of my life.

Standing there was Pamela Myers, glowing in the soft light of the street lamps reflected off the snow that had fallen the previous night. My mouth dropped open and I couldn't make myself say anything. Actually, there were about a half-dozen things that were warring in my find, each fighting for first place, but I couldn't pick one to say first.

She smiled with a warmth that made me feel like the room was way too hot. She said, "Then, I'll just come in, if it's OK?"

I was still in shock and just stepped aside as she stepped in. Mum asked, "Who is it this time?"

By this time Pamela had walked into the living room. As I followed her, I heard both my mum and dad rise and greet her. Dad said, "I'm glad you found your way here without problems."

This gave me even more questions to ask and no better idea of where to begin. Mum asked me, "Where are your manners? Please take Miss Myers coat."

I had nothing better to say or do, so I did – that is, nothing. As I got back, I discovered that she had sat down on the couch, which was the only unoccupied seat in the living room. She had sat squarely in the middle of it, which left room for me on either side, but just. I had to sit next to her, whichever place I chose.

Mum was asking, "Just when did you get to know Dudders."

Her smile blazed out, and she gave a brief but accurate story, "I started noticing him early in the term. Most evenings he sat in the Common Room of Gryffindor and was reading Shakespeare."

Dad commented, "That's our Dudders, always the student in school or out."

There was far too much to respond to already. Where could I begin? But she was continuing, "But I really spent time with him for the first time at the Halloween party. I was standing at the punch bowl when he walked up, and I realized just how handsome he was. He asked me to dance and . . ."

I couldn't let this go on, so I interrupted, "Look. We did dance at the Halloween party, but it was you who asked me." Somehow that was not really what I wanted to object to, but there were so many things to cover and that just came out of my mouth.

She immediately looked deep into my eyes and said, "Yes, Dudley, I think that is right. I just didn't want to seem too forward to your parents. Anyway, we spent the rest of the evening, dancing and talking."

Mum was eating it up. It fit in perfectly with her picture of me as a desirable son. I had to start taking on this crazy story or who knew where it would lead, "Really, I think you did most of the talking, but . . ."

Mum interrupted me, "Are you going to contradict everything this charming young lady says?"

My mouth opened and closed a couple of times. When Pamela finally finished with the story, which omitted the little matter of our visiting with the Head in her office before the evening was over, I decided to try another approach. "Mum, you're right, Pamela. . ."

At that, Pamela patted my knee briefly and said, "You know, I prefer Pam with my close friends."

I just completely let that one pass, "Yes, Pam. You see that evening . . ."

Again, Pam interrupted, "Was a small slice of heaven. I'll never forget it the rest of my life."

Then, Dad interrupted both of us, "Let's go into the dining room and start dinner or we'll be here in the living room the whole evening."

So, we moved to the dining room. Mum asked Pam to help her with the meal, and Dad and I were left on our own at the table. The first thing he said to me was, "Don't forget to hold Pam's chair for her when she comes back." That was all right. I wasn't going to start explaining things to Dad and then have to turn around and repeat the explanation to Mum.

They came back both carrying trays. Both Dad and I stood to help, but Pam put a free arm on my shoulder and pressed down gently, "Now, just sit back and relax. Your mom and I have this handled." None the less, Dad helped Mum and held her chair for her. I couldn't remember when I'd seen him do that last.

The meal started with grace and small talk about passing this and that and isn't the Yorkshire Pudding great and so on. Mum asked me to go on telling about our first "date." It looked like I'd gotten a lucky break, so I started.

"Well, the first time that I saw her was actually in a class she was taking – English Literature. Professor Wendt had left the door open for some reason."

For once Pam's mouth dropped open and she exclaimed, "I remember that day. It was unusually warm and Professor Wendt left the door open so we would get a cross draft." Then she gasped, "You saw me reading the Cordelia part for the first time. Oh, I was so awful. I didn't have any feeling in the part."

For the first time that night I said something that was completely true, "Pam, I thought you were the most wonderful actress I'd ever seen."

She broke in laughing and said, "Oh, you are far too generous, I muffed that reading terribly." She reached across the table and patted my hand, "It's nice of you to pretend I did well."

Again, I was temporarily caught speechless. But Dad broke in and said, "We can go on over coffee in the living room, but your Mom has made her special desert." He turned to Pam, "You haven't lived until you've had Pet's Treacle Tart." Then he turned to Mum and said, "Don't waste any more time. Bring it out. I can't wait."

So, she went to the kitchen to get the Treacle Tart, and I could see that I'd have to wait until coffee to finish my side of the story. The tart was good, and Pam particularly seemed to enjoy it. Mum insisted that we just stack the dishes in the sink and let them soak, and she sent Dad scurrying to find the photo albums. My heart sunk at that. If there's anything that all kids (whatever their age) agree on, it's that there's nothing more embarrassing than going through the photo album and there's nothing that parents like to do more with guests than to inflict that embarrassment on their kids.

Mum insisted that we sit on the sofa, her on one side, Pam in the middle and me beside Pam. Dad stood behind the sofa as Pam browsed through the pages and Mum narrated. Dad volunteered information occasionally. There were the usual "ooh"s and "ahh"s at the "cute" pictures. Give me a break. Of course, opening a new topic had to wait until we'd struggled through the entire book.

An amazing thing happened. After we'd finished with the album, Mum asked a question that let me talk about what I wanted to. "Dudders, why didn't you mention this utterly charming young woman until she showed up on the doorstep?"

I had the floor, and I wasn't going to give it up until I had set everything straight. "OK. Here's the real story. That night of the Halloween party," I noticed Pam shake her head "no" very slightly. I stopped for a minute to consider. Mum and Dad were waiting, hanging on my words.

That imp, Pam, had the nerve to ask me, "Familiar got your tongue?" and smiled that blazing smile of hers.

I went on, "Well, that night, the Headmistress noticed that we were spending a lot of time in each other's company. She took us aside and reminded me of the school rule that staff and students couldn't . . uh . . what's the word."

Dad provided it for me, "Fraternize."

"Right. Anyway, she told us that she was really serious and that we couldn't see each other again until Pam graduates in the Spring.'

Pam said, "She was very definite, BUT she was talking about school grounds. I'm sure that she wasn't thinking about away on Holiday. After all, we're both adults."

That seemed to sober Mum. She said, "You're not an adult are you?"

Pam said in the closest that she'd been to what Aunt Marge calls impudence, "I am so. I turned 17 last year just after school started."

Suddenly, I wanted to know what that date was, but I didn't have the courage to ask. I was thinking furiously. Just after school started. That would be the first week of September. So that could be what? September 1 through 7? Maybe a bit later.

Pam interrupted my thoughts, "Dudley, what is it?"

"Oh, sorry. I just had a strange thought. Nothing."

Mum seemed to look at Pam in a new light. I went on, "But regardless, I didn't want to take any chances. The Head . . uh . . Mistess made it quite clear that I could lose my job over this."

That seemed to call for a change in topic, and Dad provided it. "Well, it's getting late, and we haven't even started opening presents."

That reminded me of a fear that had been building up as the evening went on. I didn't have a present for Pam! I immediately added, "Yes, it is late. I don't want to keep Pam out too late. Surely you have to get home soon."

She stared at me as though I'd turned into a toad. "I just said I was an adult. I don't have a curfew."

Mum agreed, "Yes, we always open presents on Christmas Eve. Let's get started."

110

I glumly agreed. Mum went on, "The guest always has the honor of handing out Christmas presents." And she looked meaningfully at Pam.

"Why thank you." And she stood and walked to the table covered with presents. She seemed to have a method in her choice. She did a little searching as she picked each one. "Ah, here's one for Mrs. Dursley from Dudley."

Mum instantly corrected her, "Please, dear, Pet."

It was a box of fancy stationery from Hogwarts. Mum always loves that kind of thing. She mostly writes thank you notes for presents with it.

Then she picked a present from me to Dad. He took it and said, "I'll bet I know what this is." He opened it and discovered he didn't. It was a clear glass ball. Dad stared at it.

However, Pam instantly knew what it was. She chuckled, "That's a remembrall. It gets cloudy when the owner has forgotten something important."

Mum chuckled too, "You mean like our anniversary?" Dad flushed but then a tear came into his eye. He turned to her and said, "Do you know what this is?"

She said, "Pam just said it was a remembrall. My memory isn't that bad."

"No, No. It's the first time that Dudders has gotten us Christmas presents all on his own."

Frankly, I wish he'd not thought of that. I was kind of trying to avoid embarrassing stuff, and this was sure one of those things. I'd like Pam to have thought that I'd always gotten Dad and Mum presents.

Then there was a present from Pam to Mum. That surprised me but I suppose it shouldn't have. It was a quill pen that corrected itself as you wrote with it. Mum read the manufacturer as she opened the box, "A product of Weasley and Weasley."

I jumped up, "Wait. Don't open that. The Weasleys are notorious jokers."

Pam said reasonably, "No. They do make gags gifts, but they also have some serious things. This is one of them. I gave one to Dad last Christmas. He loves it. But he did have to get the spell renewed this year."

Mum picked up a sheet of her new note paper and started to write, dictating as she did, "Dearest Dudders, Thanks for." Then she stared at the note sheet and said, "This misspelled your nickname. It wrote Dudley instead."

Pam kind of went slightly red, "Maybe that's because he prefers to be called Dudley."

Mum cast a questioning gaze toward me, and I could only shrug and nod.

Then came the really embarrassing presents from Dad to Mum but with my name on the FROM line. And then the other way around. Finally there was a large stack of presents – most of which were for me. It wasn't as bad as when I was younger when I'd get dozens of presents. As I thought of that, I was really kind of ashamed at how much I cared about presents.

Anyway, the first was from Dad to me. I opened without enthusiasm. It turned out to be a PlayStation 2. I suddenly realized that I didn't even know what kind of games you played on it. I tried to be enthusiastic. Then came present after present. Each seemingly more expensive and gaudy than the last. By the end I could hardly do anything but stare at the floor.

Then something that I didn't expect happened. Pam called out her own name. It was a gift from Mum. She opened it, and it turned out to be a red scarf. Pam immediately put it on. I was forced to say, "I think it looks beautiful on you." Pam flushed a bit.

Then the next gift was from Dad to Pam. It was a bottle of perfume. He said in an aside to me, "I picked it out myself."

Pam tried it on her wrist, "Really, I thought Pet had picked it out." Dad blushed himself a bit at that.

There were still two packages on the table. I was really glum. The first was wrapped and was to me from Pam. I slowly opened it, hoping that I could put off the inevitable, "I'm sorry, Pam, I don't have anything for you."

When I'd unwrapped it, I discovered that it contained a bill fold. It was made of leather that the little tag that was attached said was dragonhide. I felt its supple black smoothness. It was gorgeous. Pam impatiently said, "Open it up."

"OK. OK, already." I did and found in the place that an operator's license would ordinarily be that instead there was a photo of Pam. All I could say was, "Wow!" Mum and Dad both wanted to see, so I walked over to them and showed them.

Dad nodded and Mum was speechless for once. But she did recover and said, "There's something strangely beautiful about this photo."

I interrupted, "Yes, it's Pam."

"No. I mean there is something strange or unworldly about it but I just don't know."

Pam had a smile like the Cheshire cat. I noticed and said, "There is something different about that photo. What is it?"

She walked over and looked over Dad's shoulder. "Look at the background carefully."

Dad caught it first, "The shadows. They look like the shadow of a tree but darn it, I'd swear they're swaying a little in the wind."

Pam nodded a self-satisfied nod. "It's all the rage these days for portraits. Up until a couple of years ago, the idea in portraits was to have the subject wave or look off to the side as though something were going on, but a couple of years ago, a Muggle wanted a photo of his girl friend that he could show to his Muggle friends and not freak them out. The thing was that the photographer couldn't resist putting a little motion in the photo. It turned out to be really popular. There's something haunting, pun intended, about that little bit of motion in a photo. But you have to look really hard to find it if the photographer is good."

Dad said, "It's easy if you have a good subject.", meaning Pam, of course.

Then we'd really reached the end. I couldn't put it off any longer. The last present wasn't even wrapped properly and it was addressed to me. Pam picked it up and said, "Finally a parcel for Dudley."

I couldn't stand to sit there and open one more present to me. "Really, it's late. And this isn't even really wrapped. I'll open it tomorrow."

Pam was not to be put off, "You will not, Mr. Dudley. You open it up this instant, and we'll finish up."

Mum added, "It's bad luck to leave a present unopened."

I sighed in resignation and took it. Mum had to get me a pair of scissors to cut the tape on the package. I opened it slowly and discovered that there was a present wrapped in Christmas wrap inside. I pulled it out and glanced at the label and then looked harder. I looked up at Pam, and she shook her head again vigorously. Mum and Dad were looking at me and didn't notice. I shrugged and said, "And finally but certainly not least a present for Pam from Dudley er me." I handed it to her, and she carefully opened it, taking care not to tear the paper or cut the wrapping.

Inside was a small oblong box. Inside the box was a necklace! I couldn't make out what hung from it. But Pam had no trouble seeing it. She gasped the most realistic gasp I could imagine. Whoever says that she isn't an actress can stuff it.

She immediately opened the cameo pendant hung from the necklace. I couldn't make it out, but she immediately turned to my Mum, "Look!" Mum gasped herself. Then she showed it to Dad who whistled.

Then she finally brought it to me and said, "Pretty proud of yourself, I guess."

I'd lost count of the number of times this evening my mouth had hung open. All I could say was, "Pam, it's not good enough for you."

She quickly stepped close, her arms went around me and on the side of my head away from my parents kissed me. It was a soft, quick kiss. She stepped back and said, "Well, I have to agree with Dudley, it is getting late. I really should get home."

Dad asked if we should call her a cab. I answered that she had a much better way of getting around than cab.

I went to the hall closet and got out her coat and opened the door for her. Strangely, Mum and Dad didn't come out to the hall but just called, "See you soon, I hope."

We both stepped out and I quickly said, "We've got to talk – seriously and soon."

She smiled that smile that turns winter into Spring and said, "How about coming for Christmas with my family?"

"No. We've got to talk alone. You have Christmas with your family and the day after, I'll take you out to dinner."

The smile got, if anything brighter, and she said, "Throw in a movie picture and you've got a deal."

I chuckled. "OK. But the word is 'moving picture' or 'movie'."

"Isn't that what I said?"

"Never mind. Come at 6PM, and we'll go."

She darted forward to me and kissed me quickly on the mouth. It was so quick that I didn't realize that it had begun by the time it had ended. Then she took two steps back and disapparated.

When I got back in to the house, Mum asked, "Well?"

"Well, what?"

"Well, do you have a date set?"

"Yes."

⊠

Christmas was as happy as I can remember a Christmas ever being. The next day seemed to drag by like the last day of school. At lunch I talked with Mum and Dad about a good restaurant to go to. They suggested a Chinese restaurant that wasn't too far away. I pointed out that it didn't matter how far away it was.

Dad pointed out, "The only one that I know is this one nearby."

I agreed that he had a fair point, and I decided on that one. They asked me if we were doing anything after. I said that we were going to see a movie. They wanted to make suggestions, but I had my own idea.

6 PM finally came, and Dad commented that it was strange, a girl picking up the guy. I explained about disapparation and how she could do it, but I couldn't disapparate. Dad thought that I ought to learn. I said I'd think about it, and I really did.

Pam rang the doorbell, and I reached it in record time. I said goodbye to Mum and Dad and told them not to wait up. She reached out her hand, and I was dumbfounded for a moment. Of course, we were disapparating. It was obvious.

"You don't know where we're going, do you?"

She laughed. "Where are we going?"

"Chinese." I gave her the address and then had to think of the cross streets for her. It seemed like she wasn't great at disapparating to a street number, but street corners were good.

I took her hand and was reminded of how much I hate disapparating. But we arrived at the right place. I led her to the restaurant, and we were seated quickly. She said that she'd not been to a Chinese restaurant before. I couldn't tell if she were kidding me or not, but regardless, I liked thinking that I had superior knowledge when I did something with her. She asked what I would recommend.

I told her about the custom that is common in Chinese restaurants of ordering one entrée per person and sharing. She thought that was romantic and insisted that I do the ordering for both of us. I ordered Egg Rolls and Egg Drop Soup and Snow Peas and beef for her and Mu Shu Pork for me. They brought the soup out very quickly. She was glancing at the menu and asked, "The Chinese really like eggs. You've got Egg Drop Soup, Egg Rolls, Egg Fu Yung."

I agreed, "Yes, I really like Egg Fu Yung, but I wanted to have mu shu pork and I thought you should have something with snow peas."

She laughed, "Yes, there are more things on this menu than I've ever seen on any other menu. They're numbered and they go into the hundreds!"

She then looked at the spoon that came with and commented, "This looks more like a ladle than a spoon."

"That's the way Chinese spoons are. Take a look at the chop sticks."

She pointed at the chop sticks in their paper wrapper and looked the question. I nodded, "Sure. You eat the entrée with these. I've never got the hang of these, but let me show you how they're supposed to work in theory." I removed mine from the wrapper, broke them apart, and put them between my thumb, forefinger and middle finger. I tried flexing them to show how you could grasp something with them. In theory. In fact, they went flying across the room.

She giggled and then couldn't resist outright laughter. Usually, I'd be angry about it, but I couldn't be with her. I started laughing myself, "Like I said, I never quite got the hang of using them."

Her smile that would melt a heart of stone burst forth and she asked, "Are we going to starve, then?"

"No. We'll ask for normal silver. They're very happy to have us Westerners for customers." Just then, the egg rolls arrived, and I asked for English silver. As we waited, I informed her about sweet and sour sauce and hot mustard. She didn't entirely believe me about hot, so I dared her to try some. Luckily, they'd brought us a pot of hot tea. She had quite a lot after the sample of the mustard.

She got to try a little sweet and sour on her egg roll, and the entrees arrived. As we worked on the egg rolls I started the conversation that I'd wanted to have ever since she had walked in the door of our house. "Pam, we've got to get one thing straight right away."

She smiled her disarming smile at me, and I could see this was going to be difficult. "OK. You were under the influence of love potion when, well, at the Halloween party. What's going on? Are you still? Because I can't imagine you finding me interesting – without love potion."

Her smile turned to a sigh, "I don't think so. I don't know if I'm in love with you. But I'm pretty darn sure that you cured me of the love potion. It was completely different under that love potion. You were just perfect. If I were under it, that little thing with the chop sticks would have seemed like the cleverest thing in the world. Now, I see it's just funny.

"Now, like before Halloween, you are just handsome, strong, fun to be around." The incandescent smile was coming back.

I was lost again, "Now you had me convinced that you weren't affected by the potion, and there you go and say something like that."

"But that's the way I thought about you before Halloween. What about you? How do you feel about me?"

Somehow, during this conversation the waiter had come with our entrees, and I hadn't noticed. So, I took the opportunity to show her how we could share the entrees. She was fascinated by the Mu Shu Pork. We made a perfect mess of the little pancakes and the Hoisin Sauce. The stuff was all over our hands and faces and it was another occasion for making fun of ourselves.

After we cleaned ourselves off she asked, "Well?"

"Well, what?"

She shook her head, refusing to be put off, "You know what?"

This was another awful situation. How did I answer? I didn't think I was any clearer about my feelings than she was, so I just blundered in, "Look, first of all, I want you to know how much I regret ever making that potion. I didn't know it was going to be for you when I helped Knowland make it. If I'd had the slightest inkling, I wouldn't have. I hate doing it."

She didn't say anything, which scared me, but I went on. "From the first moment I saw you, I wanted to get to know you. Now that I know you, I can't keep my eyes off you. I begin to believe that there might be a heaven, when I'm with you. And believe me, when I realized that you'd taken that potion, I knew there was a hell.

"I don't know if I'm in love with you, but I sure know that I want to spend my time with you."

A little smile cracked on her face. "Are you sure that you've not taken some of that love potion?"

I smiled, "I know it sounds pretty sappy. Sorry."

She reached across the table and took my hand, "Don't be."

We finished the meal and had to get going quickly to get to the movie. She was fascinated with everything about the theatre. She'd seen plays, so she knew about auditoriums and tickets, but she'd never seen a screen before. We got in about ten minutes before the published time of the movie. "Hurry, we'll only barely get in there in time."

"Don't worry, Pam. We'll have to sit through ten minutes of adverts and then 15 or 20 minutes of previews before the thing starts."

We found seats near the back of the auditorium, and she stared in disbelief at the adverts that were going. "Wizard plays don't have anything like this. Why do Muggles put up with it?"

I shrugged, "I don't know. I just have never seen a movie that didn't have them."

She was fascinated at the moving picture that covered all of a large wall. I was pointing at the fire escapes when I found her hand. She pulled it on top of her leg. Frankly, I'd never had a girl friend before, and this was completely surprising to me.

We were well into the previews when she asked, "Is one of these the movie we're going to see?"

"No. The movie we'll see is called 'Saving Private Ryan'. It's about World War II."

I could see her head nod although it had gotten pretty dark in the theatre. "Yes, that was Hitler wasn't it?"

"Yeh."

As the movie started, I found I was terribly aware of my hand on her leg and not much aware of anything else. Sometime during the movie, she turned to me, and I kissed her. From that point on, I pretty much missed what little I'd been seeing of the movie.

When the movie was over, we left the theatre hand in hand, our fingers intertwined. The first thing she said was, "Remind me again what the movie was about." And she broke into giggles.

All I could say was, "Like I said, it was about World War II."

She squeezed my hand and said, "Would you like to try seeing it again, soon?"

All I could do was laugh and say, "Sure, tomorrow night?"

She looked up into my eyes and I didn't even notice whether she was smiling or not, "With Chinese?"

"Sounds great!"

She dropped me off at home, and I thought again about the necessity of learning to disapparate. The next day, she picked me up again and we tried the whole date over again. It came off differently, but I still didn't quite get why they were trying so hard to find Private Ryan.

We went to a Starbucks afterward, and I was surprised to find that she'd never been to one before. It was really exciting getting to introduce her to wonderful things that she had never imagined existed. As she stared up at the board with all the variations on coffee and tea that were available, I could see her eyes widening. That was something that was nice to see.

We found a quiet corner with a little table with three chairs. I lost one of them quickly. I didn't want anyone getting the idea that it would be nice to turn our twosome into a threesome. They had her coffee and my tea ready before I'd really had time to say anything.

When I got back with our drinks, she had a thoughtful look on her face. It was sort of a looking inward expression as though she were having a conversation with herself. "There's one thing that I don't understand about that movie."

I laughed with her, "Only one. I can think of a couple of dozen."

Her smile disappeared, "No, really. There's one thing that I don't understand at all. That war went on for years and years."

I nodded. I didn't remember a lot about history, but my dad had talked about his dad who had been in that war. He said the war went on for half a dozen years. She went on, "That battle on the beach at the beginning of the movie picture." I frowned at her. "At the beginning of the movie. I've never seen or heard anything like it – except that last battle at the end of the last school year at Hogwarts. That was horrid, but I've never heard of another battle of wizards like that."

I nodded, "So?"

She stared at me. It made me feel like I was a dunce. That's not an unusual feeling for me, but it was unusual when I was with her. She just seemed to think that I ought to understand what was bothering her. I nodded again slowly and said in a slow drawn-out way, "Yeeesss?"

She was still exasperated. "Well, doesn't it bother you?" When I still didn't get it, she went on, "Don't you see? There was battle after battle in that movie picture." She was so mad that she just said, "That movie thingee. That, that whatever it is. There was battle after battle after battle. They weren't all like that, but they just kept going on and on and on without end. How did the soldiers ever live through it?"

She hurried on, "The war against He-Who-Must-Not-Be-Named." I interrupted. I wanted to show how smart I was, so I said, "You mean Valdemort?"

I regretted it even before I finished saying "Valdemort". She glared at me. Then she went on, "The war went on for years. I guess really for decades, but the battles never got like they were in this "Saving Private . . . " She had forgotten his name for a moment.

It gave me a chance to say something that turned out to be not so bad. "You're right. The wars that Muggles fight seem to go that way. The Wizard wars seem like they're mostly fought in the dark. Nobody is quite sure who is on whose side. So, you're always mucking around trying to find you friends.

"The Muggle wars are mostly different. People wear uniforms. You can tell who is on whose side." I had another thought then. "My granddad fought in the Private Ryan war. He once told me that most of the time, you never saw the enemy. You muddled along and then suddenly, you'd see some of the enemy in the distance. Then you'd start shooting, and you'd never know if you'd killed someone."

She was quiet for a long time. Then she changed the topic.

She casually asked another question that scared me, "Dad and Mom want to meet you. They're having a New Year's party. Would you come?"

I was afraid of that question. "Well, I've got this problem."

"You're afraid to meet The Parents."

"No. Well, yes. I am, but that's not my main problem. My real problem is that I could get fired if the Headmistress finds out about us. I can trust my parents. I can trust the waiter at the Chinese restaurant. I think I can trust your parents, but can I trust all their guests?"

An expression came over her face that I'd never seen before. I'd learn later that it was stubbornness. But then I was in the dark. She said more to herself than to me, "There's got to be a way around this."

I agreed, "Sure, it's simple. I meet them at your graduation party!" I thought I had a brilliant solution.

She just stared at me and said, "No. That's not it."

I mumbled, "It seemed pretty good to me."

She tried something different, "We have to leave for Hogwarts after the weekend. We'll never get to see each other after we get there." Then she brightened. "Are you going on the Express?"

"You mean the Hogwarts Express?"

"No, the Edinburgh Express. Of course, Hogwarts."

"No. I usually go by floo from Diagon Alley."

She smiled and said, "Well come by the Express. We can be together in a compartment."

"No, we can't. That's the worst place. Dozens of people will see us together."

She was quiet for a while and finally said, "That's it, then, we can't be together again until I graduate."

I asked the obvious question, "What about tomorrow?"

"Didn't I tell you, I've got some friends from Hogwarts throwing a party that I agreed to go to. I can't let them down."

The Express was beginning to sound good to me. I'd at least be able to see her from a distance. But she agreed with me that it wasn't a good idea. We were both feeling pretty glum about the next several months. She dropped me off and we kissed good night. It was a long kiss that kept us away from reality for a few minutes. We didn't say anything. What was there to say? She backed away a couple of paces, and I saw her disappear. I'd not see her again until we were both back at Hogwarts, and even then, it would always be at a distance.

I went back into the house and found Mum and Dad still up. They immediately noticed that I was not feeling wonderful. Mum asked, "Bad date?"

"No, great, actually. It's just that I won't see her again this Holiday. Then we'll be back at school, and we can't see each other, really."

Mum came over and hugged me. "Love is hard a lot of the time. Just hang in there. You'll get to the end of the term, and then things will be different."

I just nodded and trudged off to bed.

Lab Rats

I stayed at home until the day after New Year's. I didn't have to go back for another two days, but what was the point of hanging around after Dad had to go back to work, and Mum was catching the Mopes from me. Maybe seeing Filch would cheer me up.

So, that Sunday, I took the train into London and found my way to the Leaky Cauldron. It was a slow day for Tom. He chatted me up as I drank the obligatory butter beer. How was the Holiday? Did I have a big New Year's party to go to? No. Well, then why not come down to the Cauldron next New Year's Eve. And so on and so on.

I finally couldn't bear it anymore, so I said, "Thanks. I'll think about it next time." I walked over to the hearth, took a little floo powder and walked into the Great Hall. No one was there to welcome me. Why I thought there might be I can't imagine. I went down to say hello to Filch.

I found him in his office. When he saw me he remarked, "The Conquering Hero come home."

I shrugged and asked if he had a shot of fire whiskey. He obliged and, we compared Holidays. He commented, "Let's see. I spent the Holiday here—just me and Mrs. Norris and the house elves. I'm having a good time, and you spend it at home with family and friends and you show up with a frown on your face. Right?"

"I suppose so." He chuckled, and I downed the shot that I'd been holding in my hand the whole time. I practically gagged. That was what I needed. A shot of his "fire whiskey" is enough to cure anyone of his desire to drown his sorrows in whiskey. I set the empty glass down and refused the proffered refill, with thanks.

As we were discussing my opinion of his whiskey, a knock on the door sounded. Filch invited the caller in, and the door opened to reveal Professor Slughorn. He apologized for the interruption and said, "Mr. Dursley. I was hoping to find you here. I was wondering if I could discuss the little proposition that we discussed before the Holiday?"

I responded, "Sure."

Then we all sat for a moment. No one said anything until Slughorn clarified, "I was hoping to speak with you alone."

"Anything that you want to say to me Mr. Filch can hear."

Slughorn's mouth opened for a moment and then he said, "Oh. . . All right. Have you thought about my offer?"

Actually, I hadn't. Like a homework assignment over a holiday, I'd kept putting it off and putting it off. And then there was Pam. I had a lot of things on my mind. But I didn't want him to think that I'd not thought about it. To gain time, I suggested that we all have a drink.

Slughorn's face fell even further at the thought of drinking Filch's fire whiskey, but he manned up and squeaked, "Sure."

Filch searched in his drawer for another shot glass but came up short. Instead, he rummaged around and found a 12 oz glass. Slughorn's face fell even further, and he gulped as Filch poured a hefty portion. Filch raised his glass and said, "Bottoms up."

I have to admit that Slughorn took it like a man. This all gave me time to think about my answer, and I said, "That was a toast to our deal." It was a decision I should have made long before.

Those words made Slughorn almost happy. He quickly added, "Wonderful. Let's meet next Saturday after breakfast to get started. He rushed out of Filch's office, and I excused myself as well.

The next night, the Hogwart's express arrived, and we had the beginning of term banquet. That is usually a low-key affair according to Filch, and neither of us attended. However, after the banquet was the beginning of term staff meeting in the Staff Lounge. That was obligatory. Filch and I were the first to arrive. We took seats at the back of the room, the perquisite of the first to arrive, usually Filch and now I as well.

People filtered in, and Filch sat at the back, smug in his knowledge that we had the best seats. Finally, the Head arrived. She always came promptly to the point. In this case the point had to do with upperclassmen.

"Ladies and Gentlemen, this term is a bit unusual because of the events of the previous school year. As most of you are aware, many students at all levels took a year of sabbatical with their parents – often out of the country. Consequently, the number of students becoming adults this term is much larger than it normally is. Usually, only 7th years and a smattering of 6th years turn adult during the school year. Most of those happen in the second term. However, this year, in addition to those, there will be most 6th years and a smattering of 5th years.

"Let me remind you that we cannot restrict adults from Hogsmead weekends except for gross discipline problems. So, this year, we will have twice as many students eligible for unlimited Hogsmead weekends during the Spring term. So, I've decided that we'll have to double the number of teachers chaperoning during weekends, especially normal Hogsmead weekends when all 3rd years and older can go to Hogsmead.

"I've posted signup sheets. Those sheets will be filled completely before this weekend, or I will take the liberty of volunteering folks myself." There was a collective groan at that announcement. Of course, no one wasted any time after the meeting signing up for the minimum required tours of duty. Most people don't like early Saturday or Sunday morning shifts, so I had it rather easy. I don't mind either.

The rest of the meeting covered topics that were both boring and not of interest to me. They were things like the schedule of OWL and NEWT exams. The requirement to sign up to be a proctor only applied to teaching staff. There was an announcement that held some interest for me. It was that there would be an instructor from the Ministry to teach Disapparation on Saturdays during the term. The announcement was dull news for everyone because everyone (except me) knew how to Disapparate. But, the announcement said nothing about its being limited to students. I would have to think about it.

After the meeting and after everyone had finished signing up for the various duties, I was about to head to Huffelpuff when a tap on my shoulder practically scared the pants off me. It turned out to be Professor Slughorn. "Mr. Dursley, would you come to my office for a few minutes to discuss this weekend?"

I agreed, and we went directly there. When we had settled, he offered a drink, and I'd reluctantly accepted. I had had my fill of drinks from Filch and was always suspicious of other "free" drinks. But Slughorn offered a glass of elf-made wine. I've never been a fan of wine, but this was good. After a few sips, he spoke.

"I'm very happy that you've agreed to this project."

I nodded agreeably but added mentally, "But. . . "

It came of course, "But, I am really anxious to get this project off to a good start. As a matter of fact, I'd like to for us to agree on a schedule to complete the project."

I nodded again and new that this would be bad. He went on, "I want to have a final draft ready to go by the end of the term." He paused and waited expectantly.

I thought about the time table. Was it reasonable? I did a little mental calculation. There were about 200 potions in the book. I could surely edit one a night – if I were determined – who knew, maybe more. One a night, 5 nights a week would make it. . . uh . . . about 40 weeks. That would take us into the summer. But I'd gotten better the more I read that book. Maybe I could end up averaging two a night. That would make it 20 weeks. That would be possible for sure. So, I said, "That's a bit tight, but I think we could do it."

He bounced up out of his chair, "Capital! I want to get started right away. If you can translate one or two a night during week nights and two a day on weekends, we can do it! We'll be in the Potions Room and I'll do one potion a night on weeknights and two or three a day on the weekends!"

What was he talking about! He doing one a night! He was supposed to be helping me. My confusion showed on my face, and he asked, "I've done my math right, haven't I?"

"Yeh, but what are you doing one a night while I edit?

"Why, making the potions." Then he added, "And testing them, of course."

"Why would you do that? These potions are perfect."

He stared at me, "My dear boy, you don't understand the scientific method. Everything must be tested. We must prove that the formula works and doesn't have bad side effects."

I found that I too was standing, and as the enormity of the project struck me, I fell back into my chair. "But we'd have to work like slaves to finish on this stupid timetable if we have to test everything." He just nodded in response.

That left me thinking as I sipped a little wine. I made a decision and looked up, "Couldn't we extend the timetable a bit. You know, maybe until the end of the year instead of the end of the school year?"

His face fell. Then, he brightened a bit as a thought occurred to him, "My dear boy, think of what you could do with the mountains of galleons that you'll earn when we publish. Surely that's worth a big chunk of your time?"

I did think about it. But I couldn't see myself working like a dog for the rest of the term to meet this stupid schedule. I didn't say that. He had another idea. "Why don't we just get started? You can go at your own pace and we'll see how things go. For the time being, let's just have our first session in the Lab on Saturday as planned and we'll see how it goes."

I decided that wasn't awful, and we agreed to it.

▽

The next couple of days, I worked on my own schedule. Each night after work, I edited one potion. One night, I finished two simple ones. I had plenty of time. Some of it, I used in the Huffelpuff Common Room. I taught some Huffelpuffs the finer points of gambling with cards.

In return, some of them taught me a few simple spells. It really worked out pretty well for all of us. The only problem I had that week was that I kept seeing Pam. You'd think that between work, potion translation, and time in Huffelpuff, I'd be safe. But it just didn't seem to work out that way. During the days, when I was on duty, it seemed like I would run into her whenever I had to clean the armor or dust the portraits.

Some of those portraits were really ticklish. I had one of them going crazy laughing. I looked over and found Pam gazing at the show convulsed in mirth. When our eyes met she stopped laughing, and for a second that seemed to stretch into eternity, I was gazing into her eyes. I turned and practically sprinted off in the opposite direction. If this went on for the next five months, I'd be a candidate for crackerbox palace.

After several days, I was actually relieved when I could retreat to Huffelpuff to edit potions. The weekend finally came and Slughorn was pleasantly surprised by the number of potions that I'd finished. He set up the equipment and ingredients necessary. When he'd assembled it all, he looked at it and said, "I think this is an historic moment. To the best of my knowledge this is the first time that anyone has made every potion in a potion book from beginning to end."

That surprised me, "How is that possible? What happened to your wonderful Scientific Methodist?"

"That's Method not Methodist."

He wasn't offended. He just explained, "Every potion book is made up of a combination of a lot of standard potions along with a few innovative potions. It's only the innovations that get tested. This book is ALL innovation. Get ready to make history."

The first potion in the book was a fun potion. It caused the user to have the giggles. When we'd finished it, he volun-told me to try it. I was dubious, but I took a deep breath and down it went. It was a delightful potion. Using it was like being drunk without the hangover. I loved it. There were a variety of effects beside giggling. You sometimes broke out into laughter for no apparent reason. You talked loud. It was a gas.

The other potions that we made that weekend could be tested on animals safely. We used an old rabbit that Slughorn kept for demonstrations in class. The first weekend was a complete success.

Over the next couple of weeks, I found that I was spending more and more time editing potion formulae. The third week, we started making potions in the evening after I'd edited a couple. I got ahead during the week, and we caught up on the weekend.

I ran into Pam less and less. It wasn't any less embarrassing when we met, but it happened less frequently. We actually started to make more progress each week than Slughorn had proposed to do at the beginning. It was grueling, but the joy of taking a bunch of scribbles on a crowded page, converting it to neat, easy-to-read instructions on a fresh page of parchment, and then watching Slughorn turn the instructions into a potion that actually did what it was supposed to was truly exciting.

I had a real problem putting the book aside when my bed time came. I would discover that I was a third of the way through transcribing a potion, and I just couldn't put it down until I was finished.

On the third week of our project, something happened that really bothered me. It was on Sunday afternoon. We'd just finished a potion called ditaney that heals wounds quickly. Slughorn asked, "Who's going to take a cut for the cause?" I looked around because it was clear that he wasn't. I grumbled a little but picked up the silver knife, sterilized it in the flame of a Bunsen burner and ran it across my left arm above the elbow. It hurt a little, but Slughorn was ready with an eye-dropper of the potion. It hit the wound, and two things happened at the same time. The wound closed, and I couldn't see the slightest scar. The pain disappeared without a trace.

Slughorn examined it closely and nodded. "Yes, that's as good as I've ever seen ditaney work. There is always at least a little scarring. This is good." We patted each other on the back, and I was actually feeling pretty good about it.

As a matter of fact, I asked Slughorn if I could have some of it. He found a clean flask. He always seemed to have some in an inside robe pocket. He poured about half out for me and took the rest himself.

He glanced at his watch and smiled, "I think that we have enough time for one more potion. Let's see what we've got." There were a couple of edited potions left. He rifled through them and pulled one out of the stack. "Yes, this should be good. It's the one that I usually assign to advanced classes for the first session. It's good for evaluating where students are at the beginning. Really good students will be able to do it, and there are a couple of tricky points that will identify where the weaknesses of the rest are. That lets me do lesson planning to help them improve."

With that he handed me the parchment and I read the title, Draft of Living Death. What in the world did that mean? He had already started getting the equipment lined up. I asked him, 'Just what is this 'Living Death'?"

"Oh, it's a poison."

"Do we have an antidote for it?"

"Of course not. It's instantaneous. Even if we had it right at the victim's lips, it would be too late."

"Well, I sure hope you don't have the idea that I'm going to try this."

"Ohhh, no, dear fellow. We don't need a person to test this."

That relieved me greatly, and I took my usual post, overseeing the operations and reading the steps off. Slughorn had a lot of trouble with this one. Some of the other potions were pretty small variations on the original recipe, and others were so different from the original that they were really completely new potions. They just did what the original did more effectively or quicker or something. But this one was close to the original with just enough changes that Slughorn kept going on to the next step without waiting for me to give directions. It was frustrating for both of us.

We did reach the end of the process, and Slughorn looked at it and proclaimed, "There have been only two people who have brewed such a perfect Draft of Living Death – Snape himself and Harry Potter. That caused him to pause, seemingly puzzled by something.

So, I was ready to celebrate, "Great! Let's call it a day."

Slughorn frowned, "No. You're too anxious. We're not done yet."

"Well, what is there left to do?" As soon as I said those words, I knew the answer. There was the test to perform. I quickly added, "You said that we weren't going to test this on anyone."

"Right. We won't test it on anyone." He put emphasis on the 'one'. "I've got a test animal ready." With that, he walked over to a table where a cage had been sitting throughout the afternoon. "I obtained this rat from a student." He apparently saw my face. It must have looked awful. So, he quickly added, "Oh, you don't think that I took it from him. I gave him a very fair price. He can buy two for the price I paid him."

I regained my speech and said, "NO! I don't care if you paid him enough to buy an owl. It's just wrong to kill an innocent animal just to prove that a potion will kill you."

Slughorn shook his head violently, "It's not just that. Yes, we could use a mosquito for that. The Draft of Living Death produces a state of embalming so complete and so quickly that you would never realize that the victim were dead without taking their pulse. It's really amazing to see."

I couldn't believe my ears. I glanced at the rat and just shook my head. "I can't allow that. There's got to be another way."

"Dear boy, this is something that happens all the time with Science. Animals are used for testing all sorts of things – cosmetics, food preservative spells, hand cream. You've just got to get used to it. Once we've done this a couple of times, you'll think nothing of it."

I was beside myself, pacing up and down, "You're right, I'll think nothing of it, because I won't be doing it!"

Slughorn lips compressed, and I suppose he was holding back a sharp comment, but he didn't say anything. Then he said, "We've got to go ahead and do it. It would be unethical to publish an untested book."

I had as much as I could stand. I strode to the door and on the way said over my shoulder, "Well, maybe WE don't have to publish this book." I slammed the door behind me. As I did, I heard Slughorn's shouted, "I'm going to do it right now."

I ran up the stairs a flight to find Filch's office. I threw the door open and was happy to see him there. Without another word I shouted, "Pour us a shot of your worst."

Filch raised his eyes in mock surprise, "Yes, sir!" He opened the desk draw, got out the bottle and his two shot glasses and quickly poured two generous shots. I swallowed mine in a gulp. Filch seemed to think that a toast was appropriate, "To good whiskey."

I gagged and spit half of it out, "To the Hell with it."

Filch said, "Whatever you say." I turned, threw the door open, left, and slammed it closed again. I don't know what Filch made of it. I didn't care. If I was going to get drunk, I was going to do it with decent whiskey, and the only place that I knew that I could get decent whiskey in this damned castle was Wendt's. He might even listen to me shout.

I ran up the stairs, reached the main floor, and then took the stairs up to the next level. I was boiling mad and was staring down at the steps. When I reached the landing where the staircase turned, I ran into somebody. I looked up and discovered that it was Pam. I'd knocked her over and scattered her books over the staircase. "I'm so sorry!" I started to help her pick them up.

"You look like you were being chased by a banshee!"

I was so mad that I forgot about the fact that I was trying to not get fired, "No, I'm. I'm. Oh, the hell with it." I couldn't bring myself to tell her about Slughorn and the book and everything. I was way too mad to make sense. I apologized again. "I really didn't mean to knock you down. I'm so so sorry."

She smiled, "That's OK. Why don't you tell me what's going on." She encouraged me by taking my hand.

I took a deep breath and thought a minute. "It's way too complicated. If I did that, we'd be here a half an hour."

"I don't mind." The warm pressure of her hand convinced me that she really wouldn't mind sitting there on the staircase a half hour or more listening to my problems.

A little sense returned to my skull, and I shook my head, "No. You can't imagine how much I'd like to do that, but I've got to do my duty to the school and keep clear of you for the term." I added, "You know that I'll tell you everything you want to know and a whole lot more on the day that you graduate."

She pouted a pretty little pout, "Oh, I suppose I'll have to wait. But I don't have to wait for this." With that she quickly moved close and kissed me on the lips and stood up. "Be seeing you."

I nodded mutely, got up, and started up the stairs without thinking about where I was going. Then I remembered that I was on the way to see Wendt.

I reached the office and opened the door without knocking. I had gotten used to that while I was doing my "time" in Coventry the previous term. I got the shock of my life when I opened the door.

What I found was Professor Wendt seated on his sofa where I slept. That didn't surprise me, but what did was seeing that the Headmistress was also seated there—but not exactly on the sofa. She was more seated on his lap. They weren't kissing. but they were gazing into each other's eyes. She was saying something softly.

I immediately turned to go, but the very unsoft, even strident voice of the Head said very clearly, "Don't leave Mr. Dursley. Professor Wendt and I have some business, and you might as well be here because it concerns you to a certain extent as well."

I slowly turned and mouthed more than I said, "Me?"

"Yes. You. Go sit down at the desk, and Wendt and I will join you there."

I took one of the yellow chairs. Wendt took his chair behind the desk, and the Head took the red leather chair. Then she began, "Professor Wendt, I've come to get your advice on something that happened yesterday in my office."

I wondered how that could concern me, and even what it was that happened there. Did it involve Wendt? She quickly filled in details and relieved my fear that I was going to hear some sort of confession.

"Yesterday, I had a visitor. His name was Mark Burbage. Does that name mean anything to you?"

I had no idea who it was and began to say so, but the Head clearly intended the question for Wendt who replied, "Sure. The name's familiar. I'm sure that I've heard . . . it." He paused in concentration and then said, "Yes. Charity Burbage. She was the Muggle Studies professor until she." He hesitated again. "Didn't I read that she had been killed by a Deatheater?"

The Head filled in details, "Yes. She was killed the summer before last. We didn't know for sure what had happened to her. She was one of the many 'disappeared' victims of the Deatheaters. Her body still hasn't been recovered, and I suppose never will. But recently, the Aurors determined that Professor Snape killed her with the *Adavra Kedavra* curse."

Wendt nodded, "I suppose by using the *Priori Incantatum* spell."

She sighed. "Yes, the Truth Commission that was set up to give closure to the many people who had relatives, friends, lovers disappear obtained as many of the Deatheater's wands as possible. It has been systematically using the spell to determine what happened to many of the victims."

Wendt nodded and said, "It must be gruesome having to review all the hundreds of spells done with those wands over the years.

"And what did Mr. Burbage want?"

I'd begun to be interested in this story. I wondered for a moment what would have happened if my family hadn't been taken away by the Order of the Phoenix. Would I have been one of the spells in that awful review?

The Head answered the question, "He was very distraught, of course. The fate of his sister had just been published in the *Prophet*." She stopped, as though trying to choose words. "He wanted some sort of revenge."

Wendt commented, "Understandable, but completely out of the realm of possibility. What could he possibly want you to do?"

"He wanted me to remove all records of Snape from the records of Hogwarts. He actually wanted me to take his portrait down from the walls of my office."

Wendt reached a hand out and patted her hand, "Hideous." I didn't understand what was hideous about it, but the Head seemed to understand him.

She said, "There's no reasoning with people in that state. I let him go on and on ranting about the injustice and agreeing with him. There's really nothing else that you can do for people in that place.

"Finally, he gave me a moment to say something and I just said that I'd take it up with the Board of Governors. Their decision would be final."

"Did that satisfy him?"

She squeezed her mouth down into a line and said, "Give yourself some credit, Wendt, for intelligence. What do you think?"

He just shook his head.

I'd not said anything much up to this point, but I thought that I ought to ask a question that had been bothering me for a while, "Headmistress, I don't understand just why it is that I should be concerned about any of this."

She looked at me and then looked up at the ceiling as if call for assistance from the divine. She said something like, "Why am I always surrounded by morons?" Then she said aloud, "Tell me, Mr. Dursley, just whose book are you and Professor Slughorn getting ready to publish, hmmm?"

The light began to dawn on me. "You mean that this Burbage fellow might not like that?"

She smiled a sweet smile that I didn't think was intended to encourage me, "I think that's possible."

130

Then another idea occurred to me, "How do you know about that book anyway?"

She glanced skyward again and said, "Every Headmistress worth her salt knows ALL of the important things that are going on inside her Castle, Mr. Dursley, and don't you forget it."

I wondered for a moment if she knew about the little meeting that Pam and I had had a few minutes before. I didn't see how it was possible, but who knew?

She was going on, "I don't think that he'll pay much attention to the two of you as long as he's concerned with Hogwarts but there may come a time when he pays attention to you."

That was a disgusting thought. I had enough to think about for a while, so I didn't object when Wendt went on with his questions.

"Minerva, what can the Board of Governors do? What can you do?"

She was not in a good mood by now. She answered curtly, "I've absolutely no intention of doing anything, and I don't know what they'll do, but I hope it's nothing as well.

"As to the portrait of Snape, there's absolutely nothing I can do about it. It's an ancient spell on the office of the Head. I think it may go back to the original founders of Hogwarts. One of them or all together created this spell that causes a portrait of each Head to be created on her or his death. There's no known way to interrupt it. There was a terrible fire in the 16th Century at Hogwarts that destroyed a number of the portraits of the Heads. Overnight, they reappeared, stacked neatly in a corner waiting to be re-hung.

"There's absolutely nothing that can be done about that. And you know very well," at that point her voice rose. I'd never heard that tone before, but I knew that I was happy that it wasn't directed at me. She went on, "that I have absolutely no desire to interfere with that spell."

Here I interrupted, "Pardon, Headmistress, why is that? This Snape seems to have been a really nasty type. I remember Harry being so angry at him once or twice that he was swearing at the top of his voice in his room."

I was immediately sorry that I'd asked the question. She turned her gaze on me. Her stare would have frozen a charging rhino in its tracks, "MR. DURSLEY, I wasn't aware that YOU paid any attention to Mr. Potter."

I could say nothing, but my mouth wagged open. She calmed a bit and said, "Everything that you've heard about Headmaster Snape is true. But what you don't know is that he was the bravest man who ever opposed Tom Riddle. He stood in his presence year after year and spied for Headmaster Dumbledore and the rest of the Order of the Phoenix. He was hated by nearly all of the Order, but he went on despite being the man without a friend."

I guess that I just don't learn from my experiences because I asked another question, "Who is this Tom Riddle? I don't think I've ever heard of him."

I'd driven the Head to speechlessness. She just put her head in her hands and lowered her head to the desktop. She slowly hit her head on it. Wendt rolled his eyes and said simply, "Tom Riddle was the most powerful and dangerous dark wizard – probably in the entire history of Magic. He was also known as Valdemort."

I knew the name, Valdemort. I had heard Harry use it, and I'd occasionally heard it at Hogwarts. I just formed a large "O" with my mouth and leaned back into my chair, hoping to disappear.

Wendt was more of a glutton for punishment than I was. He asked the Head, "OK. I know why you don't want to help Burbage and, frankly, I don't want to either. Is there anything the Board could do if they wanted to?"

She lifted her head from the desk and her eyes looked tired, "I don't know. There is an official logbook of the Heads. I've seen a few entries in it and have made a few myself. Could Snape's pages be removed? I don't know. And, I don't care.

"There's a few places in the school where the Head's names are magically placed – there's the trophy case. The Great Hall has a row of stones fairly high up that have the names chiseled into it. Maybe there are a couple more. I'd oppose any changes to the end. Maybe I'd even resign in protest if the Board tried to remove any of them."

Wendt agreed. Since we'd completely covered the topic, we were all left staring around at each other. I suppose we were all wondering who'd get up and leave. I didn't have any intent to do so. Nobody did. Finally, the Head said that obviously Wendt and I had business, and she didn't want to get in the way of THAT.

Wendt opened his mouth to say something, but nothing came out. The Head rose and walked to the door. She opened it and turned to look in over the sill. "Well, Professor, when you and Dursley have finished your important business, maybe you'll have a little time for the Headmistress."

I found myself a bit embarrassed, but I had waited through all their problems. I wanted to get a drink or two in and talk about mine!

Wendt turned to me after the door had closed and asked, "I suppose you had something else that you came to see me about. You didn't get lost on your way to Hufflepuff, I suppose?"

"No. I came because I need a drink."

Wendt smiled at me, "And you can't find one from Filch? He's normally quite happy to drink with pretty much anyone."

I frowned at Wendt, "I can't believe that you'd suggest that anyone share a drink with Filch."

"No, I suppose not. What brings you up to see me?" Then he remembered about the drink. "Would you like a shot of real whiskey?"

I nodded. He got out a glass from a little wet bar that was built into a bookshelf and pulled a bottle out of the drawer of his desk. "I think that you might like this a little better than Filch's." He poured a couple of fingers and apologized. "Sorry. No ice. You've got to go to real magicians for that." He handed me my glass and asked what the issue was.

I nodded. "Here's the thing." By now, after all the business about Burbage, I wasn't quite so hot about my argument with Slughorn but I sure wasn't going to drop it. "Slughorn and I have been re-writing the potions textbook AND doing experiments to be sure that the potions work right." I went on to tell him about the last experiment and how angry I was about experimenting on animals. I wanted to make sure that we didn't do it again.

Wendt listened throughout and didn't say a word – just sipped his whiskey until I reached the end. Then he asked some questions.

"What do you want? "

"I don't know." I thought for a minute and just repeated that.

"Do you want to publish the book without checking the potions?" It was really a question. I had the feeling that if I'd said yes, he'd have said, "OK." But I didn't want to do that.

His next question was, "Do you want to not publish the book at all?"

That was a hard question. I'd done so much work and I really did enjoy working with Slughorn. He had a sense of humor and didn't mind being told what to do when I read out my potion instructions. I finally decided that I did want to publish a book. "But do we have to put all the bad potions in it – the ones where things get killed or injured? What kind of book is that anyway for kids to be learning from!"

Wendt's eyes lifted at that. "Yes. That's a good question. I think I'll take that up with Minerva er the Headmistress."

I laughed at that. So, they were an item. She was so down on my dating a student – and an adult one at that. But she was dating a teacher. Didn't that break some kind of moral rule? I wondered what they would have been doing if I'd not walked in when I did.

Wendt went on, "Why don't you ask Slughorn about that? Another thing. Do you mind making potions that are harmful if you can also make the antidote and test it at the same time? Would it be OK to test animals that way?"

I thought about those questions for a while. "I don't know. Those are good questions. I think I'll talk with Slughorn about them." I discovered that I'd not finished the whiskey – which was really pretty good. I swallowed it down in a gulp and immediately regretted it. It was too good not to take your time with. But, I'd finished here and wanted to move on. I got up and said, "Professor, I really appreciate your talking with me." I hesitated and decided to say the other thing that I wanted to, "And this whiskey is too good to gulp down."

He smiled, "No problem. It's always good to share with someone who appreciates good liquor. And good luck with your book. Let me know when you're ready to publish. I know it would do me no good in the world to own a copy, but I'd like to anyway."

I walked to the door and turned as I left to wave goodbye. He returned the wave.

I opened the door and was interrupted by Wendt, "Oh, one more thing."

I partially turned and asked, "Yes?"

"Can you disapparate?"

It was such an odd question that I closed the door and asked, "No. Why?"

"Do you want to learn?"

I was startled by the question. I almost laughed at the thought that Wendt might teach me. However, I asked, "You're not teaching are you?"

Wendt did laugh, "No, no. But there are going to be classes coming up very shortly here."

"Really?"

"Yes, you haven't heard about them?" He paused and answered his own question, "Of course, you and Filch don't usually eat in the Great Hall. Miner . . uh . . . The Headmistress announced that the Ministry was going to send an instructor to teach eligible students. I think the lessons start in a few days."

I walked back to the desk and took the red leather chair. "But am I eligible. I'm not a student here."

Wendt seemed confident, "Sure, why not? It's not taught by any Hogwarts professor. It's a Ministry of Magic instructor."

I asked, "Is it free."

Wendt answered quickly as though by rote, "It's free to all eligible students." He hesitated again, "Maybe non-students have to pay a fee."

I drummed my fingers on the desk. "How do I sign up?"

Wendt wasn't so sure of his answer. "There should be a signup sheet in every house's Common Room. There should be one in the Huffelpuff Common Room."

I nodded. Maybe I would sign up. I said, "Thanks for the tip. I'd not have had time for one more thing, but now that Slughorn and I are stuck, I guess I might have time. Do you know how long the lessons are? How many days they take? Is there homework?"

Wendt laughed again, "Remember, I've never taken lessons. I've not the slightest idea of any of that."

I nodded and rose to leave the room, "Be seeing you."

"You bet."

Disapparation 101

I reached Huffelpuff and found that the entrance code had been changed. Why wasn't I being informed of these things? So, after "Black" didn't work, the painting gave me a hint, "The code is a number."

I sighed, "How many numbers are there?"

It actually answered me, "You may be glad to know that the number has only two digits."

I thought that couldn't be too bad. All I had to do was start from ten, and it couldn't take me more than 89 more guesses to find it. So, I said, "ten."

The door said, "That's not a bad guess. You'll no doubt be glad to know that the correct answer is the number of chess men on the chess board at the beginning of the game."

I asked, "Both sides counted?"

The painting almost seemed offended. It said, "Of course."

I started trying to count chess pieces. There was the Queen of course, the King, there were those castle things. Then it occurred to me that the number of squares on a chess board was the same as the for checkers. I jumped to the conclusion that the number must be the same as the number of checkers pieces, "Twenty-four." I said confidently.

The painting was even more disgusted, "Common, Dudley, you know better than that!" She was staring down at me. I was afraid she might try to throw that bag that she was always carrying at me.

Then, I remembered that chess pieces started in two rows on each side of the chess board. Eight squares per side must make, "Thirty-Two."

The painting exclaimed, "Finally!"

I muttered, "Well, you try to work it out when you're in a hurry."

I went to the bulletin board in the Common Room that I'd never paid attention to before. There was a calendar on it that seemed to have important dates, like the next Quidditch Match that Huffelpuff had. On the Saturday of the week that we were now in, there was a note about first disapparation lesson. The following Saturdays all had the same notice for the rest of the month.

I thought to myself that it looked like it might be a lot of work. Also on the bulletin board was a parchment for signing up for disapparation lessons. There were a number of lines on the long parchment. You had to sign your name, tell your school year, and date that you would be seventeen.

I pulled out a ball point pen and wrote my name. For school year, I wrote "staff", and for 17th birthdate I wrote, "I'm 19. None of your business."

A small crowd had gathered around. As I was writing somebody asked, "You don't know how to disapparate yet?" It didn't sound like I was being made fun of. Whoever asked seemed to be genuinely curious.

I just said, "Nope." I didn't offer any other explanation. The crowd broke up except that somebody stayed behind.

As I finished writing she said, "I signed up too. I'm up near the top." She reached past me to point out her name. It was Mary. As she pointed, her arm brushed my side very noticeably.

I took a step back and returned my pen to my breast pocket. She was still talking. "I think it will be SUPER to learn to disapparate – especially in the same class with you."

I gave a non-committal grunt and turned to go up to the boys side of the dorm. She called after me, "Look forward to seeing you in class."

I grunted again.

<hr>

On Saturday morning, Filch and I had breakfast as usual in the kitchen. One of the house elves approached us and asked, "Are you remembering sirs that we are having to clear the Great Hall after breakfast for disapparation practicing?"

Filch said, "Sure, we've got lots of time. Just don't get excited." Then he turned to me and said, "I hear that you're going to learn disapparation."

I asked, "How did you know?"

"Oh, I get the list of people to take lessons so that I'll know how much space I have to clear.. I just happened to notice your name."

I suddenly realized that I might have an audience for the practice other than students and the teacher. So, I asked, "You got something going this morning?" I added to myself, "I hope."

Filch stretched and lazily said, "Nope. I thought I might just drop in and see how the lessons go. It's usually good fun."

I thought to myself, "Yeh, good fun if you're not taking the lessons."

Breakfast ended, and we went up to the Great Hall. About the only thing that Filch had to do was scratch his chin and say, "Well, I reckon that we should move the Slytherin table and the Huffelpuff table. There are a lot of students this time." Then the house elves did the work.

That gave me some hope that maybe I'd just get lost in the crowd. That hope was dismissed when Filch knocked me on the back and said, "Just remember, I'll be there rooting for you."

Oh, great! That's all I needed. How could it be more perfect than Mary there watching and Filch rooting me on.

I sat on a bench at the Gryffindor table that was not being moved. I just hoped the instructor would get there quickly, and we'd get this first lesson over. Maybe the next one would be easier and even fun.

The teacher arrived followed by a pile of things floating along that looked like hula hoops. He dumped them, and shortly students started drifting in. There was a lot of them as Filch had promised.

At the stroke of 9, the teacher introduced himself, "I'm Wilke Wycrosse. I work for the Ministry, and I'll be teaching you lot how to disapparate."

He had copies of the parchments from the various houses. He scanned down them and then stopped. He looked up and asked, "Is there a Duddle Dursten here?"

No one spoke up. He repeated the question a couple of times and sighed. Then it occurred to me that he might mean me. I stood up and shouted, "Could that be Dudley Dursley, sir?"

He looked at the list again and said, "I guess it is. Would you please come up here?"

Oh, great! Was he going to tell me that I had no business in his class. I walked up as quickly as I could to get it over with. When I arrived, he said, "Since you're not a student, the fee for lessons will be ten galleons per lesson, payable in advance."

I had forgotten about the possibility of a fee. I turned out my pockets, hoping to find ten galleons. What I found was a five galleon piece, four galleons, and a lot of sickles and knuts. I gave up trying to count them. I just dropped the whole mess in his hands. He patiently counted them and declared, "You have me two silver sickles and a knut more than the fee. Please have the proper change in the future."

I nodded and then he said, "As long as you're up here. Why don't you stay right where you are? I've got a feeling that you might need some extra help."

He had to say that, didn't he? He couldn't just say, "Why don't you stay here."

Then he gave his canned speech about disapparation. The only thing I got out of it was that you had to have a Destination (well, duh), Determination, and Deliberation. I think those were the three D's. Oh, yeh, and you spun around when you disapparated.

After going through that he told everyone to give it a go. The destination was to be to get out of the hula hoop that you would first step into. We stepped in, picked our destination, deliberated about getting there, and decided that we were determined and gave it a go.

I spun around and nothing happened. I think that was what happened to everyone. One guy near me thought that he'd disapparated but Wycrosse simply told him that in spinning around violently, he'd kicked the hula hoop away.

We tried several more times with hardly any better results.

This was discouraging. Then something happened that gave me a whole new perspective on discouragement. Someone ran into the Great Hall (I'd got the name right by now). She called out to Wycrosse, who turned around to look at her. Everyone else did too.

When I did, I realized that things could get worse. It was Pam. I now had the prospect of making a fool of myself in front of her. I had no idea why she was there. She obviously was great at disapparation. Why did she need to take a class? But there she was picking up a hula hoop and getting inside it.

Well, there was nothing I could do about it. After Wycrosse got her set up he gave us a bit more instruction, "You need to visualize the target location. It may help if you close your eyes. So this time, try again, closing your eyes."

I was ready to try anything. As I was getting ready for my next attempt – san voir – I glanced around and happened to notice Pam smiling her best multi-million kilowatt smile in my direction. I couldn't help thinking that I would like to be with her right then. In the background I heard Wycrosse slowly say, "Destination, Deliberation, Determination. . . go."

I didn't have to shut my eyes. I spun, and something happened. I heard a pop and felt the pressure that presses in on you when you disapparate. When I stopped spinning, I tried to orient myself. I looked down and found myself squarely in my hula hoop. Nothing had happened, and yet, I was very sure something had happened. I looked around to see where I was.

It was then that I realized that something had happened. Pam was not on my right side several hoops away. She was on my left side several hoops away. Of course, she had disapparated. No surprise there. Why she'd gone so far I couldn't figure.

Then I heard Wycrosse crossly say, "Ms Myers, Mr. Durkley, please follow me." I wondered what I'd done now.

He took us outside the Great Hall and looked us both up and down. Then he said, "You look like you've not splynched anything. What kind of a prank is this? You two obviously already have your licenses. Why did you come down here to disturb my students?"

We looked at each other in surprise. I'd been here before. I recovered first and spoke first. "I don't know what you're talking about. I've never disapparated before. I don't know about Pam, but . . ."

He interrupted me, "Don't give me that! Let me see your licenses."

Pam was still a bit flummoxed. "I went on. I don't have a license. I've never disapparated on my own today."

By this time, Pam was talking. "He's right. He's never disapparated before. I have. As a matter of fact, I've learned but never gotten my license."

Wycrosse nodded, "Finally, a believable story. Why don't you have a license? That was a perfect performance."

Pam said, "Well, you remember that last year, when I would normally have taken the class, there wasn't one here at Hogwarts. The year was so disrupted, and for some reason the instructor wasn't available. So Dad and Mum decided that for my protection I needed to learn."

Wycrosse asked, "Did they teach you?"

"Oh, no. they hired a retired instructor. He couldn't grant me a license, but he taught me well."

She glanced over quickly at me. I nodded, "Believe me. She's good."

Wycrosse said, "Yes. The reason that the instructor couldn't come last year was that I was the instructor, and I was sent to Azkaban."

Pam gasped involuntarily.

Wycrosse went on, "You needn't worry. I wasn't there long. We were rescued from Azkaban. It was your English Literature professor who did it."

Both of us stared at him. I didn't know anything they were talking about but Professor Wendt breaking someone out of Azkaban, whatever that was, seemed unlikely.

Pam said, "Anyway, I didn't turn 17 until September. I decided to just wait for the class to get my license."

Wycrosse told us to wait there. He went back into the Great Hall and was back in a minute with a sheet of parchment on a clipboard. He started writing on it.

I interrupted, "Please don't give her detention. She didn't have much choice did she?"

Wycrosse laughed, "I'm not giving her detention. I'm not a Hogwarts teacher. I can't give detention. I'm signing her disapparation license. Would you please sign as well Ms. Myers?"

She took the quill and signed her name. He tore a section off the parchment and handed it to her. He then said, "You can go now."

She stuck around and asked, "What about Mr. Dursley?"

"Yes, what about you Mr. Dursley? What do you have to say for yourself? What kind of trick was it that you just played?"

I looked from one to the other of them. "It was no trick. Like I said, before today I'd never disapparated on my own. I don't quite know how I did it. As a matter of fact, where did I disapparate to?"

Pam smiled. "You disapparated into my hoop."

I scratched my head, "How is that possible? You weren't there."

She smiled the megawatt smile again and said, "I wasn't there because I disapparated into your hoop."

I pondered that. "Then I really did disapparate into your hoop?"

She nodded. "A pretty neat trick for the first time."

Wycrosse broke in, "This is really your first time? How do you account for such precise disapparation?"

"You're asking me!" I thought a moment and tried remembering exactly what had happened. It came to me, "You were always talking about Destination, Deliberation, and Determination. Well, I guess I had a Destination that I was really Determined to get to."

Pam's smile notched up a few gigawatts and she said, "Really!"

Wycrosse then gave me a really close exam. He got out a magnifying glass and examined me up and down. He even looked closely at my eyelashes. He finally said, "I suppose that you're not splynched at all. I don't see how I can deny you a license."

I was a little bothered by that. "Wait a minute. I've only done it once. Don't I have to do two out of three or something?"

Wycrosse frowned and said, "That was so perfect, I don't have a choice. You know, I don't think I've ever seen anyone take so quickly to disapparation. Your parents should be proud." With that he took the quill back from Pam and started writing on the parchment. He asked me to sign. I did. Then he tore off the section of the parchment and said, "Here's your disapparation license. Don't go overboard. You can't disapparate here in Hogwarts except in the Great Hall while classes are going on."

I shook my head. Wycrosse said, "OK. Get out of here. I don't want the two of you demoralizing the class with your fancy disapparation."

Pam walked away down the hall. Wycrosse looked at me and asked, "Well, I meant you too. What are you doing hanging around?"

I shook my head. "The Head . .. uh . . . Mistress has a strict policy against staff and students uh fraternizing. I don't dare seem to be walking away with her."

Wycrosse frowned at me. "Well, do you suppose she's had enough of a head start?"

I walked away and decided that I'd have to talk with Wendt about that Azkaban thing. Could he really have broken people out of it?

As I was walking another thought occurred to me. I did just fine disapparating into Pam's ring. I really wanted to be there with her. But what about everyday disapparation? What would happen when I just wanted to disapparate to the corner chip shop? Would I be able to?

Worse, would I splynch, whatever that was. Wycrosse had mentioned splynching more than once during the brief lesson that I'd had. It sounded like you might leave a part of you behind. What did that mean in practice – a patch of hair? A fingernail? Something really vital?

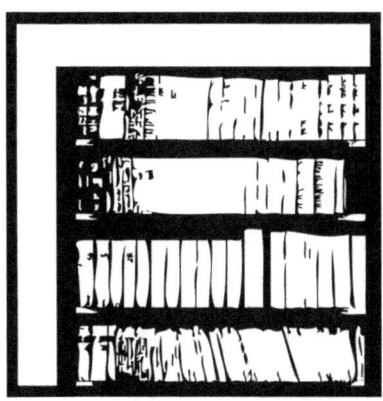

Experimental Biology

The following week, I was trying consciously and unconsciously to avoid everyone. I knew that I'd have to get together with Slughorn sometime, but I wasn't anxious to right away after my explosion in the potions lab. I had been and continued to try to avoid Pam, of course. When you came down to it, there was only one person whom I was not trying to avoid – Filch. I spent a lot of my time in the office when I wasn't actually working.

After a couple of days, I thought of another place that I could hide out with safety and I wouldn't even have to spend time with Filch. I went to the Library after dinner. The Library had cubicles where a student could go to study in peace. Needless to say, there were precious few students who wanted to go someplace to study and not be interrupted.

The first night, though, things didn't go quite as I'd expected. I'd snuck in so that no one would know I was there. I don't think that even the Librarian, Ms. Pinz, noticed me. I later discovered that that was quite a feat. Anyway, I had brought along the potions book and parchment so that I'd have something to do while I was there by myself. Just because we weren't experimenting didn't mean that I couldn't keep working.

I'd been in the carrel for about forty-five minutes when I heard a scream behind me. I looked up in time to see Ms. Pinz, examining every nook and cranny of the little cubicle. She was saying something like, "Got you. Now where is she Mr. Dursley?"

It was such an unexpected assault that it took me a minute to understand what she wanted to know. In the meantime, she just repeated, "Where is your girlfriend?"

By this time I understood enough to ask, "Who are you talking about?"

Pinz raised her nose in a superior gesture, "I know that you've got a girl in here. Why would you be so quiet? You can't fool me. Where is she?"

I looked around the small cube and shrugged. Where could she be?

"Don't you play dumb with me. You've used some sort of cloaking spell to hide her. Just don't waste any more of my time. I know you students. The only reason that you'd be so quiet back here is because you're doing something forbidden," she said indignantly.

I tried to look indignant myself, but I'd never had any practice. I suppose I just ended up looking dumb. "Ms. Pinz, I never went to Hogwarts as a student, and I can barely use the *Wingardium Levioso* spell. How can you expect me to use a cloaking spell?"

She cast a quick glance around and harrumphed. She stepped out of the cubicle and looked back. "Well, I've got my eye on you. Don't you ever try to fool me again."

All I could do was nod and say, "No, Ma'am."

From then on, I was always sure to make noise when I came into the Library, when I went into the carrel and when I was writing, I tried to make the pen scratch as much as possible. However, she never suspected me again.

▽

The following Friday, I was leaving the kitchens after dinner for the Library. On the way past the Great Hall, I saw Slughorn standing at the main entrance. I knew that he must be looking for me. I decided that it wouldn't do any good to try to avoid him any longer. So, I walked directly to him as though it were what I'd intended to do all along.

He smiled sheepishly as I approached and asked me if I'd care to join him for a drink.

I nodded, and we walked silently to his room. After he'd poured us both a glass of white wine (which, by the way, wasn't bad), he got down to the point, "Well, Mr. Dursley, I want to say that I've been doing a lot of thinking about what we talked about.

"Uh . . . I should have discussed with you in advance what I intended to do with live animal tests. But, you see. . . Oh, it doesn't matter. I just want you to know that I'm willing to compromise—if we can come to an agreement."

I was happy that I hadn't had to start the discussion. I felt the same way as he did. I asked him one of the questions that I'd come up with at Wendt's office. "Do we have to include killing potions in the book? I think that if there were potions that just did harm that could be turned around by an antidote AND if we brewed that antidote and had it ready to use immediately, I think I could get along with that."

Slughorn's eyes sparkled at that. "Yes, my boy. I've been thinking about that very idea. The Draught of Living Death has to be in. It has a number of good techniques in it, and every potion-master uses it when teaching. But after you left, I completed the test. It worked perfectly."

I simply commented, "Congratulations."

"Yes, well, anyway, I agree. We don't need any more killing potions. There are only two more in the book, I think, and I've never used them in teaching. I completely agree about brewing antidotes and using them just as soon as we're sure that the original potion has done what it was supposed to."

I nodded slowly. We were both silent for a moment, and he asked THE question, "Does that mean that we can start again?"

I agreed. He added some wine into both our glasses and proposed a toast. Then he got right down to the next important question, "I suppose that you've not edited any more potions?"

I could smile broadly at that, "Yes, I have. As a matter of fact, I've really been trying to stay out of everyone's way, and I've been using the extra time to work on potion formulas."

He almost bounced out of his armchair, "Capital! That means we can start again tomorrow." It must have occurred to him that he didn't want to seem too pushy, so he added, "That is, if you are agreeable to that?"

I agreed. So, it was decided that we'd start the next day on the potions that I'd worked out.

———

⊠

The next couple of weeks flew by. We were on what had started out as a marathon where we were not pushing ourselves too hard, knowing we had a long race. It had now turned into a sprint to the end, but a sprint that had started at the 7 mile mark. I don't know how Slughorn kept it up. He had classes, papers, exams to grade, and lessons to plan. Besides those, we were working not just on the weekends but he trying to get at least one potion in most weekday nights.

The one good thing about the schedule was that I didn't have time to think about Pamela or Filch or even much about the day job I had. I just got through my duties as quickly as I could so that I could take most of the noon hour to work on a potion.

One day, Filch asked me, "You've been acting like a man possessed by a fire demon lately. You'd think you were studying for your Owl exams the way you've been hitting that book! I could understand if you were trying to impress your lady friend, but who would this impress?"

I didn't even look up but just mumbled, "Almost done. We can talk in a minute." But when I looked up, I discovered that Filch had walked out – apparently in disgust at my distraction.

Portraits

We'd been working along for a couple of weeks, and we were beginning to feel really good about our progress. I had been spending what little spare time I had with Filch. He was always doubtful about the partnership that Slughorn and I had, but even he'd begun to get used to it. One evening, we were sitting in the office and talking. Filch was having some of his wretched fire whiskey. I had excused myself from sharing.

As we were having a laugh at the expense of Flitwick, there was a knock on the door. Filch welcomed him with a curse, "Bloody interruptions, come in, already!"

A boy, looking like a 5th year, entered and spoke to Filch, "The Headmistress wants you to come up to her office to clean up a mess." Filch rolled his eyes and said, "She's a bleeding witch isn't she? Oh, well."

Then he turned to me and with a wave of the hand said, "Oh, you go. The headmistress is waiting."

"Why me? She asked for you."

Filch laughed, "But you're my assistant. I'm delegating this job to you. Anyway, how hard could it be? What kind of a mess would the Head make?"

I had to admit that she was very particular, so what Filch and I might regard as a perfectly acceptable level of disarray, she might be unhappy about. So, I got up, lifted a bucket and mop with the windardium leviouso spell and I was off. As I worked my way up flight after flight of stairs, I wondered what kind of mess could possibly happen in her office.
I entered the outer office and found that I was not alone. Wendt was there. The Head was sitting on the desk in the outer office, and as I entered, she said, "What happened to Filch?"

I opened my mouth to explain that rank had its little privileges when she just shook her head and said, "Never mind. I'm sure Filch is doing something really important with a bottle of fire whiskey."

She turned to Wendt and sent him down to the floo in the Great Hall. He was to welcome an Auror who was being sent to investigate. That, of course, raised the question in my mind – what had happened that required law enforcement?

I asked where the mess was. She answered that I'd have to wait a bit for the Auror to examine the scene of the crime, her inner office. We didn't have to wait long. Wendt came up with someone whom I'd never seen before. He wore a distinctive robe with an unusual catch at the throat that I couldn't quite make out.

The Auror introduced himself as constable Bartholomew. He looked around and asked, "Who discovered the crime?"

The Head said she had.

He turned to Wendt and me and asked why we were there.

The Head announced, "Professor Wendt has been very useful when there have been mysteries here at Hogwarts, and this is Mr. Dursley, the Assistant Groundskeeper. He's here to clean up."

The Auror didn't seem very happy about the two of us being there, but he proceeded to question the Head. "Ms. McGonagall, please tell me about the circumstances around your discovering this act of vandalism."

The Head described coming to her office and discovering that one portrait had been vandalized by having been slashed and blood splashed on it and everything nearby. Her desk had been upset, and there was debris everywhere in the room. She tried to volunteer suggestions about who might have done it. But the Auror insisted, "Madame, you should leave investigation to the professionals. There will come a point when I'll want to hear about possible suspects, but that time hasn't arrived yet.

The Auror went on, "What time did you discover this vandalism?"

She had discovered it about twenty minutes before and had immediately sent her patronus to the Auror Office to ask for assistance.

After a few more questions to discern if there had been suspicious characters seen in or around the school (No, none had been seen), the Auror asked to see the damage. We all walked through to the inner office and saw the horrible state it was in. All sorts of things were scattered throughout the office. There seemed to be blood everywhere, but it was mostly concentrated around the portrait – as though someone had taken a bucket of blood and threwn it at the portrait, hitting it dead center.

The portrait itself had several broad gashes running through it, mostly from lower left toward upper right. It was obvious that there was a healing process that was happening. A couple of gashes were already mostly closed. Another had just started healing itself.

The Auror walked around the room with his wand pointed at various splashes of blood and then the portrait itself. After a while he walked over to the Head and asked, "Do you have any idea of someone who would want to harm you or Hogwarts."

She harrumphed and exclaimed, "Well, finally. Yes, we know someone who had a clear and extreme prejudice against the Headmaster in that portrait. At the beginning of this year, he tried to convince me to get rid of the portrait and expunge all references to Headmaster Snape in the history of Hogwarts. I thought that he might come back for another attempt. I just didn't think it would be so violent."

"Yes, Madame. What's his name?"

"Mark Burbage, the brother of the Hogwarts Professor who was killed by Snape."

The Auror frowned and agreed, "Sounds likely."

She asked, "Are you going to investigate him?"

Instead of answering, Bartholomew took a slow walk around the room, examining everything again. Then he asked, "Do you believe that anything of value is missing?"

I could tell that the Head was becoming exasperated, but she answered civilly, "Not to the best of my knowledge."

He turned to Wendt and me and asked, "And you two, are you aware of any other damage done or valuables missing."

We looked at each other and answered in unison, "No."

He nodded slowly and turned back to the Head, "Well, Ma'am, here's the thing. As I see it – and I invite you to correct me if I'm wrong – there has been some minor vandalism done. The blood is not human. It's dragon blood. It can be easily cleaned with a simple Scourgio spell." He turned to me and said, "Pay attention here young man.

"The mess is unsightly but it can be straightened. If anything is irreparably damaged, please report it.

"The portrait would be something of value but it seems to be healing itself. It will be fine by tomorrow.

"The truth is that this is simply minor vandalism. I can't justify starting a major investigation for that."

Wendt interrupted, "But isn't it easy to find out whose wand was used to do this damage! All you have to use is a *Priori Incantatum* spell on a wand. And we've given you the name of a good suspect."

Bartholomew frowned and turned on the Professor, "Well, sir, that would be true were it not for two simple facts. In the first place, most criminals today use stolen wands – never their own – and they destroy the wand after the crime is committed."

Wendt objected, "But I thought that a wand would only obey its owner?"

Bartholomew shook his head derisively, "That's a common misunderstanding of a true principle. It is true that wands only obey their master, BUT wands that are stolen, usually change allegiance to the one who stole them."

Wendt just made a big "O" with his mouth and didn't say anything.

Bartholomew went on, "The second fact is that I could never get a judge to give me a search warrant to do the *Prioiri* spell on a wand that was suspected of being involved in minor vandalism. Besides that, my Chief Inspector would demote me for spending any more effort on this stuff than I already have."

Just then, I remembered about my experience as a gang leader, and I blurted out, "What about Breaking and Entry?"

Everyone looked over at me and apparently no one had really paid attention to what I'd said. The Constable asked, "What did you say?"

I repeated it. He turned to the Head and asked, "How did the perpetrator get in here?"

The Head perked up, "Well, I have the door from the outer office locked at all times."

"Are there other entrances?"

"The other door leads to my private quarters, which are sealed I'll have you know!"

Bartholomew looked around the room, "Is the floo connected to the network?"

She gasped, "Yes. I didn't have it sealed. I suppose Burbage could have come through it."

Bartholomew released a sigh of relief, "Well, there you are. He just walked into any public floo, said, 'Hogwart's Headmistress' office' and walked out here as easy as 'Bob's Your Uncle'!"

This seemed to settle it; he went on, "No Breaking and Entry. Can't investigate further. Ma'am, you'll be well advised to put a password on your floo so that no one can use it whom you don't want to."

He went on in a speech that was as practiced as any, "Well, Ma'am. That's about it. We'll get in touch if anything new turns up about your case." He reached into an inner pocket and pulled out a business card, "Here's my card. If there's any significant development, don't hesitate to get in touch." But the tired mechanical way that he said it left no doubt that he was hoping that we all would hesitate to get in touch.

Wendt cleared his throat and said, "Constable, you should realize that this Burbage is a dangerous man. Anyone who would break into. . ."

At that point Bartholomew broke in with a cleared throat of his own. Then Wendt corrected, "Anyone who would enter an office without permission and do such damage is clearly a dangerous person who might do something desperate and much more harmful! Surely, this calls for more action than, "Get in touch if there's significant developments'! You could find that you are investigating a bloody attack on a person the next time."

Bartholomew just looked around at us and finding no sympathetic face to bid goodbye to, just stepped to the door and said goodbye to the room in general.

▽

We looked at each other, and everyone had something to say at once. The Head told me to go ahead and clean up in her office and don't forget about the *Scourgio* spell. Wendt walked next to the Head and said something about getting the floo secured and talking. I asked the Head for some help knowing where things should go when I straightened up.

I cleaned up. It wasn't as bad as I feared it would be. I got back to the office before the night was over. Filch wanted to know why it had taken so long to clean up. I told him about what had happened. He thought that I had made it up, but I assured him it was all the truth.

The next day, when I finished dinner, I found someone waiting for me. She turned out to be a reporter for the *Prophet*. She wanted to know what had happened in the Head's office. I decided that she should get a toned-down version of the story. No one was hurt, no one knew who had done the minor vandalism. I'd cleaned up everything, and it was as good as new.

Her name was Barbara. She seemed to think that there must be something more to the story than I'd told her. "Come on, Dursley, there must be something more to it. An Auror was called in. Were you there when he arrived?"

I had to think fast and decided that the best idea was to tell only the truth – maybe not all the truth, but I'd not say anything that wasn't true. "Sure. Someone had gotten past a locked door to do the deed. That was something beyond your ordinary student." I hesitated a minute.

She leapt onto that, "I knew there was something. What is it?"

Again, I stuck to the truth. I'd actually been thinking that the Weasley twins and their abilities were legend around here, "Oh, I was just thinking that there were a couple of students recently who would have been up to it."

"Give. Who are they?"

"Well, they're no longer students. They're the Weasley twins. I don't remember their names. Maybe, Frank and Earnest – something like that."

She was disappointed, "Oh, yeah. Everyone knows about the Weasleys. They. . . " Then she hesitated. "I mean George has a joke shop in Diagon Alley. But there's something else isn't there? How did the vandal get in?"

151

Again, honesty is the best policy, "I don't know."

She looked down at her Quill writing away on its own. "There's something more that you know that you're not telling me. I'll find out. There's no point in holding it back."

I didn't say anything. She just kept staring. She gave up before I did. I'd had a lot of practice staring down principals who tried to intimidate me.

The next day there was a note in my mailbox in the Teacher's Lounge. It was simple, "Who was the girl I saw you with yesterday?" It was unsigned, but I had a good idea whom it was from. I couldn't send her an answer. It was a real problem trying to decide what to do about it.

Fortunately, the next day, an article showed up in the *Prophet* about the break-in. The byline was Barbara's, and I was quoted in a couple of paragraphs. She was not exactly complementary to me. But that was fine with me.

Publishing

Slughorn and I seemed to work with even more determination than we ever did before. He shared his plans for the day at the beginning of each brewing session, and I sometimes suggested changes – especially when his plans seemed too hard on the experimental rat that we'd obtained.

We were practically flying through the book. I began to believe that we would not only finish by the end of the term, but possibly even a few weeks before the end of the term. As a matter of fact, at the beginning of May, Slughorn began a session in the lab by talking about our next steps.

"Dursley, we need to think about publishing."

"All right. How do we do that? And aren't we a bit ahead of ourselves? I haven't even finished all the potions."

"Not at all. We'll be done in a week or so. We have to decide on publisher and think about what terms we want. They' may want us to assign all our copyrights to them. There may be other choices."

I had rarely even read a book, let alone published one. I had to depend on Slughorn to make good decisions. I just shrugged, "Well, I don't know about any of that. Go ahead and decide what publisher you think is good, and let me know. I doubt that I'd ever object to it."

Slughorn rubbed his hands together in glee as he considered. He then started out, "Well, the first decision is whether to go with an educational publisher like Scholarly or maybe St. Brutus's. It might seem reasonable, but we want to appeal to a wider audience than Scholarly."

It's amazing to hear him when he gets going, so I just relaxed and let him go. "For a general audience publisher, I think Harbottle, Grace, and Saturnovich is good. Though, there's also Harcourt, Fenton and Mudd. I don't know. I can't decide. You pick."

That surprised me—but what the heck—I could guess as well as the best of them. "I like . . uh . . Mudd. Yes, Harbottle, whatever Mudd."

Slughorn must have been wondering if I was making it up but he decided that I must have meant Mudd. "Yes, I like Mudd too. I'll send our manuscript to them right away."

That bothered me, "You'll send our only copy to them? What if it gets lost in the post? What if they steal it!"

Slughorn just laughed, "No such thing will happen. The owl post never loses anything. Plus, don't forget that we've got your copy."

I stared at him in disbelief, "We've got my copy? What copy are you sending them? There isn't any other. Well, beside the original in Snape's hand."

He cleared his throat, "Oh, yes. I guess I didn't mention that I'd been copying over the potions as we tested them. It's purely to correct a few minor issues. You know, just spelling of technical words, making abbreviations into the full words and such."

I wasn't happy with that, but I had to admit that it was a good idea to have an extra copy – just in case. I actually thanked him kindly and decided that I'd just swallow my objections. We then turned to the potions again and did three of them that day. I wanted to see his copy before it went out the window on its way to our publisher – for that was how I thought of Mudd – our publisher.

The next week, I went to work at full bore to complete the last potions of the book. I was delighted when I finished them Thursday night and delivered them to a tired Slughorn. He would have preferred that I not drop them off at 11:30, but he was the one who was in a hurry.

▽

On Saturday, I was looking forward to a weekend when we'd just about finish off the testing of new potions, but instead, Slughorn intercepted me outside the potions classroom and led me up the stairs. He refused to tell me what we were doing, but I noticed that he had a large manila envelope under his arm. We walked to one of the highest points in the castle. I'd never been up there before, but even before we reached it, I had a guess as to what it was.

The smell of rank bird droppings reached me before we rounded the last curve of the stairs. Slughorn opened the door for me to the owlery. I walked in gingerly, hoping to avoid stepping in a pile of droppings. As I watched where I stepped carefully, Slughorn reached a large table and opened the manilla envelope. Inside, there was a sheaf of parchments. A glance at them revealed potions that I'd worked on.

I asked him, "I see one problem. We've not completed testing the last potions. How can you send the book off without its being completely verified?"

He smiled, pulled a sheet off the pile and handed it to me. It was a letter of explanation. It said that we had enclosed the draft of an advanced potions textbook that we were offering to Harcourt, Fenton and Mudd to publish. It explained that the final version would be available in a week or two at most, allowing them to get it published in time for the next school purchase cycle.

Finally, at the bottom were blanks for signatures. Slughorn handed a quill to me so that I could sign. I started to put quill to parchment but he grabbed my arm shook his head, "You are the main author. You sign first."

That was news to me, "What are you talking about? You're the real authority."

Slughorn shook his head. "No, this is your project from first to last. You're the main author. I'm just a technical expert, helping you with details."

I objected, "But Snape's the real author."

He shook his head, "Snape is no longer with us and has no next of kin. He was the end of his line. There's no one even to sign for him – no executor of his estate. Of course, his estate was pretty much minimal. He had a small vault at Gringotts. I imagine that all the contents were used to pay for his funeral and burial. Sad, really."

I shrugged and signed. He put everything back in the envelope, sealed it and summoned an owl. He tied on the owl's leg and sent it on its way. "Well, we should know what they have to say in a couple of days. Let's go back down to the classroom and get cracking on the next tests."

That weekend we finished everything except the last potion. We had done a record number and tried to finish the last one, but we were both so fagged that we just couldn't get the steps to work for us. We must have tried starting three times and each time we made a mistake. By common consent we just stopped and called it quits until the next weekend.

On Thursday, I went up to the Teacher's Lounge to check my pigeon hole for announcements and letters. I found a note from Slughorn. He wanted me to join him in his office after dinner.

That evening, I walked up to his office wondering what they would offer us. Would we have to negotiate a better deal? I had gotten used to just walking in unannounced. I did that this time.

He was sitting at his desk examining a parchment. He didn't notice me at first, but then realized that I was there. He said nothing but handed me the parchment. I took it and as I did, he said, "Read it aloud."

I shrugged and read, "Gentlemen. We thank you for the consideration of your submittal but regret to inform you that it does not meet our current needs. Please feel free to resubmit it at a later date for consideration. Sincerely yours, Greg Manoni, Managing Editor, Harcourt, Fenton and Mudd"

I suddenly felt like I'd come to a blank wall at the dead end of a street.

Slughorn gazed at me and simply said, "I don't understand." Then he went further, "I mean, I'm a respected Potion Master. I have friends in publishing. How did they pass this gem by?"

I was apparently much more accustomed to disappointment than Slughorn was, "Well, let's pick another publisher and try again."

He stared at me as though I were talking in a foreign language, but after a minute or so of staring, he sighed and said, "I suppose so. You spend a lifetime building up your contacts, and when you need them most, they fail you."

"So, who's next?"

Slughorn shrugged and said, "Saturnovich."

So, he wrote a new letter, addressed a fresh envelope and we signed the letter. Up to the owlery we went, and off into the blue the owl went.

We got a response on Friday. Slughorn didn't do anything fancy. He just found me on the third floor dusting paintings and simply said, "No good. Scholarly is next. I've sent them a lot of good business over the years. I don't see how they can turn us down."

Fortunately, there wasn't time to get a response by the weekend. We finished the last potion test and Slughorn polished up the last pages and declared that the book was print-ready. He suggested that we celebrate by going out to dinner that night. I was not about to object.

We changed into better robes and met at the Great Hall. Slughorn announced that we were going to an exclusive restaurant across the Channel in Brittany. "I had the lad who is the chef there twenty years ago. What he does with shellfish is Magic."

We both laughed at his little joke. Then he said, "I'm sorry that I can't share the name with you. You'll have to take my hand. I'll get us there by floo."

I've never been a big fan of shellfish, but I agreed to do the Bouillabaisse. It was good enough to make me re-think my refusal to have shellfish. We had a bottle of good white wine and I had to admit that I completely enjoyed the evening. I had had my doubts about going out with an old codger, but we talked about sports (Football and Quidditch). We laughed about our little differences over the term and what a good job we'd done with the book.

We convinced ourselves that we should have gone to the educational publishers from the start, and we came back to Hogwarts with the confidence grown of wine and good company that we'd have our book contract on Tuesday or Wednesday at the latest.

⊠

Tuesday came and went. Wednesday came, and I could hardly work with anticipation of the owl post. That evening, I went down to the potions classroom and found Slughorn just sitting there and staring at the door. I didn't have to ask whether mail had come, and he didn't say anything. I just turned around and left the classroom.

The next day, I was having breakfast as usual in the kitchen. Amazingly, Slughorn knew that. He walked over close enough to our table to be sure that I saw him. He just shook his head. Then he turned and left. Filch noticed my attention was directed over his shoulder. He turned and asked no one in particular, "I wonder what old Sluggy wanted down here."

I just shrugged. That evening, I visited his office and found him laboring over a stack of parchments. I asked him, "Grading parchments?"

He just frowned and said, "Come on over and start signing these." They turned out to be cover letters to a whole list of publishers that I had never heard of.

"I decided that we might as well be prepared for the flood of rejection that's coming our way. Sign them all and I'll just send to the next one without bothering you."

I picked up a quill and started. When I'd finished, I asked the obvious question, "What do we do when we've been rejected by all these?" I'd not asked, "What do we do IF we've been rejected by all these?" I was convinced that we'd not be published by any of them.

Slughorn looked at me forlornly and said, "I don't know. I suppose it's about time to start thinking about that." But that was all that he had to say. The rest of that week and the next week was really quiet. Slughorn sent the manuscript out and received it back multiple times. If we encountered each other in the hall, there was just a shake of Slughorn's head and my nod of understanding.

During this time, I'd not been waiting for Slughorn to come up with another idea. I'd hardly had the question out of my mind the whole time. I just couldn't think of any ideas. But then, I had an idea. It was kind of a long shot, so I decided to wait until Slughorn had completely given up. That didn't take a long time. By the end of that next week, he'd run out of publishers and he really looked down-in-the-mouth whenever I saw him. But I was determined to wait until he came to me and we agreed on complete defeat.

That weekend, I was in the Great Hall having breakfast on Saturday, as I often did. I really didn't need to worry about running into students – especially one particular student. None of them got up early enough for breakfast on the weekends. So, I was there enjoying a pastry and coffee when Slughorn sat down beside me.

"Well, professor, why aren't you at the head table?"

"It's not necessary for breakfast. Most people are in such a hurry that nobody pays any attention – even in the good old days of Professor Tippett." He picked up a croissant and poured a cup of tea. Then, he went on, "I suppose that we've got to give up. I just can't think of anything to do.

"All my contacts have failed me. I just don't understand it. What's the use of spending your career developing high-placed friends if they don't help you when you really need them?"

"I guess you're right, Professor."

He must have been really disconsolate because he answered back, "Oh, don't 'Professor' me. I might as well be a garden gnome as much good as that title has done me."

This was the time, "Well, my friend, an idea occurred to me. Would you like to hear it?"

He wasn't anxious but he did say, "Sure, I could use a laugh. What are you thinking about?"

I was just about ready to keep the idea to myself – a laugh, indeed – but I went ahead, "I just thought that we might talk to Professor Wendt. He seems to have a good idea every now and then."

Slughorn wasn't excited by the idea, but I could see that he had a glint of hope in his eye. He said, "It certainly couldn't hurt. Is he in the hall?"

We both looked around but didn't see him. After breakfast, we went our separate ways but agreed to be sure to be in the Great Hall for lunch in case Wendt showed up. If he didn't, we'd go up and try to find him in his office.

As it turned out, Wendt did come down for lunch. Slughorn used the informal nature of weekends to sit beside him at the Head table. It looked like they had had an animated discussion, and they left lunch together by way of the Hufflepuff table where I, of course, was sitting.

Slughorn slapped me on the back and said, "Come along." We went up to Wendt's office. He invited us to sit and got out the whiskey for us.

"Well, gentlemen, what can I do for you two?"

Slughorn looked over to me, and I looked to him. I guess since it was my idea to consult Wendt, he must have decided that I should explain the situation. I went over our problem, Slughorn nodding all the time. Wendt was leaning back in his chair with his eyes mostly closed, staring off into the distance. When I finished, he asked some questions.

"All right, you've tried all the publishers that you know of. You, Horace, have tried pulling all the strings that you have, right?"

We both agreed.

He looked from one to the other of us and then suggested, "I have an idea that's pretty far out. So, I don't want to discuss it with you until I've done a little research and have a better idea whether it might work. Is that all right with you?"

I nodded but Slughorn thought a while in tight-lipped silence. Then he agreed that it would be OK.

Wendt continued, "It will probably take me a couple of days, but don't give up hope just yet."

We agreed not to, and we parted.

It's Only Two Hundred Thousand Galleons

Slughorn took to having meals with Filch and me except for dinners when attendance was required of teachers in the Great Hall. Each meal began with a silent prayer that one of us would have news from Wendt. We were not patient in our travail. Every meal contained speculations as to what Wendt was doing and when he'd get back with us.

The favorite theories were that he was approaching American publishers or that he had gangster friends that he would get to apply pressure on one of the English publishers or that he had some Muggle electronic way of publishing books (that was my theory). They were good for passing the time but, of course, they weren't anything like the truth when it finally surfaced.

By this time it was late May, and we were checking our mailboxes in the Teacher's Lounge three times a day. Even Filch had gotten into the spirit.

When the answer came, it was in the form of a summons in our boxes but not a summons to Professor Wendt's office. Instead it was to dinner on Friday night at the Leaky Cauldron.

Slughorn and I traveled together by floo. We arrived and were greeted by Wendt, who was standing at the bar waiting for us. He had a reserved table in a dark corner away from the fire, and we sat immediately. Tom took our drink orders quickly as well. Slughorn wondered if this were a Dutch treat.

Wendt shook his head, "No. I'm treating. Don't argue." Well, he wouldn't have gotten an argument from me, anyway.

"My last guest should arrive within a few minutes. I don't think that either of you know him, so I'll handle introductions."

Our drinks arrived and shortly afterwards, the fourth diner arrived. He was older than any of us at the table. He was tall with disorderly grey hair. He wore a chain around his neck that held a strange work of art the like of which I'd never seen before. It looked like some sort of geometric symbol. It consisted of a bisected equilateral triangle with a circle around the triangle. His robes were old but clean if not terribly neat.

Wendt introduced us all, "This, gentlemen, is Xenophilius Lovegood.

"Mr. Lovegood, here is Professor Horace Slughorn, current Potion-Master of Hogwarts, and Mr. Dudley Dursley, Assistant to the Groundskeeper of Hogwarts."

Tom was there to take Lovegood's drink order, and we looked at the menu so that we could order when his drink came to the table.

After we'd ordered, Wendt began to explain the situation all around. By this time, it was becoming dark outside, and the main source of light in the Cauldron was candles and the fire. We were in a dark corner to start with, and it was now too dark to read menus easily.

Wendt explained, "The situation is that Professor Slughorn and Mr. Dursley are authors who want to publish an advanced potions textbook. But they've not been able to interest a publisher in their book. Mr. Lovegood is a publisher, who might be willing to publish the book."

Slughorn and I nodded vigorously, and he asked, "What do you know about the book?"

Lovegood was quite blunt, "For one thing, I know why you can't get it published."

We were surprised. None of the rejection letters had hinted at the real reason. Lovegood went on. "Although the two of you are the authors in name, the author in fact is Severus Snape."

Slughorn was surprised, "How do you know this? Did Wendt tell you?"

"Oh, no. I may be at the fringe of the publishing world, but even I hear rumors. The thing that they will not say to your face is that the problem with your book is the author."

Slughorn almost rose at that. Instead his voice became strident, "Professor Snape was an excellent student of mine, perhaps the best Potion Master of his time. I ought to know. I taught him."

Lovegood seemed to shrink into himself at the forceful answer but he replied, "Don't transfigure the messenger. Because of my daughter, I know more about Snape than most people do. I am not prejudiced against him, but I am the rare exception.

"The vast majority of wizards know that he killed several innocent people as a Deatheater and that one of them was Professor Dumbledore. Dumbledore's popularity increased and fell off with politics but at the end he was as popular as anyone in the Ministry. His murderer is not going to get a sympathetic hearing anywhere."

Slughorn went back to something he'd said, "Who was the daughter who knew more about Snape?"

The first genuine smile came to Lovegood's face at the mention of his daughter, "Yes, Luna. She was just before your recent time as Potion Master of Hogwarts, as I was before your original time. She didn't take advanced potion-making in her 6th or 7th year, which is when you came to Hogwarts."

Slughorn slapped his forehead, "Of course, Luna Lovegood. You're right, I never had her in a class, but I recognize the name now." Then he came back to the point of the meeting, "Are you willing to publish our book? And, come to think of it, what publisher do you work for?"

Lovegood sat a little taller in his chair, "I am the publisher myself. I self-publish."

"But what have you published?"

Lovegood simply answered, "Have you never read the *Quibbler*?"

Slughorn's mouth opened wide, and he was speechless for a time. I stepped in and asked the question, "What's the *Quibbler*?"

Wendt jumped in at this point, "Well, I don't want to impose on Mr. Lovegood's modesty, so I'll tell you.

"The *Quibbler* is a weekly journal. It contains articles of general interest to the wizarding community. However," here Wendt looked over at Lovegood, "excuse my providing a critique of your work that you might not agree with. However, the viewpoints expressed in articles are pretty far out of the mainstream of the wizarding press. The *Quibbler* is known for taking up causes and theories when the evidence is somewhat shaky."

Lovegood looked to be on the verge of saying something, but he didn't.

Wendt continued, "You can see that such a publisher would be the only one to help you in this situation."

Slughorn's face seemed to be torn between outrage and gratitude. When it settled down he asked, "You would actually be willing to publish our book?"

Lovegood nodded silently.

"How many copies could you do in the first run?" He hastily added, "It would have to be available by August to fill orders from wizarding schools."

Lovegood smiled, "I'd be happy to publish. I think I could turn out a half dozen, perhaps as much as ten copies per week."

Slughorn's face fell at that. "It would take you all the time until August just to turn out enough copies for Hogwarts for the fall. It's not possible."

Lovegood answered, "Beggars can't be choosers. I have the press that I have. It's not possible to turn out more than that. I'd have to cut back on the *Quibbler* even to do that much!"

"The *Quibbler*! How can you compare the *Quibbler* to a serious book on potion making?"

"I'll have you know . . . Oh, if you don't want my help, you don't have to have it!" With that Lovegood stood, and it looked like he would leave.

But Wendt interrupted, "Our food is just arriving. Let's not ruin our appetites over this." So, everyone sat down, and our plates were laid before us. Wendt continued as we began eating, "I think there is a way that we can work through this difficulty." He simply left it there without saying more.

After everyone had cut the edge from their appetites, both Lovegood and Slughorn wanted to know Wendt's idea.

"Before I tell you, I need to ask a couple of questions." With some grumbling both agreed. "All right, Slughorn, just how sure are you that this book will do as well as you've assured our friend, Dursley, here?"

Slughorn looked around and said positively, "I'm sure."

Wendt followed up instantly, "So sure that you'd co-sign a loan to help Lovegood get a serious printing press?"

That took Slughorn back a bit, but he said, "Yes. Just how much would you need to spend on a press?"

Lovegood shot back, "How many books printed by August?"

Slughorn thought, "We really have to have a first printing of at least a thousand."

"But do you have to have them all available by August?"

Slughorn thought. "Maybe not. We'd probably not sell all by August. Considering how unpopular we are with publishers maybe not that many. It will take time to build up sales."

Lovegood thought. "I think that I could get a decent printing press – used, of course – for maybe 200,000 galleons. We'd have to rent a building. There would be materiel costs too."

Slughorn sighed, "Where in the world would we get two hundred thousand galleons?" He giggled and then laughed outright and then could hardly get his breath. It was infectious. Before long we were all laughing.

Wendt, laughing as much as any of us, asked, "Just what's the joke?"

Slughorn controlled himself, "I thought we might rob Gingrott's."

Everyone continued laughing, but Wendt stopped first. "Maybe that's not so preposterous as you think."

Slughorn stared at him as though he'd turned into a mermaid.

Wendt was undeterred, "No, I mean it. We could get a business loan from them."

Lovegood was the one to stare now, "Don't you think that I've ever tried to get a loan from Gringott's?"

"I'm sure you have. I just think that you should try again. You've not had Slughorn to help you before."

This brought an end to a discussion and a return to serious eating, but at the end of the meal Wendt simply said, "Let's set a time for the four of us to go talk to a banker at Gringotts."

Slughorn shook his head scornfully, "I've never had a student who went anywhere in Gringott's. I don't know what difference I could make."

Wendt just said, "What's the worst thing that could happen – they throw us out on our ears?"

No one said anything for a while as the check came. Wendt pulled out his purse and poured galleons into the hands of Tom. With that example of extreme extravagance, Slughorn said, "Well, I've never done anything at Gringott's but put galleons in my vault and take them out – and a lot more taking out than putting in. OK, but it's got to be after finals are finished and graded."

Wendt agreed to that as did Lovegood. I was strictly along for the ride because I wasn't bringing anything to the table. So, it was decided that we'd meet three weeks from now for breakfast here before we went into Gringotts.

―――

The next couple of weeks were busy for everyone. Both Wendt and Slughorn had to prepare final exams and grade final parchments. I had my usual duties and we had to prepare for the graduation ceremonies. This year was to be especially grand because the previous year, the castle had practically been demolished and there had been no graduation ceremony. Most people hadn't even had final exams. So, there was going to be a grand joint graduation a week after the end of final's week.

Filch and I had to find out how many people were going to attend. It was obligatory for all students. But then there were families and friends. Just sending owls out to families to get reservations was time-consuming and boring. We had all sorts of lists – lists of attendees, lists of lists for the graduation reception and dinner. We couldn't just get out an old plan and use it because there were so many extra people.

It was hard enough helping people find accommodations for graduation in a normal year. In a double graduation year, it was hideous. We ended up deciding to put up a lot of people in Huffelpuff house and Gryffindor house.

I don't think I saw anyone of our little group until exams week itself. Even then, it was just a quick check-in to make sure everyone still remembered our breakfast meeting the Saturday after exam week.

And to top it all off, I ran into Pam Wednesday afternoon of exam week. She was casually walking along the 3rd floor hall near the Room of Requirement.

Her face lit up and mine turned some shade of crimson. I thought desperately of something to say. I wanted it to be clever and express how much I wished it were a week later after the end of term and . . .

She walked up to me and said not a word. Instead, she gave me a quick, almost imperceptible kiss as we passed and kept on walking as though nothing had happened.

⊠

Saturday came but not until after a hard, nearly sleepless night. It was filled with half-dream, half-waking nightmares of being in Gringotts and being laughed out of the place. I finally was hopelessly awake at about 5:17 AM. I took a shower, fumbled into my best dress robes, and went out to the Great Hall. We hadn't arranged a time to meet, and nobody was there. I arrived about ten to and sat on one of the benches – I think Slytherin – to wait for my companions.

The time passed. I supposed it did, but when I glanced at my wrist, the minute hand of my watch hadn't seemed to move in the least since the last time that I'd seen it. After repeating that exercise a couple of times and only being rewarded by a minute passing, I decided that I'd rather wait at the Cauldron. So, I got up, walked to the fireplace and took a handful of floo powder. I closed my eyes (traveling by floo goes a lot easier for me if I close my eyes and don't have to see the world spinning around me). I thought the happy thought of the Leaky Cauldron in my head, threw the floo powder at my feet, heard the sizzle of the powder exploding in flames, spun around and opened my eyes. The cheery sight that greeted them was the Great Hall of Hogwarts.

I stared around to make sure that my eyes weren't deceiving me. They weren't. That was disgusting. I walked out of the fireplace, as sooty as though I'd traveled a thousand miles, and sat down on a bench. Wendt and Slughorn would show up in a while, and one of them would give a perfectly reasonable explanation why I was still sitting on the Slytherin bench.

They turned out to be almost as anxious to get it over as I. About five minutes after six, the two of them arrived in quick succession. Wendt looked me over and asked, "Where have you been at this early hour?"

165

"Professor, only here."

"But you've obviously traveled somewhere by floo."

Slughorn smiled. "I think I know what happened. You arrived here before 6 and tried going to the Cauldron, right?"

I shrugged, "Sure, so?"

His smile widened, "Well, the Cauldron closes around 1 AM and then re-opens at six for the breakfast trade. During their off-hours, they close the floo connection."

I nodded and asked, "Are you guys ready to go already?"

Wendt agreed, "Who do I go with?"

I put out my hand as I stood, "Let's just get going!"

The two of us walked into the fireplace, I grabbed a handful of floo powder on the fly, and I spoke our destination. The world spun around and we emerged from the hearth of the Cauldron. Slughorn was close behind.

Tom was standing behind the bar as he always seemed to be. He greeted us with a wave that turned to expansively include the entire dining area, "Take your pick. You're the first customers this early Saturday."

We picked a spot in the corner away from the hearth. Tom suggested that we have the breakfast burritos, something new that he was trying. Wendt asked him, "I didn't know that you were interested in TexMex?"

He just looked puzzled and said, "What?"

"Never mind. I think I'll have my usual breakfast."

Tom nodded, "Poached egg on bagel?"

Wendt agreed, and none of us tried the breakfast burros or whatever they were.

Our breakfasts arrived, and Lovegood still hadn't. We didn't hesitate to begin and were well along when people began to arrive. Everyone looked up when someone arrived, but it was never Lovegood. Slughorn remarked, "Well, we didn't actually agree on a time. It's still before seven."

He went on, "By the way, I got an appointment with a loan officer at Gingrotts at 9:15, the earliest available."

Wendt asked who we were going to meet with. Slughorn didn't know.

We had lots of time to kill, so we didn't feel rushed, and we finished our breakfasts leisurely. Tom dropped by and asked if we wanted a change of beverage. Wendt asked for tea to replace his orange juice. I already had tea and I just asked for some more hot water. I don't remember what Slughorn had.

The conversation turned to sports. There was a lively discussion between Went and Slughorn about the relative pleasures of Quidditch vs. Football. The time passed somewhat faster. However, we were still trying to figure out ways to pass the time when Wendt noted that it was only 15 minutes before nine. "Gentlemen, we have a problem. I don't see how we can apply without all the applicants being present."

Slughorn sighed, "I think we've got to go to Gringotts and hope that Lovegood shows up on time."

Wendt just stood, pulled out his purse and tossed a fifty galleon coin on the table and said, "Let's go." Slughorn looked like he might object, but he didn't say anything. We rose and strode out the back door.

We reached Gringotts just after the opening hour of 9. There was no sign of Lovegood, and we were all feeling embarrassed as we opened the door and walked in. We stopped at the welcome table, and Slughorn was about to announce our arrival when the door flew open and Lovegood walked in. He saw us and shouted, "Oh, glad to see that you've arrived. I was waiting in Flourish and Blotts for you."

He looked around at our amazed faces, seemingly oblivious of the fact that we'd agreed to meet for breakfast. Slughorn seemed ready to say something explosive but restrained himself. Meanwhile the attendant at the welcome desk had to ask us, "Did you have some business with Gringotts?"

Slughorn turned his attention to the goblin and said, "Oh, yes. I'm Professor Slughorn. I made an appointment with a loan officer at 9:15."

The goblin glanced at his open ledger and nodded, "Please take seats over there, and I'll inform Grasnick that you're here." Then he seemed to notice Professor Wendt for the first time. He stood and extended his hand, "Good to see you Professor. What business can we help you with?"

Wendt just shook his head and said, "Oh, I'm with them," indicating us and walked over to join us.

After about twenty minutes, a young goblin approached us and announced that he was Grasnick. Would we come with him. He led us to a small conference area just off the main lobby. We took hard wooden chairs around the low table that was obviously designed to be perfect for goblins. Grasnick smiled a smile that had a lot more sneer in it than good fellowship as he said, "Now, please tell me about your loan request. IF." He placed quite a lot of emphasis on the IF. "IF your business sounds interesting, we'll start an application."

Slughorn told his story about Snape's book. He may have mentioned Snape's name, but I don't recall his doing it. He painted his usual rosy picture of the minimum profits that he expected and why he expected them.

Grasnick listened impassively to the entire recitation like a music critic listening to a piano recital by a very young and not very precocious child. Finally, when Slughorn had finished he spoke.

"I don't understand why you're coming to me for a loan. Your book – if it is truly as exceptional as you say – should be grabbed up by any of a number of publishers and you shouldn't need any money. What am I missing?"

Slughorn seemed flummoxed, but Lovegood spoke up at this point, "Well, I can answer that question. Professor Slughorn has graciously granted me the right to publish his book. However, I don't quite have the capacity currently to publish a first run as large as they really need. It's really I who need the loan to expand my current publishing capacity to fulfill this very lucrative order."

"And what publishing house do you represent?" the goblin asked with a smile that had positively turned wicked.

Lovegood seemed unfazed by the question, and he promptly answered, "Why the House Lovegood."

For the first time, the goblin looked puzzled. "I'm not familiar with that publishing house. What are some examples of what you have published?"

Lovegood sat a bit straighter and said, "I publish the *Quibbler*."

Grasnick stared a moment, seemingly not comprehending what Lovegood had said. Then he leaned back and emitted a sound that might have been a laugh. I think I might have made such a sound sometime in my old life when I was about to steal the milk money from a runt of an eight-year-old.

Grasnick got control of himself and closed the portfolio that he had brought to the meeting, "Oh, my. I must admit that I've never seen such a group come to steal money from Gringotts in a long, long time. Because it is simply theft that you propose. How you think that we would ever help you on the basis of such a tale is completely beyond me."

He started to rise and at that moment professor Wendt cleared his throat and said, "You're new to this branch of Gringotts, aren't you."

He stared at Wendt as though he'd never seen anything like him before, but he gave him an answer, "Yes, that's right. I've come from the Cairo branch of Gringotts just in the last two months."

Wendt nodded and said, "Please do me one last favor. Please send a message to Gorblatt that Professor Wendt would like to meet with him. We'll wait for his answer." Wendt was sitting back in his chair as though at perfect ease and in complete certainty that he would be there for quite some time.

Grasnick stared at Wendt without moving a muscle or making a sound for more than a minute, and then he did something that completely surprised everyone at the table. He asked, "How do you know of Glorblatt?"

"Oh, just mention my name to him. He doesn't need to know details."

Grasnick looked around the table at the four of us and backed away uncertainly, but he didn't have us ejected either. After he'd gone, Slughorn turned to Wendt and asked, "Do you actually know something about this Glorblatt?"

The slightest smile crossed Wendt's face, and he said, "Oh, we go back a long time." And he refused to say anything more.

After about fifteen minutes, Grasnick returned and simply signaled to us to follow him. We got up and walked off into the bowels of Gringotts. We passed the exit to the subterranean vaults and kept going further back into the main building. We passed into a door that didn't have a lock but seemed to require someone to pass a long fingernail around the door handle counterclockwise to open it. We walked down a fairly narrow hall and passed a couple of crossing halls.

After the second, Wendt asked, "Does Glorblatt have a new office?"

The goblin turned to face him with a strange look on his face. "How did you know?"

"Oh, he used to have an office down that hall." As he said this, he motioned vaguely down the passage to the right.

I think that a watcher would have found an expression on all of our faces similar to that on Grasnick's visage. He said no more, but led us to the next crossing hall and took us to the left. At the end of the hall was a large door that opened as we approached. Grasnick stopped at the door and motioned us in. Inside, there was a waiting room with a sofa – normal size – and a couple of chairs – all goblin-sized. There was what I guessed to be a female goblin at a desk. She said, "You're expected inside. Please go directly in."

Wendt opened the door, and we entered a large office with a large desk that was made of some dark wood. There was a window that faced on a courtyard. There was some sculpture in the courtyard, but I couldn't make out what it was.

The goblin seated at the desk rose and came around it with a hand extended. As he did, he said to Wendt, "Well, what do you think of my new office?"

Wendt smiled and said, "It's fitting, I'm sure, of your status in Gingrotts. I hope business has been good."

The goblin's expression that might have been a smile changed. It would have been grim on a human. He said, "I suppose you're going to gloat that you were right last year about the disastrous effects on business of sitting out the war on Riddle?"

"No. You've suffered enough. I've brought you a little business that might compensate for that disastrous war."

The goblin seemed to brighten a bit and asked for introductions, which Wendt supplied although it was quite scanty in detail about Glorblatt. It appeared that he was an officer of the bank. That was about all that we learned.

Glorblatt wanted a quick description of our business opportunity. Slughorn talked about the sales potential of the book. Lovegood talked about needing a better, faster press. Then Glorblatt looked to me and asked what I had to bring to the table.

I was stumped for a minute, and then I told him, "Well, I guess that I bring the book." I held up my folder that had the loose-leaf parchment sheets. "I found the original book as modified by Headmaster Snape." I didn't know how to approach the ultimate authorship of the book. Would Glorblatt hold it against the book that Snape had been a Deatheater? I didn't know and had no way of deciding, so as Wendt sometimes quotes someone as saying, "Lie if you must or lie if you want, but never lie because you have nothing better to say." So, I told the truth.

I went on, "Besides finding it, I recognized its value and started translating it into normal readable formulas."

Glorblatt asked, "What? Was it in code?" This seemed to interest him greatly.

I've found that people think something is worth more if it is a secret than if it is known. I almost wanted to lie, but I decided to tell the truth again. I began to worry that it might become a habit that I couldn't break, but I continued. "No, it was just that Snape frequently had many changes to potion instructions, and there wasn't a lot of room to spare on the pages. So he had to abbreviate things, and sometimes, he'd just say, something like, 'See page 54.'

"I had quite a time at first just deciphering his tiny writing and then figuring out all the abbreviations and getting all the references to other pages."

Glorblatt twisted his head so that it almost rested on his left shoulder and asked, "You didn't happen to bring the original, did you? I'd like to see it myself."

I shook my head, "I'm afraid not. It's not much to look at – cover frayed, marked on, binding starting to loosen."

Glorblatt said, "Still . . " listlessly and then went on in a more business like tone and pace, "Well, I'd like to have one of our experts have a glance at your manuscript before I make my decision. May I send it out for, oh, a half-hour?" He hastened to add, "I won't let it leave the sight of a trusted associate, and if it were accidentally lost or destroyed, I'd reimburse you fully for the value that you've described." He nodded in the direction of Slughorn.

I was about to agree to it, but Slughorn interrupted, "I just want to tell you that the text is copyrighted, and we've applied for patents on the more commercial processes."

Glorblatt frowned at Slughorn. Wendt spoke up, "Mr. Glorblatt is an ethical businessman. You can trust any promises that he makes you. I've had a number of business transactions with him, and I've always found him to be true."

Glorblatt seemed mollified. He pressed a button on his desk. His secretary came in and took some brief instructions in a language that I later learned was gobbledegook. He then handed her the folder with my "translation."

She left the room, and the discussion turned to other things—how the loan would be repaid, precisely how much should be the net amount to us, having the press as collateral and so forth. Glorblatt seemed to think that the loan wouldn't be a problem. He said that the papers would be drawn up, and he'd send them to us by owl for us to review. Then, if we were satisfied, we'd come back to sign them. He thought that it all could be done by the following weekend.

We were still discussing details when the secretary returned with the manuscript and exchanged a few words in gobbledegook. She handed the folder to him, and he returned it to me. Slughorn was glaring at me, apparently trying to communicate something to me. I opened the folder and flipped through the pages, satisfying myself that all was in decent order. All the pages appeared to have been individually gone through. They were all slightly misaligned but didn't seem worse for the wear. I couldn't imagine how anyone could have read all of them in a half hour.

When I'd finished glancing through them, I looked up and discovered Slughorn still glaring at me. I just nodded slightly, and he seemed to relax.

We finished our discussion, and we left the way we came. As we walked, I realized that Mr. Wendt had hardly said a word during the whole time. It was puzzling.

When we left the bank, Everyone looked at Wendt and began a barrage of questions. He simply said, "It's close to lunch. Why don't we visit the Cauldron, and we can talk over a little light lunch."

Everyone agreed, and we were off to the Cauldron. We arrived and Tom was happy to have a second meal out of us. He actually bought a round for us all. When we were seated, the questions resumed. Wendt sat impassively letting the waves of questions wash over him, like the tide at a beach washing over a large rock.

When it subsided he said, "I think it would be simpler to tell you how Glorblatt and I are so well acquainted than to try to answer all your questions.

"Like you, I had a simple relationship with Gringott's for a couple of years. I rented a vault and deposited my earnings from Hogwarts there. From time to time I made withdrawals and converted galleons to pounds sterling or vice versa.

"After a few years, I decided that I should open a credit card account and discovered that there was no such thing in wizard banking, so I suggested a way that I could open a Muggle credit card account and have it draw against my deposits in my vault.

"Originally that was only for me. . ."

Here Slughorn interrupted excitedly, "You mean to say that when Gringotts introduced credit cards that it was really you who invented them?"

"Well, I didn't exactly invent them, but I did suggest to Gringotts how to use Muggle Credit cards so that wizards could use them."

Slughorn went on, "Well, I can see why you have such a reputation at Gringotts. I think that's been very profitable for Gringotts and has given them a real leg up on all the other wizarding banks."

Lovegood added, "As though they needed an additional leg up on the rest!"

Wendt continued, "I had an idea or two in addition that proved useful to them, so they usually listen very carefully when I approach them with a new idea."

Slughorn shook his head, "And to think that I spent decades building up friendships among the children of well-placed wizards and witches, and you just walked into Gringotts with an idea or two."

Wendt shrugged, and Tom approached our table to take our lunch order. When we'd finished, Slughorn declared that he wasn't going to be shy about accepting meals on Wendt from time to time.

Wendt smiled and harrumphed mildly, "No, you needn't. I'll pick up this meal as well." He hesitated for emphasis, "BUT you will have to pay in inside information from time to time."

The Parents

We were pleasantly surprised when a large parcel arrived by owl on Tuesday of the next week. It turned out to contain the loan agreement. We all looked it over. No one could find a problem with it, but Slughorn insisted that we hire a lawyer to review it. Of course, he had had a student who'd studied law after Hogwarts and was apparently quite good. Slughorn sent it to him by owl for review.

It didn't take long. The lawyer asked to meet with us Thursday night. We agreed, and he even volunteered to meet in Hogsmeade. We decided to meet in the Broomsticks for a drink and the review.

He showed up about ten minutes early and Slughorn greeted him effusively. He was a young middle-aged man with a light grey pinstripe robe. He looked ready to walk into a school board meeting to propose the latest in discipline measures. .

Introductions were made, and he was surprised that Wendt was present, "Excuse me, Professor, but you're not mentioned in the loan papers anywhere. What brings you to our meeting?"

Slughorn immediately intervened. "Oh, Randolph, Wendt has been our advisor almost from the beginning. In a way, he's responsible for our having this deal that we're reviewing now. Please, let's sit down and start."

Randolph seemed to be suspicious still, but we took seats near a window, and we started to discuss. Madame Rossmeurta appeared and recited our usuals by way of asking for our orders, "Let's see. Professor Slughorn will have a brandy, Mr. Dursley will have a butter beer, Professor Wendt will have a Dewars 'on the rocks' as you Americans say and what can I get for the rest?"

Lovegood ordered a white wine, and Randolph asked for a scotch and soda. When she'd left, Randolph started, "Well, gentlemen, the contract doesn't have anything that looks like a trick. Gringotts loans you the gold for the prime rate, which is fairly decent of them, considering that the only thing that you offer by way of collateral is the used printing press that you're going to buy.

"You're all separately and jointly obligated to repay the loan." He looked around at us all, inviting questions with his eye. Finally, it settled on me, "Mr. Dursley, you're ready to repay the entire loan if your partners flee the country?"

I involuntarily gulped and nodded my head.

"But – and here's the rub – they want a half of a percent of the gross of the book in perpetuity. That's not much for most books, but if you think that this is going to be a standard potions text for a long time, it could mount up to quite a lot over time. Those Goblins always take the long view when they're doing business."

Slughorn asked, "There's nothing else worth noting in the contract?"

Randolph sort of waved a hand dismissively, "Oh, you know, whenever the Goblins are dealing, they have a couple of standard things that they like to throw in. They always throw in things like agreements are binding on your heirs to the 3rd and 4th generations and so on. I've never heard of Gringotts ever trying to enforce those terms."

Lovegood gulped.

I asked, "So, is this a contract that you'd sign if you were in our place?"

Randolph looked around the table speculatively and said, "I think you might better ask that question of Mr. Wendt. I hear that he does a fair amount of dealing with the Goblins. What do you think, Professor?"

Wendt smiled, "Well, the Goblins are hard bargainers, and they do have you over a barrel. They know that you'd have published elsewhere if you'd had a choice. I think the ½ percent is not burdensome. I'd go along with it, provided that Mr. Randolph thinks there aren't any traps in the contract."

Everyone's eyes turned back to Randolph. He shrugged, "I think it's OK. As a matter of fact, for a Goblin deal, it's down-right generous. Sure, I'd take it."

With that opinion, everyone relaxed, and we spent the rest of the evening speculating on the World Cup of Quidditch that was approaching the first round. The general thinking was that the Irish had a lucky run the last World Cup, and somebody else was due. Maybe it would be some African team. Nobody thought that the other World Cup finalist from the previous Cup, Bulgaria, would make it past the first round either.

Randolph was the only one who gave the English a shot at getting past the first rounds either. He insisted that the recent naturalization of the Brazilian keeper would make the English a contender, but he was practically laughed from the table. I didn't know enough to have a decent opinion, but I liked to be in the majority, so I downplayed the English team as well.

The evening ended when Wendt reminded everyone that we had a graduation coming up the next week. There were still some grades to finish and preparations for the double graduation were running a little behind. Randolph commented, "Well, I'm well out of that. Good luck with your school homework."

▽

The following day, Slughorn sent an owl with our acceptance of the contract. The return owl accepted the time that we proposed to sign on Saturday. We took Randolph along, so Wendt declined to go along. It was a quick very business-like meeting. We met with Grasnick again in the little conference room off the main lobby of the bank. He was in a hurry. He had all the copies of the contract neatly stacked and handed us each a copy. There were places on it for all signatures. He had two copies in front of him.

When everything was laid out, a look of avarice came over his face. That look seems to translate across all cultures and creatures. "Anyone plan on dropping out?"

No one said anything, so he said, "Let the signing party begin."

We all signed the copy in front of us on our line. Then we shifted one position around the table and signed the next copy and then the next and so on until we had all finished. Grasnick then paper clipped each set of copies together and said, "You can keep the quill that you used as a memento of this significant day. I advise you to put your copy of the contract in your vault as long as you are here.

"As agreed, your money will be delivered to Mr. Lovegood's vault on the next business day. Good luck with your business."

Then he quickly turned and called over his shoulder, "If you've got any questions, don't hesitate to get in touch." And he disappeared into the depths of the bank.

No one seemed to be in a particularly good mood. Somehow Gringotts seems to do that to you. We didn't even get together afterwards for a drink. I went back to Hogwarts and checked in with Filch who had a list of things for us to do to get ready for the big graduation.

It was lucky that we did have a lot to do between getting dorm rooms ready for guests, setting out under tents chairs, ready to be set up on the coming Friday, and setting up tables and chairs in the Great Hall for the reception after graduation. The House Elves wanted help with preparing canapés that were going to be preserved by some spell or another to be served.

Filch was adamant that that was not in our job descriptions. He even led me up to the Head's office to protest. We didn't get very far. She just waved a hand airily at us and said, "Oh, this only happens about once a century. You could help out like everyone else just this once."

She, of course, won the dispute. We ended up on Wednesday and Thursday in the kitchen peeling potatoes and apples.

On Wednesday night, we were sitting in our office resting from the hardest day's work that either of us had done in a very long time. Filch was reading the *Prophet*. He was constantly looking for good deals in the want ads. But that evening, he was reading the front section. He had his feet up on his desk when he whooped and tried to get up too fast. His chair fell over backwards and I ran around the desk to help him up.

He was laughing and said, "Well, me lad, you've made the papers."

"What do you mean?"

He opened the front section to page eight and folded it several times so that there was only one advert visible. It said that Lovegood Publishing, LLC was about to release a new Potions textbook that was appropriate for upper levels of Potions and use in general practice. All schools were invited to send for a complimentary copy. There was an address, of course.

Filch exclaimed, "Look, look!" and gestured at the authors. And there it was as clear as the nose on my face, "translated by Mr. Dudley Dursley from notes of Severus Snape, edited by Horace Slughorn."

I hadn't heard that we were going to advertise, but it was a pleasant surprise. Filch was clapping me on the back and asked what I was going to do now that I was rich and famous.

I could hardly talk, my mouth was smiling so broadly, but I managed to allow that I wasn't quite rich yet, and it wasn't clear that I was famous either. Filch wouldn't have any of it, and the only thing that we could do was open a fresh bottle of his fire whiskey and have a toast or two or ten.

I managed to come away that night, having only had two shots of the retched whiskeys but he had several. I didn't have a really bad hangover in the morning, but it certainly made our extra work all the harder to do.

The day of graduation dawned bright and early. The day was lovely, which was good. I didn't fancy having to wait for the last minute to see if we'd have bad weather and have to scramble to set up in the Great Hall for both graduation and reception. We set up chairs, helped the House Elves and managed to finish shortly after lunch. The graduation was set to begin at 3 PM. We actually had time to help the teachers greet guests who were going to spend the night to find their rooms. Most had attended Hogwarts, so they really didn't need help finding their rooms other than being given the temporary passwords for all Houses – Zen. They could hardly forget. There was a sign over the entrance of all houses announcing the password.

There were surprises. Lovegood showed up shortly after lunch, levitating several cardboard boxes. I asked him what they were.

"Why they're programs for the graduation, dear boy. What else would I be carrying?"

I just stood with my mouth agape. Just then, the Head arrived and exclaimed, "Good! Just in time. Mr. Filch and Mr. Dursley will show you where we want the programs."

Filch asked my question for me, "You printed the programs?"

Lovegood looked slightly hurt, "Of course. I'm a publisher. Why wouldn't I?"

Lovegood went along with me to where I was taking the programs at the entrance to the field where the graduation was to happen. He nudged me gently in the ribs and said, "This is the first run from our new printing press!"

I was surprised, "You sure didn't waste any time."

"No, somehow, Professor Wendt got me the job, and I barely had time to pay for the press, get it delivered, and run off these. We didn't make a lot of money, but it's a start."

I had another bigger surprise. Back at the castle, there was a commotion going on. As I approached the entrance to the castle, I made out a short wizard in a cape that seemed about 6 inches too long for him. He was shouting and gesturing wildly. Filch was standing defiantly with his chin stuck out. I couldn't make out what they were saying, but as I approached, Filch turned and noticed me.

"Mr. Dursley, this madman seems to want you."

At the sound of my name, he turned instantly and strode to me. I couldn't make out everything that he said, but it boiled down to something like this, "Dursley, you're the one who is publishing that cursed book by that . . that . . Deatheater."

"Well, yes. But it's not just me. I have help . . "

He stepped forward and drew his wand, pointing it at my nose, "Do you realize that he killed my sister?"

I was trying to get myself oriented to this strange claim. "What are you talking about?"

"Snape," he spit the word out, covering my robe with spittle, "Snape slaughtered my sister with the *Adavra Kedavra* curse. And you want to make his name famous in every wizard home in the world!!"

While I was concentrating on what to say to that, he went on, "Nothing to say. How could you. He's indefensible, and his memory should disappear without a trace the way my sister did!"

He sobbed at that and seemed ready for a new harangue when Professor Hagrid arrived. "Filch, what's going on here?"

Hagrid is intimidating to anyone, but alongside Hagrid, Burbage seemed a pygmy. But Burbage looked up at the mountain and was unmoved. As a matter of fact Burbage turned on him and said, "And you! I suppose you were here when Snape was the Headmaster!" It seemed to be an accusation as damning as any that Burbage could utter.

Hagrid practically snarled, "See here. Have you got a ticket?"

It was such an unexpected question that Burbage hesitated and asked, "Ticket?"

"Yes, a ticket for the graduation."

Burbage barked a laugh, "We're talking murder and you want a ticket?"

Hagrid rarely lost his temper, but this was one of the times. He took the man's robe in his hand, bunching up the material just below Burbage's face and lifted him slightly from the ground. "You will leave the grounds of Hogwarts now, or I will assist you to. And if you return, I won't wait to be polite."

Burbage tried to free himself for a few seconds and then said, "All right for now! But we'll see later."

Hagrid let him drop and watched as he turned slowly and strode determinedly off.

He'd gotten a good distance away and I was turning from watching him walk to the edge of the castle property where he could disapparate when I suddenly found arms around my waist and something wet on my neck. I whirled around and the arms let me slip around without letting me go and I found myself looking straight into the eyes of Pam.

"You're still a student. Do you want to get me in trouble?"

Her eyes sparkled as she whispered, "I am not, I'm an adult and this is graduation day! I'm a graduate." She had determination in her voice as she spoke.

"Well, you're not a graduate until you cross the stage and get your delicate hands on that diploma."

She kissed me on the lips and then said, "I'll show you delicate hands."

I disengaged her hands as gently as I could, which was not easy. She was determined. But Filch intervened, and his voice was full of menace, "No you aren't dearie. You're still a student until the Headmistress declares all you guttersnipes to be graduates. Now, move along and don't bother my assistant." Filch has a patented threat voice that is amazing.

She pouted and turned to leave. I wasn't sure whether I should thank Filch or not, but she disappeared into the castle and it was over. I looked around as though I were assessing the state of the grounds.

Filch smirked at me, "Oh, get out of here. You're no good to me now and we've done all the damage we can anyway."

Another surprise was that the Weasley family was there. It shouldn't have been if I'd taken time to think, but I'd not realized that the youngest Weasley was in the year '00 graduating class. I watched them idly. I'd never seen so much flaming red hair in one spot in my whole life.

Along with the Weasleys was another big surprise – Harry Potter. When we saw each other, I don't know which of us was more surprised. We both stood transfixed for at least five minutes, each trying to decide what to do. Finally, Harry walked over toward me. I was not going to be outdone by him, so I started to walk toward him.

When we got within handshaking distance, neither of us appeared to know what to do, but Harry spoke first, "Well, Big D, I guess I should have guessed that you might be here. I never seem to have a summer when I don't have a run-in with you, but frankly, you're the last person in the world that I expected to see.

"How can you possibly be here?"

I had to smile. Here was something that he didn't know. "I work here now."

Harry's jaw dropped, "Never!"

"I'm afraid so. I'm Filch's assistant."

"Filch." He shook his head, "I guess that would have to be it. A Muggle working for a Squib."

My smile broadened as I relished the news that I was going to give him. "Oh, no. Not a Muggle. A Wizard working for a Squib."

As if his jaw hadn't dropped enough, it descended further. He looked at me very closely, "Yes, I suppose you are." He leant back and nodded his head slowly. "And McGonagall puts up with you?"

I shrugged, "Sure. I'm not any dumber than the average Wizard."

He stared some more and said, "No, I meant. . . " He hesitated and seemed to think better of what he was going to say. "I meant that there was a time when you'd have ended up in Slytherin House, but maybe not now."

I just nodded dumbly and tried to think of something to say. I finally asked, "What have you been doing since, well, I guess it's almost two years now?"

Harry nodded and said, "I've been trying to decide what to do with my life."

Something occurred to me to say, and it was actually kind of good, "Well, when you've saved the world, what is there left to do?" That seemed to have broken the ice. We both laughed, and we actually shook hands.

He said, "I wish we'd gotten off to a better start all those years ago."

"Me too. I was pretty much a pill. I don't know what happened. I guess I just needed to get into a place where I had to win my way."

He looked at me quizzically, "So you like it here?"

I shrugged, "Yeh. I do."

Harry laughed and nodded, "There was a time when I thought that I didn't want to do anything else than spend the rest of my life here."

"But no more?"

"No. I've lost too many friends here. I can't look down the Great Hall without thinking of them – Fred Weasley, Cedric Diggery," He hesitated again and blinked something away. "I can't believe I'm saying it, but I even miss Snape."

I corrected him, "Headmaster Snape."

"OH, yeh. I could never get that right. He was another that I wish I'd gotten off to a better start with." He turned away for a minute and when he'd composed himself he turned back.

"Funny you should mention him. I've kind of been working on a project with him."

Potter stared at me and asked, "What are you talking about!"

"Well, he had this book, you see. It was an advanced . . ."

Potter interrupted me, "An advanced Potion-making textbook, right?"

"Sure, how did you know?"

He looked away again and took his time returning my gaze. "I had that book a couple of years ago. It was the textbook I used in 6th year, but I was sure that it was destroyed in the fire in the Room of Requirement. I guess I have to explain that to you."

I surprised him, "Oh, no. I know all about the Room of Requirement. You're right, there was a fire there, but it didn't destroy the book. As a matter of fact, there was a lot that survived OK. I got a neat desk out of the Room of Requirement and the book was pretty much undamaged except for the cover being a little singed."

He shook his head—sadly? "Maybe it would have been better if it had been destroyed. There were more than potions in it."

"Oh, I know." I declared happily, "But the only things we're doing for now are the potions."

He snapped to attention, "What do you mean, 'doing'?"

"Oh, we're about to publish a book based on Headmaster Snape's potion notes. Don't you read the *Prophet*?"

Potter seemed to be engrossed in his thoughts and only answered absently, "Not when I can help it." He looked up at me then and said, "I suppose that's OK. I used those things without a second thought about their safety and without knowing whether they worked or not."

I agreed, "Oh, I know. We tested them all."

Potter looked at me again, carefully, "Just who is 'we'?"

I laughed, "Why the only potions master around here these days – Professor Slughorn."

He seemed to consider that a bit and then said, "Well, good luck with the book. I'm out of the potions business myself. I doubt I'll buy a copy.

"Well, I've got to catch up the Weasley's. I'd be in so much trouble if I missed being with Ginny's family for her graduation. Maybe I'll see you at the reception after."

I wished him goodbye and good luck, but I doubted that he'd go out of his way to find me at the reception.

After everyone else was seated, I took a chair in the back row next to the far right side. I watched the procession of the two classes of graduates. The class of '99 was in red robes, and the class of '00 was in green. After they were all seated on the front rows – the class of '00 on the right and the '99's on the left, the Head took the podium and welcomed everyone. She explained that as this was a double graduation, there would be two salutatorians speak and two valedictorians. The class of '99 would go first. Finally, there was some sort of agreement struck among the speakers that the order would not be traditional. The valedictorian of the class of '99 would go first and the valedictorian of the class of '00 would be last.

She then introduced the honorees, although everyone could read in the program that they were:

- Valedictorian '99 – Hermione Grainger
- Salutatorian '99 – Neville Longbottom

- Salutatorian '00 – Pamela Myers (woohoo!)
- Valedictorian '00 – Padma Patil

Grainger strode up to the podium and apparently had to stand on a low stool to be seen above the podium. She spoke smoothly at first,

"Professors, Staff, Parents, Students, my fellow speakers have agreed to drop the normal speech traditions for this joint graduation. There are so many of our classmates both recent graduates and those who would have been graduates that have died in the War that we've decided that we will honor them by simply naming them. I will take the odd number years backwards from my class to the graduating class when we were first years. Neville will take the even number years. Pamela will take the odd number years forward to the year of graduation of those who were first years last year. Likewise, Padma will take the even years likewise."

Then she looked down to the paper and began naming names. She held up quite well at first. When she reached the class of '97, she faltered once or twice and stopped when she tried to read the name, Fred Weasley. She stood there trying to read that name but failing. Someone jumped up, walked to the podium, patted her on the back, and said, "Let me finish yours."

She nodded and sat down. It turned out that he was Neville Longbottom. He read the names starting with Fred Weasley and continuing through the class of '99 and then back down the even number classes.

Pam took the podium and started with the class of '01, and I was proud of her. She obviously had lost a good friend or two, and with a catch or two of voice, kept going. Padma took over with the even years and ended with her own year. She had a cold fury in her voice at the end that made me happy that I'd never crossed her this year.

The only applause was the soft respectful applause that each name received as it was named. After Padma had left the podium, the Head returned to it. She looked around the audience and took a deep breath as if preparing for something that she didn't relish. Then, she spoke.

"I have to ask for your forbearance for an overlong introduction of our speaker." I immediately glanced down at my program and realized that I didn't recognize the name. She was continuing, "He is a Muggle, of course. I chose him to speak because his experience in the Muggle Second World War gives him a perspective that is very valuable for us just coming away from our own great war.

"He never fought on a battle ground. He never led an army. He never was on the same continent where the great war was fought, but he is probably as responsible for the end of that war as any single man is. He didn't invent the terrible nuclear weapon that brought the war to an end. But my adviser tells me that he just made it work.

"He is an expert in the Muggle study called, 'Elemental Participle Physics', whatever that is. He invented some kind of diagram named after him." She hesitated as if puzzled and then said, "Oh, yes. I see. He's also something of an artist. He painted and his painting can be found in museums and bars all around Pasadena, California. He also won a Nobel Prize, which Professor Wendt tells me is quite a big deal.

"So, please give a warm welcome to Professor Richard Feynman."

An old man with scant white hair stood and came to the podium. He looked around the audience and began to speak, but I couldn't hear him. The Head jumped up and came to the podium. She took out her wand and placed it against his throat and spoke a spell that I didn't hear. Then, when he spoke, everyone could hear him clearly.

"That wand thingee is pretty handy. I wish I had one." Everyone laughed.

"The Headmistress has left out one of my main accomplishments. I'm a crack lock pick." More laughter.

"At the end of World War II, there were many people who wanted to inflict on the losers retribution that would be remembered for generations. And it was hard to argue against them. The Axis countries had bombed London mercilessly. They killed six million non-combatant prisoners who had only the fact that they worshipped God against them. They intended to rule the world for a thousand years. And they came closer to achieving that than many people would admit.

"Luckily for the world, they didn't. The victors did not impose on the losers the usual revenge that victors are so effective at doing. That was lucky for the vanquished AND it was even luckier for the victors.

"In the history of the world, almost uniformly, the merciful truly do inherit the Earth. I'm not speaking metaphorically where the good in heart have the comfort of being good in heart. NO! I speak literally. At the end of World War I, the Muggle "Great War", the revengers won out. Germany was treated to revenge that they probably didn't deserve. That sewed the seeds of World War II, which very nearly reversed the revenge onto the victors of World War I.

"By contrast, the victors of World War II treated the vanquished with real mercy and more than mercy. They helped them rebuild so that the vanquished, the Germans and the Japanese, are among the strongest countries in the world. That success did not impoverish the victors. Indeed, the victors became even more successful that the vanquished had. The Americans, of whom I am one, became the strongest nation on the face of the earth. You English became what Shakespeare always dreamed you would become,

'This royal throne of kings, this scepter'd isle,
This earth of majesty, this seat of Mars,

183

This other Eden, demi-paradise,
This fortress built by Nature for herself
Against infection and the hand of war,
This happy breed of men, this little world,
This precious stone set in the silver sea,
Which serves it in the office of a wall,
Or as a moat defensive to a house,
Against the envy of less happier lands,
This blessed plot, this earth, this realm, this England'

"Or consider America's great Civil War. The victors of that internecine struggle, far more fierce even than World War II, imposed on the losing Southerners vile retribution. We have suffered from the consequences of that retribution ever since. We stand about to enter the second Century after that conflict and still are rent by its consequences.

"So it goes throughout history.

"I ask three things of you students about to become full adults:

"First, I ask you to extend mercy to all the Deatheaters with malice toward none, to steal a phrase from America's greatest leader, Lincoln. That mercy should include a measure of justice for the very worst, but a justice leavened with mercy.

"Second, I ask you to extend mercy to your own people who did not stand bravely beside you when you fought your Civil War.

"Finally, I ask you to have a thumping wonderful party, which I intend on joining with you."

With that, he walked away from the podium and took his seat, but the crowd leapt to its feet and gave him an ovation that was thunderous. He rose slightly, bowed, and sat again. The crowd was not to be satisfied with such a little gesture. They continued to applaud as though they expected an encore. Finally, he stood fully and ambled to the podium.

"I thought you English were so very restrained. Well, since you insist on hearing something more, I'll give you a bit of the speech that didn't make the 'cut'."

The crowd had largely quieted and then became utterly still.

"I decided not to give you the usual tripe that commencement speakers dish out. You know, 'Yours is the greatest class, you're the smartest, you're bound for certain success, blah, blah, blah.' Instead, I'll tell you something that will really be useful to you if you only have enough sense to think about it.

"The truth is that you will NOT succeed at everything you try. You will face fear of failure. Yes, whether it's fear of failing to get a date with that pretty redhead sitting next to you—yes, I mean you in the second row —or if it's fear of the ultimate failure of life, being unable to live as anything other than a beggar on the streets of Diagon Alley.

"You will face such fears not once, but often in your life. And, more than that, those fears will come true at least once in your life if not often. When those failures happen, especially if they are the worst of fears, you still can maintain a degree of happiness in your life. That happiness will proceed, if you let it, from exercising the power that you have and cannot be taken from you to extend mercy to the people around you.

"Further, it's possible to start the exercise of that power right now.

"Anyone can serve in a food pantry—even if you need the food pantry's services yourself. Almost anyone can help someone else learn to read. Anyone can be a friend to someone who is friendless.

"You can practice it and become so good at it that it becomes second nature to you—a second nature that will not fail you in your worst moments."

He stepped away from the podium, and this time, no amount of applause would tempt him back to it. The rest of the graduation proceeded. The graduates marched across the stage and received their diplomas. The Assistant Head read each one's two greatest achievements while at Hogwarts, and then the next graduate took her place to receive her diploma.

I learned a lot at that graduation. I learned that Hogwarts has an alma mater. I tried to forget as quickly as I could after singing it. I learned that there was a tradition of the graduating class doing a practical joke on the next class. This year, the two graduating classes had filled the hourglasses that show the score of points that each House earns with stones from the beach so that no points could be added to any of them.

As the crowd broke up and headed back to the castle for the reception, I just stayed seated. I didn't want to jostle with parents and graduates to get in a line that wound all the way around the Great Hall to reach the refreshment table. So, I sat, gazing off at the lake and was surprised when something hit my knee. I looked up and found that Feynman was standing over me swinging his cane like Charlie Chaplin.

When I noticed him, he asked, "Aren't you going up to have something to eat?"

"Sometime."

"Well, we're at the end of the line. Why don't we do it now? I hear that the House Dwarves of Hogwarts make a 'mean cuisine' as we would say in the States, and I don't want to miss it."

Fully awake now, I nodded, "Yes, sir, you're right. But it's . . . uh . . . House Elves, not Dwarves."

"Whatever, let's go!"

185

As we walked up slowly - he seemed to feel his age – I tried to think of something to say. "Well, I'm surprised you didn't walk up with the Head . . Headmistress."

He seemed to be cantankerous by nature. He just said, "I sent her on along. It will be a sad day when I can't walk up a little hill without a nurse to escort me." I didn't mention the fact that I was sort of nursing him.

I asked, "How did she find you? It's unusual for anyone to know Muggles."

"Oh, it was that Muggle Professor that she likes. He suggested me."

So, it was Wendt. Interesting. We reached the castle, and I led him in to the Great Hall. He could hardly have missed it, but he seemed happy that I'd brought him along. As we went, he asked questions about the moving portraits that he'd spotted. There are none on the main floor but all you have to do is pass a staircase, and you're close to several. He was fascinated by them, and fascinated by the fact that you could have a conversation with one of them.

He actually stopped at one staircase and took a couple of steps up to be at eye level with the portrait. He asked it a couple of questions but didn't get much in the way of answers. He asked, "Where are you?"

The old man in a large ruff said, "Well, I'm in the main hall of Hogwarts, of course."

"No. I mean your surroundings in the portrait where is that?"

"Oh, it was a room in the artist's studio. All this backdrop is stage-dressing."

Feynman thought about that for quite some time. Then he asked, "Can you leave the studio?"

"Of course. I'm also in a portrait hanging in my home in the Lake Country. I can go there."

"Is that what the background of that painting shows?"

"No. No. That portrait was done in a drawing room of a house that I used to own."

Feynman became excited at that, "How do you go from one to the other?"

The portrait laughed, "I walk. The backgrounds are connected, but I can move from one portrait here to another." In demonstration he turned away and walked out of the portrait and showed up in the portrait next to him. As he appeared in it, he addressed the portrait he'd just entered, "Pardon, ma'am, I'm just demonstrating something to this gentlemen."

186

She was a much later portrait. The clothes seemed relatively modern, and in the background was a window that showed a cloudy sky over the Thames.

Feynman asked, "When were you first conscious?"

The portrait thought a moment, "I guess my first memory was when I was a child in the park with my Mother. Probably."

Feynman was getting excited again, "No, I mean when were you first aware of being in this portrait?"

The portrait shrugged, "I don't know exactly. I remember coming to and from the studio and my home. Then one day as I was sitting, the artist seemed to walk away. Afterwards, he never returned. I got up and tried to find him, but I couldn't leave the studio for a very long timed. Then, one day, there was that other home that I could enter. And then, maybe twenty years later, there suddenly were all these other paintings here that I could get into. I don't have a clear idea of when that happened because there didn't used to be so many places that I could go."

"Doesn't it get boring in there?"

"Oh, sure, but I must have hundreds of acquaintances now. I can go anywhere from the African Veldt to Hong Kong, from the 10th century to the 20th. I can make or receive visits. Not bad, what?"

Feynman took a deep breath and said to me, "Let's go. I could spend months here but I really need to be on my way."

We proceeded and entered the Great Hall, which was crowded, noisy, and full of happy conversations. Most, I supposed, were students happy to be out of Hogwarts for good. I led him to a table of hors d'oeuvres and we had all the delicacies that the House Elves could devise. We hadn't browsed long when I was happily surprised to see Pam approach with a man and woman whom I supposed to be her parents.

When they arrived, Pam made introductions. Their names were Roger and Hildegard. They were both surprised when I introduced Feynman. He asked if they were Wizards. When they admitted it, he congratulated them and would have turned back to the hors d'oeuvre table, but Roger wanted to know more about Elemental Participle Physics.

Feynman laughed, "There's a little misunderstanding here. It's Elementary Particle Physics. That means the study of the smallest building blocks of the world."

Roger became animated, "OOH. I know about that. You're talking about atoms, right?"

Feynman nodded and said, "You've pretty much got the idea."

Roger continued, "Then what are these diagrams of yours?"

Feynman scratched his head and said, "Well, suppose that you wanted to calculate the power of the forces between two uh atoms."

Roger asked, "Why would I want to do that?"

Hildegard (who liked to be called Hilde by friends), "Now, Roger, let the poor man get something to eat. We'll come back later and talk about these Participle atoms."

She then took my arm and said, "What we really want is to talk with you, Mr. Dursley."

As we walked, Hilde asked, "Are you really publishing a book with Professor Slughorn or is that a cousin or something?"

I agreed, "Yup, that's me."

She squeezed my arm a bit tighter and enthused, "Really!"

Roger added, "Of course, it is Hilde. I told you that Pam was a sensible girl and would get a practical boyfriend."

Of course, this was a development that I never dreamed of when Slughorn and I started working on the book. It seemed too good to be true!

Meanwhile Pam wanted to take my arm as well, so I was walking between Mother and Daughter as they navigated me to a table where we sat and the Myers introduced me to some of their friends. They were apparently mostly Ravenclaw alumni. The inevitable question came up and came up quickly of what house I was from. I decided to play a little game with them and started by saying, "When I first came to Hogwarts, I was in Gryffindor, but an unfortunate incident happened and the administration required me to move to Huffelpuff. Though, come to think of it, I had to stay for a while with one of the professor, while they looked for a house that would take me."

One of the former Ravenclaws commented, "Well, you couldn't have done anything too bad, or they wouldn't let you in Huffelpuff."

Roger added, "They'd have begged for you in Slytherin." There was general laughter at the joke.

Pam just gazed at me speculatively and, being devious, asked, "How many OWL's did you get?"

That made me think fast, but my old motto to tell the truth whenever possible during a lie came to my rescue. "I'm not proud of it, but I didn't earn any OWL's."

She laughed at that. Everyone stared at her as though she'd struck me when I was down, but I smiled and assured them that I wasn't offended in the least. I added, "What's important is what a man does with what he has – not what he doesn't do with what he doesn't have."

That set them all to thinking and seemed to be generally approved. Mrs. Myers invited me to visit now that summer was here. And she demanded dates. I hadn't thought about the possibility that family would want to spend time with me. I thought about it and came up with an answer that would put the real decision off a bit.

"Well, this weekend, Mr. Filch and I . . ."

But just at that moment I heard a voice behind me that was very familiar. As I turned, he was saying, "Well, Mr. Dursley, are you going to introduce me or do I need to." He didn't give me a chance to perform that duty but started directly in, "I'm Argus Filch, Department Head of Facilities Maintenance—Mr. Dursley's boss. I take a lively interest in Mr. Dursley's concerns being as you might say 'a loco parents'." He extended a gnarled hand toward Mrs. Myers who took it tentatively.

I inserted names, "Mrs. Myers, Mr. Myers. You know Miss Myers, I believe."

He nodded and replied briskly, "Yup."

The rest of the people at the table introduced themselves, which was lucky for me, since I needed a refresher. Filch continued to stand there and said, "You go right ahead with your talk, and don't mind me."

So, I went on, "I'll be involved with cleaning up after this party this weekend and next week we'll be getting things in order after the school year. Maybe the following weekend I can visit."

Filch added, "Yes, sir. I depend greatly on Mr. Dursley to keep the castle ship-shape. But if we move ass that next weekend ought to be good for an outing for him."

Mr. Myers said that he'd keep that in mind and that he thought that weekend would be fine for a visit. It was embarrassing enough without Filch hovering over me, and I searched my mind for some scheme to get him away. But relief came from a completely unexpected direction.

Another voice that I knew sounded and was addressing Filch, "Mr. Filch, there you are. I've been looking for you. There's someone that I want to introduce you to – a Mr. Beam, J. Beam. Would you join us?" It was Professor Wendt. When he reached us, he put his arm around Filch's shoulder and urged him away with him.

Filch's eyes switched back and forth between Wendt and me. Finally, he decided with Wendt. As they left, Wendt said to me, "I'll catch you up later" and winked at me.

There was never a more grateful student receiving an "O+" on a paper in his class than I was at that moment. The atmosphere at the table completely changed, and one of the Ravenclaws asked, "How does a published author put up with it?"

That struck me as extremely rude, especially since Filch wasn't there. I was conflicted how to answer. I didn't want to embarrass Pam or her family, but I didn't want the comment to go unanswered either. Finally, I just said, "Every beginning author has to have a 'day job', and I could hardly have a better one. I'm here at Hogwarts. I am surrounded by the finest people—every single one of them." I tried to put emphasis on that last phrase.

It's true that Filch is boring, drinks bad liquor, is bigoted, and has a million other bad habits, but he has always been good to me and looked out for my best interest. I truly think that he was there at the table for that very reason. He wanted to look out for me in his self-assigned role *in loco parentis*.

Time flew in the presence of Pam as on a jetliner. Before I noticed, the Great Hall had nearly emptied, including the Ravenclaw couple from our table. I stood and fumbled for something to say, "I really have to look up Filch, and we need to get started straightening up after the reception."

Pam rose from the other side of her mum and walked around to me. She spoke to me in a low voice, "Please send an owl, and we'll get together before your visit." With that, as quick as lightning, she took my forearm and leaned in to plant the breath of a kiss on the cheek facing away from the table.

I stumbled away backwards saying goodbye, and the parents waved. I had no idea where I was going, but I turned and strode out of the Great Hall not even trying to think of a destination.

The Manor

The weekend was a blur of cleanup and wild imaginings of what Pam and I might do on our first real, official, legal date. Filch was constantly complaining of my sleep-walking through work. On Saturday we cleaned up everything from the reception and got the chairs organized from the field where the graduation had happened. We were lucky that it didn't rain – we'd have had to get the chairs inside the Great Hall in a hurry.

On Sunday, I started to think about a date with Pam. It was at that moment that I realized just how isolated that we were here at the castle. How could I discover anything to do with Pam other than go out to dinner? Without a newspaper, there were no movie listings, no shows advertised, nothing. Sure, there was the *Prophet*. It listed concerts and things, but I was determined to impress Pam with all the unique things that Muggles do.

I was moping around the Great Hall after lunch when an idea occurred to me. I went to Slughorn's office and found that he was not in. Not surprising. As I was ambling back upstairs another thought occurred.

Professor Wendt WAS in his office. He had the one double-window thrown wide, and the sunlight of a beautiful summer day flooded his office. I'd never been there during the day when the weather was nice and the window wide. It lifted my spirits just to be there. And the fact that he was present helped as well.

"What can I do for you Mr. Dursley?" Wendt was sitting at his desk, quill in hand, apparently writing something.

"I've noticed that you often have *The Times* in your office. You don't happen to have a recent one, do you?"

He beamed, "I have a subscription, and today's is over there on the sofa torn apart so that I could find the sports page. Have a look at whatever you like."

I immediately started looking for the Culture section. I found it and looked for music. There was a listing of clubs and some concerts. I glanced at the movie section. I soon realized that I needed a sheet of parchment to make notes on. Wendt was happy to give me one and loan me a quill. He noticed the section that I was looking at and asked, "You looking for some kind of treat for your fancy lady?"

I must have turned red. My face was certainly warm. I nodded.

"Summer seems to offer all sorts of possibilities – especially when you can disapparate almost anywhere."

And there was the rub. I still hadn't learned to reliably disapparate even though I had a license. With all the extra hours that I'd been putting in on the book, I just hadn't had time to learn. It was very embarrassing to have to ask your date for a lift.

Wendt seemed to sense what my problem was, "You haven't learned to disapparate yet, right?"

I shook my lowered head. "Oh, I have a license, but I wouldn't take a chance with . . . uh . . . Pam." I suddenly realized that I could actually use her name safely.

"Well, you've been very busy. The summer is a good time to practice. Without students, Hogwarts is a much quieter place."

I'd made all the notes that I needed, so I thanked the Professor and, taking my notes, left. I'd study them in the office and send off an owl to Pam.

▽

It was Tuesday before I finally got the note off. I still hadn't quite the knack of tying a note on the leg of an owl. At least, I remembered to bring some owl treats up to bribe one of the little beggars. I watched him fly off into the bright sun and wondered when I'd hear from Pam.

That evening, the teachers and staff who were still at Hogwarts were in the Faculty Lounge. We typically ate meals in the Faculty Lounge – especially when the group was fewer than a dozen. It was a compact cheerful group. There was almost always – except in real cold or foul weather – a window open. Its function was allowing owls in to deliver. That evening, as we approached the end of the meal, an owl flew in and came directly to me.

Of course, I was expecting an owl from Pam and was eager to rip open the envelope that was addressed, Mr. Dudley Dursley, Hogwarts Castle, Faculty Lounge, third chair from right. It was a little strange that it was a package rather than a simple note. Also, the address was a little formal compared to the few other owls that I'd had from Pam, but I could have cared less. I ripped open the envelope and found a book with a folded note protruding from it.

192

I glanced at the cover. The book was *Advanced Potions* by Eldridge Cleaver. It was old and fairly tattered. Why in the world would Pam send me that? Then I had a happy thought. Perhaps, it was sort of a reverse Graduation gift. It was hers and she was graduated and no longer needed it AND it was an old version of what Slughorn and I were about to publish. Very fitting.

I pulled the folded piece of parchment out of the book and unfolded it.

⊠

My eyes expected to see her fine flowing quillmanship. And for a moment, I thought it was hers. But as I began to read, I saw immediately that it couldn't have been from her.

Wendt, who always seems to observe things that you wish he never would, must have noticed something suspicious because he immediately asked me, "Something the matter, Dursley?"

I looked up from the note, and for a moment all I could do was gape. The Head was instantly up and beside me. "Would you like to come to my office?"

Almost as quickly, Slughorn rose and was on his way around the table. I controlled my voice with an effort and said, "Yes."

The Head took me by the arm and we started for her office. When she noticed that both Wendt and Slughorn were following, She turned to face them down directly, but Wendt just frowned, and the Head relented, "Very well, perhaps you two should come."

When we got into her inner office, she did something to seal the door to the outer office and commented, "I don't want to be interrupted. Now, please tell us what has disturbed you so."

I said, "I'll just read the note.

"Mr. Dursley, you may think that you and Slughorn have triumphed over me, but I think not. I know who the apple of your eye is. You will collect all manuscripts, the original potion book, and any notes that you have. Then, grasp the potions book that I've sent you. It is a port key. It will activate at 10 PM this night. It will bring you to the place where you may trade them for Ms. Myers' life.

"Don't make the mistake of thinking that bringing Aurors or anyone else will help you. I've administered a poison that will kill her by midnight unless I administer the antidote. You may kill me or capture me but you can't force me to give it her.

"Be prompt. Bring everything."

193

Wendt immediately asked Slughorn, "Does Lovegood have any copies?"

Speechless, he just shook his head. Then he added, "He didn't want the manuscript until he'd finished printing the programs for the graduation."

I asked him, "Is that possible? You can surely brew an antidote?"

Slughorn's speech failed him again. He shook his head and sighed, "IF I had a sample of the poison, which Burbage has surely destroyed. Even if I had a sample, I can't guarantee that I could brew the antidote in less than half a day."

The Head asked, "What about a Bezor? That's effective against almost all poisons."

He was becoming testy. He compressed his lips and spit out, "MOST poisons, and I'll surely bring several, but there's no guarantee that he hasn't picked one that a Bezor would not be effective against."

Everyone started speaking at once. Then Wendt stopped and said in a tone that commanded one to listen, "Here's the way we have to work this.

"First, you two, get every scrap of paper that you ever wrote anything about the book on. I mean absolutely everything. Return here then."

"Second, I'll go get something that might be useful in this situation." The Head sniffed her apparent disdain for whatever Wendt was off to get.

"Third, everyone meet back here no later than a quarter to ten."

I took off for my office and then on to my quarters in Hufflepuff. When I arrived, I pulled all the drawers out of my desk and pulled anything that even looked like a piece of parchment out of them and stuffed them in a sack.

Filch was surprised and wanted to know what I was doing. I just screamed at him, "Never mind. I'll tell you later." I added to myself, "If there is a later."

I then went to Hufflepuff. When I got there, I gave the password, and the painting smiled and said, "I just changed the password."

"When?"

"About thirty seconds ago."

"I don't have time for games. Open up!"

She just smiled.

I turned to face the painting directly, "Goddammit! If you don't open up and open up right now, I'll use this wand to blast a hole in that wall, and I won't bother to take you off it." I knew that my wand would do that for sure. There was a hole in the moon to prove it.

That seemed to be an effective threat because the painting opened immediately, and I ran through as soon as there was a crack that I could squeeze through. In my room, I overturned my trunk and quickly scattered the contents around looking for anything that might have notes on it. I emptied my armoire and looked everywhere. I threw some things in the sack, and I glanced at my wrist. It was 9:30 already. I scanned the room one more time. Thank goodness everyone had left Hogwarts except staff!

I made it to the Head's office in record time. When I arrived, she and Wendt were talking. As I entered, they stopped. Slughorn wasn't in the office yet. He arrived in a couple of minutes carrying a sack even larger than mine. He was huffing and puffing, "I . . whoo. . . had lots of notes. I hope I got everything." He gasped again, and I could see perspiration rolling down his face.

Wendt nodded and immediately spoke, "Minerva and I have been discussing this, and we've agreed on a plan. The three of us will take the port key. She will stay in contact with me and try to send help when we discover where we are."

Slughorn asked, "How will she stay in contact?"

Wendt cut him off, "No time for explanations.

"Do both of you have your wands with you?"

We nodded.

"Good." He reached inside his robe and pulled a handgun out. The Head shook her head, but he talked to me, "You know what this is?"

I nodded.

"Have you ever used one?"

For a moment, I thought about whether to tell the truth but Wendt cut my thoughts off, "Spare me your modesty. Yes or no?"

I never had owned one, but a gang member had one that he'd stolen from his dad. We'd gone to an empty field and set up cardboard box with a couple of cans on it as targets. We both shot all the ammunition that we had trying to hit one of them. We never did. But technically, I had used one. I said, "Yes" somewhat uncertainly.

He said and demonstrated, "This is the safety. ON. OFF. ON. OFF.

"This cocks the trigger." A bullet ejected from the chamber.

"And the trigger fires it." He pointed the gun at a piece of blank wall and squeezed the trigger. The sound deafened us for a moment. The Head swore but I couldn't make out what she said. There was a small hole in the stone wall where the bullet hit.

"Now, this is a resource that we have that can be used by any of us in a real emergency." He returned it inside his robe. While he said that the Head shook her head violently.

He went on, "Let me do the negotiating. My intention is to give everything he wants to him." He looked around at all of us, daring any of us to disagree. None of us did. "When we have Ms. Myers, Slughorn, you'll disapparate her and any of the rest of us still standing to St. Mongo's. Come back with help but she goes first."

I heartily agreed with that. I glanced at my wrist. There were three minutes until ten. I held the port key up, and Slughorn and Wendt took firm grip of it. At the last minute, the Head came, kissed Wendt and held him for a second. Then she was back at her hearth.

The port key activated.

⊠

We spun and for a moment, I agreed with Wendt about traveling magically. We landed in a large dark room. My eyes didn't reveal any details at first. They became adapted to the dark, and I slowly perceived that we were in a large vaulted room near a large dining table.

A voice that reverberated in the room so that I wasn't sure of its direction spoke, "I know Slughorn, and I know Dursley, but I don't know you. Why are you here?" He was strangely relaxed in his way of speaking. Why?

Wendt mumbled something at first that I couldn't make out. I hoped to God that he wasn't cracking under the stress. Then he said in a voice that anyone could have understood, "I'm Professor Wendt of Hogwarts. I'm a Squibb and have absolutely no magical abilities. You have nothing to fear from me."

Burbage, if it were Burbage, seemed to digest that and then said, "Why are you here?"

Wendt's answer was perfectly flat, "I'm here to provide moral support for Slughorn and Dursley."

Burbage digested that a bit as well and then said, "Well, just so long as you all know that you can't talk me out of my threat, and there's no way that you can prevent it other than to co-operate."

Wendt answered quickly, "That was obvious from the beginning. We come with two sacks of parchment fragments, manuscripts, and the original book. We have no intent of doing anything other than co-operate."

Burbage almost seemed sorry about that. By this time, my eyes had dark adapted enough to see more detail. Something that I had completely missed before became apparent. There was a person hanging in midair over the table.

Burbage noticed my attention, "I wondered when you'd notice my other guest. Ms Myers hangs there. She has exactly 100 minutes left."

Wendt added, "Unless we co-operate. We are and will. What do we need to do?"

Burbage pointed his wands at the bags that we carried and said, "*Accio* bags." Mine flew out of my hands and landed beside him. He pulled them to the hearth that had wood laid for a fire. Then he said, "I'm going to burn these now, but first, we have to be sure that there are no others in existence."

Slughorn broke in, "How can you be sure?"

Burbage laughed, "It's very simple. I thought you were smart. How would you be sure in my place?"

Slughorn looked from Burbage to me and the Professor.

Burbage said, "Come, come. Time flies. How?"

Slughorn said, "I'd make everyone swear the unbreakable oath that there weren't any others."

Burbage nodded, "Exactly. So let's go."

I had never heard of this unbreakable oath thingee and said so. Burbage chuckled, "Do one of you want to explain it?"

Wendt wasted no time. "It's a magical contract. If anything you swear to is false, you die. I've never seen anyone actually die, but I've seen it administered a ton of times. People take it very seriously."

"Very good, Professor. They didn't make a Squibb a Professor at Hogwarts for nothing."

I immediately said, "No more wasted time. Let's go."

Burbage instructed us. Slughorn and I would clasp arms. He would say the oath, and we would repeat it. Slughorn and Wendt would follow.

Slughorn and I clasp arms, and he began the oath, "I swear that there is not another copy of . . ." At that point, Wendt shouted, "Stop!"

Burbage glanced up from us, "What! I thought you were here to co-operate?"

Wendt quickly said, "I am, but not in their death. Your oath is unnecessarily strong. I believe that they've brought all copies of the manuscript that they have any least idea of, but that doesn't mean that there isn't another fragmentary copy that exists that they don't know about. The only thing that does you any good is to be sure that all copies that they have any knowledge of are here."

Burbage thought about that for a long time. He seemed to be examining it, looking for flaws. Then he said, "But suppose there is another copy somewhere that they don't know about?"

Wendt smiled a little smile that crossed his face so quickly that I wasn't sure that I'd seen it. He answered, "If there is, but they don't know anything about it, how can they help you find it?"

He pondered that again. Finally, he said, "At least I'd know that it existed. I could go after it."

Wendt seemed stumped for a minute. Then he gazed around, and he said something that seemed completely crazy as an answer. "This is the Malfoy mansion, isn't it?" His voice was loud enough to resound around the hall.

Burbage strangely seemed on the defensive, "What if it is?"

"Oh, it just seemed like the kind of ironic thing that you tend to do —threaten to kill Ms Myer in the very room where your sister died."

"Well, you're right," he said with vehemence, "It is ironic, and it is where she was murdered."

I was going crazy wondering why Wendt was taking so much time, "Well, to answer your question, if you make them swear that oath, and they die, you'll die even before Ms. Myers does. Now, we don't want that, do we?"

I was puzzled, and then I thought of the handgun that Wendt had in his robe.

Burbage was silent for a long time, his eyes traveling back and forth between the three of us. It was driving me crazy sensing the minutes tick away while Slughorn and I stood stupidly holding hands. Finally, he said, "No, we don't. You're right. I'll rephrase that oath."

He began again, "I swear that I have no knowledge or belief." He paused as we repeated, and he went on, "that another copy whole or partial. . .". He paused again as we repeated. All the time there were lines that seemed to be of fire, pulsing and tightening around our arms. ". . .of the manuscript or original. . ." The lines of fire squeezed our arms mercilessly. ". . .of Severus Snape's potion book." My arm ached excruciatingly. ". . .Outside this room."

With our final repetition of the oath, the lines of fire disappeared, and we had our arms back. Burbage nodded at Wendt, "Now you."

Wendt simply said, "Certainly." However, I interrupted, "Do it with me, Professor. I think Slughorn's arm might not take a repeat of that ordeal."

Wendt said, "Sure." And Burbage just nodded at us. I took Wendt's right arm in mine, and we repeated the agony.

When it was over, nobody was dead. I shouted, "OK. The antidote!"

Burbage simply said, "Not so fast. I have to destroy the manuscripts."

I glanced at my wrist. It was 11:35. "God man, get moving. There's only 25 minutes left."

He flicked his wand at the hearth, and the logs burst into brilliant flame. The additional light let me see Pam's face clearly. She was pale and her hair hung down and almost reached the table. Meanwhile, he glanced at manuscript pages of parchment and tossed them in the flame where they caught fire, curled, and turned into ash that flew upward.

At least Burbage was quick. He'd emptied one sack in a couple of minutes, and I began to realize the loss that I was suffering. He began on the second sack and shortly whistled as he pulled the original textbook out.

"Hello, hello, hello. What do we have here?" He set it aside and kept shoveling manuscript into the flame.

When it was all gone, he picked up the book and opened it. "The Half-Blood Prince, eh? Is that what he fancied himself?

"Well, Half-Blood Prince, meet the prince of darkness." He almost lovingly tore pages out of the book somehow using his wand and flung them into the fire. I heard Slughorn gasp with each page. I was past caring —other than that he hurry so that he would have time to give Pam the antidote. I didn't dare urge him on—who knew what he would do.

Finally, the cover of the book went into the fire, which was now roaring and so hot that I didn't believe that he could stand so close. There were still more than five minutes left when the cover was no longer recognizable in the flames. He turned and said, "I am honorable even if Snape wasn't." He somehow conjured a syringe from thin air and with the other hand, motioned Pam to lower. She did slowly, and her head gently touched the table and then the rest of her. He used the syringe on some sort of port in the crook of her left elbow. Then he said, "It's finished."

Suddenly, the air was filled with coruscating beams of red. I dropped to my knees and saw Burbage fall. I rolled under the table and saw Wendt jump behind a chair but be struck. Then my eyes filled with red.

St. Mongo's

I had a splitting headache and seemed to be having a hard time moving my hands to my head. Somebody shone a bright light in my eyes and said, "Don't try to move just yet. You've been stunned and it will take several minutes more for it to completely wear off." I then realized that someone was holding an eyelid open, and I had enough control of my hand to swat his away.

"O.K. O.K. I'm coming around. Take the bleeding light out of my eyes."

It turned off. The voice asked, "Do you know where you are?"

I tried looking around. It looked like an emergency room. Then I began to remember. I said, "I hope this is Saint Mongrel's or something like that."

The voice said, "Close enough. You seem to be coming around pretty well. You should be able to be questioned by the Aurors shortly."

I leaned on one arm and raised myself enough to see that there were two others in the ward – Professor Slughorn and Professor Wendt. They seemed to be coming around too. However, before they were well enough to start talking themselves, an Auror helped me stand and said, "We'll go into a room where you can tell me your story."

I had to know, "What happened to Pam er Ms. Myers?"

"She's in the ICU. It's not clear how she'll come out of it, but she will live."

He took me to what looked like a small office. The Auror kicked its inhabitant, who seemed to be a nurse, out and had me sit. He took the seat behind the desk, and we talked about what happened. He had me tell my story frontwards and then backwards and then sideways and then upside down. Of course, it didn't look the same from each of those perspectives, but we worked on it so that the Auror finally admitted that he couldn't get anything more out of me.

"You're free to go. Don't leave the country." He handed me a card that had his name and owl post address on it. It also had that funny symbol that the Aurors wore instead of badges on their lapels. "If you need me at any time, you can get in touch by using this disk. Just touch it with your wand, and it will signal me that you want to talk. Then, I'll send my patronus."

I'd never heard of a patronus. "Oh, you'll know it when you see it," was the only thing that he would say. I asked what was going on with Slughorn and Wendt.

"They're still being interrogated. They'll be released shortly."

He wouldn't say anything else and left immediately. I went to the nearest nurse's station—although they called them Healer's Stations—and got directions to ICU. When I arrived, the Healer at the Healer's Station told me what room Pam was in but asked, "Are you family?"

"Not exactly."

"Well what are you *exactly*?" She looked rather cross.

"Close friend?"

"Not good enough. They're only allowing immediate family to visit for now."

"Can you tell me how she is?"

"Are you family?"

I had run the drill already, "I know, I know. Only family get to know how she is."

Then the Healer turned friendly, "The parents are with her now. If you stay in the waiting area, you should be able to catch them and find out from them how she is."

I nodded and took a seat. I didn't stay in it really long. I found that I couldn't stay seated. I stood, paced, went to the water fountain, got a drink, came back, sat, got up, and paced. My worst enemy wasn't the Healer, it was the clock on the wall. I don't know how long it went on.

Eventually someone I knew showed up, but it wasn't any of the Myerses. It was Professor Wendt and the Head. They asked me how Pam was.

I could only shake my head and admit that I had no idea other than that she was in the ICU.

Wendt asked, "And they won't let you visit because you're not family?"

It wasn't necessary to answer.

He nodded and inclined his head briefly toward the Head, "We've been involved with something like that. Don't worry. You have sympathetic friends at Hogwarts."

The Head said, "Of course, Mr. Filch is hopping mad that his assistant isn't available. He has to do some real work now, but you should stay here as long as you need to. I'll deal with Filch. If Ms. Myers is still in the ICU when school starts, we'll talk about that at the time, but for now, don't worry."

I was surprised that she'd let me take so much time off, but I could only thank her. Wendt had a practical suggestion. "Have you been eating while you've been here?"

I thought about it. Had I? I guess that I hadn't. I shook my head no.

Wendt went on, "Why don't you return to Hogwarts for meals – at least breakfast and dinner. You wouldn't take any more time than if you went down to the hospital cafeteria. I admit that hospital cafeteria food isn't bad, but why have good when you can have superb?"

That was a possibility that I'd not thought of. "I can use the floo network to travel?"

The Head nodded.

"That's a good idea. I think I'll do it."

Wendt asked me to go back with them as it was close to dinner. I agreed.

We arrived and were a little early. At the Head's urging, I ran up to my room and showered and changed and came down to the Teacher's Lounge in time for supper. Everyone wanted to know what had happened—most of all—I. So after dinner, we rearranged tables and chairs and each of us told our version of what happened. Slughorn went first and I followed.

When Wendt's turn came up, he suggested that he and the Head give their story together. After they started, it became clear why. Wendt started, "Well, when we learned about the danger that Ms. Myers was in, I stayed in the Headmistress's office while you went on your errands.

"After you were out of earshot, I suggested a plan. Both Miner. . ., that is, the Headmistress and I have cell phones."

I started to object, and Slughorn just ogled him and said "What?"

Wendt just said, "That's a completely different story. I'll tell you both about it sometime but not now. The critical thing is understanding what cell phones do. Mr. Dursley does, I"m sure. For you, Professor Slughorn, it's enough to know that cell phones let you talk to people at great distances."

Slughorn didn't look satisfied, but he didn't say anything. Wendt went on, "The idea was that I would use my cell phone to call the Headmistress's as soon as I had an idea of where we were."

I couldn't help interrupting then. "That was your brilliant idea! How could you dial without attracting attention?"

Wendt laughed, "That was easy. I had a speed dial # set up for the Headmistress's phone already. I turned the volume down to nearly zero, so there wouldn't be any sound made. All I had to do was figure out where we were, dial, and work the location into the conversation."

Slughorn nodded, "Clever. You guessed where we were and got Burbage to confirm it. Then, you, Minerva, got the Aurors to go to the Malfoy mansion and . . ."

The Head interrupted, "NO! I led them there. We used the disillusionment charm to make ourselves invisible and disapparated to outside the wall. I dissolved the gate, and we crept in as quietly as we could." She laughed at this point. "It was hardly necessary. The kidnapper had the fire roaring by this time. We could have marched in completely visible, and he probably wouldn't have noticed.

"But we had a whispered argument outside the castle."

I held my hand up to stop the progress into the manor house. The Auror, Ripley, barely held her voice to a whisper, "What now, Minerva?"

"We have to wait until the girl has been revived or it's certain that she'll be dead before we act," I said as I tried to restrain my anger myself. "We can't just go in there blasting away with stunning spells."

In the dim light of my wand, I could see that she was angry that I'd challenged her right to run the raid. "But, he may get away if we don't act right away. He can disapparate in a moment."

I could feel myself slipping into my highland brogue. "But you kenna be sure the girl will live if you do that."

We were at loggerheads. I would not have Ripley and her Aurors barging in and taking chances with the life of Ms. Myers. I cast around for an argument that would convince her. And then I thought of one. "Myers is the niece of the new Minister of Magic"

Ripley was as mad as an insulted Hypogryph, but she couldn't make a peep. Her lips compressed to keep herself from making a noise that she'd regret, and she simply nodded. We could see which room was occupied because it was the only one with lights, but none of us had been in the house, so we didn't know how to get there from the entrance.

Now that Ripley had determined to follow my plan, she didn't consider any other possibility. She led us up the main steps and said, "I disapparate in first, and I'll return if it's safe. Then we'll all go in."

She disappeared and after a seeming eternity, she reappeared. She lit her wand very dimly and signaled us to disapparate after her. Again she disappeared but this time, we followed. The inside was illuminated slightly by her dim wand tip. Our eyes were dark-adapted, but I still had trouble seeing my way around. There was a stairway that led up to the lighted room, and there was a passage behind the stairs. Rooms opened off to the right and left but our path led up. Ripley told us to follow her up at a distance of half the length of the staircase.

When she reached the top of the stairs, she looked about while clinging to the wall. She then signaled us up. She drew us near and whispered almost inaudibly. "From here on we go invisible. When we find them, hold off stunning until I stun the first. Stun everyone. We're taking no chances. Hold hands and stay together until I release Minerva's hand. Then separate and prepare. I take Burbage, and the rest fire at whatever target of opportunity lies closest to you."

She hesitated and looked about at us. Then she nodded and one by one applied the disillusionment charm to the rest of us. We then took hands and proceeded. We went first into a small anteroom. Light leaked from the banquet hall into it. Holding hands we went through that anteroom and into the banquet hall itself.

The sight that greeted us was horrible. Ms. Myers was suspended in air above the banquet table, and her long blond hair extended down from her back and poured almost to the table. She was facing down with her head toward the opposite end of the table. Wendt, Slughorn and Dursley were standing around the table while Burbage sat.

What Burbage said excited my worst fears. He would not give Myers the antidote until all copies of the book were destroyed. Wendt made what seemed to me to be a pointless suggestion for an oath but Burbage accepted it. Then I stood by while the last shreds of Snape's existence were systematically and almost lovingly destroyed.

I'd been so shocked by the atrocity that I didn't realize for a moment that it was over. But Ripley's first stunning spell woke me, and I remembered that I was supposed to stun whoever was closest. Everyone had scattered at the first bolt, but I had eyes only for Wendt. He eluded one or two bolts but I had a good angle at him. I almost lovingly aimed my wand and stunned him. I immediately ran to him and was almost stunned myself by a bolt that hit Dursley. Then it was all over.

We undisillusioned ourselves, and we each chose someone and disapparated with him or her to St. Mongos. I took Wendt, of course. Ripley took Ms. Myers, and the rest were handled by other Aurors.

The Head finished her story, and she turned to Wendt and asked, "What was that all about with the unbreakable oath?"

He shrugged, "I thought it was obvious. I didn't know what would happen if there were another copy someplace un-beknownst to us. Would we immediately die or only when its existence became known to us? I just didn't want to take the chance."

"Then you were quite confident that I'd rescue you, eh?"

"I have complete confidence in you always." He said softly, almost inaudibly. I saw what seemed a light in his eyes as he said those words.

Slughorn's Story

Slughorn said, "I really don't have much to add to this story. When Wendt sent us off, of course, I immediately went to get my potions bag and all the notes that I could find on our book. I didn't think of anything else and had a hard time to get back in time to take the port key.

"When we arrived, I started to think about how to do something to prevent this atrocity of destroying Snape's book while avoiding the greater tragedy of the death of Ms. Myers.

"I considered several possibilities. I thought about veritas serum to force Burbage to tell us how to use the antidote."

I broke in, "That sounds good! Why didn't you do that?"

I struggled with the idea of veritas serum. In the end, I gave up that idea for a couple of reasons. For one, it was entirely possible that Burbage had prepared by giving himself a dose of antidote for veritas before we arrived.

When I went back to Hogwarts to teach a couple of years ago, I always carried a small vial of veritas antidote with me just in case Dumbledore would try to spike my pumpkin juice with it and learn my dark secret. I wouldn't talk about it with anyone – not even you, my partners in crime. I never had to use it. I had absolutely no trouble believing that Burbage would carry the antidote as well. He was obviously good at potion-making.

Then there was another problem with veritas serum. It only makes you tell the truth. It doesn't keep you from disapparating or anything else. Even more importantly, it can't make you retrieve the antidote for Ms. Myers. It was too dangerous to try using it.

Another possibility was using the imperious curse. I really thought hard and long about that. You might not think that I had time to consider all these possibilities, but in emergency, time either passes very quickly or very slowly. I thought about using the imperious curse to force Burbage to give Myers the antidote. But there were two problems with that. The thing that drove me crazy was that neither of those problems would necessarily kill the plan but . . .

The imperious curse is one of the forbidden curses. It will land you in Azkaban if you use it. That wouldn't have mattered to me if I were sure I could save Myers. Also, Wizard law allows lots of exceptions for real emergencies – and for lots of things that aren't emergencies.

The real problem with the Forbidden Curses is that you have to really want to use them. I had a friend once who used a forbidden curse – the *Crusio* curse – to torture someone he had real reasons to despise. It didn't work very well. He said the spell, and there was hate in it, but you have to really want it and enjoy it to make it work. I wasn't sure that I had that desire and pleasure in dominating someone else's will to do it.

And then too, it's possible to train yourself to resist the Imperious curse. It's not easy, and you maybe can't resist it for a long time, but maybe long enough to disapparate. And then it would be all over.

I know what you're thinking. What about the *Crusio* curse? Couldn't I torture that son of a bitch into giving the antidote to Myers? God, there was a moment when he started to burn the pages that I wanted to. I wanted to so, so much. But it was such a stupid idea that even I, in my moment of anger and fear, couldn't bring myself to do it. He'd probably take any amount of torture to see his revenge.

I finally gave up trying to think of things to do. And as the pages burned one by one, I felt the life drip out of my heart one drop at a time. It's funny; I thought that I could live out my life in retirement perfectly happily if I just had enough galleons to live comfortably and write my little letters to the editor of the *Prophet* and see them printed and get my occasional tickets to a Harpies game and take a friend.

But now, I had the chance to do something really good and that would live on after I'd gone. It would be something that people would respect and admire. It would be something that was better than the dreams of my youth. Now that's gone, and I don't see any way to bring it back.

After Slughorn finished, the Head had nothing to say. Actually none of us had anything to say. The obvious truth of what he had to say and the fact that, in a way, it was true for all of us, made us all feel like we'd lost something that could never be returned.

My Mum always used to say that nothing was ever lost. I think she was talking about socks and keys. Oh, yes, she once lost an earring and wouldn't replace the pair for months. Finally, she gave up and bought a new pair that was very much like it. Then the next week, the lost earring showed up at the bottom of Potter's sock drawer. How in the world it got there, we'll never know. When she saw it, she broke out in tears. I don't know why, but you'd think that she'd lost her best buddy.

Anyway, she would never give up on finding something that was lost – ever.

But this was different. We were never going to find our lost future again.

Wendt tried to convince us that it would be possible to recreate the lost book. "Look, it's variations on the text that you have on your bookshelf in the potions classroom. You must have a dozen copies of it. Surely you can remember a lot of the formulas."

Slughorn shook his head sadly. "You don't understand. The formulas are not obvious extensions of the standard recipes. I can probably remember a dozen or so and test those. Probably young Dursley here can remember more, eh?"

I was taken by surprise but sputtered out, "Well, well, I don't know. Sure, I could probably do another dozen or so."

Wendt looked from one to the other of us and said, "You worked through all of them. Both of you performed them. Call up muscle memory. I'll bet that if you started actually doing a potion that neither of you think that you can remember, you'd find yourself doing it correctly.

"Slughorn, make the potion, and Dursley, you record it as he goes."

Slughorn and I looked at each other, and there seemed to be an unconscious communication. I started to object, and Slughorn came in and added to what I was saying. What we said was something like, "Look it just doesn't work that way. Oh, you could probably remember 80, 90, maybe even 95% of the potion recipe that way, but you make the slightest mistake, and it almost always comes out wrong – sometimes fatally wrong.

"Oh, we could work our way through a recipe as best we remembered, and then when it came out wrong, try again with slight variations. Eventually we'd get it right. But that would be a lifetime's work."

The Head was clearly disgusted, "Oh, come on. Snape did it as a student. He didn't have a lifetime to work on his versions."

Slughorn fumbled for words. He was pretty clearly disgusted himself. "But, but," he stuttered, "Look, Snape was a genius. Now, don't misunderstand. I've got a fair-sized ego, myself. But I don't have the kind of intuition that he had about potions. Someone like Snape comes along maybe once or twice in a generation. Dumbledore was one of those. Snape, in his generation, was one of those. Lilly Evans was another. Two in one generation – amazing when you think of it.

"You know, when I do think about it, Snape and she were something of an item for a while. I wonder if the two of them collaborated on that book." Slughorn paused and seemed deep in thought but then came out of it, "Oh well, I suppose we'll never know.

"Anyway, for a while I thought that Potter was another. He could have inherited it from Lilly, but in the end I was disappointed by him. He just used the book that he'd. . . " Slughorn paused again and his eyes unfocused for a moment. They returned to the present, and he said, "That book! I gave him that book. I'd had it all those years from the time that Snape was my student until Potter added my Advanced Potion Making class in his sixth year. To think that I had that treasure trove all that time and never realized it!"

That seemed to leave him speechless. There didn't seem to be anything to add. Both Slughorn and I were convinced that we'd never recreate it. So our meeting broke up. I headed for the Great Hall to take the floo express to St Mongos. I don't know what the others did.

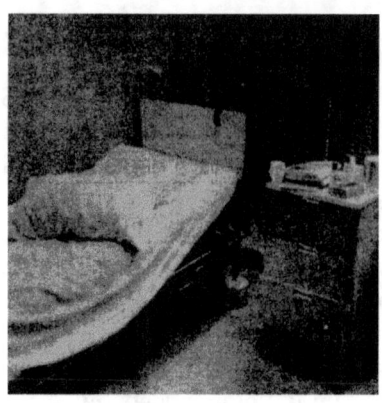

The Myerses

I arrived at St. Mongos and immediately headed up to ICU. I had an insane hope that maybe Pam had been removed from the ICU, but when I checked with the Healer's station in the ICU waiting area, I found that she was still there with her parents.

There was a coffee table in the waiting area. I glanced through the magazines there. There were a couple of copies of *Witch Weekly* that were months old, a *Prophet* from the day before yesterday and a *Healer's Quarterly*. I tried reading one of the Witch Weekly's. I barely got past the table of contents. It had an article about making a DIY wrinkle-removing potion. There was an interview of some author who had been in Saint Mongo's for a long time, recovering from a memory modification scheme that had gone wrong. There was an article about a beauty contest that *Witch Weekly* was running.

I tried the article about the recovering amnesiac. He appeared to have been quite the heart-throb of most witches who still had a heartbeat a couple of years ago. He talked about what he intended to do next in his career. He seemed to think that he'd been quite the thing when it came to fighting the Dark side of magic. He even claimed that if he'd only been out of the hospital, he'd have kept the Dark Lord from taking over the Ministry. It was then that I realized that the article was about the Lockhart that I'd met at Hogwarts.

With his background, he'd decided that he'd go into the Ministry and become an Auror. It was at that point that I couldn't stand reading the article any more. I tossed the magazine onto the coffee table in some disgust and looked around for something else to do.

As before, I ended up just pacing the room. That seemed to bother the Healer at the station. She asked me if I couldn't just go outside and walk it off. To that suggestion, I just snarled and sat down for a while.

I don't remember how long it took, but Pam's parents eventually did walk out the door to the ICU unit. When they did, I almost missed them, I was that bothered. I wouldn't have noticed them if Mrs. Myers hadn't recognized me.

"Why, Mr. Dursley, we didn't know you were out here. Why didn't you come in to Pammies' room?"

I started to answer, but she supplied her own answer, "Of course, you're not really family are you. It's just that I've been thinking of you as family for a while now. Please feel free to come in and sit with her whenever you want to."

I looked up at the Healer, hoping that she'd heard that conversation. I don't know if she did, and I didn't care. I'd been invited. Mrs. Myers was going on, "We were going down to the cafeteria to have something, won't you come?"

I was surprised by this pleasant greeting. I had been preparing what I'd say when they arrived, and now this friendliness had flummoxed me. So, I went on with what I intended to say from the beginning, "I can't tell you how sorry I am that Pam was hurt. It's my fault, and I want to apologize from the bottom of my heart for what happened."

Mr. Myers made a noise deep in his throat but Mrs. Myers hurried to say, "Oh, no, Roger, don't be that way. Mr. Dursley isn't responsible for what happened to Pammie. Is he going to be responsible for every crazy person in the world?"

Then she turned to me and took one of my hands in both of hers. "No. Dudley, you're not responsible for that poor man. As a matter of fact, I want to thank you from the bottom of my heart for saving our baby's life. You were so courageous to go into that terrible place to risk your life for her."

I didn't feel courageous. My Mum and Dad sometimes told me that I was courageous, but somehow, at school, boxing a kid in intramural sports about half my weight just didn't seem all that courageous to me. At least not now, it didn't.

As a matter of fact, I wanted to say that I hadn't done something courageous. I'd just done something that I didn't have a choice about. I don't think I could have come back to Hogwarts if I hadn't done that. I certainly couldn't have faced Mr. Filch if I hadn't gone to rescue Pam. How could I do anything else? I wanted to say that the real courageous person was Professor Wendt who certainly didn't have any reason to risk his life for Pam. He wasn't even a wizard, and he walked into that black hole.

But I couldn't say any of those things. There was something in my throat that was constricting it, and I was struggling not to let the tears escape from my eyes.

She finished by asking me to join them for something to eat in the caf. I managed to ask if I could visit Pam instead.

"Oh, dear boy, of course. If we'd known that you weren't allowed in, we'd have come out for you immediately." She led me to the door to the ICU ward.

The Healer at the desk, cleared her throat, and Mrs. Myers, turned and gave her a look that would have turned a Hypogryph to stone. She just looked down at imaginary papers on her desk, and we went on in. There was a short corridor that had a half dozen rooms entering off it. Pam was in #6.

Mrs. Myers just motioned for me to go in and said, "I'm sure you'd like to be alone with her for a bit. Roger and I will go down to get a bite and we'll be back in a while. I'm afraid she's still in a coma."

I walked in and took one of the chairs next to her bed. Her face was smooth, unlined. She might just have been sleeping. Now that I was there, I wasn't quite sure what I wanted to do. I could easily sit there all night and watch her, but . . . After a few minutes, I reached my hand out and took the one of hers that was resting on top of the cover.

I don't know how long I sat there and just watched her even breathing and holding her hand. But eventually I realized that someone else was in the room. Startled, I turned and stood. It was her Mum and Dad.

Mr. Myers shook his head and said, "Sit down. You look natural there beside her. I think that we'll just pull another chair in from the next room and watch with you."

Mrs. Myers, picked up a copy of the *Prophet* sitting on a night stand next her bed. "Dear, we read to her. Some Healers say that even in a coma people can sense their surroundings." She began reading an article about the economy and the rise in cost of good broomsticks.

After a while, she hesitated and handed it to me and went on, "Maybe you'd like to read for a while."

It felt really strange reading to someone who appeared to be sound asleep, but after the first paragraphs, it didn't seem nearly so strange. I read the weather report and the Quidditch scores. There was an article about the incident that we were all involved in. I started to read it and stopped on the first words, "Hogwarts Graduate". When I realized what the article was about, I stopped with my mouth hanging open.

Mrs Myers (I couldn't quite bring myself to think about her in any other way) tapped me on the arm and said, "What is it?"

I opened and closed my mouth a couple of times as I tried to think of a way to say why I wasn't reading the article without saying what the

212

article was about. Meanwhile, she continued, "Oh, you're reading an article about Pammie being kidnapped. Go ahead. It's therapeutic for people to talk about traumatic experiences. It's important to face these things in a safe environment."

I still didn't know what to say, but I handed the paper over to her, which she took and started to read. "Last night in a tragic series of events, a recently graduated Hogwarts student was kidnapped and held for ransom on the estate of the Malfoys. In a daring raid led by the Chief Auror Inspector Ripley, the abductee was rescued and is currently a patient at St. Mongo's Hospital. She refused to provide any further information on the victim.

"Inspector Ripley said, 'We'll provide details on the victim and the accused after we've contacted the victim's family.'

"However, confidential sources have informed this reporter that there were several Hogwarts staff members who participated in the raid that saved the victim. The *Prophet* is attempting to contact these people for comment." I was glad that they hadn't contacted me yet. Who knows what I'd have blurted out unintentionally that would have brought pain to the Myerses.

Mrs. Myers finished reading that story, and I felt that I'd relived the hideous adventure again. Mrs. Myers noticed and suggested that we go down to the cafeteria for a "cup'o". I didn't feel up to arguing, so we all went down. She had an agenda besides taking my mind off that night. She suggested that we set up a schedule of staying at Pam's bedside. We'd each have at least 12 on and the rest to recuperate and sleep. Each of us would take an overnight shift once every three days. The rest of the time we'd be in as we could always allowing for 8 hours of sleep on the days that we weren't at the bedside overnight. Even those nights, we could get a good bit of something that resembled sleep between visits by the healers to check on her condition.

With the imperial position of being Pam's mother, she declared that this night was hers, the next was her Dad's, and that mine was the third night. With that decided we all returned to Pam's bedside to watch and wait.

In the late afternoon, the Chief Healer came for a visit. He discussed Pam's case with us. Although he was not happy about talking with a mere boy friend present, he suffered my presence. He might as well just have given his little speech. He had little enough to say. I could have summed up what he knew in three sentences, "Pam's in a coma. She's physically healthy. We have no idea when she'll come out of the coma."

Shortly after his visit, an owl flew in and perched on the bedside table. I paid it no attention, thinking it was for the parents. But shortly something landed in my lap with a thud. I looked up and found that the owl was digging its left claw into my shirt, and it had its right claw extended toward me. It had a note attached to it. I addressed the owl, 'OK. OK. I get the message."

I removed the note and sent the owl on its way. The note turned out to be from Gringotts.

Mr. Dursley,

Please make yourself available at the Gringotts home office tomorrow morning at 9 AM. We wish to discuss with you and the other principles, the state of the loan that we made to Mr. Lovegood.

It was signed by some secretary that I'd never heard of. I reflected how thoroughly Burbage had wreaked his vengeance. Not only did it encompass Snape but everyone who wished to do Snape's memory a good turn.

The Myerses noticed that I was distracted and asked if something were wrong. I simply said, "I've got a meeting tomorrow morning that I can't avoid. If you don't mind . . ."

Mr. Myers interrupted, "You should go back home and get ready for your meeting, which includes a good night's sleep. I hope it's not really bad news."

I laughed mirthlessly, "The last couple of days have adjusted my scale of what's really bad news. No. It's NOT really bad news. But I do have to go into Gringotts. I suppose the main topic will be what happens to our book."

Mrs. Myers rubbed my shoulder and said, "We really hadn't thought about that. I'm so sorry that you lost your book. I know you put a lot of work into it."

I shook my head, rose and took Pam's hand in mine. "As long as Pam recovers, I'll be happy. I'll see you tomorrow."

I left the ward and found the closest floo. I showed up in the Great Hall and discovered that the evening meal was over. I knew that I could always get something to eat in the kitchen, so I headed down there. On the way, I ran into Filch – literally. I was concentrating hard on my problems – trying to think of some way to help Lovegood get out of his debt.

Filch almost knocked me over. He grabbed me and asked, "Where in the world have you been?"

"Oh, I was at St. Mongo's but . . ."

Filch frowned and said, "You look like you could use a drink."

Of course, for the first time in a long time, I really did feel like I could use a drink. However, he set his head at an angle and looked at me more carefully. "Maybe you could use something to eat first." With that he grabbed my arm, swung me around, and headed me toward the kitchen. I didn't feel up to arguing, so we went into the kitchen, and Filch ordered a house elf to get us some stew with bread and cheese. I'd never seen him be so assertive in my life.

He found a table, which he commandeered from another house elf. He pulled it over to a quiet corner and grabbed a couple of chairs that he carried over. "Sit. We had beef stew tonight. It's just the thing the Healer ordered for you." Shortly a house elf brought a large steaming bowl of the stew, several thick slices of whole grain bread, and some Swiss cheese.

I had to admit that I was hungry once I started eating.

I hadn't finished eating when the Head came storming into the kitchen. When she saw us, she came directly over to our table, 'Well, Mr. Dursley, you can carouse with your drinking buddy some other time."

Filch started to protest, but the Head shut him down with a gimlet glance and turned to me. We've been looking for you ever since that note came from Gringott's. "You come right up to my office immediately. Such a trail you've led us on!"

She set off at her normal "walking" pace, which most people would have taken for a jog. I kept close and followed her up into her office. I'd expected to find Wendt there and maybe Slughorn as well, but Lovegood was waiting too.

She began without pre-amble, "I presume that we all are agreed that the purpose of this meeting tomorrow is that the GOBLINS," she wrinkled her nose as she said the word, "want to call in the loan and they will take a pound of flesh if they can't get galleons."

Lovegood, who seemed to be the most affected by the statement, almost wailed, "They can't do that can they? Now that I have a REAL printing press, my circulation has increased. Do you know that Flourish and Blotts actually gives me some space on their newspaper stand and . . ." We never heard the other good news that his business was enjoying because the Head gave him the Evil Eye, and he shut up immediately.

Wendt stood up, and the Head hesitated and didn't say whatever she was about to. Wendt drawled out, "I think we should let the other partners speak before either of us do." He turned to Slughorn and didn't say a word, but Slughorn got the idea and spoke.

"I suppose you're right about what the Goblins want, but surely we can reason with them. We can pay back the loan slowly. I'll have to keep teaching longer than I want to, and Mr. Dursley could surely pay some each month. With Lovegood's regular publishing business going better. . ." Here he stopped and tried to signal Lovegood to say something, but Lovegood refused to take the hint.

At this point, I spoke up and agreed.

Then the Head looked pointedly at Wendt. He too didn't take the hint, but the Head didn't leave any doubt about what she wanted, "Well, Wendt?"

"Well, what?"

"Don't you have something to contribute?"

He looked around at all of us and said, "You want the bad news first or the good?"

I answered instantly, "The bad."

He nodded and looked around at the rest of the people in the room. The Head just looked up toward heaven and harrumphed. Lovegood looked lost and didn't say anything. Slughorn shrugged and said, "Why not?"

Wendt stood and walked to the largest opening in the ring of chairs and paced back and forth a moment as he tried to decide what to say. We all turned to face him. "All right. The bad news is that I'm not going to help you with money. You're going to have to work that out for yourselves."

There was a general sad sigh from everyone except the Head. However, Wendt went on, "The good news is that I will come along with you tomorrow. I have a certain amount of influence with the Goblins of Gringotts as Minerva can attest."

Everyone stared. He had used the Head's given name. He quickly waved off the surprise that was evidently on everyone's faces. "Yes, yes. She has a first name, and we might as well use it. This has nothing to do with school and we're all adults here.

"Now, I want you all to do the talking tomorrow. You negotiate the best deal that you can get, and I'll only speak if you seem to floundering. We'll have breakfast together at the Head table, and we'll leave together for Diagon Alley around 8:30. Agreed?"

No one had a problem with the plan other than the "we all speak for ourselves, and Wendt buts in only if we're floundering."

We separated to head to our rooms. On my way to Hufflepuff, I discovered that Filch had been lying in wait for me. "Did you get reamed out good? Do you want to share a bottle?"

"No No. I'm fine."

"Good, then it's time to celebrate." He said gleefully.

"Yeh." I said forlornly. We went down to his office, and he pulled out a bottle of real whiskey. His tastes had been improving lately.

Filch wanted an account of how things had gone. I couldn't think of a reason not to be honest with him. "Well, you know that I've been working on a book with Professor Slughorn?"

"Sure. It must be about ready to come out, eh? Then we'll really celebrate!"

I just frowned, "Not so much. The man who kidnapped Pam . . . er Ms. Myers did it to prevent us from publishing the book."

216

Filch scratched his head, "But the Auror's got the son of a bitch, right?"

"Oh, they got him OK, but not before he'd destroyed all the copies of the book that we had."

Filch was beginning to get it, but he still wasn't satisfied. 'You could write it again, couldn't you?"

I just shook my head and then added, "Snape was the real author of the book. We just corrected the spelling and got it into shape to print."

Filch just stared at me and finally asked, "Why didn't he do it himself?"

I looked up at the ceiling trying to search it for the secret of Snape's motivations. I answered without much conviction, "I don't think Snape cared much for fame or fortune. After Dumbledore recruited him to fight Riddle, I think he only really cared for revenge against Riddle."

Filch filled his glass again and commented, "I never really understood that. If I'd been a Deatheater, I'd sure not have hung around if I were mad at him. I'd have gone to Australia."

"Yeh. I suppose. Still." I thought about Pam. "I guess I can think of a reason to stick around."

Filch just downed the rest of the glass at a gulp and said, "Whatever." I excused myself because of the early morning meeting and went to my room in Hufflepuff.

Gringott's

We were all up plenty early the next morning and sitting around the Head table for breakfast. There were a few other professors up for breakfast, but they sat together at the other end of the table as though they sensed the bad Karma that we had and didn't want any of it to rub off on them.

Lovegood was supposed to meet us at The Cauldron but I didn't trust him to brave the Goblins in their den. However, when I walked out of the floo, there was Lovegood standing at the bar talking with Tom. We collected ourselves and walked through to Diagon Alley together looking a bit like *The Charge of the Light Brigade*.

When we arrived at Gringott's, we marched in almost in lock step and amazingly were greeted immediately. A Goblin met us and simply said, "You're expected, of course. Come with me."

We walked back into the deep recesses of Gringotts, and we felt like we'd left all hope behind as the first of a series of doors closed behind us. We eventually were taken to a conference room and asked to wait. After a few minutes a Goblin showed up and reminded us that we'd met him before. His name was Grasnik.

He began, "Well, gentlemen, you must be close to publication. I just wanted to check with you and see if we can set up a repayment schedule. I know it might be a little premature since you've not actually published yet, but you're so close . . ." He trailed off and gave us a pregnant look. He wanted us to start the conversation on schedule. He looked at each of us in turn. Lovegood's gaze was locked to the floor. Slughorn looked around searching for anyone to look at other than Grasnik.

I don't know where it came from, but I began speaking, "Mr. Grasnik, I'm afraid there's a problem. We aren't going to be able to publish. So, I guess we're going to owe money to Gringotts for most of the rest of our lives. I can't tell you how sorry we are that we won't be able to publish, but it's just not possible"

Grasnik stared at us for what seemed like hours. He blinked twice and said, "This isn't about last minute nerves, is it? Afraid that you'll be disappointed by poor sales or maybe no sales?"

Slughorn came to life and said, "No. It's worse than that – far worse. We don't have the manuscript or any copies of it. Maybe we could reproduce it – maybe – in a dozen years. But that doesn't really help you or us."

Grasnik was taking it amazing well. He politely asked how we'd lost it. Slughorn just shook his head and said, "We're not going to find them in the laundry if that's what you were thinking. They were destroyed before our eyes. We checked the ashes thoroughly – no chance of reconstituting them." Then he told the story of Pam's abduction and the ransom that was required.

Grasnik listened calmly and then rang a small silver bell that I could barely hear. Almost immediately another Goblin entered the room and came to Grasnik. They spoke at some length in Gobbledygook and the other Goblin left the room. I was wondering if they were going to get a surgeon to take a pound of flesh but no one else seemed troubled.

Lovegood looked up for the first time, "I'll sell my new printing press. I got rid of the old one. I'll never be able to buy another to replace it. That will be the end of the Quibller." He said it in a flat tone that he might have used to announce the weather prophecy for the next day.

Grasnik was strangely silent. He didn't even seem to be listening to what people were saying. Then the door to the conference room opened and the other Goblin entered the room. He was carrying a small portfolio that he handed to Grasnik. Grasnik opened it and glanced at the contents for a moment or two and then announced,

"Mr. Dursley, Professor Slughorn, this may interest you. Please take it." With that he held out the portfolio toward me. It was rather heavy. I opened it and stared at something that I thought I'd never see again in life. I riffled through the contents and could not believe my eyes.

Slughorn, becoming impatient for the first time this morning asked to see it. I simply closed it to prevent the contents from spilling out and handed it to him. He opened it, and his eyes became as big as pie tins. He exclaimed, "Why this is . is . it's our manuscript." He turned rapidly toward the Goblin and asked, "How did you get hold of this? What kind of magic is this?"

Grasnik merely smiled and said, 'Surely you didn't expect us to be so casual with the safety of a manuscript that was the real security for our loan to you?"

No one provided an answer, not even Wendt, so he went on, "You no doubt remember, when you came to us, that I sent your manuscript out of the room to be examined?" He answered his own question, "Of course you do.

"Well, checking the manuscript was not the only thing that was done. The bank owns a xerographic copying machine. We had a copy made too."

Lovegood spoke up again, "But I know a little about those machines. They're Muggle-made. Surely those zerograppling machines can't work in a building that has so much magic in it?"

Grasnik smiled again, "Of course, you're right. But the Bank rents a small office in a building on the other side of London. There is a floo connection between the two and we always send important documents there to be copied. We have a vault in another branch that we use to store these documents. I just sent my assistant, Sniverly, there to retrieve this copy. We'll give this copy to you so that you can publish."

Wendt spoke up at this point, "I think it would be prudent to have another copy made of this copy. Oh, yes, one other thing. Needless to say, you'll charge us for these copies."

The biggest smile of all came to Grasnik's face. "Yes, you can be sure that we'll be able to buy another copying machine or two with the fee we'll charge you."

Lovegood's face underwent an amazing transformation as we discussed this. He leaned forward in his seat and seemed ready to leap out at the first hint that the meeting was over. Of course, we had to haggle a little over the duplication fee, and we had to wait while a second copy for the Bank was made.

When all that was completed, we were escorted out of the inner offices of Gringotts. Lovegood asked to use a Gringott's floo connection to get to his printing press all the quicker. He was off, and Wendt invited the rest of us to join him and Minerva for a little celebratory lunch. I declined with thanks and took the floo at The Cauldron directly to Saint Mongo's. I wasn't as bold as Lovegood to ask for the use of a Gringott's floo.

▽

At Saint Mongo's, I found that I could step smartly and take the elevator to Pam's floor and right into her room. Or, at least, I intended to. Instead, I was intercepted by the Myerses who were waiting for me in the waiting room.

Sensing the possibility of a problem, my attitude changed, and I asked if there were a problem.

Mr. Myers grimaced, but said, "No major problem. As a matter of fact, we have some good news." He seized my arm as I started to pass him to get into Pam's room. He went on, "The good news is that Pam has regained consciousness."

I interrupted, "But. . ."

He looked to his wife for support and then turned back to me, "There's a complication. Let's go to the Resident Healer's office. He can probably explain it better than I can."

We walked to a small office that was just big enough for a small desk, a small cot and two guest chairs. Fortunately, he was there. After a little discussion, I convinced the Myerses to take the guest chairs, and I stood. Mr. Myers simply asked the Healer to explain Pam's condition.

"Well, Mr. Dursey."

"It's Dursley."

"Yes, yes. Anyway, Ms. Myers' condition is really quite good. She's regained consciousness and seems otherwise quite healthy. But, her memory is affected. She remembers her parents vaguely. She knows that she graduated from Hogwarts but there isn't much detail there. Her memory of vocabulary and basic Arithmancy skills seem largely unaffected but . . ."

Here Mrs. Myers interrupted, "We've talked with her a little—a very little—about you, and she doesn't really have any recollection of you."

I found myself slumping back against the wall of the office. I was almost leaning against it to start with, so there wasn't any great danger. I took a deep breath and asked, "But you expect her to improve with time. Eventually she should remember me?"

The Healer looked at me. I guess he was trying to evaluate me and then said, "Memory is funny. People who have artificially repressed memories, such as from the *Obliviate* spell, frequently recover their memories eventually, but it can take a very long time.

"There is a man here who lost his memory six years ago and has been confined here ever since. He's just been released and seems to be doing all right in the outside world but still has huge gaps in his memory.

"His was an extreme case, but it shows you something of the difficulties that Ms. Myers may face. Frequently, non-stressful exposure to old acquaintances and environments stimulate the return of memory, but there are no guarantees."

I practically whooped, "I'll live in her room if that will improve her chances."

That seemed to bother the Healer, "Remember, I said non-stressful. I would suggest short bouts – not more than an hour at a time. Don't try to talk about shared memories until she brings the topic up. Just be a good listener. Let her lead the conversation where she will."

Mrs. Myers had a question, "When can she be released?"

The Healer scratched his 4 o'clock shadow and said, "She's been bed-ridden for several days. I'd like to see her get a little physical therapy.

As soon as she seems ready to the therapist, she should get back into familiar surroundings. I'd guess that would be three or four days."

I had a question, "Can I see her now?"

"Yes, but today limit it to half an hour. Tomorrow, you can do a couple of one hour sessions but only so long as she isn't becoming tired or disturbed."

I nodded agreement, and we left the tiny office. Mr. Myers stopped me as we approached her room, "Remember. No excitement. No drama. You're just a friend of the family."

I agreed, and we entered her room.

⧗

I entered the room and found that I was smiling broadly when she looked up to see who had entered. She brightened a little and asked, "Who's the guest?" But she added almost immediately, "Oh, I know you!" And then she added a little less certainly, "Don't I?"

I nodded and asked if I could sit with her a bit. She brightened a little more at that. She asked, "I think you're from the school, aren't you?"

My heart leapt wildly but I tried to contain my face's reaction. "Yes, I am."

She smiled more broadly still, "You're one of my professors, aren't you?"

I hadn't expected that. I quickly tried to come up with a good, mild reply, despite the fact that my heart was screaming for me to say, "Oh, Pam, I love you. I'm Dudders, don't you remember?" But what I said was, "I'm actually a member of the staff – not a Professor."

She puzzled that a minute and said, "But, you seem so much like someone I should trust. If not a professor, then what?"

I couldn't believe the next words that I was saying but they seemed the right thing to say, "I'll tell you, but I don't want to tire you overly, so I'll leave afterward. I'm part of,' I hesitated a moment and thought of something that Filch had once told me that he considered his position to be, "Environmental Services."

"Oh, that sounds so important."

I had a terrible temptation to laugh but restrained it and turned it into a smile that I hoped would seem friendly. "I'll see you tomorrow if that's OK."

"Oh, please do."

Mr. Myers followed me out and commented, "Good job. We'll see you tomorrow."

222

I returned for an hour, morning and evening until the day that she was released. I usually read the *Prophet* to her but toward the end, she insisted on reading it.

On the day that she was released to her parents, she told me, "I think I remember your name. It's Dursley, isn't it?""

"Sure it is. May I continue to visit you as your recover?"

She nodded enthusiastically and asked, "You'll do that morning and evening, won't you?"

I hesitated, "I have duties at Hogwarts but I'll come as often as I can."

Her face fell a little, "Of course, I understand, I'm just being selfish wanting you with me all the time."

It cost me quite a bit of effort to only say, "I enjoy being with you too. See you tomorrow."

Publicity

While this was going on, I spent most of my time helping Filch get the school ready for the fall term. I only had time to help him and occasionally visit Pam. However, one morning at breakfast, Slughorn came over to me as I was about to begin the work day.

He pulled me aside as I was about to enter Filch's office to get the assignments for the day. "Mr. Dursley, we have an interview scheduled at lunch today."

I could only stare at him and echo stupidly, "An interview at lunch?"

"Yes. I've invited the *Prophet* to send a reporter to write an article about the publication of our book. They'll place it in next Sunday's book section of the *Weekend in Prophecy* magazine."

I wasn't happy at only being notified a few hours in advance. Slughorn just slapped me on the back, 'You'd just worry if you knew about it yesterday or the day before. Buck up! It will be fun."

I grumbled mostly to myself, "Yes, fun for you with all sorts of contacts at the *Prophet* and lots of your students reading."

Filch noticed that I was not fully paying attention when he gave me my morning assignments. "No, no, Dursley. You're to mop Moaning Myrtle's WC not the Head's. I don't know what's gotten into you."

Of course, I knew precisely what had gotten into me, and I couldn't get it out of me. Lunch hour finally arrived, and Slughorn found me and practically dragged me to the Teacher's Lounge where the interview was going to happen. When we walked into the door, there were several reporters waiting. One introduced herself as Rita Skeeter of the *Prophet*, but there were a couple from international papers.

Slughorn whispered to me that I needn't worry. He'd field all the hard questions, and I could just smile and nod to what he had to say.

After a few soft cricket pitches were fielded by Slughorn, the sticky wickets started coming to me. "Mr. Dursley, it is MR. Dursley isn't it – not Professor Dursley?"

So this was Slughorn fielding the hard questions, eh. But, I grimaced, collected my thoughts, and started, "Yes, MS. Skeeter, I am not a professor here at Hogwarts."

Someone else asked, "Then how are you an author of this book?"

"Well, I'm not exactly an author. I'm more of an editor. The real author is Severus Snape. You see I found . . ." Slughorn interrupted and explained that a former student, Severus Snape – yes, THE Severus Snape, had made copious notes in a standard text. They were so copious that they constituted a new book in itself. We – that is – Slughorn with a little assistance from me had checked all the formulas in the new book. He chuckled a bit when he admitted that I had given him some assistance.

Skeeter asked, "Did you graduate from Hogwarts, Mr. Dursley."

I gulped and tried an answer, "Well, Ms. Skeeter, I didn't attend Hogwarts."

"Then what school of Witchcraft and Wizardry did you attend?"

We all had glasses of water in front of us. I took a swallow and said, "Actually." And then an idea occurred to me. I improvised, "St. Brutus's."

Skeeter stared and seemed to be stymied for the moment. Someone else asked, "Were you good in school at potions?"

I stared over at Slughorn who seemed to have developed a thirst and was taking a long slow swallow of water. I squinted at him and said, "Not particularly."

Skeeter pointed her irritating quill at me and asked, "Then how can you write an Advanced Potions textbook?"

I was getting really irritated, and I snapped, "I've already told you that I didn't write it. I edited it. Professor Slughorn checked all the potions by doing them." I paused for a breath and said, "The real genius is Snape who perfected practically every potion in the standard potions book."

A French reporter asked, "Zen it iz zees Znape who iz ze real author?"

"Yes, yes. How many times do I have to tell you that?"

The rest of the interview went downhill from there. It ended with a photo being made by the photographer from the *Prophet*. It featured Slughorn and me with a galley copy of our book held between us by the two of us.

We finally escaped from the interview, and I was so disgusted that I didn't have a single bite of the excellent lunch that the House Elves had prepared. I was late getting back to Filch for my afternoon assignment.

I was so miserable that I didn't even go visit Pam.

The rest of the week, I tried my best to forget the whole interview. The reputation that Rita Skeeter had for taking the worst interpretation of an interview convinced me that I didn't even want to see the Sunday magazine section of the *Prophet*.

However, my visits with Pam, though brief, were extremely pleasant. She was slowly recovering her memory and could name most of her cousins, aunts, and uncles. She seemed to mostly want to walk in the roads surrounding the small town where she and her parents lived. Her world was the small sphere of memories that slowly came back to her. Once she asked me about Professor McGonagall. Did she still teach Transfiguration?

I agreed that she did and wondered for a moment if I should mention that she had become the Headmistress of Hogwarts. Pam noticed that I seemed to be holding something back. She asked about it and I just said, "Well, I was trying to decide if I should let you know that Professor McGonagall is now the Head of the school."

Pam laughed, "Well, I guess you just decided."

I smiled and agreed. She stopped us walking by putting a hand on my forearm and said, "I really can't make out why you are being so sweet to me. You must have friends that you'd rather be with."

I so much wanted to tell her that there was no person in the rest of the universe that I preferred to be with, but I thought that would be dangerous for her. I just fought to keep the lump out of my throat and said that I enjoyed being with her pretty well." She was silent after that for quite a while.

That Saturday was a Hogsmeade day at school, and I had been drafted to help keep a watch on the students invading the town. When I'd mentioned to Pam that I wouldn't be able to drop by that Saturday because of the Hogsmeade day, she'd said, "You really are a Professor and are just too modest to admit it."

I shook my head vigorously but she would not have any of it. She insisted that she had the right to punish me for missing a day with her, not to mention imposing on her with the fiction that I was "just" staff, by giving her three times as much time on the next day, Sunday.

I pretended to argue about it and then reluctantly agreed.

All three of the Myerses had insisted that I come for lunch that day, and I happily agreed. Lunch was very nearly as good as it was at Hogwarts.

I'd never have said anything like that to the Myerses because, though true, I wanted them ALL to have a favorable opinion of me.

After lunch, it seemed to be a tradition of the Myerses to attack the extra large weekend edition of the *Prophet*. Sometimes all three worked the crossword. I begged off that, claiming that it was unfair for me to help them, since I was a word-master unequalled.

All three Myerses saw through that, and Pam suggested that her parents work the puzzle together and that she and I would read the other sections. I claimed the sports section, which pleased Pam because she wanted the Magazine Section.

I was reading about the All Europe Quidditch Tournament. Pam was laughing at some article. She was laughing so hard that she stood and placed the section down flat on the kitchen table that we were still all arrayed around. I suppressed my curiosity about what had caused her laughter. It ended, and I heard a page or two turn while in the background the parents were puzzling over a clue, "Nonsense word from Finegan's Wake or Muggle Physics."

Then, I heard a gasp and looked up from the sports section. Pam had seemingly fallen into her chair and had both hands clasp over her mouth. I looked down at the Magazine Section and found a picture of myself staring out from the page with THE book held in my hand. Slughorn was looking over at me.

Pam stared at me and between her hands I heard her whisper, "Dudley." She jumped up still staring wide-eyed at me. Her hands fell away from her mouth. She said, "Oh, my God!" and ran out of the room. I heard feet on the stairs up to the bedrooms on the second floor.

Her parents had stopped their puzzling and stood to see what article had caused that reaction. Mrs. Myers simply said, "OH!". Her husband looked me straight in the eye and said, "I think you'd better go. The Healer said that it was possible that when her memory started to really return it would be a severe shock."

I left and found my way back to the school.

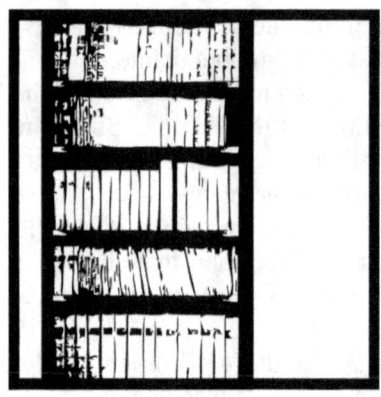

Snape

I finally got together as much courage as I could and walked up the steps from Mr. Filch's office to the main floor of Hogwarts. I changed to the staircase that led up to the second floor. I walked as slowly as I could manage because I wasn't anxious to meet Professor Wendt. It wasn't that he was unkind or mean. It was just that I had to ask him about Professor Snape, and I was afraid that he would think that I thought he was with the Deatheaters or something. Every step seemed harder than the last. I picked the longest route that I could find that didn't actually take me to the third floor.

Finally, I stopped at the very door and stood for minute after minute hoping that something would happen. I didn't now what. Maybe Professor Wendt would open the door and have to go to a faculty meeting or something. But it didn't happen. As a matter of fact nothing happened. Well, nothing happened, at least until a 5th year walked around the corner. Then, I had to do something. He'd seen me, and I didn't want to just be standing there like a dork. So, I knocked without thinking.

From the other side of the door, someone said, "Come." I had stopped thinking when the kid rounded the corner. I just opened the door and found myself walking into Wendt's office. He looked up and said, "Oh, good. I was thinking about you. I had a feeling somehow that you might want to see me."

My mouth was gaping wide, but I managed to close it and asked, "Really?"

"Yes, certainly. You've just published a book that you helped edit. That book had a major contributor - Professor Snape. You've been far too busy to really think about much other than getting it published, and then there was Ms. Myers's problems. So, you've been wondering about Snape."

He opened his desk drawer and pulled out a bottle. "I think this calls for a drink." He then pulled another couple of shot glasses out of the wet bar. He looked at me for a moment and asked, "Well?"

"Oh, yes." I said in a choked voice. Then, so I could be heard, "Yes. Please Professor."

He opened the bottle and as he did, commented, "This is Blue Label Johnny Walker. I save it for very special occasions." He then poured some in each of the two glasses and handed me one. "Ice?"

One word can make all the difference in the world – the difference between a friendly celebration and a bitter, troubled meeting.

I smiled. It was the first time since I had started up the stairs. "Yes." He went to a bookshelf and opened a little door into the lower part of the bookshelf. Something rattled as he reached his hand in. It came out with several cubes which he dropped into the glasses.

He walked back to the desk and reached across it to hand me my glass, "To your book."

We both drank a swallow. Of course, I'd had hard liquor before, but this was different. It burned like hell, but it was smooth. I laughed, "You know, it really isn't my book."

He stared at me and said, "Of course it is, whose else is it?"

I shrugged and rolled my eyes. I'd almost forgotten why I'd come, and now, he'd brought me back to that. "I suppose. . ." and left it hanging in the air.

Wendt nodded and started to speak, keeping me from having to go further. When he started to speak, I could hear his classroom voice, lecturing, but not like most teachers lecture. He was talking about something that he loved and not about something that he was paid to lecture about but didn't really care about. He turned partway away from me as he talked, swiveling his chair, maybe not wanting me to see how much he enjoyed what he was talking about.

"A good question. As I understand it, the book is largely based on the text, *Advanced Potion-Making,* by Eldridge Cleaver. But it had been amended so frequently and often by Professor Snape when he was a student here, that it is hardly Cleaver's book at all.

"Of course, Professor Snape provided the information." Here Wendt paused and seemed to be looking off into the distance. "But, you know, Snape had sat on those changes for so long. Probably more than thirty years. If he'd wanted to publish he could have." Here his tone changed and became decisive, "No. It's certainly not primarily his book. It should have been. But it wasn't. It isn't.

"And then Professor Slughorn contributed as well. He was more of a technical editor than anything else. He was like a good editor at a publishing house. He makes good suggestions. The editor of *Brideshead Revisited* made good contributions, but he isn't remembered. Evelyn Waugh is."

I couldn't keep myself from interrupting. This was getting crazy. I didn't know who this lady, Evelyn Waugh, was but I'm not an author. "Wait one minute, Wendt. You've got this all wrong. All I did was take this Cleaver's book and Snape's." I said the name. I couldn't go back now. There was no choice—we'd end up talking about Snape and what kind of person he was and then. . . what?

"Yes, what were you going to say about Snape?"

"Well, he had all the ideas. And I guess they are pretty darn good ideas too. It's his book."

Wendt looked me directly in the eye and said, "You're right. He's a big contributor, but where I come from, there's this idea. When there's a project, there are people who contribute ideas and are essential to getting the job done. They deserve credit and get some. They are called individual contributors. I'm sure Lovegood was an editor and Professor Slughorn and, of course, Snape. They all are individual contributors. But, the person who made it all happen, the one who managed it, gets the big credit. That was you."

I was surprised but this gave me a chance to ask the question that I'd come up here for, "Wendt, you keep calling Professor Snape, 'Snape'. What can you tell me about him? You keep calling him that. Were you two friends? He doesn't seem like the kind of person that you'd be friends with. Oh, I've heard you talk about him with respect, but I still don't know much about him."

Wendt nodded and picked up the bottle of Blue Label. "If I'm going to talk about Snape, it calls for more of this." He poured some more into my glass that was close to empty. This was a welcome development. I was beginning to have a taste for it. He added some into his own, took a deep sip and leaned back into his chair. He looked across his desk at me and nodded, seemingly more to himself than me.

"Yes, I was his friend. I think I was probably his only friend for a very long time. He was not an easy person to be friends with, but from the very first he was a friend to me." Wendt chuckled. "His first act of friendship was trying to prevent us from ever becoming friends."

I, of course, was puzzled and showed it in the look on my face.

"Oh, he was afraid that as a Muggle at Hogwarts that I'd get myself killed or as Ms. Grainger used to say, 'Something worse.' And I almost did a time or two. I didn't have lots of friends at the beginning here."

I wrinkled my face at that. Wendt was one of the nicest and friendliest and best-liked people I knew here. I couldn't believe that people didn't like him.

"Oh, yes. It's true. Someday maybe I'll tell you one of those stories. But for now, let's just say that when I needed a friend most, he was there. You may find this interesting. Another early friend was Mr. Filch.

'I know that you're wondering how a Deatheater could possibly be that friendly with a Muggle. Well, it's widely believed that Severus was a Deatheater in earnest to the end."

I had to ask, "And he wasn't? I heard that he was with Valdemort to the very end."

Wendt looked away quickly. Was he trying to hide a tear? He sighed and began again, "Yes, but he was a spy for Dumbledore. He started as a Deatheater pure and simple, but changed. I don't know why. He was so good at disguising his real feelings and thoughts that maybe no one knows the reason. We know that even the ultimate Legillimens, Tom Riddle, never knew the truth."

At this point, I would have killed to know for sure what a Legillimens was, but I wasn't going to break into the story at this point.

Wendt was continuing, "I don't know, but I will believe until the end that Snape was critical in some way to the defeat of Tom Riddle. I know for sure that Snape kept Dumbledore informed on the details of Riddle's thoughts and schemes and that every moment of that time the slightest slip by Snape of his iron control of his thoughts would have meant his death. That control lasted for more than twenty years, and I don't know with certainty but I believe that it held until the end. I don't know why Riddle finally killed Snape, but my personal belief is that Riddle feared that Snape might be preparing to usurp Riddle in the moment that Riddle believed to be the achievement of his ultimate victory."

This was far from what I expected. "So, you were friends with Snape and are . . . well, proud of it?"

"Yes. And that's why I'm glad that you've dropped by today. I have a couple of favors to ask."

I couldn't help laughing out loud, "Pardon me, but you want to ask favors of me? That's like, well, like your asking me for advice on Shakespeare."

"Yes, I do want favors – more than one – from you. I want you to take me to Diagon Alley and after I buy a copy of your. . ." I guess I must have made some strange face. "Yes, your book, I want you to autograph it for me."

I restrained laughter this time, but I did ask, "And just how do you want to go to Diagon Alley."

This time Wendt laughed, "Nothing easier. You'll take us there by floo."

I was still staring, but I managed to ask, "You mean right now."

With that, he got up walked over to his fireplace and motioned me to follow.

I did as he said. There was a flare of green fire, just like always. We spun around and staggered out of the fireplace. We were in a dark, large room. I was coughing and was still sort of dizzy. Wendt was hacking as badly as I was.

He got his cough under control and asked, "Did you take us through every floo in London?"

I would have laughed if I weren't still getting my cough under control and just said, "No, cough, cough. . . Where did all this dust come from?"

He didn't answer my question, but made a comment, "I thought I'd traveled in all the worst ways that Wizards travel, but this trip tops them all."

All I could do was nod because another fit of coughing had struck me. It left me as quickly as it had struck and I looked around carefully. By this time, the barkeeper who was almost the only other person in the bar, had taken notice of us.

Wendt walked over to him said something about our returning for something later. He smiled and waved us off. Wendt was leading the way. As he opened a door for me, and we walked through he said, "Well, here we are."

We walked over near the back wall of the lot. Wendt asked me, "I know that there are four bricks in that wall that you tap with your wand, and the wall opens for you. I've seen it dozens of times. How is that you know which ones they are?"

I stared at the wall and then at him and then back to the wall. "You're kidding, right? You want me to tell you how I know what four bleeding bricks to tap with my wand?"

"Yep." I was about to object, but he sped on, "I've seen it done lots of times. And no, I don't know which four they are, but I think if you concentrate, you'll see that there's something different about four of the bricks."

I shook my head, shrugged and tried to explain. "Something amazing happens. It looks like a trick of the light but four of the bricks seem to be a bit brighter than the others."

He asked, "How do you know what order to tap them in?"

He smiled, "That I have noticed the first time Minerva took me here. She always taps the highest and then go to the lowest and then the one on the left and finally the one on the right."

I tapped each brick in sequence with my wand. For about two seconds nothing happened and then the wall directly in front of me seemed to dissolve. Wendt walked forward as though he were perfectly confident that the wall would open for us, and I followed him. Beyond the wall was a street that could have been any in any of the older neighborhoods of London. Except. Except that every store front was "wrong" in some way. Sometimes they were obvious things. There was a store that looked like a pet store except that it had a large display featuring owls in the window. There was a sign that said that there was a sale on toads and newts. There was a shop that had a name that I immediately recognized – Olivander. It had wands in the display window and said that it had been in business since 1060 or something like that. London has old businesses that have been around for hundreds of years but I've never heard of one being around since before the Magna Carta.

Wendt was walking rapidly with purpose down the street. We shortly reached a store that looked as normal as any I'd seen so far. It was clearly a bookstore. Its name was Flourish & Blots. This was obviously where Wendt was going. I knew of it from Slughorn, but I'd never been. We went in and found the shelves filled with books which all seemed to have been from the 19th century. There were a few modern-looking books but even they had titles like *The Monster Book of Monsters*.

Someone approached us. He looked like he worked here, but he didn't have a name badge like all the normal book chains like Waterstone's. He seemed to be happy to see us or maybe it was just Wendt that he was happy to see. He greeted him jovially, "Professor Wendt, it's good to see you. Are you come to order next year's textbooks already?"

Wendt turned to me and introduced us, "Mr. Davies, this is a colleague at Hogwarts, Mr. Dudley Dursley. Dudley, this is the manager of Flourish and Blotts, Mr. Paul Blotts Davies." He turned his full attention to Davies and answered his question, "I'm want to buy a copy of the new *Advanced Potions-Making* textbook by Severus Snape."

Davies laughed, "Are you taking up a new career, Professor?"

"No. I just know that it's been recently published, and because its author was an old friend, I wanted a copy."

"Severus Snape? Do you really want a book written by that." He hesitated and looked down for a second and finished, "scum?"

"Yes, I do. First, he was one of the unsung heroes of the war against Riddle. Second, he was a good friend when I needed a friend. And third, I think you'll find that next year it is the text used by Hogwarts and before long by all the best schools in Europe."

"Well, I did receive a small shipment on consignment from the publisher. I almost sent them back unopened, but since you're going to buy one, I'll open it right now, sell you one and stock the rest in the education section."

Wendt thanked him, and he led us back behind the cash wrap desk and into the back of the store. There were several unopened shipping crates and shelves with a disorderly array of books. He picked up a box and put it on a work desk. He opened the box with a case cutter and pulled out a book that looked like every other textbook that I'd ever seen in a chemistry class. He handed it to Wendt and led us back to the front of the store. He stood at the cash register that didn't look like any that I'd seen. It had three sets of buttons. He punched them and said, "That'll be 63 galleons, 8 sickles and 15 knuts, including tax." Then he seemed to have an inspiration. "Oh! All purchases over 50 galleons include an offer for one galleon more, a nifty dragonhide book bag."

Wendt agreed to take it. He pulled out of his pocket what looked like a small purse, but he reached deep into it and pulled out six 10-galleon pieces and a few other coins and said, "Don't bother with the knuts. It's nuts to have such a small denomination coin."

Then he turned to me and took the book out of the book bag. He handed it to me and said, "Now, Mr. Dursley, please autograph it."

Davies eyes bugged out and said, "But he isn't Severus Snape!"

Wendt was not disturbed. He took the book back, handed it to Davies and said, "Please open to the title page and read."

He did and read, ' *Advanced Potions-Making* by Severus Snape. So?"

"Keep reading."

He went on, "Compiled and Edited by Dudley Dursley and Horace Slughorn." Davies stared at me and asked, "You're this Dudley Dursley?"

I shrugged. Davies smiled and said, "Oh, Mr. Dursley, please accept a small gift that we give to all the authors who visit our store." He handed me a slim paperback book that had the title, "Bookstone Daily Planner." He went on about it, "It's a very nice little planner. It has an alarm that rings when you get close to the appointments and to do's in the calendar. You can pick from a dozen different tones or none at all. A lot of people prefer that one."

I thanked him and turned again to Wendt who was holding out the Potions book to me and said pleasantly, "Please."

I had to think for a moment and then said, "Please give me a little time to decide what to write. I'll autograph it back at Hogwarts."

He returned the book to the book bag, and we left Flourish and Blotts. We went back to The Leaky Cauldron. There was an easy-to-see door in the brick wall with a sign over it that had the sign of the Leaky Cauldron on it. We went in and approached the bar and Tom. Tom asked what we'd have.

Wendt glanced at his wrist and said, "You know, it's close enough to dinner time that I think we might just have an early dinner." He turned to me and asked, "What do you think, Dursley?" He quickly added, "I'm buying."

I smiled and shrugged my agreement. Tom came around the bar and asked where we'd like to sit. Wendt walked over to a small table near the fireplace and asked, "OK?" Both Tom and I agreed. Tom commented that as it was a bit early. The specials of the day wouldn't be available, but all the normal fare was available now.

We sat and considered the menu. Wendt advised me that everything he'd had here was good – not up to Hogwarts standards – but good. He also advised me that he hadn't had the steak and kidney pie.

We looked over the menu and pretty quickly decided what we wanted. Wendt ordered the Sheppard Pie, and I decided to try the steak and kidney pie. We had been waiting about ten minutes after the order was placed when I was surprised by someone coming through the fireplace. It was a woman who slowly turned and scanned the room. When her head pointed toward us, I recognized the Headmistress. Wendt had seemed to recognize her sooner because he was up almost immediately and had reached her in two long steps. He took her arm and said, "Dursley and I are over here." They walked over, and Wendt pulled up a chair for her.

When they were both seated I realized that I should have risen for Ms. McGonagall but it was too late, and she motioned me to just stay seated. "Well, I wondered where you two had gone."

Wendt had a big smile on his face. He asked her, "You didn't really know it was Dursley with me until you saw him, did you?"

"I most certainly did. When I came to your office and found you gone, I examined your floo connection and found that someone had gone to The Leaky Cauldron. It didn't take me long to track down and check the few people who might have given you a 'lift' here. There was Sinistra, of course, and I even checked with Professor Slughorn. Since Mr. Dursley here had recently published a book, it seemed likely to me that the two of you had gone off to buy a copy. And what better place to do that than Flourish and Blotts?"

Wendt was laughing and said, "I see you've picked up some of my methods. Well, will you join us for dinner? We can add something for you to our order."

She smiled as well, and for a moment I saw how Mr. Wendt might just find the Headmistress very appealing. Wendt signaled to Tom who was on his way to our table anyway. He took her order which was simply, "My usual."

I blurted out, "You eat here enough that he knows your usual?"

She blushed a little and said, "I guess Mr. Wendt and I do eat here a fair amount."

Wendt changed the subject, "Mr. Dursley, have you decided on a dedication for the book?"

She looked over at me and asked, "You have a copy already?"

I just nodded and she asked, "May I see it?"

Wendt pulled up the book bag,pulled the book out, and was handing it to her just as Tom came over with her drink—a glass of wine. He

235

looked at the book and took it out of Wendt's hand. He stared at it a moment as everyone else stared at him. Then he said, "Mr. Snape wrote this?"

I said, "Yes."

Wendt added, "Yes, but it is Mr. Dursley's book at least as much as Snape's. It would never have been published without him."

Tom face showed surprise and he said, "An author in the house. The meal's on the house if I can join you. It's early, and Sally can handle the bar for a while." Wendt took the book back from Tom and handed it to Professor McGonagall. She looked it over from all sides as though she'd never seen a book before and carefully opened the book. "Yes, very nice, but there's no autograph." She handed it to me with a look of expectancy on her face.

It was at that moment that I had an idea. I opened the book and asked Ms. McGonagall if she had a pen.

"Oh, I have something better than that." She opened her purse and pulled out a quill. "Please use this."

I took the quill, wrote on the inside of the cover, and handed it to Wendt. But again, Tom took the book first. He looked on the inside and shook his head, "What is this interference thing?" Wendt took the book back and looked at the inside cover himself. He started to say something but seemed to be choking on something. McGonagall took the book from Wendt and read aloud what I'd written, "To the man whose interference in my life led to this book being written." She laid the book down and took Wendt's hand in hers. There was a tear in her eyes and she said, "That's the most beautiful inscription that I've ever read."

She went on, "Why did you want this book, though?"

Wendt seemed to have gotten whatever was in his throat out of it and he said, "Well, you all know that Snape was a loyal friend. That last year of his life, I was on the run and didn't see him at all. By the time I got back to Hogwarts, the place was a shambles and Minerva, er . . Headmistress McGonagall had moved into the Head's office and moved all of his things out."

She shook her head and said, "You know that he didn't have many personal belongings and no relatives. Everything went to charities and we didn't really have anything that was his left. Another strange thing is that we don't even have a regular portrait of him."

I asked, "What do you mean? I know there's a portrait of him. I was there after that madman despoiled it. It was almost recovered to normal before I left your office.

She turned to me and said, "Almost all of the headmasters have a portrait that appears after their deaths. They are like all the other portraits in that something of the soul of the original person persists and can give

236

advice and. . . " She hesitated, as though not sure if she should reveal this, "sometimes they're a pain in the butt.

"However, Snape's is one that is like a Muggle portrait. It just never moves or says anything. I wish I understood why."

Wendt went on, "Anyway, I would like to have had a memento of him. But there wasn't any. I'd given up hope but then, you found that potions book that had belonged to him. It was yours and I wouldn't have it from you even if you offered it. I think that you must have been intended to get it. It was such an unusual and unlikely chance that brought it to you.

"But, when you published this book, it was an opportunity for me to have a memento of Snape without taking from you an object that was clearly to be yours. I can't have him autograph it, but your autograph is fine. When I get back to my office, it will have pride of position in my bookcase. I can't thank you enough for publishing this book that Snape should have published. It gives him a sort of memorial that he would never have otherwise."

I just gaped at him, and Tom just shook his head and got up, saying that he had to go back to the kitchen to see how our food was coming. After a while, he returned carrying a tray with several dishes that he distributed to us and himself. The food was not as good as Hogwarts, but it was better than a lot that I'd had. Through the whole meal, we talked little, and Wendt and McGonagall kept touching each other's arms at breaks in the meal when we talked.

After we'd finished, McGonagall suggested that I go directly back to Wendt's office by floo on my own. She said that she and Wendt had some school business to discuss. The way they were staring into each others' eyes as she said that made me think that there wasn't a lot of school business to discuss. So, I got up and thanked them both for dinner. Wendt just shrugged and said, "Go thank the real founder of the feast – Tom."

I did, then came back to the fireplace and took a handful of powder and asked McGonagall, "I just say, 'Professor Wendt's office at Hogwarts'?"

She nodded and added, "Professor Wendt's office is enough."

I stepped into the fireplace, threw the powder down at my feet and spoke those words. I spun around and stepped out into his office. There was a lot less dust and soot in the air, and it only took a minute to get over the coughing fit.

Book Signing

I sent a few notes to the Myerses. They replied saying that Pam was well and her memory had improved immensely after the Sunday that we spent together. BUT. There was always the BUT. But she was still very disturbed and trying to sort out all the things that had happened in the last year. In the last letter from them they admitted that they had agreed that Pam should see what the Muggles called a "Psychecarist". She had just started and seemed to come home from the weekly sessions with her calmer than before.

The Fall term was working on. The Halloween party had a long-standing tradition that Professor Wendt come disguised as someone at school. This year there was a pool established, the people who guessed the disguise correctly would split the pool. The most popular choice was the new Defense Against the Dark Arts Professor. She'd had the post before when it was still cursed. Her name was Stiffie Applecart. I had no idea who would be the choice but that didn't stop me from putting a couple of Galleons on Madame Pomfrey. As a long shot choice, I thought that I'd win a lot of money because I'd not have to share with anyone else.

One day, I ran into Professor Wendt and asked if he'd entered the Pool. He just stared at me and said, "I've not decided yet. I'll put in a last minute entry after I've transformed to whomever."

Of course, everyone knew that it was really Professor Sinistra who decided who Wendt would be, and so it was silly of Wendt to put money on anyone.

On Halloween itself, a Tuesday, I had finished my assignments and had come to Filch and my office. He wasn't around, so I went up to the Great Hall for the Halloween Banquet, which was to be followed by the Ball. On occasions like this, Filch and I could take our meal in the Great Hall. I decided to eat with the Hufflepuffs whom I lived with. I couldn't see Wendt or anyone who reminded me of Wendt anywhere. I looked around for Filch and found him sitting with the Raveclaws. I wondered why. They certainly didn't seem to be his types.

Later after the banquet, the tables moved magically to the walls of the Great Hall, and a band set up that seemed to be made of Hogwarts students. They weren't great but they did have plenty of amplification so it wasn't really possible to make out the lyrics. So, it wasn't all bad.

At one point a girl who looked to be 6th or even 7th year came over and asked me to dance. I really wasn't interested, but she was very persistent and when a slow dance started, she grabbed my hand and started to drag me out onto the dance floor. Fortunately, I heard a voice cut through the music in a Scottish brogue, "Miss Penrose, I really don't think it's appropriate for you to be dancing with a member of the staff."

Miss Penrose's face fell, and she said something that reading lips looked like "Shit!" but was probably "Shoot."

The Head came around to face me and said, "If you've got to dance with someone, it might as well be me." She took my hand and dragged me out to the dance floor. She wasn't bad on her feet.

I shouted over the noise, "Why aren't you dancing with Professor Wendt?"

She just shook her head and said, "Oh, who knows where OR who he is."

I had to admit that I'd not seen him all night. A knight in armor strode by on his way to the refreshment table. Minerva commented, "I see you boss isn't wasting time finding something to drink."

I scanned the room looking for him but couldn't see him right away. Then I did. He was standing at the refreshment table next to Professor Sinistra. At that moment, Minerva slapped her forehead and marched over there. I had no idea what had occurred to her, but I decided to watch what happened. She arrived at the table and seemed to be engaged in a lively discussion with the other two standing there. Shortly after her arrival, the Librarian, Pinz made an appearance there and seemed to be as much engaged as the rest. Then, someone disguised in knightly armor strode over and joined them and seemed to have as much to say as the others.

By this time, there were a few spectators showing up and the formation began to look like a rugby scrum. I decided that I should have a closer look to see if I could figure out what the excitement was all about.

By the time I arrived, there was a layer of observers between me and the participants in the melee. I only heard snatches of conversations, such as:

"You've done this one too many times."

"You leave my, my, friend alone."

"I'M Filch!"

"Oh, Argus, who is that?"

I'm sure I saw a glimpse of a wand or two drawn but I didn't see any sign of the tell-tale red and green showers of sparks that would mean that someone had used one. I thought I'd seen as much as I could and not learned much, so I backed away and looked for a neutral corner. In doing so, I bumped into Professor Slughorn.

"Oh, pardon me." I told him.

"No, problem, dear boy. It's not surprising that there would be a few bumped elbows. There's usually some sort of excitement caused by Wendt and Sinistra at this party. It's all good clean fun, and nobody gets seriously hurt – uh, usually. Now there was that party where the fake fake Mad-Eye Moody showed up as well as the usual fake Mad-Eye."

I shook my head confused by Slughorn's non-explanation. Seeing my consternation, he explained. "You remember last year when Wendt came disguised as . . Now, who did he come disguised as?"

I remembered, "Uh, Lockhart wasn't it? Whoever that is."

"Yes, you're right. Well, he does something like that every year."

The sky, as seen through the transparent ceiling of the Great Hall, began to rain. It was a gentle, cool, sustained rain. Meanwhile the altercation at the refreshment table seemed to also have cooled a bit. It broke up, and Minerva sent the worst combatants off the field. I commented, "Game postponed for rain."

Slughorn was confused but realized that I was talking about the altercation, "What game would be postponed for a little rain?"

"Cricket, for one."

Slughorn became indignant, "Well, let me tell you a proper game of Quidditch would never be called for something so ephemeral as a little rain."

He swelled up a bit and said, "Why I remember the semifinal game of the '88 Quidditch Cup that had Russia and Argentina facing off against each other. Such a storm of lightning, thunder and wind blew up that the astounding Seeker, Botvinik for the Russians, was blown completely into another county. By this time, it was full night, and it took him hours and hours to find his way back to the Pitch.

"Some people claim that there was a tornado in that storm. It accounted for the Snitch being far away from the Pitch for hours as well."

He finished, "No! No self-respecting Quidditch team would suffer a postponement for mere weather."

We went back to the refreshment table after the combatants had withdrawn and drank a toast to the House Elves of Hogwarts.

The rest of the week was mild compared to the Tuesday night Halloween party, but on Thursday Slughorn stopped by the janitorial office that Filch and I maintained and asked me to join him in his office for some discussion.

It turned out that a publicity opportunity had come up for our book and he wanted us to take it. "Mr. Dursley, would you like to travel to Paris this weekend?"

I regarded him suspiciously but gave him a guarded "Yes".

"Excellent. We've been invited to have a book signing at a magical bookstore in a Paris suburb on Saturday afternoon. How about it?"

I was still suspicious. "Just how does it work?"

"Oh, it's a jolly good time. We'll arrive at the bookstore around 1 PM, and we'll just occupy a table. People who've just bought our book come up and get to talk with us. They usually want us to sign their copy and maybe include a simple inscription.

"It's Win-win. The book store sells books and has more patrons who may actually buy books other than ours. They get some publicity too."

"We get the royalties from book sales. We get publicity. AND." Here he leaned forward a bit and confided, 'We should get an excellent dinner at the expense of the book store."

I was pretty much won over but still had a couple of questions, "How do we get there?"

Slughorn, who was getting excited himself at the prospect, explained, "Oh, we get up early on Saturday and take the floo to an Inn that I know in Dover and disapparate across the Channel from there."

That gave me an idea, "Oh! Oh! Can we take the Chunnel across to France?"

"The Chunnel? What's that?"

"Oh, it's a train. It goes under the Channel in a tunnel. You zip along over a hundred miles an hour." Another idea struck me. "And we could have breakfast on the train!"

Slughorn was not happy about the idea, "Go under the Channel in a train under hundreds of feet of ocean? And eat tinned food to boot? Never!

"Besides, I've got a wonderful little Patisserie that I know in Rouen. You would not believe the flaky croissants that you get there."

I could see that I was not going to sell Slughorn on the idea of the Chunnel, so I agreed to go to his patisserie for breakfast. "Well, we should be ready to disapparate to Paris by 10. How do we kill a couple of hours?"

Slughorn seemed genuinely offended, "Kill time? Kill time in Paris! Incredible! There are a million things we can do in Paris. We could go to the Louvre. We could see the Cathedral Notre Dame! We could walk the Left Bank!" He sputtered and couldn't say anything more for the moment.

Then I had a question, "Can we see the Eiffel Tower?"

Slughorn was effusive, "See it? We'll go up in it and survey the city. We'll take a tour of the city from the air."

"OK. OK. I get it. Paris is wonderful. We'll have a good time." I thought a second and asked, "So, what happens after we have dinner at the fancy French restaurant? We come home?"

Slughorn sighed appreciatively, "No. We're in Paris, the City of Light. Why do they call it that?"

I couldn't resist a snappy comeback, "Because there are no fat Parisians?"

He wouldn't be provoked but simply said, 'You haven't seen Paris if you've not seen it at night. The lights along any major street, the Seine River, it's all magical." He was amused by his own joke and said, "And I don't mean magical like Hogwarts, I mean enchantingly beautiful, magically inspiring."

I accepted it all provisionally. We'd see when we got there.

The next night I had a hard time getting to sleep. But I popped awake promptly and headed down to the Great Hall. Slughorn had a brief case. When I asked him what was in it, he just said, "Oh, some business cards of mine, some quills and parchment sheets and a few odds and ends.

We were taking the floo network to the Lonely Mermaid inn in Dover. We stepped out into the Common Room which served as Dining Room and, apparently, a dance hall when there was a band present. When we arrived, the only other person there was the breakfast wait staff and a bartender. No one was having breakfast.

Slughorn apparently knew the barman. He addressed him as Mark and said, "We'll be back for a drink or two this evening."

The barman just nodded, and we went out one door that opened on a courtyard. Slughorn held out his arm and said, "You know, Dursley, you've got learn to disapparate." I nodded but didn't elaborate about my having a license. I took his proffered arm, we spun through the cosmos, and landed in a dark alley. Walking out, we discovered ourselves on a large street and, indeed, there was the Boulangerie Patisserie du Vieux Marche. It was small, but the croissants that Sughorn ordered for us were wonderful. No wonder he went here for breakfast when he was in France.

We next disapparated and found ourselves in a stand of trees. Rising above them majestically was the Eiffel tower. Although we stood among the trees and so close to its base, I had a little trouble recognizing it immediately. We walked over to the ticket office and purchased tickets for the earliest lift—at 9:30 AM. While we waited we walked around the tower, amazed by the views up through the girders that formed its structure.

We caught the lift, and I couldn't help agree with Slughorn that the view was tremendous. We got off at the highest level and walked slowly around the structure drinking in the early November view, cool and cloudy though it was.

We reached the side nearest the river and gazed down at the boats and the seemingly miniscule people walking beside the river. Slughorn nudged me, and when I looked up, he pointed over to our right where a couple was standing looking down as we were. Their arms were about each other's waists, and every now and then, they looked up at each other, smiling and sometimes laughing.

I stared silently for a while and Slughorn asked what I was thinking about. I told him the truth, "I was just thinking that I really wanted to see Paris for the first time with my love."

Slughorn turned back to gazing at the river. After a while, he said, "The first time I saw Paris I had graduated from Hogwarts and had been working for a potion manufacturer for about six months. You see:

I had discovered love in my 7th year. Oh, before that I'd had the occasional crush on a beauty whose body made you want to wrap yourself around her and protect her all at the same time. But, in my 7th year Advanced Potion-Making class, there had been a woman who was not spectacularly beautiful but whose every word excited both my head and my hands. We started out as lab partners.

Somehow even before I knew her name or came to appreciate her beauty, I knew that I wanted her as my partner. Before long we were studying together in the Ravenclaw Common Room. Oh, you weren't supposed to invite non-house-mates but few people followed the rule strictly. We didn't go to the Halloween Ball together, but we were inseparable shortly after that. We went to the Yule Ball, and we both chose to stay over at Hogwarts for the Christmas Holiday.

I guess you'd probably find it strange that we didn't go to the favorite spot for people who thought they were in love – Ms. Paddifoot's. We preferred to walk by the Lake or by the Shrieking Shack. It never held terrors for either of us, and it was pretty sure to be lonesome there.

After we graduated, Aurora visited me after work at the Potioner's where I worked. At least a couple of times a week, we'd go to dinner and talk for hours. For all the talking we did, we never talked about her family or mine.

Then one day, in October, after quite a lot of nudging, Aurora agreed to take a trip with me to Paris. She was to meet me for breakfast at a Patisserie that she knew in Rouen. Then we were to go to Paris and see all the sights that we could stuff in before 10PM. We would then. . . Well, we would see then. I hoped that I could convince her to stay the night with me.

I arrived at the Patisserie bright and early. I ordered a coffee and settled in to wait for her. Half an hour passed and then three quarters and then a full hour. I didn't know how to get hold of her and I certainly didn't want to leave just to miss her by five or ten minutes. So, I stayed. Finally, I decided that maybe I'd misunderstood and I should proceed to the Eiffel Tower which was to be our first stop on our tour.

I arrived and bought two lift tickets and waited. Finally, I decided to go up. When I arrived at the top level, I looked out on the Seine just as we are. Of course, I was hoping to be enjoying the view as they are over there.

As I stood there, looking out into the distance, I saw a dot on the horizon. I wasn't sure what had attracted my attention to it at first, but then I realized that it was drifting a bit against the background. Eventually I realized that it was actually some sort of bird flying directly at me.

In the last minute, I realized that it was an owl. It landed on the parapet that I was leaning on. It held out its claw to which was tied a message. I removed it and read something pretty much like this,

"Horace, I can't tell you how sorry I am to have to tell you that I can't join you today. I can't join you ever. My family is prejudiced against everyone who isn't a pure-born wizard. When they learned that I was coming to be with you just for a day, Mum and Dad were furious and forbade me ever to see you again. I'm breaking the agreement that I swore to them so that they would not write me out of their will by just writing this to you. Please understand that I hate this, but they threaten to disown me forever if I disobey them in this. I can't imagine never seeing them again.

"Please forgive me and don't hate me for my cowardice. You are my only true love, Aurora"

I discovered that her parents were indeed as heartless and prejudiced as that. She is my only true love as well. I tried sending owls to her and communicated through mutual friends, but I never saw, heard or spoke with her again.

I stood there astounded by what he'd said. "You really never dated another woman – ever?"

He shook his head. I asked who her parents were.

244

"Oh, they were part of the Black family. The headmaster Nigelius Black was one of her more distant relatives.

"Was it Mum or Dad?"

With a puzzled look he asked, "Mum or Dad what?"

"Mum or Dad that was the Muggle."

"Neither, it was my maternal grandmother. She died before I was old enough to really get to know her, and nobody talked about her much. The ironic thing was that that was the way that I discovered that she was a Muggle. I had no idea that I wasn't 'Pure Blood' until then.

"Now, let's get going. We need to get to the book store."

Before we disapparated I had to ask one question, "The patisserie that you were going to meet Aurora at was the one that we went to wasn't it?"

He just nodded, held out his arm for me and twisted us through space and time to land in a suburban alley. As before, just outside the alley was the bookstore that we were headed for. When we arrived, the owner greeted us effusively. He took our jackets and led us to a fairly large open area near a number of book shelves. There was a table and two chairs laid out for us. There were customers milling around but not a lot.

We took our seats. Slughorn opened his brief case and brought out quills, parchment sheets, a small stand that he put a neatly lettered cardboard sign on. It had the name of the book, the editors and authors printed on it

Almost immediately, people came by and talked with us. Actually, they mainly talked with Slughorn who knew some serviceable French. A few people talked to me. Shortly, people began approaching our table armed with our textbook. These first purchasers turned out mostly to be Professors at various schools.

However, as time went on, a wider variety of people came by to purchase our book and get inscriptions. Mainly, they just wanted simple messages, "Good Luck", "To my friend -----" and the always popular, "Mon Ami".

A rather cute brunette was chatting up Slughorn in French. I was idly observing, hoping that I could pick up some of the language. Just then, someone who must have been right in front of me said, "What do you have to do to get an inscription here?"

I jerked around and for a few seconds I couldn't place the voice or the face. It was the unfamiliar surroundings. If we were at Hogwarts or even anywhere in England, I'm sure that I'd have recognized her immediately.

When I did recognize her, my jaw went slack, and I stared like a zombie at her face. She said, "Well, I paid good Galleons for this book. Don't I get an inscription?"

My tongue loosened at that. I said, "Oh, yes. You get anything you want."

"Make it out to 'My Only True Love'."

I leapt to my feet and reached over the table to take her arms in my hands and pulled her to me. We kissed, and I thought vaguely that it was appropriate to be Frenching in the heart of France.

Someone behind her asked, "Do you think that you could stop kizzing ze girl for ze one minute to sign my book?"I paused my kiss and said, "Slughorn will be happy to help you. I'm busy."

About the Author

William Wilkin lived in a small Southern Ohio town until he began his college career. He has a Bachelor's degree in Physics from The Ohio State University and a Master's degree in Physics from The University of Chicago. He had a career in corporate Information Technology and currently lives in Dallas, Texas.

He enjoys music, both "serious" and "classic Rock". He reads classic Detective fiction and Science Fiction & Fantasy as well as trying to stay current in Physics.

He began writing seriously about 2005. He has a blog, in-mid-world, where he writes about Science Fiction & Fantasy and remotely related topics.

www.ingramcontent.com/pod-product-compliance
Lightning Source LLC
Chambersburg PA
CBHW071459170626
46811CB00007B/2643